A TEXT BOOK OF

FOUNDATIONS OF COMMUNICATION AND COMPUTER NETWORK

FOR
SEMESTER – II
SECOND YEAR DEGREE COURSE IN
INFORMATION TECHNOLOGY ENGINEERING

**Strictly According to New Revised Credit System Syllabus
of Savitribai Phule Pune University**
(w.e.f June 2016)

NITIN N. SAKHARE
M. E. (Comp. Networks)
Assistant Professor,
Computer Engineering Deptt.,
Vishwakarma Institute of Inform. Technology
Kondhwa (Bk.), PUNE

Mrs. MANISHA P. NAVALE
M.E. (Comp. Engg.)
Assistant Professor,
Computer Engineering Deptt.,
STES's NBN. Sinhgad School of Engineering
Ambegoan (Bk), PUNE

NIRALI PRAKASHAN
ADVANCEMENT OF KNOWLEDGE

N3584

FC & CN (SE IT)   ISBN 978-93-86353-24-5

First Edition   :   January 2017

©   :   Authors

Published By :   Polyplate

NIRALI PRAKASHAN

Abhyudaya Pragati, 1312, Shivaji Nagar,
Off J.M. Road, Pune – 411005
Tel - (020) 25512336/37/39, Fax - (020) 25511379
Email : niralipune@pragationline.com

☞ **DISTRIBUTION CENTRES**

PUNE

Nirali Prakashan   : 119, Budhwar Peth, Jogeshwari Mandir Lane, Pune 411002, Maharashtra
Tel : (020) 2445 2044, 66022708, Fax : (020) 2445 1538
Email : bookorder@pragationline.com, niralilocal@pragationline.com

Nirali Prakashan   : S. No. 28/27, Dhyari, Near Pari Company, Pune 411041
Tel : (020) 24690204 Fax : (020) 24690316
Email : dhyari@pragationline.com, bookorder@pragationline.com

MUMBAI

Nirali Prakashan   : 385, S.V.P. Road, Rasdhara Co-op. Hsg. Society Ltd.,
Girgaum, Mumbai 400004, Maharashtra
Tel : (022) 2385 6339 / 2386 9976, Fax : (022) 2386 9976
Email : niralimumbai@pragationline.com

☞ **DISTRIBUTION BRANCHES**

JALGAON

Nirali Prakashan   : 34, V. V. Golani Market, Navi Peth, Jalgaon 425001,
Maharashtra, Tel : (0257) 222 0395, Mob : 94234 91860

KOLHAPUR

Nirali Prakashan   : New Mahadvar Road, Kedar Plaza, 1st Floor Opp. IDBI Bank
Kolhapur 416 012, Maharashtra. Mob : 9850046155

NAGPUR

Pratibha Book Distributors : Above Maratha Mandir, Shop No. 3, First Floor,
Rani Jhanshi Square, Sitabuldi, Nagpur 440012, Maharashtra
Tel : (0712) 254 7129

DELHI

Nirali Prakashan   : 4593/21, Basement, Aggarwal Lane 15, Ansari Road, Daryaganj
Near Times of India Building, New Delhi 110002
Mob : 08505972553

BENGALURU

Pragati Book House   : House No. 1, Sanjeevappa Lane, Avenue Road Cross,
Opp. Rice Church, Bengaluru – 560002.
Tel : (080) 64513344, 64513355,Mob : 9880582331, 9845021552
Email:bharatsavla@yahoo.com

CHENNAI

Pragati Books   : 9/1, Montieth Road, Behind Taas Mahal, Egmore,
Chennai 600008 Tamil Nadu, Tel : (044) 6518 3535,
Mob : 94440 01782 / 98450 21552 / 98805 82331,
Email : bharatsavla@yahoo.com

niralipune@pragationline.com | www.pragationline.com

Also find us on [f] www.facebook.com/niralibooks

Dedicated to...

" Our Beloved Parents"

... Authors

PREFACE

It gives us great pleasure in publishing this text book on **"Foundations Of Communication and Computer Network "** for the students of Second Year Degree Course in Information Technology Engineering. This book is strictly written according to **New Revised Credit System Syllabus** of Savitribai Phule Pune University (2015 Pattern).

As per the policy of the University, Engineering Syllabi is revised every five years. Last revision was in the year 2012. New revision is coming little earlier, as university has introduced **Online System of Examination** from year 2012.

As per the **New Credit System**, the **Online Examinations** Phase-I will be conducted based on First & Second Units and Phase II on Third & Fourth Units. The **Online** examinations will have objective types of questions with multiple choices. End Sem. Theory Examination will be based on all the six units and that will be conducted in traditional way and the Theory Course will have 4 credits.

It is our objective to keep the presentation systematic, consistent, intensive and clear presentation of concept through explanatory notes and figures. So we are sure that this book will cater for all your needs for this subject.

Main feature of this book is, **Complete Coverage** of the New Credit System Syllabus with large number of **Worked (Solved) Examples and Exercises.**

We have given Separate Book of Multiple Choice Questions (MCQ's) which will be very useful to the students especially for Online Examinations.

We take this opportunity to express our sincere thanks to Shri. Dineshbhai Furia, Shri. Jignesh Furia, Mrs. Nirali Verma and Shri. M. P. Munde and entire team of Nirali Prakashan namely Mrs. Deepali Lachake (Co-ordinator), who really have taken keen interest and untiring efforts in publishing this text.

The advice and suggestions of our esteemed readers to improve the text are most welcomed, and will be highly appreciated.

Pune   **Authors**

SYLLABUS

Unit I : Introduction To Communication And Networking (09 Hrs)

Introduction To Communication Theory: Terminologies, Elements of Analog Communication System, Baseband signal, Band-pass signal, Need for Modulation, Electromagnetic Spectrum and Typical Applications, Basics of Signal (Analog and Digital,) Representation and Analysis (Time and frequency)

Introduction To basics of networking: Computer network fundamentals, ISO OSI Model: All Layers, TCP/IP Protocol Suite: All Layers, Addressing (Physical, Logical Port and other), LAN, WAN And MAN, Network Topologies. Guided Media: Twisted-Pair Cable, Coaxial Cable and Fiber-Optic Cable, Unguided Media: Wireless, Radio Waves, Microwaves and Infrared, Wireless frequency spectrum.

Noise: External Noise, Internal Noise, Noise Calculations, Communication Channel. Discrete and Continuous Channel, Shannon-Hartley Theorem, Channel Capacity, Nyquist and Shanon Theorem, Bandwidth S/N Trade off

Unit II : Amplitude And Angle Modulation (08 Hrs)

Amplitude Modulation: Amplitude Modulation Techniques (DSBFC, DSBSC, SSB), Generation of Amplitude Modulated Signals, Frequency Spectrum.

Angle Modulation Techniques: Theory of Angle Modulation Techniques, Practical Issues in Frequency Modulation, Generation of Frequency Modulation, Frequency Spectrum

Unit III : Pulse And Digital Modulation Techniques (08 Hrs)

Pulse Modulation Techniques: Pulse Analog Modulation Techniques, sampling Pulse Digital Modulation Techniques: PCM, DM, DPCM Average Information, Entropy, Information Rate. Source coding: Shanon-Fano, Huffman and Limpel-Ziv

Digital-to-digital Conversion: Line Coding, Line Coding Schemes, Block Coding, Scrambling **Digital-to-analog Conversion:** Aspects of Digital-to-Analog Conversion, Amplitude Shift Keying (ASK), Frequency Shift Keying (FSK), Phase Shift Keying (PSK), Quadrature Amplitude Modulation (QAM)

Analog-to-analog Conversion: Amplitude Modulation, Frequency Modulation, Phase Modulation

Unit IV : Error Control Coding And Data Link Control (08 Hrs)

Error Detection and Correction: Introduction, Error Detection, Error Correction **Linear Block Codes**: hamming code, Hamming Distance, parity check code

Cyclic Codes: CRC (Polynomials), Advantages of Cyclic Codes, other Cyclic Codes as Examples: CHECKSUM: One's Complement, Internet Checksum

Framing: fixed-size framing, variable size framing.

Flow control: Flow control protocols. Noiseless channels: simplest protocol, stop-and-wait protocol. Noisy channels: stop-and-wait automatic repeat request, go-back-n automatic repeat request, Selective repeat automatic repeat request, piggybacking

Unit V : Multiplexing And Multiple Access (06 Hrs)

Multiplexing: FDM, TDM, Synchronous Time-Division Multiplexing, Statistical Time-Division Multiplexing, WDM, Spread Spectrum: FHSS and DSSS **Random access:** ALOHA, CSMA, CSMS/CD and CSMA/ CA

Controlled Access: Reservation, Polling and Token Passing **Channelization:** FDMA, TDMA and CDMA

Unit VI : Physical, Mac Layer Standards And Switching (06 Hrs)

LAN hardware: (Switches, routers, hubs, bridges and their types) IEEE 802.3, Fast Ethernet (MAC Sublayer and Physical Layer), Gigabit Ethernet (MAC Sublayer, Physical Layer) Ten-Gigabit Ethernet, Token ring and token bus standards. Circuit Switched Networks, Packet (Datagram) Networks, Virtual Circuits, Structure of Circuit and Packet Switches

CONTENTS

INTRODUCTION TO COMMUNICATION AND NETWORKING

1.1 TERMINOLOGIES

We will discuss some terminologies used in electronic communication system.

1. **Signal**

- It is representation of data. Information converted into an electrical form suitable for transmission is called a signal. There are two types of signals; Analog and Digital.
- Analog signals are continuous waveforms of current and voltage whereas digital signals are those that have discrete stepwise value of 0 = Low, 1 = High.

2. **Transducer**

- Any device that converts one form of energy into another can be called as a transducer.
- In electronic communication system, it mainly refers to a device that converts a physical variable (pressure, sound, force, temperature, etc) into its respective electrical signal and gives it as an output.
- The mouth piece on the phone is a transducer which converts the sound waves into electrical signals.

3. **Attenuation**

- Attenuation refers to any reduction in the strength of a signal. The loss of quality and strength of the signal while travelling through the channel/ medium during electronic communication is known as attenuation.

4. **Amplification**

- The process of increasing the amplitude of a signal using an electronic circuit is called amplification.
- Amplitude refers to the strength of the signal.
- The electronic circuit used for amplification is called an amplifier.

5. **Bandwidth**

- Bandwidth refers to the frequency range over which the signal is transmitted or the range over which the equipment operates.

6. Modulation

- Most of the information/ messages are generated at low frequencies but such frequencies experiences heavy attenuation and hence their range is severely hampered.

- To overcome this problem, the original low frequency information is superimposed on a high frequency carrier wave which carries the information.

- This process is called modulation and there are several types of it, namely AM, FM and PM.

7. Demodulation

- The process of extraction of the original information from the modulated signal at the receiver is termed as demodulation. This process is basically the reverse of modulation.

1.2 ELEMENTS OF ANALOG COMMUNICATION SYSTEM

- Communication systems are designed to send messages or information from a source that generates the messages to one or more destinations. The term communications refers to the sending, receiving and processing of information by electronic means.

- The electronics equipments which are used for communication purpose are called communication equipments. Different communication equipments when assembled together form a communication system.

- Examples of communication system : Line telephony and line telegraphy, radio telephony and radio telegraphy, radio broadcasting, point-to-point communication and mobile communication, computer communication, radar communication, television broadcasting, radio telemetry, etc.

1.2.1 Block Diagram of Communication System

Fig. 1.1 shows the block diagram of a general communication system, in which the different functional elements are represented by blocks.

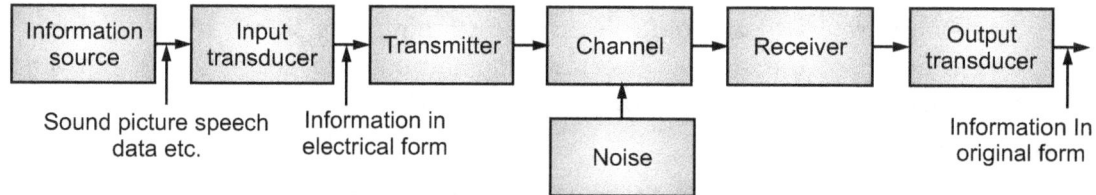

Fig. 1.1 : Block diagram of Communication System

- The essential components of a communication system are information source, input transducer, transmitter, communication channel, receiver and destination.

- Now, we shall discuss the functioning of these blocks.

1. Information Source

- A communication system work for to communicate a message or information. This information originates in the information source.

- In general, there can be various messages in the form of words, group of words, code, symbols, sound signal etc.

- However, out of these messages, only the desired message is selected and communicated.

- Therefore, we can say that the function of information source is to produce required message which has to be transmitted.

2. Input Transducer

- A transducer is a device which converts one form of energy into another form. The message from the information source may or may not be electrical in nature.

- In a case when the message produced by the information source is not electrical in nature, an input transducer is used to convert it into a time-varying electrical signal.

- For example, in case of radio-broadcasting, a microphone converts the information or massage which is in the form of sound waves into corresponding electrical signal.

3. Transmitter

- The function of the transmitter is to process the electrical signal from different aspects.

- For example in radio broadcasting the electrical signal obtained from sound signal, is processed to restrict its range of audio frequencies (upto 5 kHz in amplitude modulation radio broadcast) and is often amplified.

- In wire telephony, no real processing is needed. However, in long-distance radio communication, signal amplification is necessary before modulation.

- Modulation is the main function of the transmitter.

4. The Channel and the Noise

- The term channel means the medium through which the message travels from the transmitter to the receiver. In other words, we can say that the function of the channel is to provide a physical connection between the transmitter and the receiver.

- There are two types of channels, namely point-to-point channels and broadcast channels.

- Examples of point-to-point channel are wire lines, microwave links and optical fibers. An example of a broadcast channel is a satellite in geostationary orbit, which covers about one third of the earth's surface.

- During the process of transmission and reception the signal gets distorted due to noise introduced in the system.

- Noise is an unwanted signal which tends to interfere with the required signal. Noise signal is always random in character.

- Noise may interfere with signal at any point in a communication system. However, the noise has its greatest effect on the signal in the channel.

5. Receiver

- The main function of the receiver is to reproduce the message signal in electrical form from the partial received signal.

- This reproduction of the original signal is accomplished by a process known as the demodulation.

- Demodulation is the reverse process of modulation carried out in transmitter.

6. Destination

- Destination is the final stage which is used to convert an electrical message signal into its original form.

- For example in radio broadcasting, the destination is a loudspeaker which works as a transducer i.e. converts the electrical signal in the form of original sound signal.

1.3 BASEBAND SIGNAL

- Baseband is a signal that has a very narrow frequency range, i.e. a spectral magnitude that is nonzero only for frequencies in the locality of the origin (termed f = 0) and negligible elsewhere.

- In telecommunications and signal processing, baseband signals are transmitted without modulation, that is, without any shift in the range of frequencies of the signal, and are low frequency - contained within the band of frequencies from close to 0 hertz up to a higher cut-off frequency or maximum bandwidth.

- A baseband signal or low-pass signal is a signal that can include frequencies that are very near zero, by comparison with its highest frequency (for example, a sound waveform can be considered as a baseband signal, whereas a radio signal or any other modulated signal is not).

- Baseband signals are the fundamental group of frequencies in an analog or digital waveform that may be transmitted along a pathway or processed by an electronic circuit.

- Baseband signals can be composed of a single frequency or group of frequencies or in the digital domain composed of a data stream sent over an un-multiplexed channel.

- Examples of an analog baseband signal may be audio or composite video. Examples of a digital baseband signal may be Ethernet signals operating over a Local Area Network (LAN).

- Signals of a baseband nature often are modulated, or multiplexed, with other signals to form a composite signal. Sometimes, as in for example FM analog broadcasting, left and right channel audio signals are mixed to form a single channel (L+R) (shown in Fig. 1.2) which is then modulated on the radio carrier but still considered the baseband of the composite FM signal.

- These same two channels are also subtracted (L-R) to form a difference channel which is modulated onto a subcarrier to minimize interference with the baseband. This modulated L-R or difference signal is considered a sideband.

- It may appear to be a conflicting definition, since sometimes a baseband signal is in itself a mixed signal.

- Another way of saying this is that mixing a baseband signal with a carrier signal normally results in a modulated signal which may or may not still be considered baseband, and that depends on what else is happening in the transmission envelope.

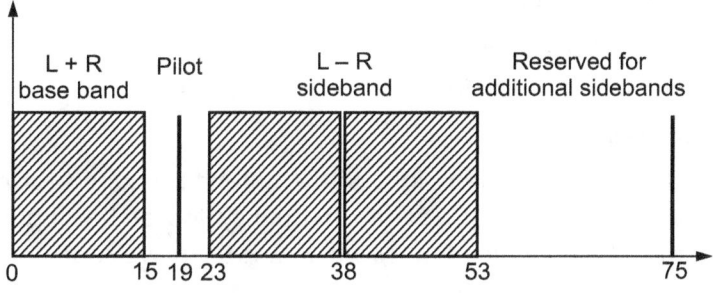

Fig. 1.2 : Baseband Signal

1.4 BAND-PASS SIGNAL

- A band-pass signal is a signal containing a band of frequencies not adjacent to zero frequency, such as a signal that comes out of a band-pass filter. The bandwidth of the filter is simply the difference between the upper and lower cutoff frequencies.

- A real-valued signal s(f) (shown in Fig. 1.3) is called a band pass signal if it has a frequency content focused in a narrow band of frequencies in the locality of a frequency fc.

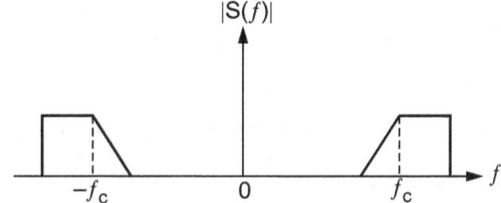

Fig. 1.3 : Representation of Band-pass Signal

- Consider a signal that contains only the positive frequencies in s (t), s+(t) , called the logical signal or the pre-envelope of s(t).

- Band-pass signals are encountered when receiving radio frequency (RF) signals such as communication and radar signals.

- In the analysis and actual processing of BP signals it is convenient to work with a related, equivalent signal called the Equivalent Low-pass Signal. This is a natural generalization of the idea of phasor used in sophomore-level circuits.

- Phasor = equivalent low-pass signal representing the sinusoid (that's why we used the subscript l–for low-pass).

1.5 NEED OF MODULATION

Main advantages of Modulation Process are as follows :

- Antenna height reduces.
- Avoids mixing of signals.
- Increases the range of communication (in kilometers).
- Multiplexing of signals is possible.
- Improves quality of reception of signal.

Antenna Height Reduces

- Antenna theory specifies that the height of the antenna required for radiation of radio waves is a function of wavelength of the frequency fed at the input of the antenna. Antenna height must be multiple of ($\lambda/4$), where λ is the wavelength.

$$\lambda = \frac{\text{Speed of light}}{\text{Frequency of signal}}$$

$$\lambda = 3 \times 10^8 / f$$

- Consider the voice as analog baseband signal with f = 4 kHz.

$$\lambda = 3 \times 10^8 / 4 \times 10^3$$

$$\therefore \quad \lambda = 75 \times 10^3 \text{ meters}$$

$$\therefore \quad \lambda = 75 \text{ km}$$

Height of antenna required = $\lambda/4$ = 75 km/4 = 18.75 km

Practically you cannot build the antenna of 18.75 km height. Consider this voice signal of 4 kHz frequency is used to modulate the carrier signal of 2 MHz frequency.

$$\therefore \quad f = 2 \text{ MHz} = 2 \times 10^6 \text{ Hz}$$

$$\therefore \quad \lambda = 3 \times 10^8 / F = 3 \times 10^8 / 2 \times 10^6 = 150 \text{ meters}$$

Minimum height of antenna required

$$= \lambda / 4 = 150 / 4 = 37.5 \text{ meters}$$

Therefore antenna height required for radio communication reduces from 18.75 km to 37.5 meters due to modulation.

Avoids Mixing of Signals

If audio signals as analog baseband signals are transmitted without modulation by more than one transmitter, then all the signals will be in the same frequency range i.e. 20 Hz to 20 kHz. Therefore at receiver all the signals get mixed together and receiver cannot separate those signals.

For this consider the baseband communication system shown in Fig. 1.4.

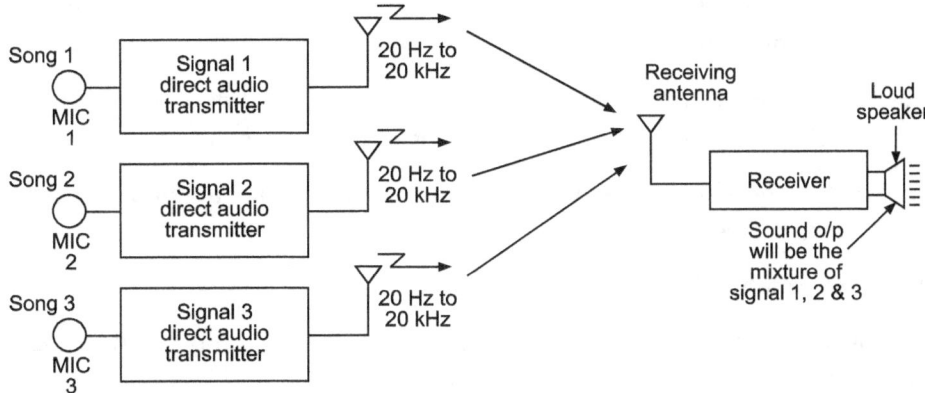

Fig. 1.4 : Baseband Communication for 3 sound signals

- The signals being transmitted by transmitter 1, 2 and 3 will be having same frequency i.e. 20 Hz to 20 kHz.

- Therefore all the signals received at receiver end will be amplified, processed and mixture of three signals will be listened at the output of speaker.

- That means the baseband radio communication doesn't have the intelligence for specific signal frequency selection and separation. But modulation techniques are going to avoid this mixing of signals as shown in Fig. 1.5.

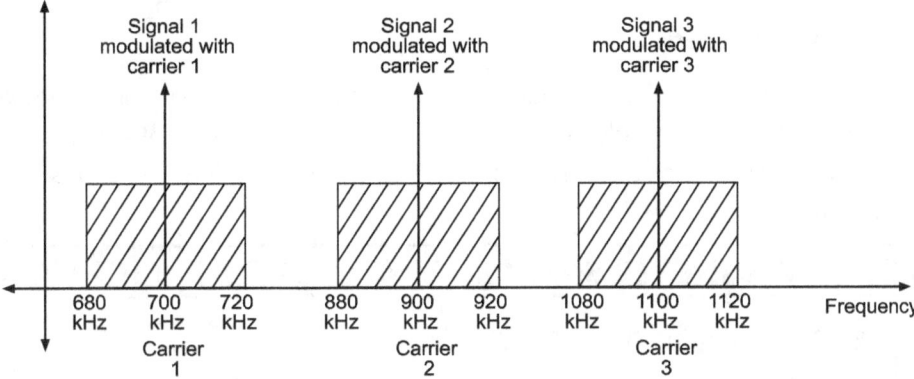

Fig. 1.5 : Modulation Avoids Mixing of Signals

Thus at receiver end, receiver can tune to specific carrier frequency and recovers the signal. If receiver is tuned to fc1, song 1 only will be listened at speaker. If receiver is tuned to fc2, song 2 only will be listened at speaker. Thus this is possible only when signal is modulated.

Increases the range of communication

The frequency of baseband signal is low. At low frequencies the signal radiation from antenna is poor or weak. Due to this reason, the signal gets attenuated and can't travel long distance when it is transmitted.

The attenuation of the transmitted signal reduces when the frequency is increased. The modulation process is also called as "frequency upshifting process."

Thus modulation increases the frequency of the signal to be radiated. Thus increase in frequency increases the range of communication.

Multiplexing of Signals is Possible

Modulation allows the multiplexing of different signals. Multiplexing means transmission of two or more signals simultaneously over the same channel.

Following are the general examples of multiplexing :

- Cable TV channels operating simultaneously.

- MW (Medium Wave) band radio channels operating simultaneously in radio broadcast.

- SW (Short Wave) band radio channels operating simultaneously in radio broadcast.

- TV channels operating simultaneously in TV broadcast.

- Thus different signals are simultaneously send over the same channel without disturbing each other using multiplexing process only. Thus modulation permits the useful multiplexing process.

Improves Quality of Reception of Signal :

There are different analog and digital modulation techniques, like frequency modulation and pulse code modulation respectively. In these techniques it is proven that they have high S/N ratio. They reduce effect of noise to great extent. Thus reduction in noise results in improved quality of reception.

1.6 ELECTROMAGNETIC SPECTRUM AND IT'S APPLICATIONS

- Electromagnetic waves are signals that oscillate.

- The electromagnetic waves vary sinusoidally. Their frequency is measured in cycles per second (cps) or hertz (Hz).

- These oscillations may occur at a very low frequency or at an extremely high frequency.

- The range of electromagnetic signals incorporating all frequencies is referred to as the electromagnetic spectrum.

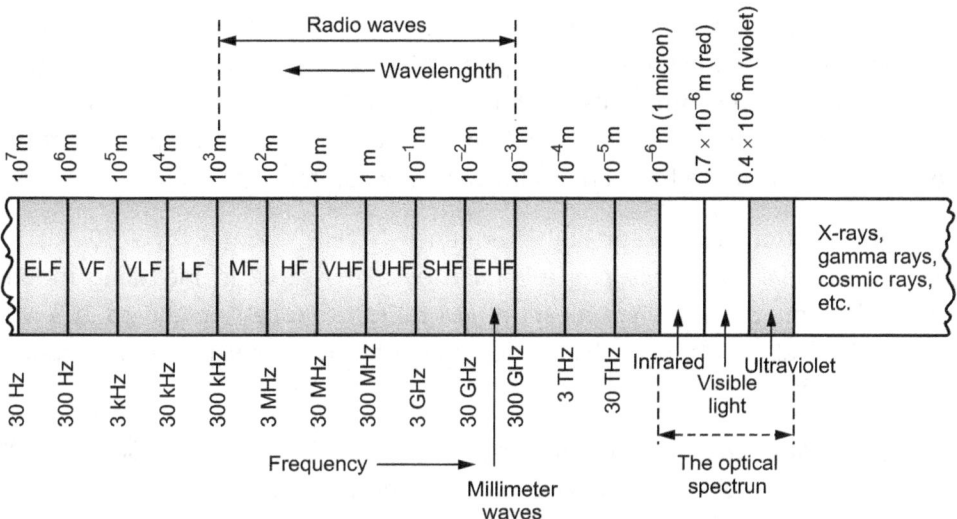

Fig. 1.6 : Electromagnetic Spectrum

For the purpose of classification, the electromagnetic frequency spectrum is divided into segments, as shown in Fig. 1.6. The signal characteristics and applications for each segment are discussed in the following paragraphs.

• **Extremely Low Frequencies :** Extremely low frequencies (ELFs) are in the 30- to 300-Hz range. These include ac power line frequencies (50 and 60 Hz are common), as well as those frequencies in the low end of the human audio range.

• **Voice Frequencies :** Voice frequencies (VFs) are in the range of 300 to 3000 Hz. This is the normal range of human speech. Although human hearing extends from approximately 20 to 20,000 Hz, most intelligible sound occurs in the VF range.

• **Very Low Frequencies :** Very low frequencies (VLFs) extend from 9 kHz to 30 kHz and include the higher end of the human hearing range up to about 15 or 20 kHz. Many musical instruments make sounds in this range as well as in the ELF and VF ranges. The VLF range is also used in some government and military communication. For example, VLF radio transmission is used by the navy to communicate with submarines.

• **Low Frequencies :** Low frequencies (LFs) are in the 30- to 300-kHz range. The primary communication services using this range are in aeronautical and marine navigation. Frequencies in this range are also used as subcarriers, signals that are modulated by the baseband information. Usually, two or more subcarriers are added, and the combination is used to modulate the final high-frequency carrier.

• **Medium Frequencies :** Medium frequencies (MFs) are in the 300- to 3000-kHz (0.3- to 3.0-MHz) range. The major application of frequencies in this range is AM radio broadcasting (535 to 1605 kHz). Other applications in this range are various marine and amateur radio communication.

- **High Frequencies :** High frequencies (HFs) are in the 3- to 30-MHz range. These are the frequencies generally known as short waves. All kinds of simplex broadcasting and half duplex two-way radio communication take place in this range. Broadcasts from Voice of America and the British Broadcasting Company occur in this range. Government and military services use these frequencies for two-way communication.

- **Very High Frequencies :** Very high frequencies (VHFs) contain the 30- to 300-MHz range. This popular frequency range is used by many services, including mobile radio, marine and aeronautical communication, FM radio broadcasting (88 to 108 MHz), and television channels 2 through 13. Radio amateurs also have numerous bands in this frequency range.

- **Ultra high Frequencies :** Ultrahigh frequencies (UHFs) contain the 300- to 3000-MHz range. This, too, is a widely used portion of the frequency spectrum. It includes the UHF TV channels 14 through 51, and it is used for land mobile communication and services such as cellular telephones as well as for military communication. Some radar and navigation services occupy this portion of the frequency spectrum, and radio amateurs also have bands in this range.

- **Microwaves and SHFs :** Frequencies between the 1000-MHz (1-GHz) and 30-GHz range are called microwaves. Microwave ovens usually operate at 2.45 GHz. Super high frequencies (SHFs) are in the 3- to 30-GHz range. These microwave frequencies are widely used for satellite communication and radar. Wireless local-area networks (LANs) and many cellular telephone systems also occupy this region.

- **Extremely High Frequencies :** Extremely high frequencies (EHFs) range from 30 to 300 GHz. Electromagnetic signals with frequencies higher than 30 GHz are referred to as millimeter waves. Equipment used to generate and receive signals in this range is extremely complex and expensive, but there is growing use of this range for satellite communication telephony, computer data, short-haul cellular networks, and some specialized radar.

- **Frequencies Between 300 GHz and the Optical Spectrum :** This portion of the spectrum is virtually empty. It is a cross between RF and optical. The Optical Spectrum Right above the millimeter wave region is what is called the optical spectrum, the region occupied by light waves. There are three different types of light waves : infrared, visible, and ultraviolet.

- **Infrared.** The infrared region is inserted between the highest radio frequencies (i.e., millimeter waves) and the visible portion of the electromagnetic spectrum. Infrared occupies the range between approximately 0.1 millimeter (mm) and 700 nanometers (nm), or 100 to 0.7 micrometer (μm). Infrared signals are used for various special kinds of communication. For example, infrared is used in astronomy to detect stars and other physical bodies in the universe, and for guidance in weapons systems, where the heat radiated from airplanes or missiles can be picked up by infrared detectors and used to guide missiles to targets. Infrared is also used in most new TV remote-control units where special coded signals are transmitted by an infrared LED to the TV receiver for the purpose of changing channels, setting the volume, and performing other functions. Infrared is the basis for all fiber-optic communication.

- Just above the infrared region is the visible spectrum we ordinarily refer to as light. Light is a special type of electromagnetic radiation that has a wavelength in the 0.4- to 0.8-μm range (400 to 800 nm). Light is used for various kinds of communication. Light waves can be modulated and transmitted through glass fibers, just as electric signals can be transmitted over wires.

- **Ultraviolet.** Ultraviolet light (UV) covers the range from about 4 to 400 nm. Ultraviolet generated by the sun is what causes sunburn. Ultraviolet is also generated by mercury vapor lights and some other types of lights such as fluorescent lamps and sun lamps. Ultraviolet is not used for communication; its primary use is medical. Beyond the visible region are the X-rays, gamma rays, and cosmic rays. These are all forms of electromagnetic radiation, but they do not figure into communication systems and are not covered here.

1.7 BASICS OF SIGNAL

- Signals are the physical representation of data. Signals are functions of time and location. Signal parameters represent the data values.

Analog / Digital, Signals and Data

- Analog signal has infinitely many levels of intensity over a period of time.

- Digital signal can have only a limited number of discrete defined values (for example 0 and 1).

- Analog data refers to information that is continuous in nature. Analog data takes continuous values.

- Digital data refers to information that has discrete state values (for example 0 and 1).

- Prototype examples for Analog signal, Digital signal, Analog data and Digital data are as shown in Fig. 1.7.

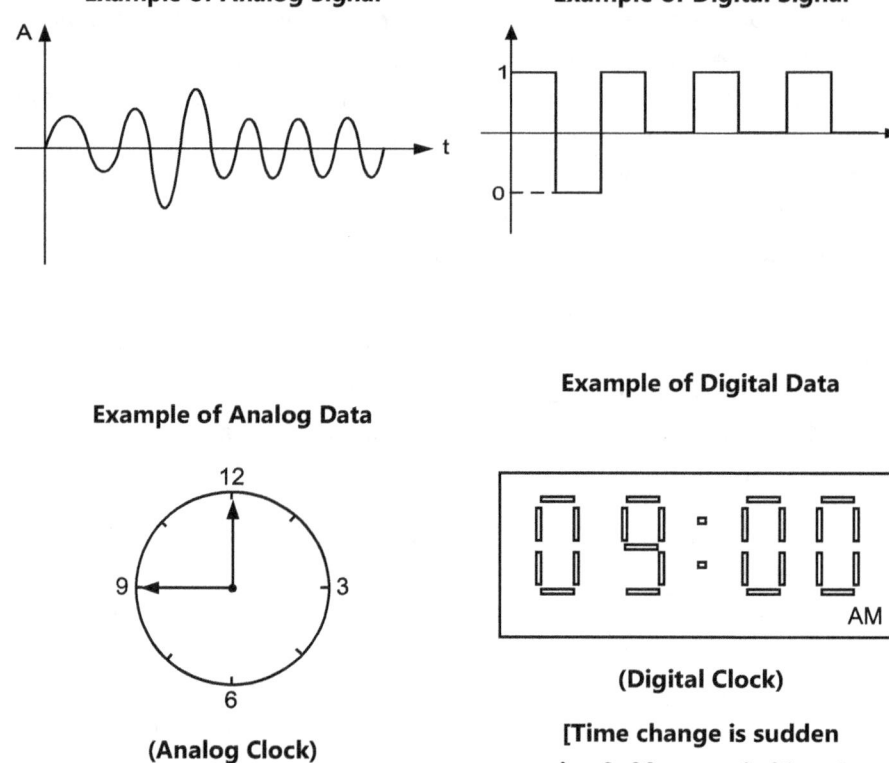

Fig. 1.7 : Analog/Digital Signals and Data Representation

1.7.1 Sine Wave Signal

- A sine wave has the same shape as the graph of the sine function used in trigonometry. Sine waves are produced by rotating electrical machines such as dynamos, power station turbines and electrical energy is transmitted to the consumer in this form.

- In electronics, sine waves are among the most useful of all signals in testing circuits and analyzing system performance. The most interesting types of signals for radio transmission are periodic signals, especially Sine waves as carriers. The general function of a sine wave is :

$$g(t) = At \sin(2\pi ft + \varphi t)$$

Signal parameters are the amplitude A, the frequency f, and the phase shift φ.

Sine wave in more detail is shown in Fig. 1.8.

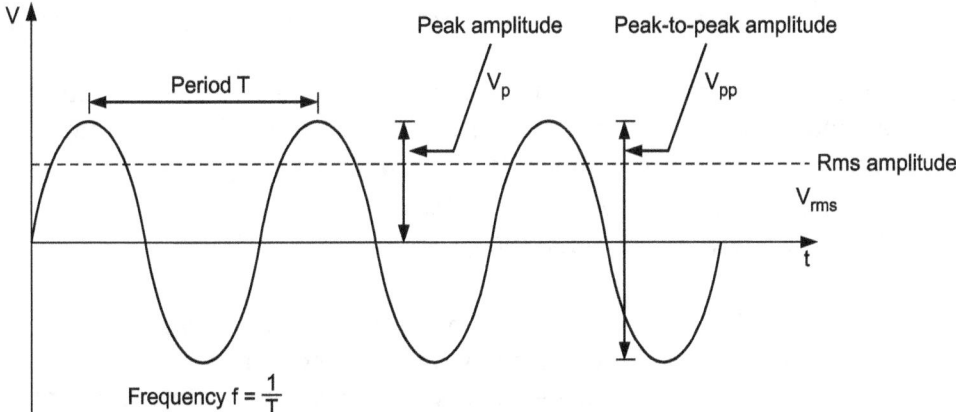

Fig. 1.8 : Sine wave representation

The terms defined below are needed to describe sine waves and other waveforms precisely :

1. Period (T)

- The period is the time taken for one complete cycle of a repeating waveform.
- The period is often thought of as the time interval between peaks, but can be measured between any two corresponding points in successive cycles.

2. Frequency (f)

- Frequency is the number of cycles completed per second.
- The measurement unit for frequency is the hertz, Hz. 1 Hz = 1 cycle per second.
- If you know the period, the frequency of the signal can be calculated from

$$f = 1 / T$$

Conversely, the period is given by

$$T = 1/f$$

- Signals you are likely to use vary in frequency from about 0.1 Hz, through values in kilohertz, kHz (thousands of cycles per second) to values in megahertz, MHz (millions of cycles per second).
- The hertz (symbol : Hz) is a unit of frequency.
- It is defined as the number of complete cycles per second. It is the basic unit of frequency in the International System of Units (SI). It is used worldwide in both general-purpose and scientific contexts.
- Hertz can be used to measure any periodic event; the most common uses of hertz are to describe radio and audio frequencies, more or less sinusoidal contexts in which case a frequency of 1 Hz is equal to one cycle per second.
- The unit hertz is defined by the International System of Units (SI).

3. Amplitude

In electronics, the amplitude, or height, of a sine wave is measured in three different ways.

The peak amplitude, V_p, is measured from the X-axis, 0 V, to the top of a peak, or to the bottom of a trough. (In physics 'amplitude' usually refers to peak amplitude.)

The peak-to-peak amplitude, V_{pp}, is measured between the maximum positive and negative values.

In practical terms, this is often the easier measurement to make. Its value is exactly twice V_p. Although peak and peak-to-peak values are easily determined, it is often   more useful to know the root mean square, or rms amplitude of the wave, where :

$$V_{rms} = V_p/\sqrt{2} \text{ or } V_{rms} = 0.7 \times V_p$$
$$\text{and } V_p = \sqrt{2} \times V_{rms} \text{ or } V_p = 1.4 \times V_{rms}$$

4. Phase

- It is sometimes useful to divide a sine wave into degrees, °, as follows :
- Remember that sine waves are generated by rotating electrical machines.
- A complete 360° turn of the voltage generator corresponds to one cycle of the sine wave.

Therefore 180° corresponds to a half turn, 90° to a quarter turn and so on. Using this method, any point on the sine wave graph can be identified by a particular number of degrees through the cycle. If two sine waves have the same frequency and occur at the same time, they are said to be in phase.

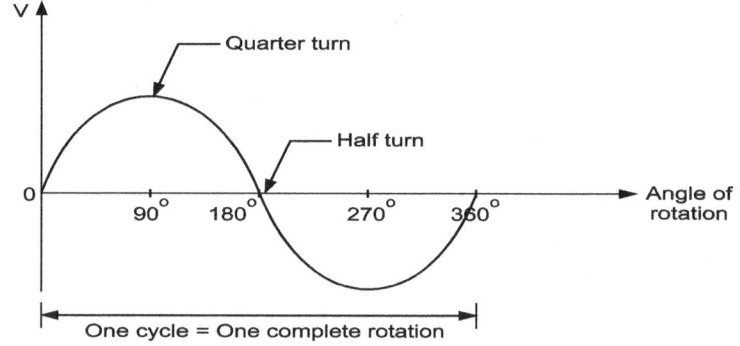

Fig. 1.9 : Phase of Sine Wave

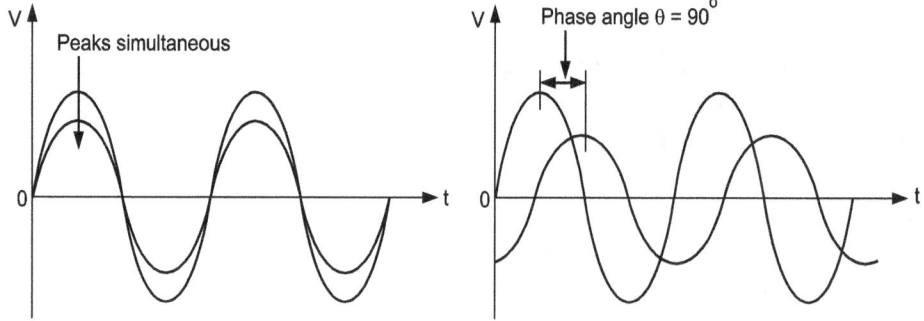

**(a) Sine waves of the same
frequency which are in phase
(b) Sine waves of the same frequency
which are a quarter cycle (90°) out of phase
Fig. 1.10 : In Phase and Out of Phase Sine Waves**

- On the other hand, if the two waves occur at different times, they are said to be out of phase.
- When this happens, the difference in phase can be measured in degrees, and is called the phase angle, θ. As you can see, the two waves in part (b) are a quarter cycle out of phase, so the phase angle θ = 90°.

Wavelength

Wavelength is the characteristic of sine wave which binds the period or the frequency of sine wave to the propagation speed of the medium.

Wavelength = Propagation speed × Period

= Propagation speed / Frequency

Where, propagation speed of electromagnetic signal = 3×10^8 m/s.

1.7.2 Digital Signals

We know that digital signal has discrete values.

Also digital signal can have more than two levels.

Two level and four level digital signals are shown in Fig. 1.11.

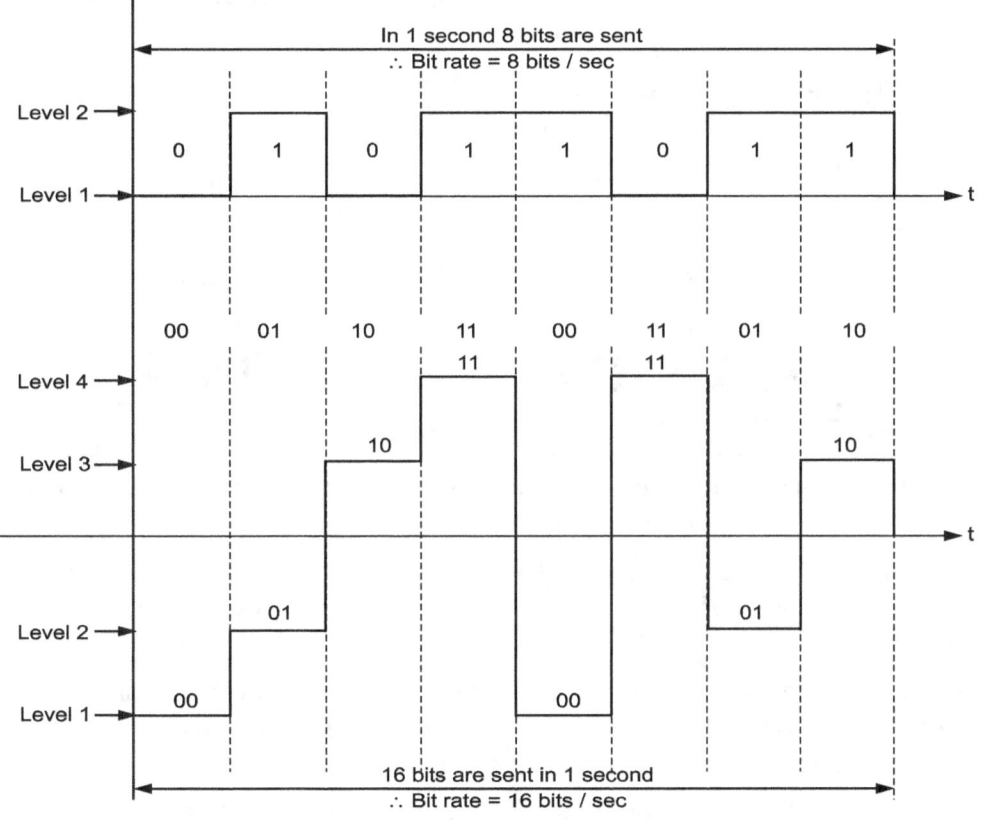

Fig. 1.11 : Two Level and Four Level Digital Signals

Bit Rate of digital signal is given as number of bits sent in one second. Hence, bit rate is given in bps.

$$\therefore \quad \text{Bit rate } = \text{ Bits/sec}$$

Bit Length of digital signal is stated as the distance one bit occupies on the transmission medium and it is given as,

$$\text{Bit length } = \text{ Propagation speed } \times \text{ Bit duration}$$

1.8 REPRESENTATION AND ANALYSIS OF SIGNALS

- A typical way to represent signals is the **time domain**. Here the amplitude A of a signal is shown versus time (time is mostly measured in seconds s, amplitudes can be measured in, e.g., volt V). This is also the typical representation known from an oscilloscope. A phase shift can also be shown in this representation.

- Representations in the time domain are problematic if a signal consists of many different frequencies.

- In this case, a better representation of a signal is the **Frequency Domain**. Here the amplitude of a certain frequency part of the signal is shown versus the frequency.

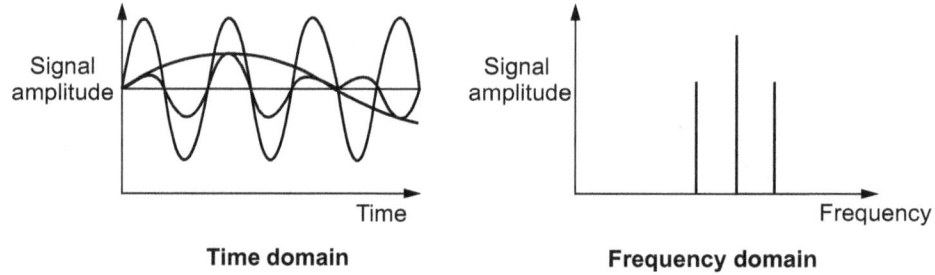

Time domain   **Frequency domain**

Fig. 1.12 : Representation of time and frequency domain

INTRODUCTION TO BASICS OF NETWORKING

1.9 COMPUTER NETWORK FUNDAMENTALS

- A network involves a number of devices linked together to form a communication system for information and device sharing.

- Local Area Networks (LANs) are small, limited to about 500 meters, and are commonly deployed in corporate offices to facilitate low-cost, high-bandwidth information transfer within a company.

- Cities and other metropolitan regions can be connected via Metropolitan Area Networks or (MANs), and Wide Area Networks (WANs) involve systems communicating across large geographic regions such as states or countries.

- Globally, computers in networks interlink to form what we refer to as "the Internet."

1.9.1 Advantages of Installing a Network

- **Speed :** Networks provide a very rapid method for sharing and transferring files. Without a network, files are shared by copying them to floppy disks, then carrying or sending the disks from one computer to another. This method of transferring files is very time-consuming.

- **Cost :** Networkable versions of many popular software programs are available at considerable savings when compared to buying individually licensed copies. Besides monetary savings, sharing a program on a network allows for easier upgrading of the program. The changes have to be done only once, on the file server, instead of on all the individual workstations.

- **Security :** Files and programs on a network can be designated as "copy inhibit," so that you do not have to worry about illegal copying of programs. Also, passwords can be established for specific directories to restrict access to authorized users.

- **Centralized Software Management :** One of the greatest benefits of installing a network is the fact that all of the software can be loaded on one computer (the file server). This eliminates the need to spend time and energy installing updates and tracking files on independent computers throughout the building.

- **Resource Sharing :** Sharing resources is another area in which a network exceeds stand-alone computers. Most institutes or companies cannot afford enough laser printers, fax machines, modems, scanners, and CD-ROM players for each computer. However, if these similar peripherals are added to a network, they can be shared by many users.

- **Electronic Mail :** The presence of a network provides the hardware necessary to install an e-mail system. E-mail aids in personal and professional communication for all personnel, and it facilitates the dissemination of general information to the entire users. Electronic mail on a LAN can enable users to communicate with others. If the LAN is connected to the Internet, user can communicate with others throughout the world.

- **Flexible Access :** Networks allow users to access their files from computers throughout the campus if it is a LAN. Users can begin an assignment in their LAN, save part of it on a public access area of the network, and then go to the media center after office hours to finish their work. Users can also work co-operatively through the network.

- **Workgroup Computing :** Workgroup software allows many users to work on a document or project concurrently.

1.9.2 Disadvantages of Installing a Network

- **Expensive to Install :** Although a network will generally save money over time, the initial cost of installation can be prohibitive. Cables, network cards, and software are expensive, and the installation may require the services of a technician.

- **Requires Administrative Time :** Proper maintenance of a network requires considerable time and expertise. Many companies have installed a network, only to find that they did not budget for the necessary administrative support.

- **File Server May Fail :** Although a file server is no more susceptible to failure than any other computer, when the files server "goes down," the entire network may come to a halt. When this happens, the entire company may lose access to necessary programs and files.
- **Cables May Break :** The Topology chapter presents information about the various configurations of cables. Some of the configurations are designed to minimize the inconvenience of a broken cable; with other configurations, one broken cable can stop the entire network.

1.9.3 Network Usage and Typical Computer Network

Networks are widely used in both the business and consumer landscapes.
- In the corporate environment, LANs are commonly used to share resources, including electronic files and devices such as printers.
- These LANs are generally connected to other networks via WANs and the Internet to facilitate global data access.
- In healthcare, LANs are used in the clinical environment to provide information such as patient's medical records and drug formularies for doctors and nurses.
- Wireless networks provide the next step in utility and convenience for many industries, including health care.
- In general, wireless networks provide the power and freedom of mobility, with the setbacks of reduced speed and unpolished functions (as compared to wired networks).
- While wireless networks have existed for decades, only the recent boom of handheld and mobile devices has spurred the demand necessary to create robust networks.
- If a home has more than one computer, then installing a computer network is a smart decision.
- Networks allow you to share an Internet connection and files among multiple PCs.

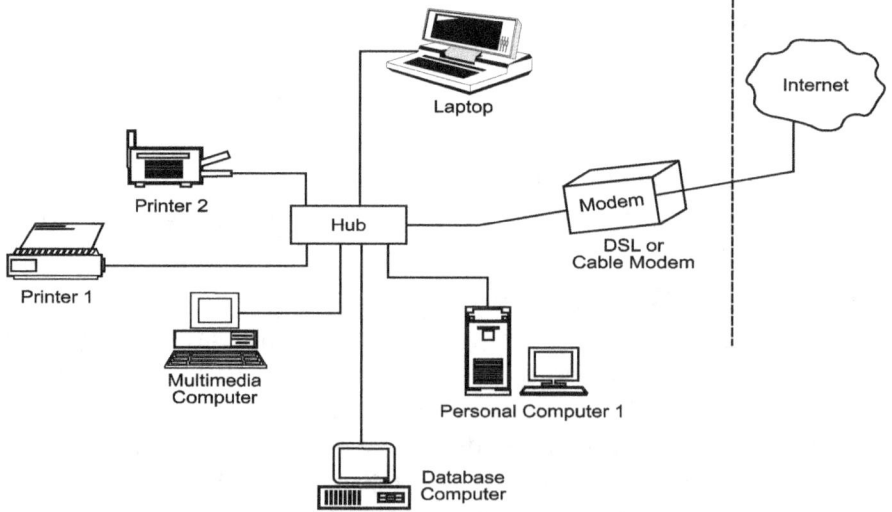

Fig. 1.13 : Typical Home Computer Network (Wired)

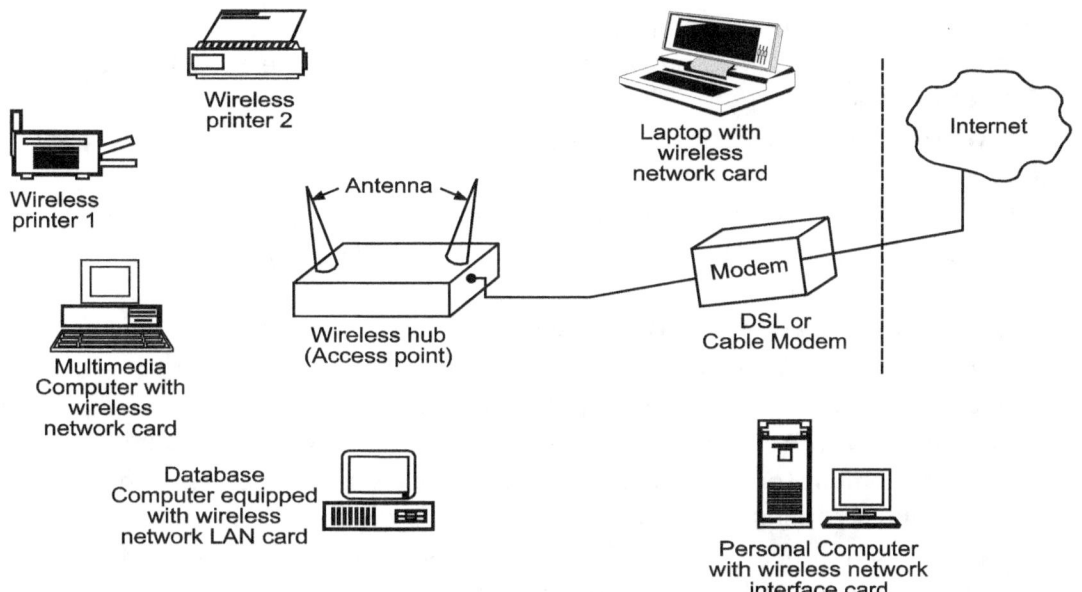

Fig. 1.14 : Typical Home Computer Network (Wireless)

- More importantly, they save time and money, and make using your computer equipment much more enjoyable for everyone in the office as well as in family.
- Let's consider the networking for the home, but all information given here applies to networking for a small business as well.
- Setting up a home network is the simplest way to get the most out of your computer equipment.
- And as your family grows or you add additional computers, expansion is no problem. Best of all, creating a network is easier than you might think.

The key benefits of networking a home include :

- Sharing a high-speed Internet connection - without anyone having to sign off, and without having another phone line installed.
- Playing games head-to-head on different computers from different rooms.
- Sharing an expensive resource like the color photo printer in office without having to interrupt any office work.
- Everyone in the family can share files from every PC in the house - no need to put files onto floppy or zip discs and swap them.

To go wireless or wired? That is the question. A wireless setup uses radio waves, while wired networks communicate through data cables. Both systems have their own advantages and disadvantages.

The following points decide whether to go for wired or wireless networks :

- **Range :** The range of the network is an important consideration while using a network.
- **Throughput :** The amount of data transferable using devices is important.

- **Integrity :** The network should have a stable form of communication. The robust designs of technology should provide data integrity performance equal to or better than other technologies.
- **Inter-Operability :** Device should provide the ability to connect to wired or wireless LAN with ease.
- **Scalability :** Networks can be designed to be extremely simple or quite complex. Networks should support large number of nodes and/or large physical areas to boost or extend coverage.
- **Simplicity of Installation and Use :** Users should need very little new information to take advantage of LANs to be used. It should be simple and easy to install.
- **Security :** Because network technology has roots in military applications and banking applications, security has long been a design criterion for network technology.
- **Power Requirement for Networks :** End-user products should be designed to run with less power and accordingly the networking technique will be decided.
- **Safety :** The used technology should be safe for human and nature. Network must meet stringent government and industry regulations for safety.

Thus Network can be Briefly Explained as follows :

- A network is a group of two or more computers that are able to communicate with one another and share data (text, sound, images), files, programs, and operations.
- The computers are able to communicate and exchange information because they use software that observes the same set of parameters, or protocol.
- There are several different types of networks.
- All networks operate using the same basic principle : Whenever a computer on network sends information to another computer or peripheral, the information is in the form of a "packet." When the packet reaches the designated station, the information is transferred to the computer.
- The basic equipment you need to set up a network includes network cards, cables, and networking software. You also need a "hub" into which all the cables are connected.

1.10 ISO OSI MODEL

1.10.1 Layered Task

- The basic need/use/application of a networking is to transfer the data from system to another system.
- It is not always data, but it can be voice, video or data.
- This is simply indicated in Fig. 1.15, that every system which is involved in data communication process is represented by a stack of layers like :
    (i)   Higher layers
    (ii)   Middle layers
    (iii)   Lower layers

- The significance of each layer and related tasks can be explained with the simple example of sending a letter by one person, which is being received by other person as shown in Fig. 1.16.
- Thus, transporting of letter from source to destination or between sender and receiver is done by carrier.
- Also each layer at the source (sender side) uses the services of the layer below it.
- The higher layer uses services of middle layer, middle layer uses the services of the lower layer and lower layer uses services of the carrier.

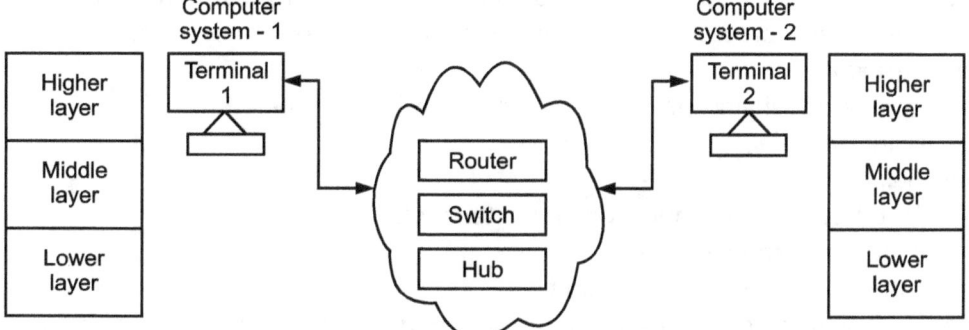

Fig. 1.15 : Network Communication System represented by Stack of Layers

- Thus, in data communication system, each system is represented by the stack of different layers. This reduces the design complexity in the networks.
- This issue is discussed in detail, in following sections.

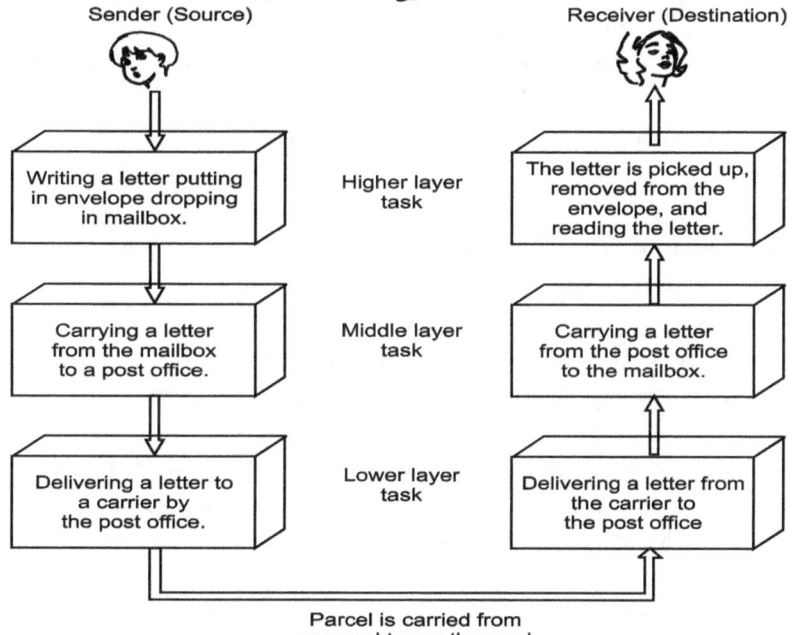

Fig. 1.16 : Tasks involved [Source to Destination] in Journey of Letter

1.10.2 Protocol Fundamentals

- In computing, a protocol is a set of rules which is used by computers to communicate with each other across a network.
- A protocol is a convention or standard that controls or enables the connection, communication, and data transfer between computing endpoints. In its simplest form, a protocol can be defined as the rules governing the syntax, semantics, and synchronization of communication.
- Protocols may be implemented by hardware, software, or a combination of the two. At the lowest level, a protocol defines the behavior of a hardware connection.

Typical Properties

Detection of the underlying physical connection (wired or wireless), or the existence of the other endpoint or node :

- Handshaking.
- Negotiation of various connection characteristics.
- How to start and end a message.
- Procedures on formatting a message.
- What to do with corrupted or improperly formatted messages (error   correction).
- How to detect unexpected loss of the connection, and what to do next.
- Termination of the session and/or connection.

Importance of Protocols

- The protocols in human communication are separate rules about appearance, speaking, listening and understanding.
- All these rules, also called protocols of conversation, represent different layers of communication.
- They work together to help people successfully communicate. The need for protocols also applies to network devices. Computers have no way of learning.

Terms and Definitions

Protocol : Protocol is agreement between the communication - communicating parties on how communication is to proceed.

Or

- **Protocol :** Protocol is strict procedure and sequence of actions to be followed in order to achieve orderly exchange of information among peer entities.

Or

- **Protocol :** Protocol is a set of rules governing the format and meaning of the frames, packets or messages that are exchanged by the peer entities within a layer.
- **Protocol Stack :** A list of protocols used by a certain system, one protocol per layer is called a protocol stack.
- **Interface :** Between each pair of adjacent layers, there is an interface. The interface defines which primitive operations and services the lower layers offers to the upper one.
- **Network Architecture :** A set of layers and protocols is called as network architecture.

- **Service :** Services and protocols are distinct concepts although they are frequently confused.
- Service is a set of primitives (operations) that a layer provides to the layer above it.
- The service defines what operations the layer is prepared to perform on behalf of its users, but it says nothing at all about how these operations are implemented.
- A service relates to an interface between two layers, with the lower layer being the service provider and the upper layer being the service user.

1.10.3 ISO OSI Reference Model

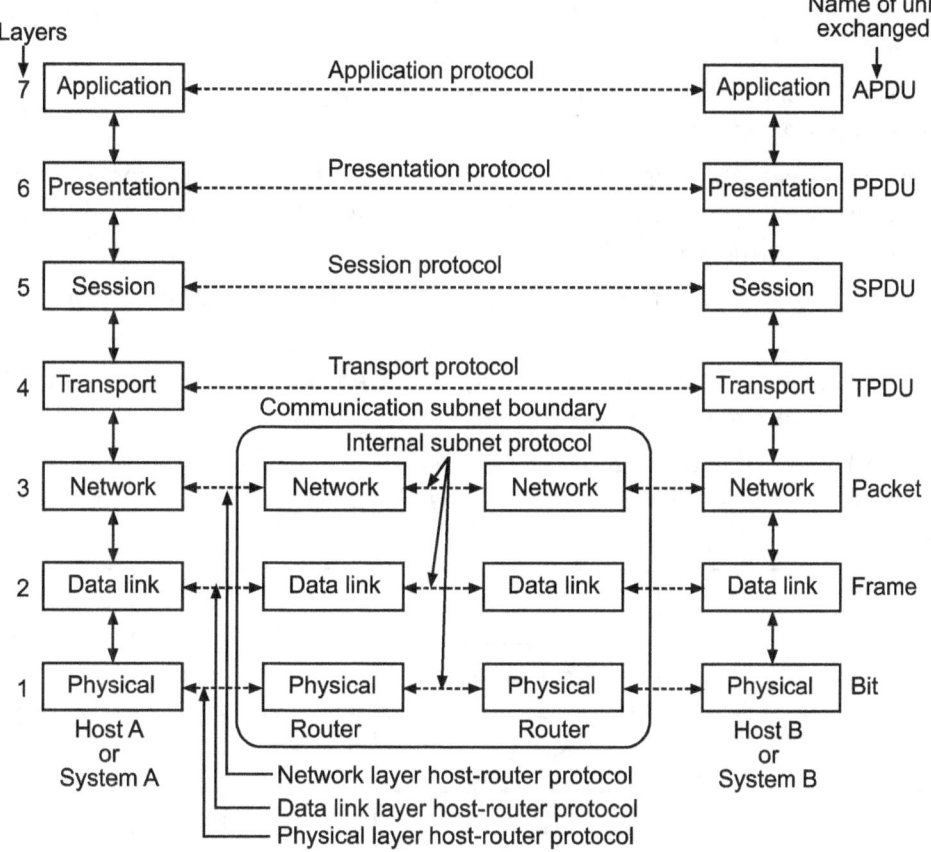

Fig. 1.17 : ISO OSI Reference Model

- This model is based on a proposal developed by the International Standards Organization (ISO) as a first step towards International Standardization of Protocols used in various layers.

- This model is called as ISO-OSI (Open Systems Interconnection) reference model because it deals with connecting open systems that is systems that are open for communication with other systems.

OSI model has seven layers. The OSI model defines a layered architecture as pictured. The protocols defined in each layer are responsible for following :

- Communicating with the same peer protocol layer running in the opposite computer.
- Providing services to the layer above it (except for the top-level application layer).
- Peer layer communication provides a way for each layer to exchange messages or other data.

Characteristics of the OSI Layers

- The seven layers of the OSI reference model can be divided into two categories : upper layers and lower layers.
- The upper layers of the OSI model deal with application issues and generally are implemented only in software.
- The highest layer, the application layer, is closest to the end user. Both users and application layer processes interact with software applications that contain a communication component.
- The term upper layer is sometimes used to refer to any layer above another layer in the OSI model.
- The lower layers of the OSI model handle data transport issues. The physical layer and the data link layer are implemented in hardware and software.
- The lowest layer, the physical layer, is closest to the physical network medium (the network cabling, for example) and is responsible for actually placing information on the medium.

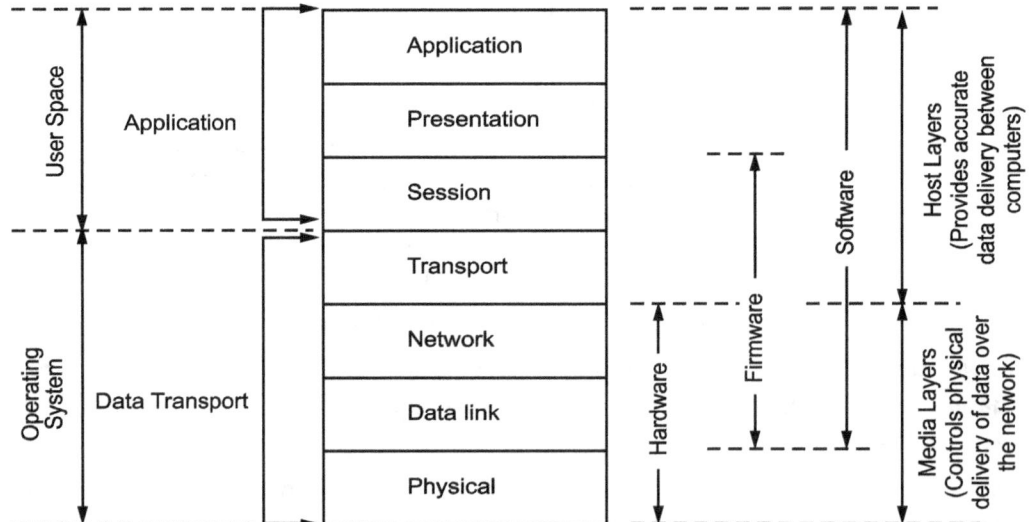

Fig. 1.18 : illustrates the division between the upper and lower OSI layers.

1.10.4 OSI Model Layers and Information Exchange

- The seven OSI layers use various forms of control information to communicate with their peer layers in other computer systems. This control information (headers) consists of specific requests and instructions that are exchanged between peer OSI layers.

- Control information typically takes one of two forms : headers and trailers.

- Headers are prepended to data that has been passed down from upper layers.

- Trailers are appended to data that has been passed down from upper layers.

- An OSI layer is not required to attach a header or a trailer to data from upper layers.

- Headers, trailers and data are relative concepts, depending on the layer that analyzes the information unit.

- At the network layer, for example, an information unit consists of a layer 3 header and data.

- At the data link layer, however, all the information is passed down by the network layer (the layer 3 header and the data) is treated as data.

- In other words, the data portion of an information unit at a given OSI layer potentially can contain headers, trailers and data from all the higher layers. This is known as encapsulation.

Information Exchange Process

- The information exchange process occurs between peer OSI layers. Each layer in the source system adds control information to data, and each layer in the destination system analyzes and removes the control information from that data.

- If System A has data from software application to send to System B, the data is passed to the application layer.

- The application layer in System A then communicates any control information required by the application layer in System B by prepending a header to the data.

- The resulting information unit (a header and the data) is passed to the presentation layer, which prepends its own header containing control information intended for the presentation layer in System B.

- The information unit grows in size as each layer prepends its own header (and, in some cases, a trailer) that contains control information to be used by its peer layer in System B.

- At the physical layer, the entire information unit is placed onto the network medium.

- The physical layer in System B receives the information unit and passes it to the data link layer.

- The data link layer in System B then reads the control information contained in the header prepended by the data link layer in System A.

- The header is then removed, and the remainder of the information unit is passed to the network layer.

- Each layer performs the same actions : The layer reads the header from its peer layer, strips it off, and passes the remaining information unit to the next highest layer.

- After the application layer performs these actions, the data is passed to the recipient software application in System B, in exactly the form in which it was transmitted by the application in System A.

1.10.5 OSI Layers in Detail

The following is a description of just what each layer does :

- The Physical layer provides the electrical and mechanical interface to the network medium (the cable). This layer gives the data-link layer (layer 2) its ability to transport a stream of serial data bits between two communicating systems. It conveys the bits that move along the cable. It is responsible for making sure that the raw bits get from one place to another, no matter what shape they are in, and deals with the mechanical and electrical characteristics of the cable.

- The Data-Link layer handles the physical transfer, framing (the assembly of data into a single unit or block), flow control and error-control functions (and retransmission in the event of an error) over a single transmission link; it is responsible for getting the data packaged and onto the network cable. The data link layer provides the network layer (layer 3) reliable information-transfer capabilities. The data-link layer is often subdivided into two parts – Logical Link Control (LLC) and Medium Access Control (MAC) depending on the implementation.

- The Network layer establishes, maintains, and terminates logical and/or physical connections. The network layer is responsible for translating logical addresses or names into physical addresses. It provides network routing and flow-control functions across the computer-network interface.

- The Transport layer ensures that data is successfully sent and received between the two computers. If data is sent incorrectly, this layer has the responsibility to ask for retransmission of the data. Specifically, it provides a network-independent, reliable message-independent, reliable message-interchange service to the top three application-oriented layers. This layer acts as an interface between the bottom and top three layers. By providing the session layer (layer 5) with a reliable message-transfer service, it hides the detailed operation of the underlying network from the session layer.

- The Session layer decides when to turn communication on and off between two computers - it provides the mechanism that controls the data-exchange process and co-ordinates the interaction between them. It sets up and clears communication channels between two communicating components. Unlike the network layer (layer 3), it deals with the programs running in each machine to establish conversations between them.

- The Presentation layer performs code conversion and data reformatting (syntax translation). It is the translator of the network, making sure that the data is in the correct form for the receiving application. Of course, both the sending and receiving applications must be able to use data subscribing to one of the available abstract data syntax forms.

- The Application layer provides the user interface between the software running in the computer and the network. It provides functions to the user's software, including file transfer access, management and electronic mail.

Thus the OSI, or Open Systems Interconnection, model defines a networking frame-work for implementing protocols in seven layers. This can be summarized in Table 1.1.

Table 1.1 : Functions of Layers

Application (Layer 7)	This layer supports application and end-user processes. Communication partners are identified, quality of service is identified, user authentication and privacy are considered, and any constraints on data syntax are identified. Everything at this layer is application-specific. This layer provides application services for file transfers, e-mail, and other network software services.
Presentation (Layer 6)	This layer provides independence from differences in data representation (e.g., encryption) by translating from application to network format, and vice versa. The presentation layer works to transform data into the form that the application layer can accept. This layer formats and encrypts data to be sent across a network, providing freedom from compatibility problems. It is sometimes called the syntax layer.
Session (Layer 5)	This layer establishes, manages and terminates connections between applications. The session layer sets up, co-ordinates, and terminates conversations, exchanges and dialogues between the applications at each end. It deals with session and connection co-ordination.
Transport (Layer 4)	This layer provides transparent transfer of data between end systems, or hosts, and is responsible for end-to-end error recovery and flow control. It ensures complete data transfer.
Network (Layer 3)	This layer provides switching and routing technologies, creating logical paths, known as virtual circuits, for transmitting data from node to node. Routing and forwarding are functions of this layer, as well as addressing,

	internetworking, error handling, congestion control and packet sequencing.
Data Link (Layer 2)	At this layer, data packets are encoded and decoded into bits. It furnishes transmission protocol knowledge and management and handles errors in the physical layer, flow control and frame synchronization. The data link layer is divided into two sublayers : The Media Access Control (MAC) layer and the Logical Link Control (LLC) layer. The MAC sublayer controls how a computer on the network gains access to the data and permission to transmit it. The LLC layer controls frame synchronization, flow control and error checking.
Physical (Layer 1)	This layer conveys the bit stream electrical impulse, light or radio signal through the network at the electrical and mechanical level. It provides the hardware means of sending and receiving data on a carrier, including defining cables, cards and physical aspects. Fast Ethernet, RS-232 and ATM are protocols with physical layer components.

Table 1.2 : Application Oriented Explanation

Iso-osi Reference Model Layers	Functions
Application Layer (Layer 7)	Computer Applications like Word processor, Presentation Graphics, Spreadsheet, Database. Network Applications like Email, FTP, Remote Access, Client-Server, Peer-to-Peer, Network management. Internetwork Applications like WWW, Data Exchange, Email Gateways, Finance transactions, Conferencing.
Presentation Layer (Layer 6)	Provides data formats, translations and code conversion. Data compression and Data encryption. Text/data (ASCII or EBCDIC). Sound/Video (MP3, Wave, Mpeg, Quick time). Graphics/Images (JPEG, Gif, BMP).
Sessional Layer (Layer 5)	Network file System (NFS), X-Windows System. Re-establishment of connection in case of failure. Connection Permission Half-Duplex, Full Duplex.

	Dialog control.
	Synchronization.
	Process to process delivery.
Transport Layer (Layer 4)	Establishes reliable End-to-End transport connection.
	Flow control, error control, connection control.
	Data error detection, recovery for end-to-end connection.
Network Layer (Layer 3)	Routing Algorithm (Routing).
	Logical addressing.
	Congestion Control Algorithm.
	Internetworking.
Data Link Layer (Layer 2)	NIC (Network Interface Card) Driver has LLC (Logical Link Control)-Framing, Flow Control, Error Control, etc.
	MAC (Media Access Control)-802.3, 802.4, 802.5, etc.
Physical Layer (Layer 1)	Handles Voltages and Electrical Pulses.
	Specifies Cables, Connectors and Media Interface Component.

1.11 TCP/IP PROTOCOL SUITE

1.11.1 Introduction to TCP/IP

- TCP/IP is a suite of protocols, also known as the Internet Protocol Suite. It should not be confused with the OSI reference model, although elements of TCP/IP exist in OSI.

- The Transmission Control Protocol and the Internet Protocol are fundamental to the suite, hence the TCP/IP title.

- TCP/IP is a set of protocols developed to allow co-operating computers to share resources across a network.

- A community of researchers centered around the ARPANET developed this TCP/IP.

- The Internet protocol suite is the set of communication protocols that implement the protocol stack on which the internet and most commercial networks run.

- The internet protocol suite like many protocol suites can be viewed as a set of layers, each layer solves a set of problems involving the transmission of data, and provides a well-defined service to the upper layer protocols based on using services from some lower layers.

- Upper layers are logically closer to the user and deal with more abstract data, relying on lower layer protocols to translate data into forms that can eventually be physically transmitted.

- The Transmission Control Protocol/Internet Protocol (TCP/IP) protocol suite is the engine for the Internet and networks worldwide.

- Its simplicity and power has led to its becoming the single network protocol of choice in the world today. In this chapter, we give an overview of the TCP/IP protocol suite.

| Application Layer |
| Transport Layer |
| Network Layer |
| (or Internet Layer) |

Fig. 1.19 : Typical four-layer TCP/IP Model

OSI-ISO Reference Model   TCP/IP Model

Application Layer (7)	Application Layer
Presentation Layer (6)	
Session Layer (5)	
Transport Layer (4)	Transport Layer
Network Layer (3)	Network Layer
Data Link Layer (2)	Layer 1 and Layer 2
Physical Layer (1)	

Fig. 1.20 : 7-Layer OSI Model and 4-Layer TCP/IP Model

Socket Application	← Application Layer
TCP and UDP	← Transport Layer
IP, ICMP, IGMP, ARP, RARP	← Network Layer
$\begin{bmatrix} \text{LAN Technologies} \\ \text{802.3, 802.4, 802.5} \end{bmatrix}$ and $\begin{bmatrix} \text{WAN Technologies} \\ \text{PPP, Frame relay, ATM} \end{bmatrix}$	← Lower layers

Fig. 1.21 : TCP/IP 4 layers and main protocols

- The main design goal of TCP/IP was to build an interconnection of networks, referred to as an Internetwork, or Internet, that provided universal communication services over heterogeneous physical networks.

- The clear benefit of such an internetwork is the enabling of communication between hosts on different networks, perhaps separated by a large geographical area.

1.11.2 Layers in the Internet Protocol Suite Stack

- The IP suite uses encapsulation to provide abstraction of protocols and services. Generally a protocol at a higher level uses a protocol at a lower level to help accomplish its aims. The internet protocol stack can be roughly fitted into the four fixed layers and are shown before.

Application Layer

- This layer is broadly equivalent to the application, presentation and session layers of the OSI model.
- It gives an application access to the communication environment.
- Examples of protocols found at this layer are Telnet, FTP (File Transfer Protocol), SNMP (Simple Network Management Protocol), HTTP (Hyper Text Transfer Protocol) and SMTP (Simple Mail Transfer Protocol).
- An application is a user process co-operating with another process usually on a different host (there is also a benefit to application communication within a single host).
- The interface between the application and transport layers is defined by port numbers and sockets.

Transport Layer

- The transport layer is similar to the OSI transport model, but with elements of the OSI session layer functionality.
- This layer provides an application layer delivery service.
- The two protocols found at the transport layer are TCP (Transmission Control Protocol) and UDP (User Datagram Protocol).
- Either of these two protocols are used by the application layer process, the choice depends on the application's transmission reliability requirements.
- Transport layer provides the end-to-end data transfer by delivering data from an application to its remote peer.
- Multiple applications can be supported simultaneously.
- The most-used transport layer protocol is the Transmission Control Protocol (TCP), which provides connection-oriented reliable data delivery, duplicate data suppression, congestion control, and flow control.
- TCP is a reliable, connection-oriented protocol that provides error checking and flow control through a virtual link that it establishes and finally terminates.
- This gives a reliable service, therefore TCP would be utilized by FTP and SNMP File transfer and email delivery have to be accurate and error free.
- UDP is an unreliable, connectionless protocol that provides data transport with lower network traffic overheads than TCP. UDP does not error check or offer any flow control, this is left to the application process.
- SNMP uses UDP. SNMP is used to monitor network performance, so its operation must not contribute to congestion.

Network Layer or Internet Layer

- This layer is responsible for the routing and delivery of data across networks.

- It allows communication across networks of the same and different types and carries out translations to deal with dissimilar data addressing schemes.

- Internetwork layer, also called the internet layer or the network layer, provides the "virtual network" image of an internet (this layer shields the higher levels from the physical network architecture below it).

- Internet Protocol (IP) is the most important protocol in this layer.

- It is a connectionless protocol that doesn't assume reliability from lower layers. IP does not provide reliability, flow control, or error recovery. These functions must be provided at a higher level.

- A message unit in an IP network is called an IP datagram.

- This is the basic unit of information transmitted across TCP/IP networks.

- Other internetwork layer protocols are IP, ICMP, IGMP, ARP and RARP.

- With the advent of the concept of Internetworking, additional functionality was added to this layer, namely getting data from the source network to the destination network.

- This generally involves routing the packet across a network of networks, known as an internet.

- In the internet protocol suite, IP performs the basic task of getting packets of data from source to destination.

- IP can carry data for a number of different upper layer protocols; these protocols are each identified by a unique protocol number.

- ICMP and IGMP are protocols 1 and 2, respectively.

- Some of the protocols carried by IP, such as ICMP (used to transmit diagnostic information about IP transmission) and IGMP (used to manage multicast data) are layered on top of IP but perform internetwork layer functions, illustrating an incompatibility between the internet and the IP stack and OSI model.

- All routing protocols, such as BGP, OSPF, and RIP are also really part of the network layer, although they might seem to belong higher in the stack.

Layers 2 and 1 (Network Access Layers)

- The combination of data link and physical layers deals with pure hardware (wires, satellite links, network interface cards, etc.) and access methods such as CSMA/CD (carrier sensed multiple access with collision detection).

- Ethernet exists at the network access layer – it's hardware operates at the physical layer and its medium access control method (CSMA/CD) operates at the data link layer.

- Network interface layer, also called the link layer or the data-link layer, is the interface to the actual network hardware.

- This interface may or may not provide reliable delivery, and may be packet or stream oriented.

- In fact, TCP/IP does not specify any protocol here, but can use almost any network interface available, which illustrates the flexibility of the IP layer.

- The link layer is not really part of the internet protocol suite, but is the method used to pass packets from the network layer on two different hosts.

- This process can be controlled both in the software device driver for the network card, as well as on firmware or specialist chipsets.

- These will perform data link functions such as adding a packet header to prepare it for transmission, and then actually transmit the frame over a physical medium.

- The link layer can also be the layer where packets are intercepted to be sent over a virtual private network.

- When this is done, the link layer data is considered the application data and proceeds back down the IP stack for actual transmission.

- On the receiving end, the data goes up the IP stack twice (once for the VPN and the second time for routing).

- The physical layer is made up of the actual physical network components (hubs, repeaters, network cable, fiber optic cable, coaxial cable, network cards, Host Bus Adapter cards and the associated network connectors : RJ-45, BNC, etc).

1.12 ADDRESSING (PHYSICAL, LOGICAL PORT AND OTHER)

In the data communication like Internet communication following types of addresses are used.

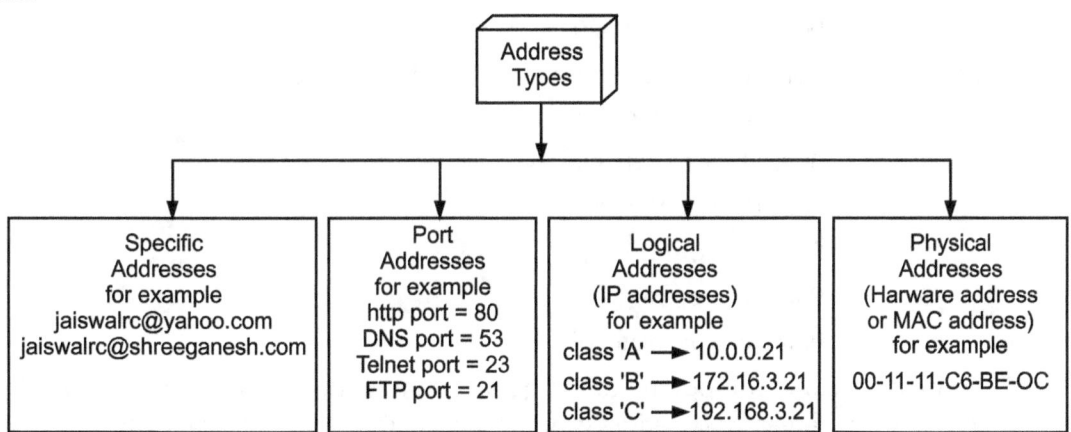

Fig. 1.22 (a) : Types of Addresses in Networking

These addresses are related to specific layer of the TCP/IP layered architecture.

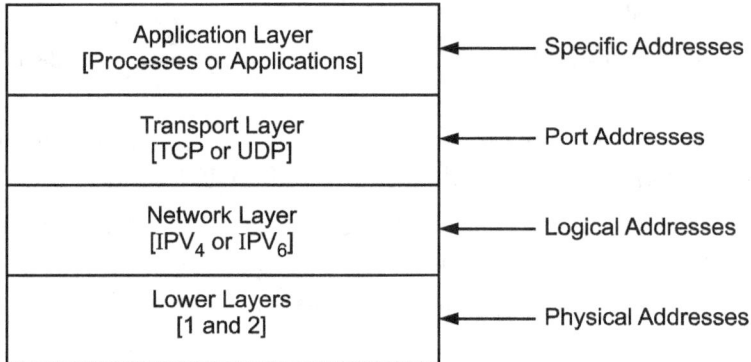

Fig. 1.22 (b) : Layer Specific Addresses are indicated

1.12.1 MAC Address

* The MAC address is a unique value associated with a network adapter. MAC addresses are also known as hardware addresses or physical addresses. They uniquely identify an adapter on a LAN.

* MAC addresses are 12-digit hexadecimal numbers (48 bits in length). By convention, MAC addresses are usually written in one of the following two formats :

    MM :MM :MM :SS :SS :SS

    MM-MM-MM-SS-SS-SS

* The first half of a MAC address contains the ID number of the adapter manufacturer. These IDs are regulated by an Internet standards body (see sidebar). The second half of a MAC address represents the serial number assigned to the adapter by the manufacturer.

* In the example,

    00 :A0 :C9 :14 :C8 :29

* The prefix 00A0C9 indicates the manufacturer in Intel Corporation.

    00000C-For CISCO

    000011- for Tektronics

    00001B- For Novell

    000048- For Epson

    0000C6- For HP

    08003E- For Motorola

* MAC addresses allow computers to uniquely identify themselves on a network at relatively low level, whereas MAC addressing works at the data link layer, IP addressing functions at the network layer (layer 3).

- It is a slight oversimplification, but one can think of IP addressing as supporting the software implementation and MAC addresses as supporting the hardware implementation of the network stack.

- The MAC address generally remains fixed and follows the network device, but the IP address changes as the network device moves from one network to another.

- IP networks maintain a mapping between the IP address of a device and its MAC address. This mapping is known as the ARP cache or ARP table.

- ARP, the Address Resolution Protocol, supports the logic for obtaining this mapping and keeping the cache up to date.

- DHCP also usually relies on MAC addresses to manage the unique assignment of IP addresses to devices.

- In Windows OS, At the command prompt, type 'ipconfig /all' without quotes and you can get MAC address of the LAN card or if using Windows XP, you can use the command '**getmac**'.

1.12.2 IP Address

- Every machine on the Internet has a unique number assigned to it, called an IP address. Without an unique IP address on your machine, you will not be able to communicate with other devices, users, and computers on the Internet. You can look at your IP address as if it were a telephone number, each one being unique and used to identify a way to reach you and only you.

- An IP address always consists of 4 numbers separated by periods, with the numbers having a possible range of 0 through 255. An example of how an IP address appears is : 192.168.1.10.

- This representation of an IP address is called decimal notation and is what is generally used by humans to refer to an IP address for readability purposes. With the ranges for each number being between 0 and 255 there are a total 4,294,967,296 possible IP addresses (4 Billions).

- Out of these addresses there are 3 special ranges that are reserved for special purposes. The first is the 0.0.0.0 address and refers to the default network and the 255.255.255.255 address which is called the broadcast address. These addresses are used for routing. The third address, 127.0.0.1, is the loopback address, and refers to your machine. Whenever you see, 127.0.0.1, you are actually referring to your own machine.

- There are some guidelines to how IP address can appear, though. The four numbers must be between 0 and 255, and the IP address of 0.0.0.0 and 255.255.255.255 are reserved, and are not considered usable IP addresses.

- IP addresses must be unique for each computer connected to a network. That means that if you have two computers on your network, each must have a different IP address to be able to communicate with each other. If by accident the same IP address is assigned to two computers, then those computers would have what is called an "IP Conflict" and not be able to communicate with each other.

- IP address classes : These IP addresses can further be broken down into classes. These classes are A, B, C, D, E and their possible ranges can be seen in table.

Table 1.3 Classes and their ranges

Class	Start address	Finish address
A	0.0.0.0	126.255.255.255
B	128.0.0.0	191.255.255.255
C	192.0.0.0	223.255.255.255
D	224.0.0.0	239.255.255.255
E	240.0.0.0	255.255.255.255

- If you look at the table you may notice something strange. The range of IP address from Class A to Class B skips the 127.0.0.0-127.255.255.255 range. That is because this range is reserved for the special addresses called Loopback addresses that have already been discussed above.

- The rest of classes are allocated to companies and organizations based upon the amount of IP addresses that they may need. Listed below are descriptions of the IP classes and the organizations that will typically receive that type of allocation.

- Default Network : The special network 0.0.0.0 is generally used for routing.

- Class A : From the table above you see that there are 126 class A networks. These networks consist of 16,777,214 possible IP addresses that can be assigned to devices and computers. This type of allocation is generally given to very large networks such as multi-national companies.

- Loopback : This is the special 127.0.0.0 network that is reserved as a loopback to your own computer. These addresses are used for testing and debugging of your programs or hardware.

- Class B : This class consists of 16,384 individual networks, each allocation consisting of 65,534 possible IP addresses. These blocks are generally allocated to Internet Service Providers and large networks, like a college or major hospital.

- Class C : There is a total of 2,097,152 Class C networks available, with each network consisting of 255 individual IP addresses. This type of class is generally given to small to mid-sized companies.

- Class D : The IP addresses in this class are reserved for a service called Multicast.

- Class E : The IP addresses in this class are reserved for experimental use.

- Broadcast : This is the special network of 255.255.255.255, and is used for broadcasting messages to the entire network that your computer resides on.

Private IP Addresses

- There are also blocks of IP addresses that are set aside for internal private use for computers not directly connected to the Internet.

- These IP addresses are not supposed to be routed through the Internet, and most service providers will block the attempt to do so.

- These IP addresses are used for internal use by company or home networks that need to use TCP/IP but do not want to be directly visible on the Internet. These IP ranges are :

Class	Private Start Address	Private End Address
A	10.0.0.0	10.255.255.255
B	172.16.0.0	172.31.255.255
C	192.168.0.0	192.168.255.255

- If you are on a home/office private network and want to use TCP/IP, you should assign your computers/devices IP addresses from one of these three ranges. That way your router/firewall would be the only device with a true IP address which makes your network more secure.

1.12.3 Port Address

- In internet communication, the actual data communication is done between two processes of the system 1 and system 2.

- For example, web browser is communicating with webserver on the internet. Hence, on one computer system web-browsing process is running and on other computer system webserver process is running.

- Hence, at both ends the logical port numbers are assigned by operating system and TCP/IP protocol stack.

- IANA (Internet Assigned Number Authority) has divided port numbers into three ranges as shown in Fig. 1.23.

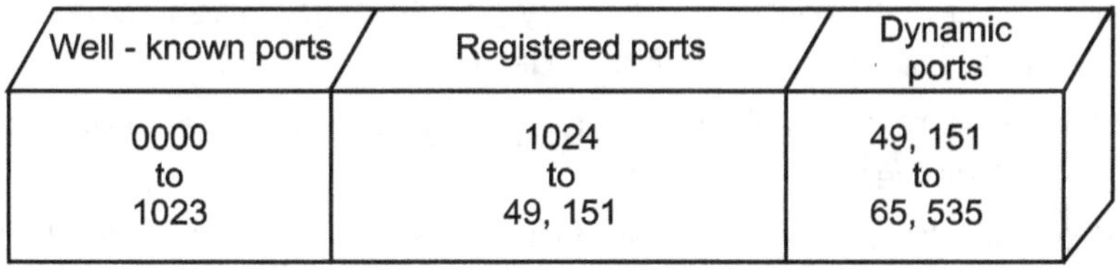

Well - known ports	Registered ports	Dynamic ports
0000 to 1023	1024 to 49, 151	49, 151 to 65, 535

Fig. 1.23 : IANA Ports Address Range

- Thus, for web-browsing process port no. 1023 above numbers are used whereas for webserver process well known port – 80 is used.

- Well known port for webserver process is 80, for FTP is 21, Telnet – 23, DNS – 53 and for SMTP is 25.
- Port addresses used by computer systems can be checked using command netstat – n – a on command prompt.

1.12.4 Node to Node, Host to Host and Process to Process Delivery

Thus, MAC address, IP address and port addresses are used by different layers like data link layer, network layer and transport layer respectively.

This concept is easily explained in Fig. 1.24.

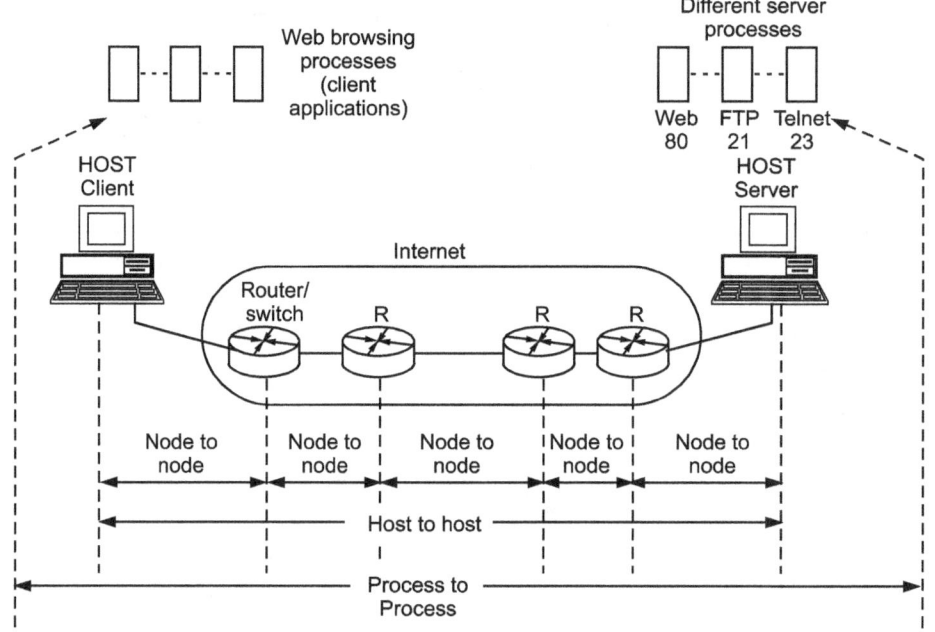

Node to Node : Data link layer.

Host to Host : Network layer.

Process to Process : Transport layer

Fig. 1.24 : Layers and Data Delivery

- The data link layer is responsible for delivery of frames between two neighboring nodes over a link. This is called as Node-to-Node delivery.
- The network layer is responsible for delivery of datagrams between two hosts. This is called host to host delivery.
- Communication on the Internet is not defined as the exchange of data between two nodes or between two hosts. Real communication takes place between two processes or application programs. We need process to process delivery.
- The transport layer is responsible for process-to-process delivery. Two processes communicate in a client/server relationship.

1.13 TYPES OF NETWORK (LAN, WAN MAN)

1.13.1 LAN

- Networks used to interconnect computers in a single room, rooms within a building or buildings on one site are called Local Area Network (LAN).

- LAN transmits data with a speed of several megabits per second (106 bits per second). The transmission medium is normally coaxial cables.

- LAN links computers, i.e., software and hardware, in the same area for the purpose of sharing information.

- Usually LAN links computers within a limited geographical area because they must be connected by a cable, which is quite expensive.

- People working in LAN get more capabilities in data processing, work processing and other information exchange compared to stand-alone computers.

- Because of this information exchange, most of the business and government organizations are using LAN.

Major Characteristics of LAN

- Every computer has the potential to communicate with any other computers of the network.

- High degree of interconnection between computers.

- Easy physical connection of computers in a network.

- Inexpensive medium of data transmission.

- High data transmission rate.

Components of LAN

1. Workstations

- In LAN, a workstation refers to a machine that will allow users to access a LAN and its resources while providing intelligence on board allowing local execution of applications.

- It may allow data to be stored locally or remotely on a file server.

- Obviously, diskless workstations require all data to be stored remotely, including that data necessary for the diskless machine to boot up.

- Executable files may reside locally or remotely as well, meaning a workstation can run its own programs or those copied off the LAN.

2. Servers

- A server is a computer that provides the data, software and hardware resources that are shared on the LAN.

- A LAN can have more than one server; each has its unique name on the network and all LAN users identify the server by its name.

- **Dedicated Server :** A server that functions only as a storage area for data and software and allows access to hardware resources is called a dedicated server. Dedicated servers need to be powerful computers.

- **Non-Dedicated Server :** In many LANs, the server is just another work station. Thus, there is a user networking on the computer and using it as a workstation, but part of the computer also doubles up as a server. Such a server is called a non-dedicated server. Since, it is not completely dedicated to serving. LANs do not require a dedicated server since resource sharing amongst a few workstations is proportionately on a smaller scale.

- **Other Types of Servers :** In large installations, which have hundreds of workstations sharing resource, a single computer is often not sufficient to function as a server.

Some of the other servers have been discussed here under :

File Server : A file server stores files that workstations can access and it also decides on the rights and restrictions that the users need to have while accessing files on LAN.

Printer Server : A Printer server takes care of the printing requirement of number of workstations.

Modem Server : It allows LAN users to use the modem to transmit long distance messages. Server attached to one or two modems would serve the purpose.

3. Clients

- A client is any machine that requires something from a server.

- In the more common definition of a client, the server supplies files and sometimes processing power to the smaller machines connected to it.

- Each machine is a client.

- Thus a typical ten PC local area network may have one large server with all the major files and databases on it and all the other machines connected as clients.

- This type of terminology is common with TCP/IP networks, where no single machine is necessarily the central repository.

4. Nodes

- Small networks that comprise of a server and number of PCs.

- Each PC on the network is called a node.

- A node essentially means any device that is attached to the network. Because each machine has a unique name or number (so the rest of the network can identify it), you will hear the term node name or node number quite often.

5. Network Interface Cards

- The Network Interface card, or LAN adapter, functions as an interface between the computer and the network cabling, so it must serve two masters.

- Inside the computer, it controls the flow of data to and from the Random-Access Memory (RAM).
- Outside the computer, it controls the flow of data in and out of the network cable system.
- An interface card has a specialized port that matches the electrical signaling standards used on the cable and the specific type of cable connector.
- One must select a network interface card that matches your computer's data bus and the network cable.
- Token ring LANs require token ring NICs, Ethernet LANs require Ethernet NICs, etc.
- The peripheral component interface bus (PCI) has emerged as a new standard for adapter card interfaces.
- It is advisable to use bus PCI-equipped computers and PCI LAN adapters wherever possible.
- Software is required to interface between a particular NIC and an operating system called as Network Interface Card Driver.

6. Connectors

- Connectors used with TP included RJ-11 and RJ-45 modular connectors in current used by phone companies.
- Occasionally other special connectors, such as IBM's Data Connector, are used.
- RJ-11 connectors accommodate 4 wires or 2 twisted pairs, while RJ-45 houses 8 wires or 4 twisted pairs.

7. The Network Operating System :

- The Network Operating System software acts as the command center, enabling all of the network hardware and all other network software to function together as one cohesive, organized system.
- In other words, the network operating system is the heart of the network.
- It can be client-server or Peer-to-Peer Network Operating System.

Advantages of LAN

- The reliability of network is high because the failure of one computer in the network does not affect the functioning for other computers.
- Addition of new computer to network is easy.
- High rate of data transmission is possible.
- Peripheral devices like magnetic disk and printer can be shared by other computers.

Uses of LAN

Followings are the major areas where LAN is normally used :

- File transfer and Access

- Word and text processing
- Electronic message handling
- Remote database access
- Personal computing
- Digital voice transmission and storage
- Office automation
- Factory automation
- Distributed Computing
- Fire and Security Systems
- Process Control
- Document Distribution.

1.13.2 WAN

- The term Wide Area Network (WAN) is used to describe a computer network spanning a regional, national or global area.
- For example, for a large company the headquarters might be at Delhi and regional branches at Mumbai, Chennai, Bangaluru and Kolkata.
- Here regional centers are connected to headquarters through WAN.
- The distance between computers connected to WAN is larger. Therefore the transmission mediums used are normally telephone lines, microwaves and satellite links.

Characteristics of WAN

Following are the major characteristics of WAN.

1. Communication Facility

- For a big company spanning over different parts of the country, the employees can save long distance phone calls and it overcomes the time lag in overseas communications.
- Computer conferencing is another use of WAN where users communicate with each other through their computer system.

2. Remote Data Entry

- Remote data entry is possible in WAN. It means sitting at any location you can enter data, update data and query other information of any computer attached to the WAN but located in other cities.
- For example, suppose you are sitting at Chennai and want to see some data of a computer located at Delhi, you can do it through WAN.

3. Centralized Information

* In modern computerized environment you will find that big organizations go for centralized data storage.

* This means if the organization is spread over many cities, they keep their important business data in a single place.

* As the data are generated at different sites, WAN permits collection of this data from different sites and save at a single site.

Difference between LAN and WAN

* LAN is restricted to limited geographical area of few kilometers. But WAN covers great distance and operate nationwide or even worldwide.

* In LAN, the computer terminals and peripheral devices are connected with wires and coaxial cables. In WAN there is no physical connection. Communication is done through telephone lines and satellite links.

* Cost of data transmission in LAN is less because the transmission medium is owned by a single organization. In case of WAN the cost of data transmission is very high because the transmission mediums used are wired, either telephone lines or satellite links.

* The speed of data transmission is much higher in LAN than in WAN. The transmission speed in LAN varies from 0.1 to 100 megabits per second. In case of WAN the speed ranges from 1800 to 9600 bits per second (bps).

* Few data transmission errors occur in LAN compared to WAN. It is because in LAN the distance covered is negligible.

1.13.3 METROPOLITAN AREA NETWORK (MAN)

* A Metropolitan Area Network (MAN) is a bigger version of a Local Area Network (LAN) and usually uses similar technology.

* A MAN can cover a group of corporate offices or a town or city, and can be either privately or publicly owned. A MAN can support both data and voice, and may be related to the local cable television network (CATV).

* A MAN employs one or two cables, and does not contain switching elements, which simplifies the design.

* A standard has been adopted for MANs called Distributed Queue Dual Bus (DQDB) and is defined by IEEE 802.6.

* DQDB consists of two unidirectional buses (cables) to which all of the computers on the network are connected.

* Each bus has a head-end that initiates transmission activity.

* In the following diagram, traffic that is intended for a computer to the right of the source computer uses the upper bus, while traffic intended for a computer to the left uses the lower bus.

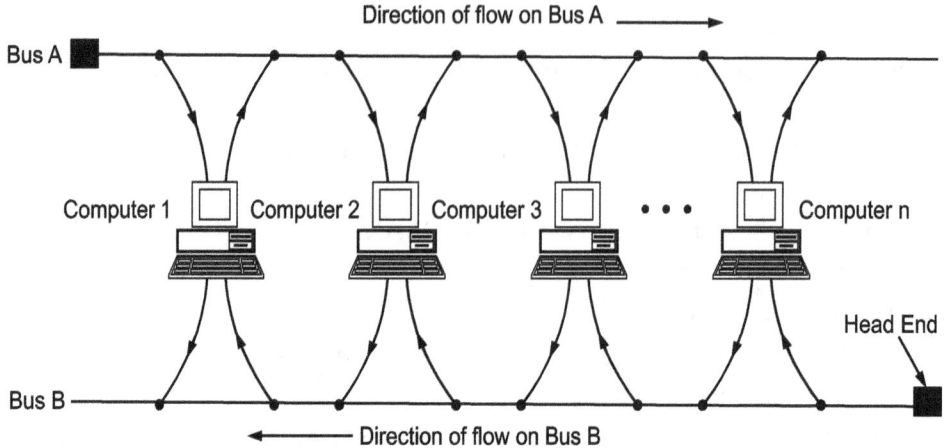

Fig. 1.25 : Typical MAN Network (also known as 802.6 DQDB network)

- The network is based on fiber-optic cable in a dual-bus topology, and traffic on each bus is unidirectional, providing a fault-tolerant configuration.

- Bandwidth is allocated using time slots, and both synchronous and asynchronous modes are supported.

1.14 NETWORK TOPOLOGIES

- The physical topology of a network refers to the configuration of cables, computers, and other peripherals.

- Physical topology should not be confused with logical topology which is the method used to pass information between workstations.

- Every LAN has a topology, or the way that the devices on a network are arranged and how they communicate with each other.

- The way that the workstations are connected to the network through the actual cables that transmits data and the physical structure of the network is called the physical topology.

- The logical topology is also called as signal topology.

- The logical topology is the way that the signals act on the network media, or the way that the data passes through the network from one device to the next without regard to the physical interconnection of the devices.

- Logical topologies are bound to the network protocols that direct how the data moves across a network.

- The Ethernet protocol is a common logical bus topology protocol.

- LocalTalk is a common logical bus or star topology protocol. IBM's Token Ring is a common logical ring topology protocol.

- A network's logical topology is not necessarily the same as its physical topology. For example, twisted pair Ethernet is a logical bus topology in a physical star topology layout. While IBM's Token Ring is a logical ring topology, it is physically set up in a star topology.

1.14.1 Network Topology (Physical)

- The way, in which the connections are made, is called the topology of the network.
- Network topology specifically refers to the physical layout of the network, especially the locations of computers and how the cable is run between them.
- It is important to select the right topology.
- Each topology has its own strengths and weaknesses.

The four most common topologies are :

(i) Bus   (ii) Star (iii) Ring   (iv) Mesh

1.   Bus Topology

Bus topology is often used when network installation is small.

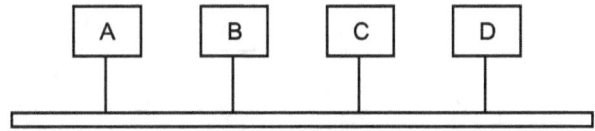

Fig. 1.26 : Bus Topology

Advantages

- Simple and reliable in very small network, easy to use and understand.
- Least amount of cable required to connect computers, so it is less expensive.
- Extension of bus is easy by joining cable and using BNC connector. So more computers can be connected.
- A repeater can also be used to extend a bus, boost the signal and allow it to travel a longer distance.

Disadvantages

- Heavy traffic (network traffic) can slow a bus considerably, because any computer can transmit data any time, uses entire B.W. and interrupts each other instead of communicating.
- Each barrel connector weakens the signal power.
- It is difficult to troubleshoot bus. A cable break or loose connector will also cause reflections and bring down the whole network and network activity stops.

2. Star Topology

Star networks are used in concentrated networks, where the end-points are directly reachable from a central location. When network expansion is expected and when the greater reliability is needed, Hub may be used.

Advantages

- It is very easy to modify and add new network without disturbing the rest of the network.

- Center of a star network is good place to diagnose network faults.

- Single computer failure does not bring down the whole network.

- With hub, you can use several cable types - UTP, STP, coaxial, fiber, etc.

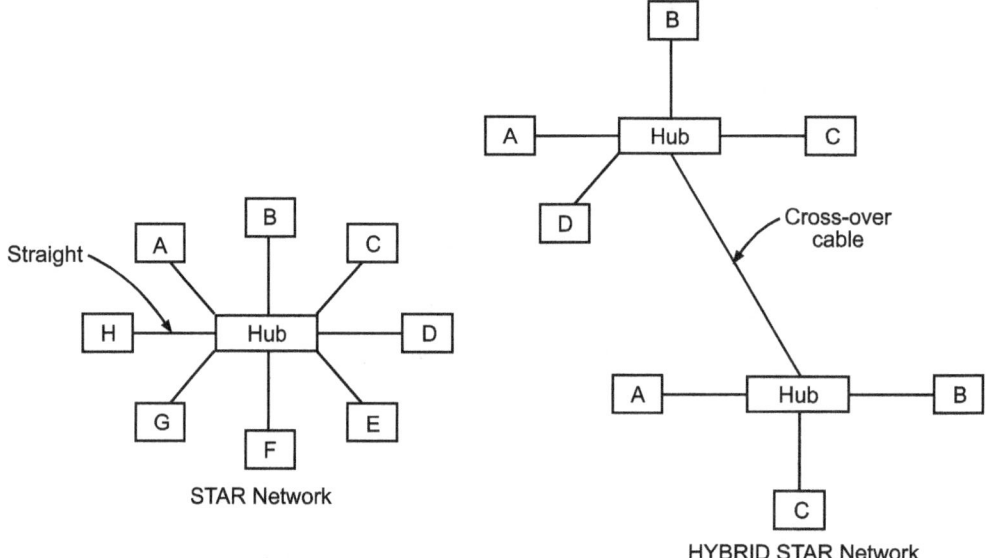

Fig. 1.27 : Star and Hybrid Star Topology

Disadvantages

- If central hub fails, the whole network fails to operate.

- Cost is more than bus network because network cables must be pulled to one central point. Thus cable requirement increases.

3. Ring Topology

In ring network, each computer is connected to the next computer, with the last one connected to first. Messages flow around the ring in one direction. Since each computer retransmits what it receives, signal loss problems are there. There is no termination because there is no end to ring.

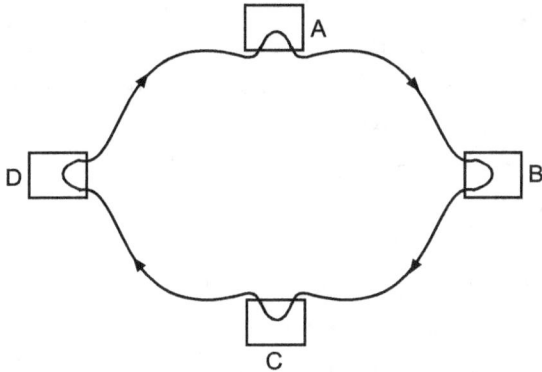

Fig. 1.28 : Ring Topology

Advantage :

- When more users are added, system slows but doesn't fail.

Disadvantages :

- Failure of one computer on the ring can affect the whole network.
- It is difficult to troubleshoot ring network.
- Adding or removing computers disturbs the entire network.

4. Mesh Topology

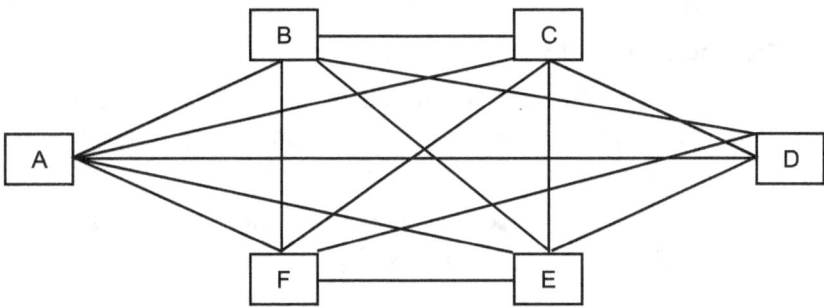

Fig. 1.29 : Mesh Topology

Each computer is connected to other with separate cable.

Advantages

- Guaranteed communication.
- High channel capacity.

Disadvantages

- Difficulty of installation and reconfiguration.
- Maintenance cost.

1.15 GUIDED MEDIA

- Telecommunication links can broadly be classified into two categories, namely, guided media (wired) and unguided media (wireless). Both media are used for short distance (LANs, MANs) and long distance (WANs) communication.

- Electrical/Optical signals are passed through a solid medium (different types of cables/wires).

- As the path traversed by the signals is guided by the size, shape and length of the wire, this type of media is called guided media.

- Also, in guided media, the signals are confined within the wire and do not propagate outside of the wire/media.

- It is the transmission media in which signals are confined to a specific path using wire or cable.

1.15.1 Twisted Pair Cable

- This cable is the most commonly used and is cheaper than others. It is lightweight, cheap, can be installed easily, and they support many different types of network.

Twisted Pair is of two types

    (i)   Unshielded Twisted Pair (UTP)

    (ii) Shielded Twisted Pair (STP)

1. Unshielded Twisted Pair Cable

•   It is the most common type of telecommunication when compared with Shielded Twisted Pair Cable which consists of two conductors usually copper, each with its own color plastic insulator.

•   Identification is the reason behind colored plastic insulation. UTP cables consist of 2 or 4 pairs of twisted cable. Cable with 2 pair use RJ-11 connector and 4 pair cable use RJ-45 connector.

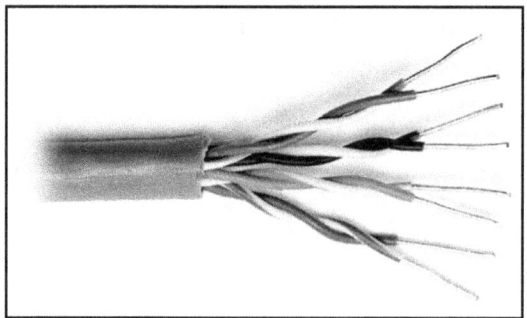

Fig. 1.30 : Unshielded Twisted Pair Cable

Advantages

- Installation is easy
- It is Flexible
- It has low cost.
- It has high speed capacity,
- 100 meter limit
- Higher grades of UTP are used in LAN technologies like Ethernet.
- It consists of two insulating copper wires (1mm thick). The wires are twisted together in a helical form to reduce electrical interference from similar pair.

Disadvantages

- Bandwidth is low when compared with Coaxial Cable
- Provides less protection from interference.

2. Shielded Twisted Pair Cable

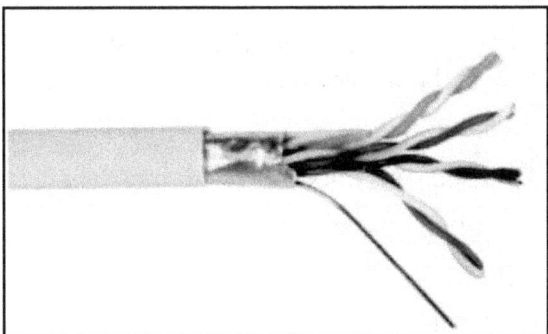

Fig. 1.31 : Shielded Twisted Pair Cable

- This cable has a metal foil or braided-mesh covering which covers each pair of insulated conductors.
- Electromagnetic noise penetration is prevented by metal casing. Shielding also removes crosstalk.
- It has same attenuation as unshielded twisted pair. It is faster the unshielded and coaxial cable. It is more expensive than coaxial and unshielded twisted pair.

Advantages

- Easy to install
- Performance is adequate
- Can be used for Analog or Digital transmission
- Increases the signaling rate

- Higher capacity than unshielded twisted pair

- Eliminates crosstalk

Disadvantages

- Difficult to manufacture

- Heavy

1.15.2 Coaxial Cable

- Coaxial is called by this name because it contains two conductors that are parallel to each other.

- Copper is used in this as center conductor which can be a solid wire or a standard one.

- It is surrounded by PVC installation, a sheath which is encased in an outer conductor of metal foil, braid or both.

- Outer metallic wrapping is used as a shield against noise and as the second conductor which completes the circuit.

- The outer conductor is also encased in an insulating sheath. The outermost part is the plastic cover which protects the whole cable.

Here the most common coaxial standards.

- 50-Ohm RG-7 or RG-11 : used with thick Ethernet.

- 50-Ohm RG-58 : used with thin Ethernet

- 75-Ohm RG-59 : used with cable television

- 93-Ohm RG-62 : used with ARCNET.

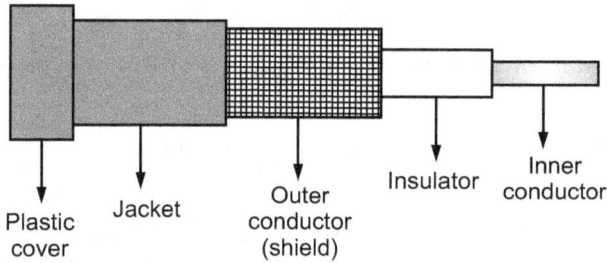

Fig. 1.32 : Coaxial Cable

There are two types of Coaxial cables

1. BaseBand

This is a 50 ohm (Ω) coaxial cable which is used for digital transmission. It is mostly used for LAN's. Baseband transmits a single signal at a time with very high speed. The major drawback is that it needs amplification after every 1000 feet.

2. BroadBand

This uses analog transmission on standard cable television cabling. It transmits several simultaneous signal using different frequencies. It covers large area when compared with Baseband Coaxial Cable.

Advantages

- Bandwidth is high

- Used in long distance telephone lines.

- Transmits digital signals at a very high rate of 10Mbps.

- Much higher noise immunity

- Data transmission without distortion.

- The can span to longer distance at higher speeds as they have better shielding when compared to twisted pair cable

Disadvantages

- Single cable failure can fail the entire network.

- Difficult to install and expensive when compared with twisted pair.

- If the shield is imperfect, it can lead to grounded loop.

1.15.3 Fiber Optic Cable

- These are similar to coaxial cable. It uses electric signals to transmit data. At the center is the glass core through which light propagates.

- In multimode fibers, the core is 50microns, and in single mode fibers, the thickness is 8 to 10 microns.

- The core in fiber optic cable is surrounded by glass cladding with lower index of refraction as compared to core to keep all the light in core.

- This is covered with a thin plastic jacket to protect the cladding. The fibers are grouped together in bundles protected by an outer shield.

- Fiber optic cable has bandwidth more than 2 gbps (Gigabytes per Second)

Fig. 1.33 : Fiber Optic Cable

Advantages

- Provides high quality transmission of signals at very high speed.
- These are not affected by electromagnetic interference, so noise and distortion is very less.
- Used for both analog and digital signals.

Disadvantages

- It is costly
- Difficult to install.
- Maintenance is expensive and difficult.
- Do not allow complete routing of light signals.

1.16 UNGUIDED MEDIA

- Here information is transmitted by sending electromagnetic signals through free space and hence the name unguided media, as the signals are not guided in any specific direction or inside any specific medium.

1.16.1 Wireless Transmission

- All unguided media transmission is classified as wireless transmission. Wireless transmission can be used as the medium in both LAN and WAN environments, as illustrated in the diagrams below :

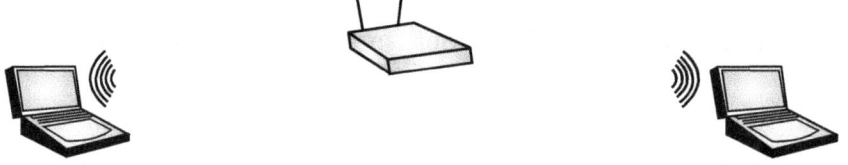

Fig. 1.34 : Two laptops communicating within a LAN using a wireless Access Points

Fig. 1.35 : Two laptops communicating via. a long distance WAN using a WiMax Wireless transmission network

Different forms of wireless communication used in the internet vary mainly based on the following attributes :

- Distance separating the end stations
- Frequency spectrum used by the electromagnetic signals
- Line Encoding technique used

1.16.2 Radio

- Radio waves are easy to generate, can travel long distances, and can penetrate buildings easily, so they are widely used for communication, both indoors and outdoors.
- Radio waves also are omnidirectional, meaning that they travel in all directions from the source, so the transmitter and receiver do not have to be carefully aligned physically.
- 10 Khz to 1 Ghz. It is broken into many bands including AM, FM, and VHF bands.
- The Federal communications Commission (FCC) regulates the assignment of these frequencies.
- Frequencies for unregulated use are :
  - ➢ 902-928Mhz - Cordless phones, remote controls.
  - ➢ 24 Ghz
  - ➢ 5.72-5.85 Ghz

1.16.3 Microwave

- Above 100 MHz, the waves travel in nearly straight lines and can therefore be narrowly focused.
- Concentrating all the energy into a small beam by means of a parabolic antenna (like the familiar satellite TV dish) gives a much higher signal-to-noise ratio, but the transmitting and receiving antennas must be accurately aligned with each other.
- In addition, this directionality allows multiple transmitters lined up in a row to communicate with multiple receivers in a row without interference, provided some minimum spacing rules are observed. Before fiber optics, for decades these microwaves formed the heart of the long-distance telephone transmission system
- In summary, microwave communication is so widely used for long-distance telephone communication, mobile phones, television distribution, and other uses that a severe shortage of spectrum has developed.
  - ➢ Terrestrial - Used to link networks over long distances but the two microwave towers must have a line of sight between them. The frequency is usually 4-6GHz or 21-23GHz. Speed is often 1-10Mbps. The signal is normally encrypted for privacy. Two nodes may exist.
  - ➢ Satellite - A satellite orbits at 22,300 miles above the earth which is an altitude that will cause it to stay in a fixed position relative to the rotation of the earth. This is called a geosynchronous orbit.
  - ➢ A station on the ground will send and receive signals from the satellite. The signal can have propagation delays between 0.5 to 5 seconds due to the distances involved.
  - ➢ The transmission frequency is normally 11-14GHz with a transmission speed in the range of 1-10Mbps.

1.16.4 Infrared

- Infrared is just below the visible range of light between 100 GHz and 1000 THz. A light emitting diode (LED) or laser is used to transmit the signal. The signal cannot travel through objects. Light may interfere with the signal. The types of infrared are

  - Point to point - Transmission frequencies are 100GHz-1,000THz. Transmission is between two points and is limited to line of sight range. It is difficult to eavesdrop on the transmission. The speed is 100Kbps to 16Mbps

  - Broadcast - The signal is dispersed so several units may receive the signal. The unit used to disperse the signal may be reflective material or a transmitter that amplifies and retransmits the signal. Normally the speed is limited to 1Mbps. The transmission frequency is normally 100GHz-1,000THz with transmission distance in 10's of meters. Installation is easy and cost is relatively inexpensive for wireless.

- Unguided infrared and millimeter waves are widely used for short-range communication. The remote controls used on televisions, VCRs, and stereos all use infrared communication. They are relatively directional, cheap, and easy to build

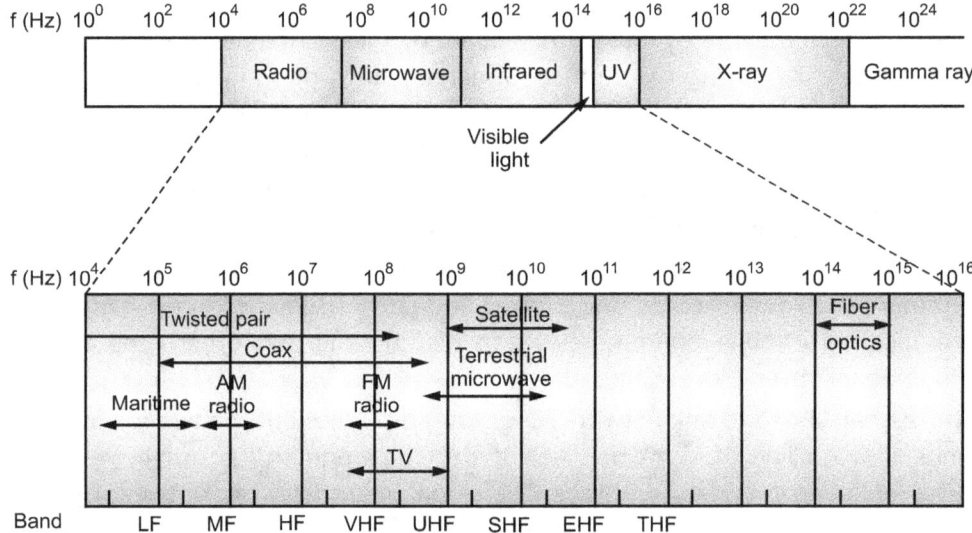

Fig. 1.36 : Wireless frequency Spectrum

NOISE

Noise is defined as the unwanted form of energy which tends to interface with the proper reception and the reproduction of transmitted signals. Electronic Devices unwanted random addition to the signal are considered as Noise.

There are various types of Noise presents. The Acoustic Noise is observed when the signals are converted into sound which is generally known as snow in TV or video Images.

In signal processing or computing noise can be considered random unwanted data without meaning that is, data that is not being used to transmit signal, but is simply produced as an unwanted by-product of other activities.

"Signal to noise ratio" is sometimes used to refer to the ratio of useful to irrelevant information in an exchange.

In common use, the word noise means any unwanted sound. Unwanted signal are called noise.

Classification of Noise

- There are several way to classify Noise, but conveniently Noise is classified as
  1. External Noise
  2. Internal Noise

1.17 EXTERNAL NOISE

- External noise is defined as the type of Noise which is general externally due to communication system. In simple way external noise is noise whose sources are external.

- External Noise is analyzed qualitatively. Now, External Noise may be classified as

1.17.1 Atmospheric Noise

- Atmospheric noise is also known as static noise which is the natural source of disturbance caused by lightning, discharge in thunderstorm and the natural disturbances occurring in the nature.

- Atmospheric noise consists of forged radio signals with components spread over a wide frequency range.

1.17.2 Industrial Noise

- It is also called as man-made noise. Sources of Industrial noise are auto-mobiles, aircraft, ignition of electric motors and switching gear.

- The main cause of Industrial noise is High voltage wires.

- These noises are generally produced by the discharge present in the operations.

1.17.3 Extraterrestrial Noise

Extraterrestrial Noise exists on the basis of their originating source. They are subdivided into

1. Solar Noise
2. Cosmic Noise

- The primary sources of extraterrestrial noise are the sun, which radiates a wide range of signals in a broad noise spectrum.

- The noise intensity produced by the sun varies with time. In fact, the sun has a repeatable 11-year noise cycle.

- During the peak of the cycle, the sun produces an awesome amount of noise that causes tremendous radio signal interference and makes many frequencies unusable for communication. During other years, the noise is at a lower level.

1.18 INTERNAL NOISE

- Internal Noise is the type of Noise which are generated internally or within the Communication System or in the receiver.

- They may be treated qualitatively and can also be reduced or minimized by the proper designing of the system. Internal Noises are classified as

1.18.1 Shot Noise

- These Noise are generally arises in the active devices due to the random behavior of Charge particles or carries. In case of electron tube, shot Noise is produces due to the random emission of electron form cathodes.

- It is produced by the random arrival of electrons or holes at the output element.

1.18.2 Partition Noise

- When a circuit is to divide in between two or more paths then the noise generated is known as Partition noise. The reason for the generation is random fluctuation in the division.

1.18.3 Low- Frequency Noise

- They are also known as FLICKER NOISE. These types of noise are generally observed at a frequency range below few kHz.

- Power spectral density of these noise increases with the decrease in frequency. That why the name is given Low- Frequency Noise.

1.18.4 High- Frequency Noise

- These noises are also known TRANSIT- TIME Noise. The noise that occurs in transistors is called Transit-Time noise.

- They are observed in the semi-conductor devices when the transit time of a charge carrier while crossing a junction is compared with the time period of that signal.

1.18.5 Thermal Noise

- Conductors consist of a large number of free electron and ions and that are bounded by molecular forces.

- The noise is generated in any resistance due to random motion of electrons is called thermal noise.

- Thermal Noise is random and often referred as White Noise or Johnson Noise. Thermal noise is generally observed in the resistor or the sensitive resistive components of complex impedance due to the random and rapid movement of molecules or atoms or electrons.

1.19 NOISE CALCULATIONS

1. **Signal-to-Noise Ratio**

    A signal-to-noise ratio compares a level of signal power versus a level of noise power and is most often expressed as a measurement of decibels (dB).

    Higher numbers generally mean a better specification, since there is more useful information (the signal) than there is unwanted data (the noise).

    For example, when an audio component lists a signal-to-noise ratio of 100 dB, it means that the level of the audio signal is 100 dB higher than the level of the noise. A signal-to-noise ratio specification of 100 dB is considerably better than one that is 70 dB (or less).

2. **Noise Figure and Noise Factor**

- Noise figure (NF) and noise factor (F) are measures of degradation of the signal-to-noise ratio (SNR), caused by components in a radio frequency (RF) signal chain.

- It is a number by which the performance of an amplifier or a radio receiver can be specified, with lower values indicating better performance.

- The noise factor is defined as the ratio of the output noise power of a device to the portion thereof attributable to thermal noise in the input termination at standard noise temperature T_0 (usually 290 K).

- The noise factor is thus the ratio of actual output noise to that which would remain if the device itself did not introduce noise, or the ratio of input SNR to output SNR.

- The noise figure is simply the noise factor expressed in decibels (dB)

1.20 COMMUNICATION CHANNEL

- A communication channel refers either to a physical transmission medium such as a wire or to a logical connection over a multiplexed medium such as a radio channel.

- A channel is used to convey an information signal, for example a digital bit stream, from one or several senders (or transmitters) to one or several receivers.

- A channel has a certain capacity for transmitting information, often measured by its bandwidth in Hz or its data rate in bits per second.

- Communicating data from one location to another requires some form of pathway or medium.

- These pathways, called communication channels, use two types of media : cable (twisted-pair wire, cable, and fiber-optic cable) and broadcast (microwave, satellite, radio, and infrared).

- Cable or wire line media use physical wires of cables to transmit data and information. Twisted-pair wire and coaxial cables are made of copper, and fiber-optic cable is made of glass.

1.21 DISCRETE AND CONTINUOUS CHANNEL

Discrete and Continuous Systems

- Systems by which signals are recorded, communicated, or displayed may represent the data in discrete form (integers) or in continuous form (real numbers).

- An important classification results from the choice of discrete or continuous representation of the amplitude, and of discrete or continuous representation of the time at which the amplitude occurred.

- Analog computers employ physical quantities that are approximations to continuous representations.

- Discrete representations of both time and amplitude are required by digital computers.

1.21.1 Discrete Channel

- A communication channel whose input and output each have an alphabet of distinct letters, or, in the case of a physical channel, whose input and output are signals that are discrete in time and amplitude.

- The size of the alphabet, or the number of amplitude levels, is usually finite.

- There are two types of discrete channel

  ➢ The discrete memory-less channel (DMC) has the property that its treatment of a symbol input at a certain time does not depend on the symbols input, or its treatment of them, at any earlier time.

  ➢ The discrete channel with memory (DCM) has the property that its action depends on its inputs at a number of earlier times.

1.21.2 Continuous Channel

- The modulating signal X (t) (which is the set of messages to be transmitted from an information theoretical view point) is invariably a continuous speech or picture signal.

- This message can be treated as equivalent to a continuous sample space whose sample points form a continuum, in contrast to the discrete case.

- A continuous channel as one whose input is a sample point from a continuous sample space and the output is a sample point belonging to either the same sample space or to a different sample space.

- A zero memory continuous channel as the one in which the channel output statistically depends on the corresponding channels without memory.

1.22 CHANNEL CAPACITY

- How fast can we transmit information over a communication channel? Suppose a source sends r messages per second, and the entropy of a message is H bits per message. The information rate is R = r H bits/second.

- The "capacity" of a channel is the theoretical upper-limit to the bit rate over a given channel that will result in negligible errors. Channel capacity is measured in bits/s.

- One can intuitively reason that, for a given communication system, as the information rate increases the number of errors per second will also increase. Surprisingly, however, this is not the case.

Shannon's Theorem :

- A given communication system has a maximum rate of information C known as the channel capacity.

- If the information rate R is less than C, then one can approach arbitrarily small error probabilities by using intelligent coding techniques.

- To get lower error probabilities, the encoder has to work on longer blocks of signal data. This entails longer delays and higher computational requirements.

- Thus, if R ≤ C, then transmission may be accomplished without error in the presence of noise. Unfortunately, Shannon's theorem is not a constructive proof—it merely states that such a coding method exists.

- The proof can therefore not be used to develop a coding method that reaches the channel capacity. The negation of this theorem is also true : if R > C, then errors cannot be avoided regardless of the coding technique used.

1.23 SHANNON-HARTLEY THEOREM

- Consider a bandlimited Gaussian channel operating in the presence of additive Gaussian noise :

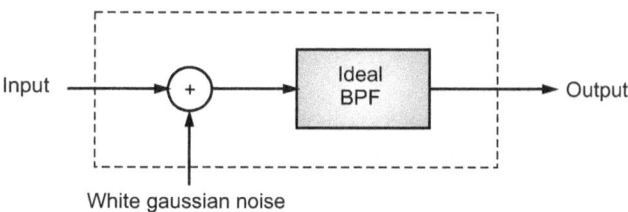

Fig. 1.37 : Gaussian Channel

- The Shannon-Hartley theorem states that the channel capacity is given by

$$C = B \log_2 (1+S/N)$$

Where C is the capacity in bits per second, B is the bandwidth of the channel in Hertz and S=N is the signal-to-noise ratio.

- We cannot prove the theorem, but can partially justify it as follows :

Suppose the received signal is accompanied by noise with a RMS voltage of σ, and that the signal has been quantized with levels separated by a=λσ.

If λ is chosen sufficiently large, we may expect to be able to recognize the signal level with an acceptable probability of error. Suppose further that each message is to be represented by one voltage level. If there are to be M possible messages, then there must be M levels. The average signal power is then

$$S = \frac{M^2 - 1}{12} (\lambda\sigma)^2$$

The number of levels for a given average signal power is therefore

$$M = \left(1 + \frac{12}{\lambda^2} \frac{S}{N}\right)^{1/2}$$

Where, $N = \sigma^2$ is the noise power.

Example :

The bandwidth of a communication channel is 12.5 kHz. The S/N ratio is 25 dB. Calculate (a) the maximum theoretical data rate in bits per second, (b) the maximum theoretical data channel capacity, and (c) the number of coding levels N needed to achieve the maximum speed. [For part (c), use the y^x key on a scientific calculator.]

a. $C = 2B = 2(12.5 \text{ kHz}) = 25 \text{ kbps}$

b. $C = B \log_2 (1 + S/N) = B(3.32) \log_{10} (1 + S/N)$

$$\log P = \frac{25}{10} = 2.5$$

$$P = \text{antilog } 2.5 = \log^{-1} 2.5 = 316.2 \text{ or } P = 10^{2.5}$$

$$= 316.2$$

$$C = 12,500(3.32) \log_{10} (316.2 + 1)$$

$$= 41,5000 \log10 \, 317.2$$

$$= 41,500 \, (2.5)$$

$$C = 103,805.3 \text{ bps or } 103.8 \text{ kbps}$$

c. $C = 2B \log_2 N$

$\log_2 N = C/(2B)$

$N = \text{antilog}_2 C/2 (B)$

$N = \text{antilog}_2 (103,805.3)/2(12,500) = \text{antilog}_2 4.152$

$N = 2^{4.152} = 17.78$ or 17 levels or symbols

1.24 NYQUIST AND SHANON THEOREM

- Sampling is a process of converting a signal (for example, a function of continuous time and/or space) into a numeric sequence (a function of discrete time and/or space). Shannon's version of the theorem states :

  "If a function x(t) contains no frequencies higher than B hertz, it is completely determined by giving its ordinates at a series of points spaced 1/(2B) seconds apart".

- A sufficient sample-rate is therefore 2B samples/second, or anything larger. Equivalently, for a given sample rate fs, perfect reconstruction is guaranteed possible for a bandlimit B < fs/2.

- When the bandlimit is too high (or there is no bandlimit), the reconstruction exhibits imperfections known as aliasing.

- Modern statements of the theorem are sometimes careful to explicitly state that x(t) must contain no sinusoidal component at exactly frequency B, or that B must be strictly less than ½ the sample rate. The two thresholds, 2B and fs/2 are respectively called the Nyquist rate and Nyquist frequency. And respectively, they are attributes of x(t) and of the sampling equipment.

- The condition described by these inequalities is called the Nyquist criterion, or sometimes the Raabe condition. The theorem is also applicable to functions of other domains, such as space, in the case of a digitized image. The only change, in the case of other domains, is the units of measure applied to t, fs, and B.

- The normalized sinc function : $\sin(\pi x) / (\pi x)$ ... showing the central peak at x= 0, and zero-crossings at the other integer values of x.

- The symbol T = 1/fs is customarily used to represent the interval between samples and is called the sample period or sampling interval. And the samples of function x(t) are commonly denoted by x[n] = x(nT) for all integer values of n.

1.25 BANDWIDTH S/N TRADE OFF

- The tradeoff considerations are especially important in medical and other applications where dynamic signal analysis is performed. As with most analog systems, the greater the bandwidth, the lower the S/N ratio becomes.

- While this is generally understood, the impact of the compensation method on the bandwidth to S/N curve is less obvious.

- As Shotter explains, "In general, a basic sensor (which has no factory compensation), has the greatest potential for the highest performance when viewed in terms of the bandwidth to S/N curve.

- "However, this design approach also has the greatest cost and effort to amplify, calibrate and compensate for temperature effects.

- To solve the problem, users cannot settle for the standard amplification that most MEMS pressure sensor companies supply. In most cases, for high performance applications, users will have to perform the amplification and signal conditioning themselves to get the performance they need.

- An All Sensors solution to this problem is provided in its BLVR Series Basic series and Low Pressure Millivolt Output family.

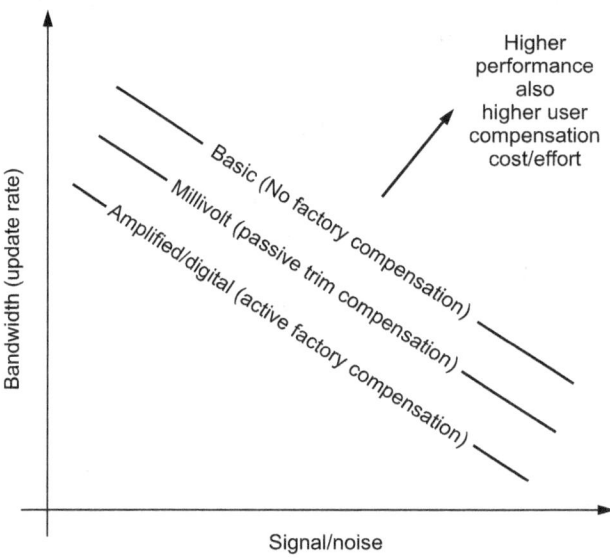

Fig. 1.38 : Performance for bandwidth and S/N ratio

- Fig. 1.38 shows the highest performance for bandwidth and S/N, users may have to tradeoff an amplified version provided by the supplier and develop their own additional circuitry. Alternative pressure sensor products, such as All Sensors' Millivolt and Basic series (shown) provide an improved starting point.

- General purpose amplified and digital sensors offer excellent calibration and thermal compensation however their S/N tends to be lower (compared to a Basic or Millivolt sensor) due to the use of lower power op amps and quantization noise.

- "Also, digital devices may suffer from factory prescribed update rates (bandwidth) which may or may not follow the application requirement unless the factory includes appropriate options for the update rate, "says Shotter.

- A trimmed Millivolt sensor has good compromise when considering the bandwidth to S/N. In this case, the part only needs user provided amplification and the amplifier noise can be tailored to the application.

- The output level of the Millivolt sensor is generally lower than a basic sensor, so the overall S/N curve is impacted compared to a Basic sensor even if the same op amp is used for both.

EXERCISE

1. Which terminologies are used in communication?

2. Explain analog communication system and elements of that system.

3. Explain baseband signal and band-pass signal.

4. What is the need for modulation?

5. Explain in detail electromagnetic spectrum and applications of each spectrum.

6. What are the applications of electromagnetic spectrum?

7. What is signal? Explain basics of signal by using sine wave signal.

8. Explain the representation of signal with respect to time and frequency.

9. What is network, computer network and explain fundamentals of network?

10. Explain ISO OSI reference model in detail.

11. Explain functions and applications of OSI reference model.

12. Explain layers in TCP/IP protocol suite.

13. Which are the addressing modes used in networking?

14. Write a short note on

    (i) LAN

    (ii) WAN

    (iii) MAN

15. What is topology? Which are the basic types of network topology?

16. What is guided media? Explain fiber optic cable in detail.

17. What is unguided media? Explain radio waves and infrared waves in detail.

18. Compare twisted pair cable, coaxial cable and fiber optic cable.

19. What is the difference between guided media and unguided media?

20. What is noise in communication system? Explain types of noise.

21. What is communication channel? Explain channel capacity.

22. Explain shanon-Hartley theorem.

23. Explain Nyquist-shanon theorem.

24. Explain tradeoff between bandwidth and S/N ratio.

AMPLITUDE AND ANGLE MODULATION

AMPLITUDE MODULATION

- In Amplitude Modulation, the information signal varies the amplitude of the carrier sine wave. The instantaneous value of the carrier amplitude changes in accordance with the amplitude and frequency variations of the modulating signal.

- Fig.2.1 shows a single frequency sine wave intelligence signal modulating a higher–frequency carrier.

- The carrier frequency remains constant during the modulation process, but its amplitude varies in accordance with the modulating signal.

- An increase in the amplitude of the modulating signal causes the amplitude of the carrier to increase.

- Both the positive and the negative peaks of the carrier wave vary with the modulating signal.

- An increase or a decrease in the amplitude of the modulating signal causes a corresponding increase or decrease in both the positive and the negative peaks of the carrier amplitude.

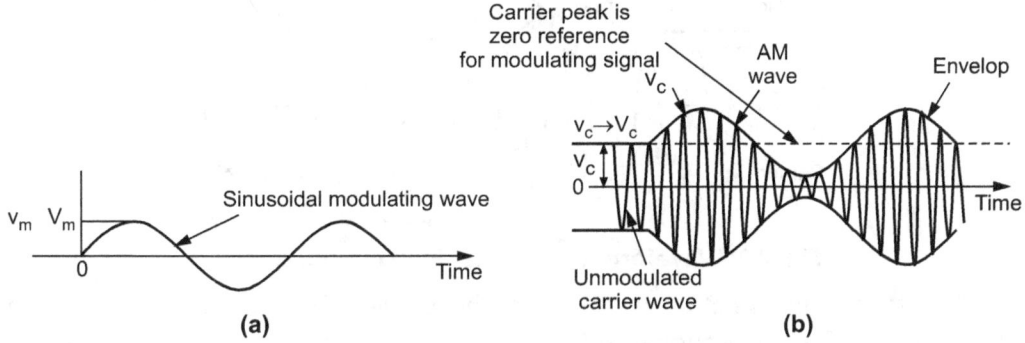

Fig. 2.1: Amplitude Modulation waveform

2.1 AMPLITUDE MODULATION TECHNIQUES

2.1.1 DSBFC

- Although there are several types of amplitude modulation, AM double–sideband full carrier (DSBFC) is probably the most commonly used. AM DSBFC is sometimes called conventional AM or simply AM.

- When the carrier is amplitude modulated by a single sine wave, the resulting signal consists of three frequencies i.e. original carrier and two sidebands.

- In the normal AM system, both sidebands and full carrier are transmitted. The system is commonly known as Double Sideband Full Carrier System (DSBFC).

- The modulated signal in the DSB–FC system contains unmodulated carrier and two sidebands. The unmodulated carrier conveys no information, but consumes around two–third of total power.

- The two sidebands carry the information. Since the two sidebands are images of each other, they carry the same information.

- Thus only one sideband is capable of carrying the same information that would be carried by DSB–FC system.

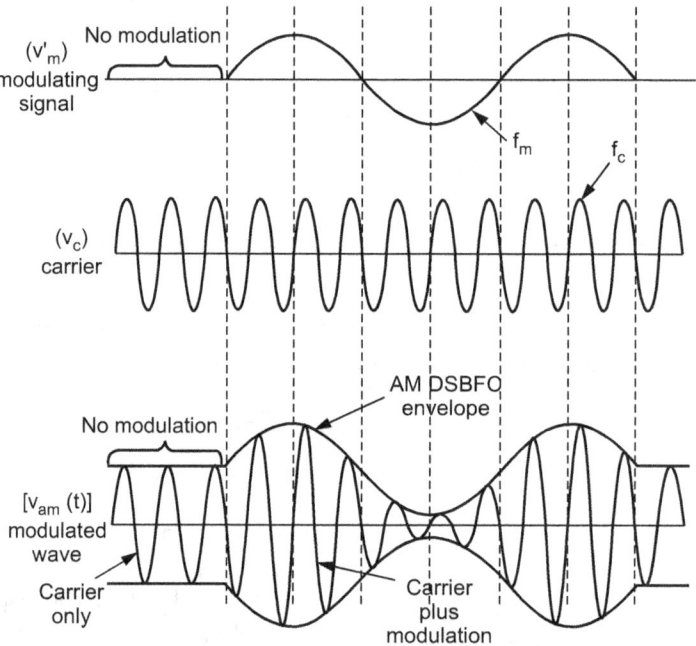

Fig. 2.2: Waveform for double sideband full carrier

- Fig. 2.2 illustrates the relationship among the carrier, the modulating signal and the modulated wave for conventional AM.

- The Fig. shows how an AM waveform is produced when a single–frequency modulating signal acts on a high– frequency carrier signal.

- The output waveform contains all the frequencies that make up the AM signal and is used to transport the information through the system.

- Therefore, the shape of the modulated wave is called the AM envelope. Note that with no modulating signal the output wave–form is simply the carrier signal.

- However when a modulating signal is applied the amplitude of the output wave varies in accordance with the modulating signal. Note that the repetition rate of the envelope is equal to the frequency of the modulating signal and that the shape of the envelope is identical to the shape of the modulating signal.

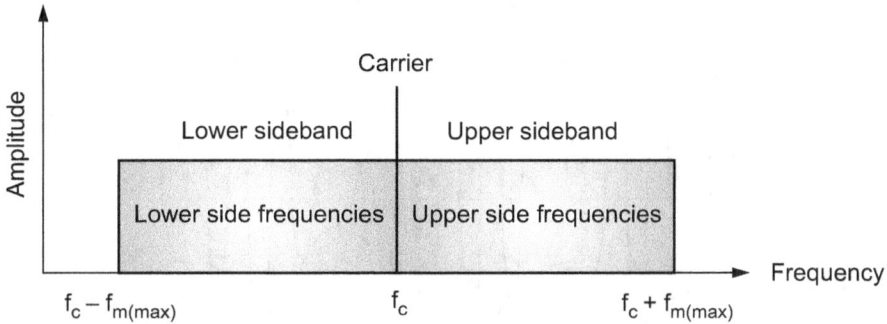

Fig. 2.3 : Frequency spectrum of an AM DSBFC wave

- Fig. 2.3 shows the frequency spectrum for an AM wave. The AM spectrum extends from $f_c - f_{m(max)}$ to $f_c + f_{m(max)}$, where fc is the carrier frequency and $f_{m(max)}$ is the highest modulating signal frequency.

- The band of frequencies between $f_c-f_{m(max)}$ and f_c is called the lower sideband (LSB) and any frequency within this band is called a lower side frequency (LSF).

- The band of frequencies between f_c and $f_c+f_{m(max)}$ is called the upper sideband (USB) and any frequency within this band is called an upper side frequency (USF).

- Therefore the bandwidth (B) of an AM DSBFC wave is equal to the difference between the highest upper side frequency and the lowest lower side frequency or two times the highest modulating signal frequency (i.e., $B = 2f_{m(max)}$).

2.1.2 Double Sideband Suppressed Carrier (DSB–SC)

- Double–sideband suppressed–carrier transmission (DSB–SC) is transmission in which frequencies produced by amplitude modulation (AM) are symmetrically spaced above and below the carrier frequency and the carrier level is reduced to the lowest practical level, ideally being completely suppressed.

- In the DSB–SC modulation, unlike in AM, the wave carrier is not transmitted; thus, much of the power is distributed between the sideband, which implies an increase of the cover in DSB–SC, compared to AM, for the same power used.

- DSB–SC transmission is a special case of double–sideband reduced carrier transmission. It is used for radio data systems.

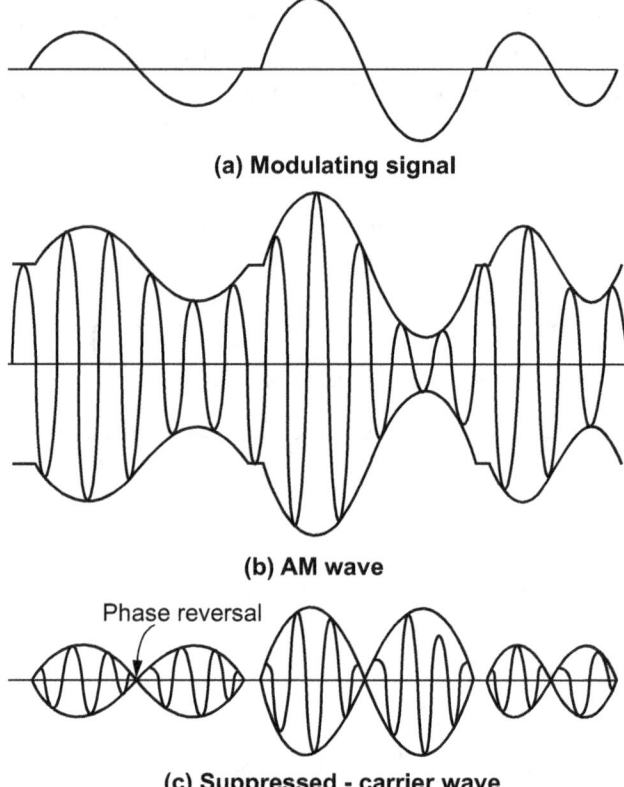

(a) Modulating signal

(b) AM wave

Phase reversal

(c) Suppressed - carrier wave

Fig. 2.4 : Waveforms for double sideband with suppressed carrier

- It is important to note that; carrier signal does not convey any information. Therefore, two–third of the transmitted power which appears in the carrier is wasted.

- The real information is conveyed by two sidebands. To make AM more efficient we can simply suppress the carrier. Since the carrier does not provide any useful information, there is no reason why it has to be transmitted.

- When carrier is removed, the remaining signal contains simply upper and lower sidebands such a signal is referred to as a double sideband suppressed carrier (DSBSC) signal.

- With this signal no power is wasted on the carrier and the saved power can be put into the sidebands for stronger signals over longer distances.

- As shown in the Fig.2.5 signal is sine wave at the carrier frequency varying in amplitude. A frequency domain display of a DSB signal is shown in Fig. 2.5 (b). Here, dotted line indicates that the carrier is suppressed.

- Looking at Fig. 2.5 we can note that the spectrum space occupied by a DSB is 2 f_m, or 2ω which is same as that for a conventional AM signal.

The equation of AM wave in its simplest form i.e. single tone modulation, is expressed as

$$s(t) = A \cos \omega_c t + A \frac{m_a}{2} \cos (\omega_c + \omega_m) t + A \frac{m_a}{2} \cos (\omega_c - \omega_m) t$$

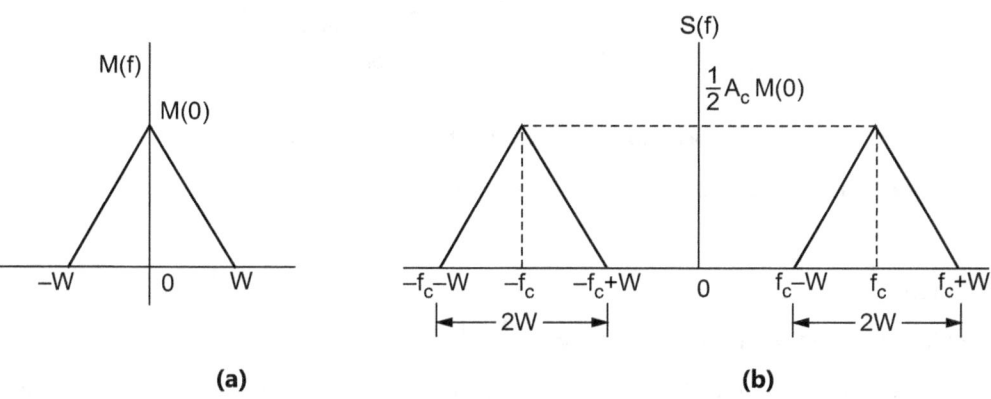

Fig. 2.5: Frequency Spectrum for DSBSC

- From this equation, it is obvious that the carrier component in AM wave remains constant in amplitude and frequency.

- This means that the carrier of amplitude modulated wave does not convey any information.

- In power calculation of AM signal, it has been observed that for single–tone sinusoidal modulation, the ratio of the total power to the carrier power is:

$$\frac{P_t}{P_c} = 1 + \frac{m_a^2}{2}$$

Where m_a is the modulating index.

- Thus, for 100% modulation about 67% of the total power is required for transmitting the carrier which does not contain any information.

- Hence, if the carrier is suppressed, only the sidebands remain and in this way a saving of two–third power may be achieved at 100% modulation.

- The resulting signal obtained by suppressing the carrier from the modulated wave is called Double sideband suppressed carrier (DSB–SC) system.

Generation of DSB–SC Signal

- A DSB–SC signal can be obtained by simply multiplying modulating signal x(t) with carrier signal $\cos \omega_c t$. So we need to use a device called product modulator for the generation of DSB–SC waves.

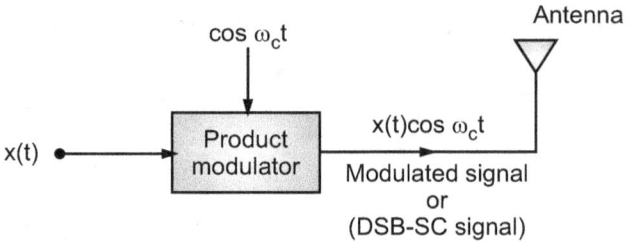

Fig. 2.6: Generation of DSBSC signal

There are two forms of product modulators as under:

• Linear Modulator

• Non–linear Modulator

(i) Linear Modulator for DSB–SC Generation

• A linear modulator is a system whose gain or transfer function can be varied with time by applying a time varying signal at certain points.

• The gain is proportional to signal f(t) .

$$G = K\, f(t)$$

Where G = gain

                     K = constant of proportionality

          $f(t)$ = gain varying signal

Let us consider Fig.2.7 in which the carrier signal $\cos\omega_c t$ is applied at the input terminal and x(t) is applied as the gain varying signal .

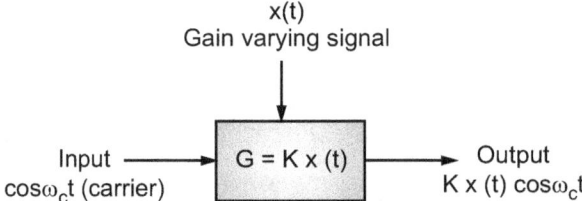

Fig. 2.7: Linear Modulator

The gain of the modulator is $G = K\, x(t)$.

Therefore, the output is given by :

$$V_o = G \times input$$

Or, $V_o = K\, x(t) \cos \omega_c t$

This is a modulated signal (DSB–SC).

As an alternative we can use the carrier as gain varying signal and x(t) as the input signal as shown in Fig. 2.8.

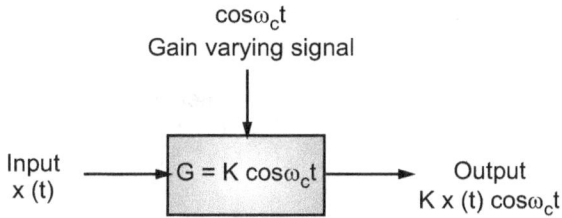

Fig. 2.8: Another variation of Linear Modulator

The gain of the modulator is given by:

$$G = K \cos \omega_c t$$

Therefore, $V_o = K x(t) \cos \omega_c t$

Balanced Modulator (Suppression of Carrier)

The balanced modulators are used to suppress the unwanted carrier in AM wave.

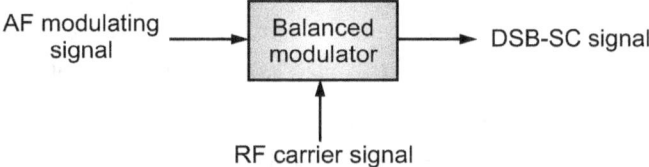

Fig. 2.9: Block Diagram of Balanced Modulator

- The carrier and modulating signals are applied to the inputs of the balanced modulator and we get the DSB signal with suppressed carrier at the output of the balanced modulator. Hence, the output consists of the upper and lower sidebands only.

2.1.3 Single Sideband Modulation (SSB)

- Single sideband modulation is a form of amplitude modulation. As the name implies, single sideband, SSB uses only one sideband for a given audio path to provide the final signal.

- Single sideband modulation, SSB, provides a considerably more efficient form of communication when compared to ordinary amplitude modulation.

- It is far more efficient in terms of the radio spectrum used, and also the power used to transmit the signal.

Single Sideband Modulation Basics

- Single sideband modulation can be viewed as an amplitude modulation signal with elements removed or reduced. In order to see how single sideband is created, it is necessary to use an amplitude modulated signal as the starting point.

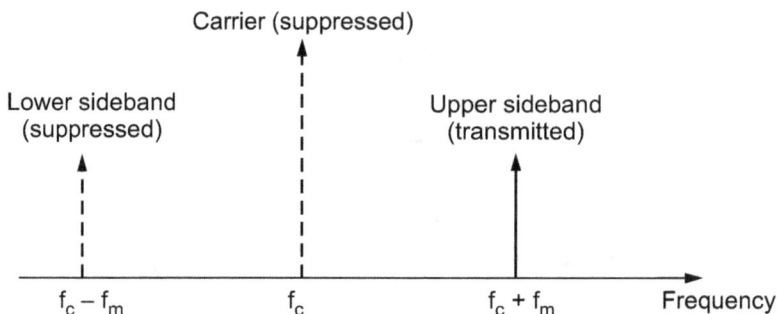

Fig. 2.10: Frequency Spectrum for SSB

- From this it can be seen that the signal has two sidebands, each the mirror of the other, and the carrier.

- To improve the efficient of the signal, both in terms of the power and spectrum usage, it is possible to remove the carrier, or at least reduce it, and remove one sideband – one is the mirror image of the other.

- A single sideband signal therefore consists of a single sideband, and often no carrier, although the various variants of single sideband are detailed below.

Forms of SSB, Single Sideband Modulation

There are a number of different formats of single sideband modulation that are used:

- Single sideband suppressed carrier, SSBSC: SSBSC is the form of single sideband modulation that is most widely used for communications applications on the HF portion of the radio spectrum. There is only one sideband – the other sideband and the carrier are both removed. Having no carrier, this needs to be re–inserted within the receiver. Any slight differences in carrier re–insertion frequency give rise to changes in pitch of the audio. However it gives the most efficient spectrum and power usage of any single sideband modulation format.

- Single sideband reduced carrier: This form of single sideband modulation removes one sideband, but retains a small amount of carrier. The reduced carrier element can then be used to lock a local oscillator for carrier re–insertion and the demodulation of the sideband with the correct audio pitch. Naturally the power efficiency of this form of single sideband modulation is not as high as single sideband suppressed carrier.

- Single sideband full carrier: This form of single sideband modulation is normally used where receivers may not have the ability to re–insert the carrier – it can be demodulated using a simple diode detector. However, having one sideband only, it occupies only half the bandwidth. Power efficiency is very poor, because the full carrier is required, but only one sideband is present to carry the modulation.

- Single sideband vestigial carrier: Vestigial sideband is a form of single sideband modulation where one sideband is present, but the other has been only partly cut off or suppressed. Vestigial sideband is used for analogue AM television transmission and is used to reduce the overall bandwidth while still keeping one sideband with the lower frequency information.

- Independent sideband, ISB: This form of single sideband is not strictly "single" sideband because it has two sidebands. However each sideband carries different modulation, and therefore provides a doubling in the spectrum efficiency.

2.2 GENERATION OF AMPLITUDE MODULATED SIGNALS

2.2.1 Amplitude Modulation: Double Sideband Suppressed Carrier (DSB–SC)

- In amplitude modulation, the amplitude A_c of the unmodulated carrier $A_c \cos(\omega_c t + \theta_c)$ is varied in proportion to the baseband signal (known as modulating signal).

- The frequency ω_c and the phase θ_c are constant. We can assume $\theta_c = 0$ to simplify the analysis.

- If the carrier amplitude A_c is made directly proportional to the modulating signal m(t), the modulated carrier is

m(t) cos(ω_ct)

- This type of modulation simply shifts the spectrum of *m(t)* to the carrier frequency (see Fig. 2.11; that is, if

$$m(t) \leftrightarrow M(\omega)$$

$$m(t) \cos(\omega_c t) \leftrightarrow \frac{1}{2}[M(\omega + \omega_c) + M(\omega - \omega_c)]$$

- The bandwidth of the modulated signal is 2B Hz, which is twice the bandwidth of the modulating signal m(t).

- From the Fig. 2.11, we observe that the modulated carrier spectrum centered at ω_c is composed of two parts: a portion that lies above ω_c, known as the upper sideband (USB), and a portion that lies below ω_c, known as the lower sideband (LSB). Similarly, the spectrum centered at $-\omega_c$, has upper and lower sidebands.

For instance, if m(t) = cos(ω_ct), then the modulated signal

$$m(t) \cos(\omega_c t) = \cos(\omega_m t)\cos(\omega_c t)$$

$$= \frac{1}{2}[\cos((\omega_c + \omega_m)) + \cos((\omega_c - \omega_m))]$$

- The component of frequency $\omega_c + \omega_m$ is the upper sideband and that of frequency $\omega_c - \omega_m$ is the lower sideband.

- Thus, each component of frequency ω_m in the modulating signal gets translated into two components, of frequencies $\omega_c + \omega_m$ and $\omega_c - \omega_m$, in the modulating signal.

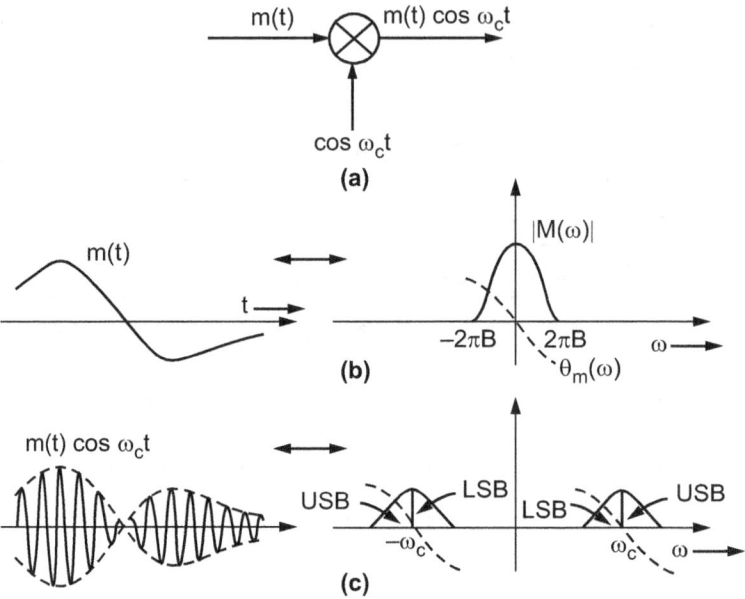

Fig. 2.11: Amplitude Modulation: DSBSC

- Note that the modulated signal m(t)cos(ω_ct), from the above equation, has components of frequencies $\omega_c \pm \omega_m$ but not have a component of the carrier frequency ω_c. For this reason, this scheme is referred to as double–sideband–suppressed carrier.

2.2.2 Amplitude Modulation: Double Sideband Transmitted Carrier (DSB)

- We now explore a modification of the AM DSB–SC modulation where we add a portion of the pure sinusoidal carrier to the modulated waveform.

- We will see that this addition greatly simplifies the demodulation process. The block diagram is shown in Fig. 2.12.

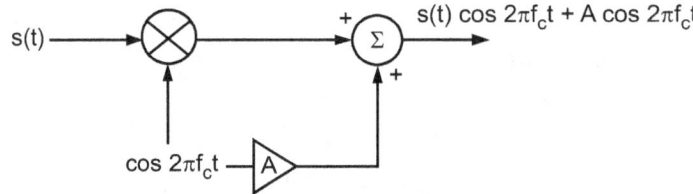

Fig. 2.12: Amplitude Demodulation Circuit

The resulting waveform is given by

$$s_m(t) = s(t) \cos(\omega_c t) + A\cos(\omega_c t)$$

- The Fourier transform of transmitted carrier AM is the sum of the Fourier transform of suppressed carrier AM with the Fourier transform of the pure carrier.

- The transform of the carrier is a pair of impulses at ±*fc* in frequency. The complete transform of the AM wave is therefore as shown in figure 3.

Figure 4 shows the time waveform.

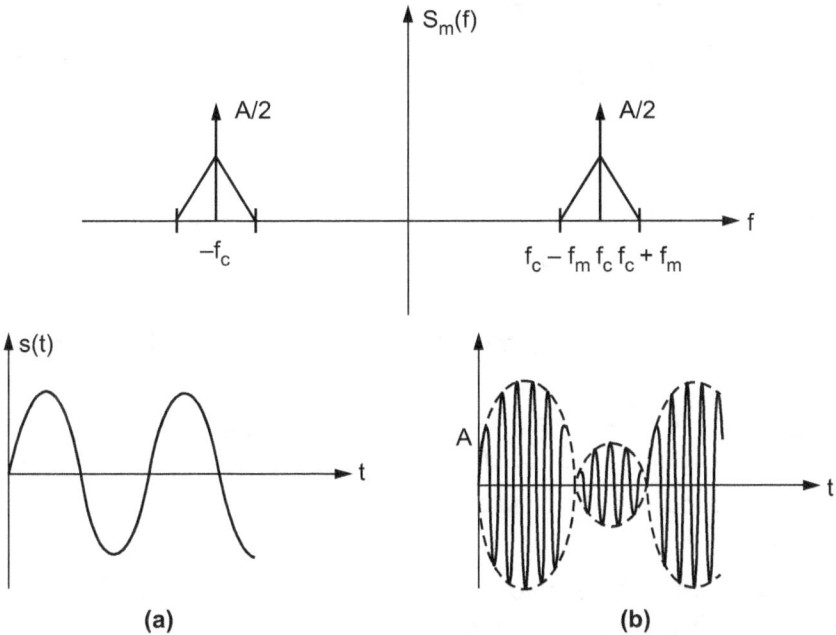

Fig. 2.13: Amplitude Modulation: DSB Transmitted Carrier

2.2.3 Modulation Factor

- A modulating wave that has low amplitude will produce a smaller amplitude variation in the modulated wave than a high amplitude modulating wave will.

- This fact gives to a need for expressing the degree of modulation produced by a wave of some particular amplitude. This is expressed by a ratio called the modulation factor, Ma.

- The modulation factor is simply the ratio of the peak amplitude variation used (Am) to the maximum design variation (Ac).

- Under proper operating conditions Am will always equal or less than Ac, therefore, the modulation factor, Ma will not be allowed to exceed unity.

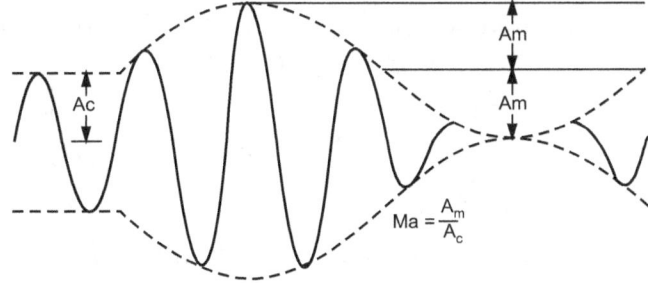

Fig. 2.14: Modulating Factor

2.3 FREQUENCY SPECTRUM OF THE AM WAVE

- The frequencies present in the AM wave are the carrier frequency and the first pair of sideband frequencies, where a sideband frequency is defined as

$$f_{SB} = f_c \pm nf_m$$

and in the first pair n = 1.

- When a carrier is amplitude–modulated, the proportionality constant is made equal to unity, and the instantaneous modulating voltage variations are superimposed onto the carrier amplitude.

- Thus when there is temporarily no modulation, the amplitude of the carrier is equal to its unmodulated value.

- When modulation is present, the amplitude of the carrier is varied by its instantaneous value. The situation is illustrated in Fig. 2.15, which shows how the maximum amplitude of the amplitude–modulated voltage is made to vary in accordance with modulating voltage changes.

- Fig. 2.15 also shows that something unusual (distortion) will occur if V_m is greater than V_c (this distortion is a result of overdriving the amplifier stage).

- This, and the fact that the ratio V_m/V_c often occurs, leads to the definition of the modulation index.

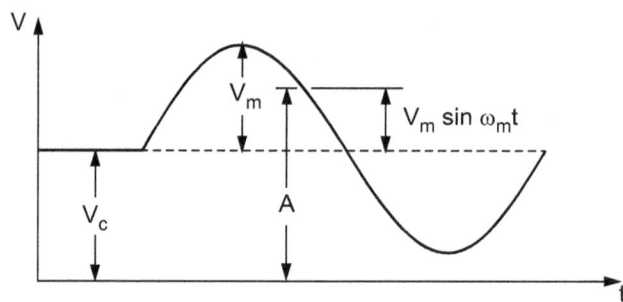

Fig. 2.15: Amplitude of AM wave

$$m = V_m/V_c$$

- The modulation index is a number lying between 0 and 1, and it is very often expressed as a percentage and called the percentage modulation.

An equation for the amplitude of the amplitude–modulated voltage is

$$A = V_c + V_m = V_c + V_m \sin \omega_m t = V_c = mV_c \sin \omega_m t$$

$$= V_c (1 + m \sin \omega_m t)$$

The instantaneous voltage of the resulting amplitude–modulated wave is

$$v = A \sin \theta = A \sin \omega_c t = V_c (1 + m \sin \omega_m t) \sin \omega_c t$$

- The frequency of the lower sideband (LSB) is $f_c - f_m$, and the frequency of the upper sideband (USB) is $f_c + fm$.

- The very important conclusion to be made at this stage is that the bandwidth required for amplitude modulation is twice the frequency of the modulating signal.

- In modulation by several sine waves simultaneously, as in the AM broadcasting service, the bandwidth required is twice the highest modulating frequency.

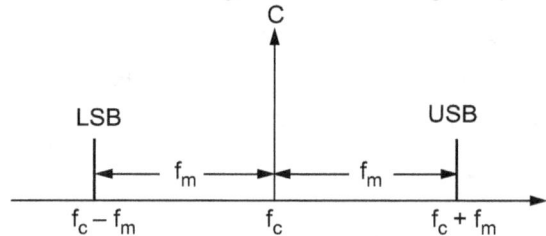

Fig. 2.16: Frequency spectrum of AM wave

Angle Modulation Techniques

There are two types of continuous–wave modulation; amplitude modulation and angle modulation. Angle modulation may be subdivided into two distinct type i.e. frequency modulation (FM) and phase modulation (PM). It is possible to obtain frequency modulation from phase modulation by the so–called Armstrong system. Phase modulation is not used in practical analog transmission systems.

2.4 THEORY OF ANGLE MODULATION TECHNIQUE

2.4.1 Theory of Frequency Modulation

- Frequency modulation is a system in which the amplitude of the modulated carrier is kept constant, while its frequency and rate of change are varied–by the modulating signal.

Description of System

The general equation of an unmodulated wave, or carrier, may be written as

$$x = A \sin(\omega t + \phi)$$

Where x = instantaneous value (of voltage or current)

A = (maximum) amplitude

ω = angular velocity, radians per second (rad/s)

ϕ = phase angle, rad

Note that ωt represents an angle in radians.

- If any one of these three parameters is varied in accordance with another signal, normally of a lower frequency, then the second signal is called the modulation, and the first is said to be modulated by the second.

- Amplitude modulation is achieved when the amplitude A is varied. Alteration of the phase angle ϕ will yield phase modulation.

- If the frequency of the carrier is made to vary, frequency–modulated waves are obtained.

- It is assumed that the modulating signal is sinusoidal. This signal has two important parameters which must be represented by the modulation process without distortion, specifically, its amplitude and frequency.

- It is understood that the phase relations of a complex modulation signal will be preserved.

- By the definition of frequency modulation, the amount by which the carrier frequency is varied from its unmodulated value, called the deviation, is made proportional to the instantaneous amplitude of the modulating voltage.

- The rate at which this frequency variation changes or takes place is equal to the modulating frequency.

- The situation is illustrated in Fig. 2.17, which shows the modulating voltage and the resulting frequency–modulated wave. Fig. 2.17 also shows the frequency variation with time, which can be seen to be identical to the variation with time of the modulating voltage.

- The result of using that modulating voltage to produce AM is also shown for comparison.

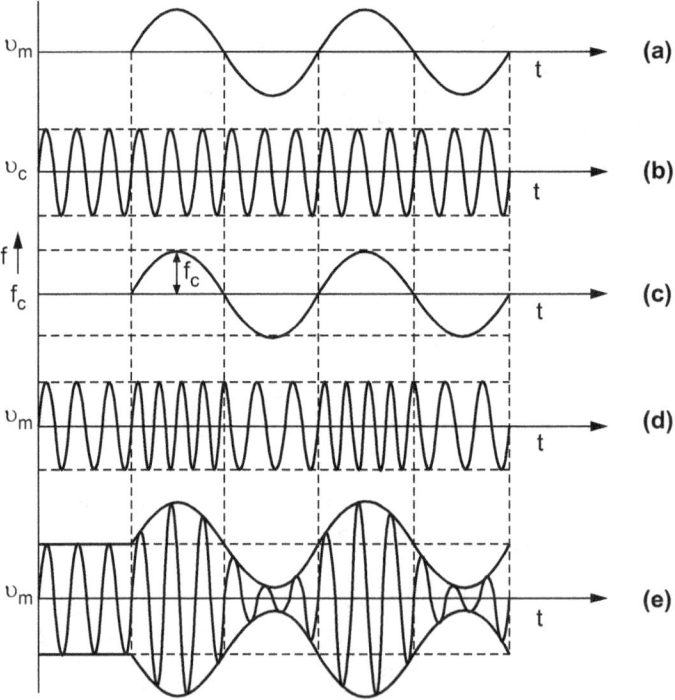

Fig. 2.17: AM and FM signals

- As in FM, all signals having the same amplitude will deviate the carrier frequency by the same amount for example, 45 kHz, no matter what their frequencies. All signals of the same frequency, for example, 2 kHz, will deviate the carrier at the same rate of 2000 times per second, no matter what their individual amplitudes.

- The amplitude of the frequency–modulated wave remains constant at all times. This is the greatest single advantage of FM.

2.4.2 Theory of Phase Modulation

- Phase modulation is a system in which the phase of the carrier is varied instead of its frequency as in FM, the amplitude of the carrier remains constant.

- If the phase ϕ, in the equation $v = A \sin(\omega ct + \phi)$ is varied so that its magnitude is proportional to the instantaneous amplitude of the modulating voltage, the resulting wave is phase–modulated.

- The expression for a PM wave is

$$v = A \sin(\omega ct + \phi m \sin \omega mt)$$

- Where ϕm is the maximum value of phase change introduced by this particular modulating signal and is proportional to the maximum amplitude of this modulation.

- For the sake of uniformity, this is rewritten as

$$v = A \sin(\omega ct + mp \sin \omega mt)$$

Where mp = ϕm = modulation index for phase modulation.

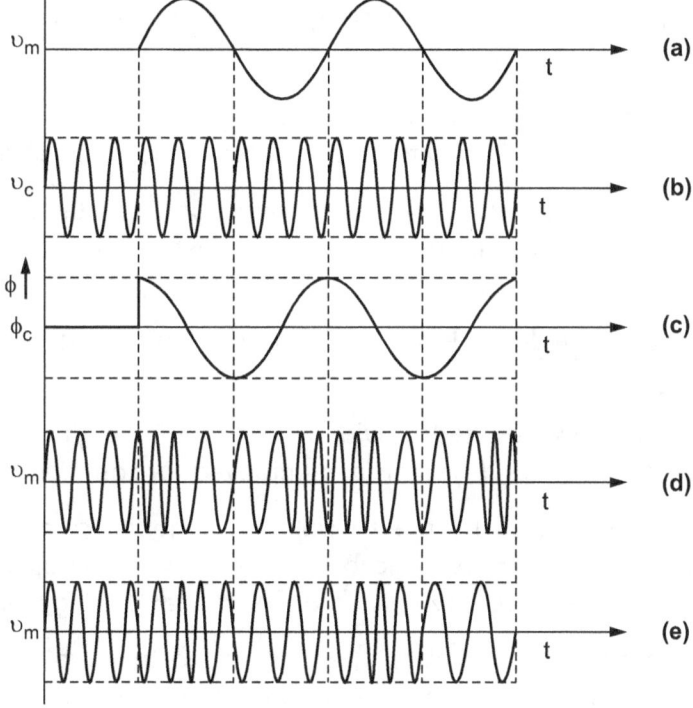

Fig. 2.18: PM and FM signals

- To visualize phase modulation, consider a horizontal metronome or pendulum placed on a rotating record turntable.

- As well as rotating, the arm of this metronome is swinging sinusoidally back and forth about its mean point.

- If the maximum displacement of this swing can be made proportional to the size of the "push" applied to the metronome, and if the frequency of swing can be made equal to the number of "pushes" per second, then the motion of the arm is exactly the same as that of a phase–modulated vector.

- Actually, PM seems easier to visualize than FM.

2.5 PRACTICAL ISSUES IN FREQUENCY MODULATION

2.5.1 Wideband and Narrowband FM

- Depending on the bandwidth occupied by the FM for practical transmission, FM is classified into wideband and narrowband cases.

- The bandwidth is also directly proportional to the modulation index value.

- By convention, wideband FM has been defined as that in which the modulation index normally exceeds unity. Since the maximum permissible deviation is 75 kHz and modulating frequencies range from 30 Hz to 15 kHz, the maximum modulation index ranges from 5 to 2500.

- The modulation index in narrowband FM is near unity, since the maximum modulating frequency there is usually 3 kHz, and the maximum deviation is typically 5 kHz.

- The proper bandwidth to use in an FM system depends on the application. With a large deviation; noise will be better suppressed, but care must be taken to ensure that impulse noise peaks do not become excessive.

- On the other hand, the wideband system will occupy up to 15 times the bandwidth of the narrowband system.

- These considerations have resulted in wideband systems being used in entertainment broadcasting, while narrowband systems are employed for communications.

- Thus narrowband FM is used by the so–called FM mobile communications services. These include police, ambulances, taxicabs, radio–controlled appliance repair services, short–range VHF ship–to–shore services and the Australian "Flying Doctor" service.

- The higher audio frequencies are attenuated, as indeed they are in most carrier (long–distance) telephone systems, but the resulting speech quality is still perfectly adequate.

- Maximum deviations of 5 to 10 kHz are permitted, and the channel space is not much greater than for AM broadcasting, i.e., of the order of 15 to 30 kHz.

- Narrowband systems with even lower maximum deviations are envisaged. Pre–emphasis and de–emphasis are used, as indeed they are with all FM transmissions.

2.5.2 Noise and Frequency Modulation

Frequency modulation is mu.ch more immune to noise than amplitude modulation and is significantly more immune than phase modulation. In order to establish the reason for this and to determine the extent of the improvement, it is necessary to examine the effect of noise on a carrier.

Effects of Noise on Carrier–Noise Triangle

- A single–noise frequency will affect the output of a receiver only if it falls within its bandpass.

- The carrier and noise voltages will mix, and if the difference is audible, it will naturally interfere with the reception of wanted signals.

- If such a single–noise voltage is considered vectorially, it is seen that the noise vector is superimposed on the carrier, rotating about it with a relative angular velocity $\omega n–\omega c$. This is shown in Fig. 2.19.

- The maximum deviation in amplitude from the average value will be Vn, whereas the maximum phase deviation will be $\phi = \sin^{-1} (V_n/V_c)$.

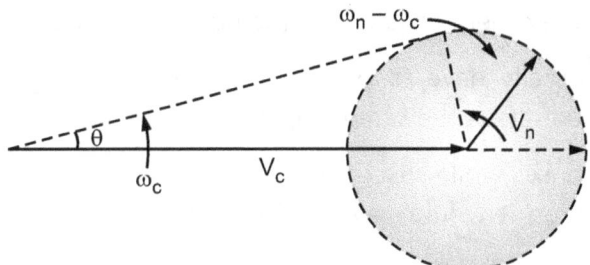

Fig. 2.19: Vector effect of noise on carrier

- The effects of noise frequency change must now be considered. In AM, there is no difference in the relative noise, carrier, and modulating voltage amplitudes, when both the noise difference and modulating frequencies are reduced from 15 kHz to the normal minimum audio frequency of 30 Hz (in high–quality broadcast systems).

- Changes in the noise and modulating frequency do not affect the signal–to–noise (S/N) ratio in AM.

- In FM the picture is entirely different. As the ratio of noise to carrier voltage remains constant, so does the value of the modulation index remain constant (i.e., maximum phase deviation).

- It should be noted that the noise voltage phase modulates the carrier. While the modulation index due to noise remains constant (as the noise sideband frequency is reduced), the modulation index caused by the signal will go on increasing in proportion to the reduction in frequency.

- The signal–to–noise ratio in FM goes on reducing with frequency, until it reaches its lowest value.

2.5.3 Pre–emphasis and De–emphasis

- The noise triangle showed that noise has a greater effect on the higher modulating frequencies than on the lower ones.

- Thus, if the higher frequencies were artificially boosted at the transmitter and correspondingly cut at the receiver, an improvement in noise immunity could be expected, thereby increasing the signal–to–noise ratio.

- This boosting of the higher modulating frequencies, in accordance with a prearranged curve, is termed pre–emphasis, and the compensation at the receiver is called de–emphasis.

- An example of a circuit used for each function is shown in Fig.2.20. Take two modulating signals having the same initial amplitude, with one of them pre–emphasized to twice this amplitude, whereas the other is unaffected (being at a much lower frequency).

- The receiver will naturally have to de–emphasize the first signal by a factor of 2, to ensure that both signals have the same amplitude in the output of the receiver.

- Before demodulation, i.e., while susceptible to noise interference, the emphasized signal had twice the deviation it would have had without pre–emphasis and was thus more immune to noise.

- When this signal is de–emphasized, any noise sideband voltages are de–emphasized with it and therefore have correspondingly lower amplitude than they would have had without emphasis. Their effect on the output is reduced.

- The amount of pre–emphasis in U.S. FM broadcasting, and in the sound transmissions accompanying television, has been standardized as 75 μs, whereas a number of other services, notably European and Australian broadcasting and TV sound transmission; use 50 μs.

- The usage of microseconds for defining emphasis is standard. A 75–µs de–emphasis corresponds to a frequency response curve that is 3 dB down at the frequency whose time constant RC is 75 µs.

- This frequency is given by f = 1/2πRC and is therefore 2120 Hz.

- With 50–µs de–emphasis it would be 3180 Hz. Fig. 2.21 shows pre–emphasis and de–emphasis curves for a 75–µs emphasis, as used in the United States.

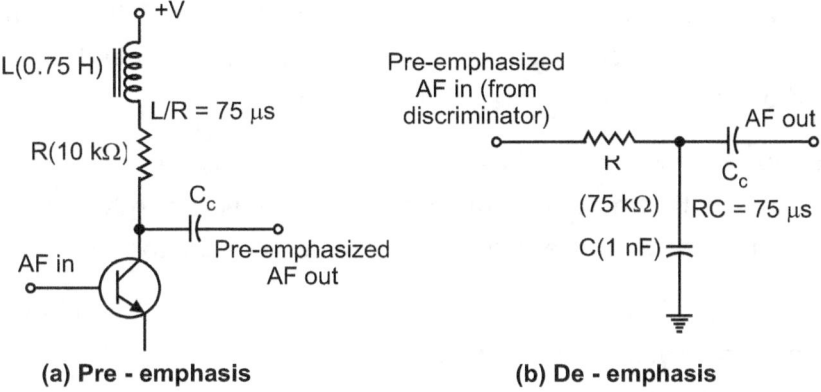

(a) Pre - emphasis   **(b) De - emphasis**

Fig. 2.20:75µs emphasis circuits

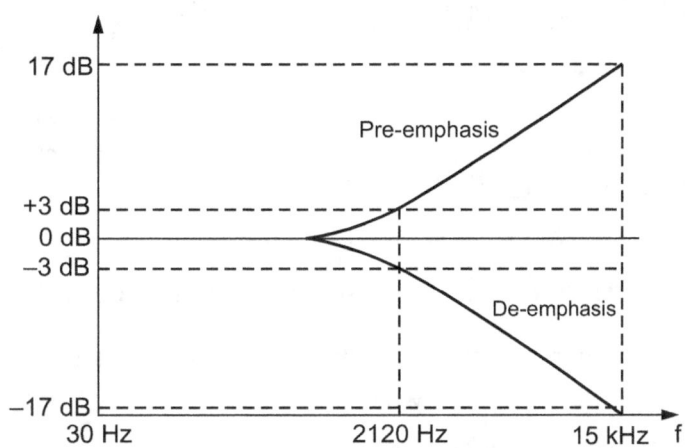

Fig. 2.21: 75µs emphasis curves

- If emphasis were applied to amplitude modulation, some improvement would also result, but it is not as great as in FM because the highest modulating frequencies in AM are no more affected by noise than any others.

- Apart from that, it would be difficult to introduce pre–emphasis and de–emphasis in existing AM services since extensive modifications would be needed, particularly in view of the huge numbers of receivers in use.

2.5.4 Stereophonic FM Multiplex System

- Stereo FM transmission is a modulation system in which sufficient information is sent to the receiver to enable it to reproduce original stereo material.

- It became commercially available in 1961, several years after commercial monaural transmissions.

- Like color TV (which of course came after monochrome TV), it suffers from the disadvantage of having been made more complicated than it needed to be, to ensure that it would be compatible with the existing system.

- Thus, in stereo FM, it is not possible to have a two–channel system with a left channel and a right channel transmitted simultaneously and independently, because a monaural system would not receive all the information in an acceptable form.

- As shown in the block diagram of Fig.2.22, the two channels in the FM stereo multiplex system are passed through a matrix which produces two outputs.

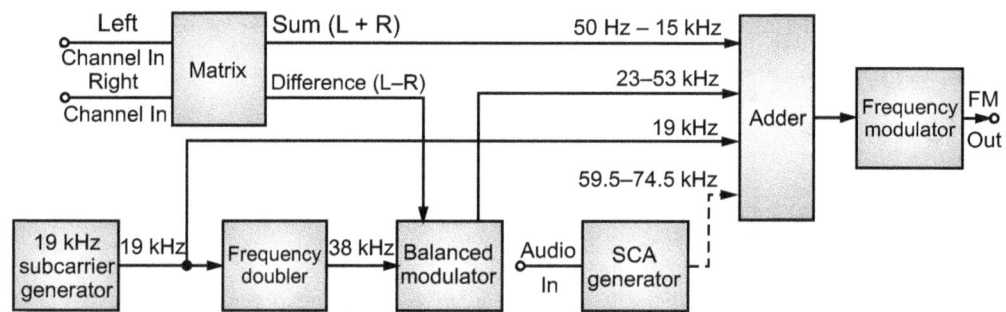

Fig. 2.22: Stereo FM multiplex generator with optical SCA

- The sum (L+R) modulates the carrier in the same manner as the signal in a monaural transmission, and this is the signal which is demodulated and reproduced by a mono receiver tuned to a stereo transmission.

- The other output of the matrix is the difference signal (L–R). After demodulation in a stereo receiver, (L–R) will be added to (L+R) to produce the left channel, while the difference between the two signals will produce the right channel.

- What happens, in essence, is that the difference signal is shifted in frequency from the 50– to 15,000–Hz range (which it would otherwise co–occupy with the sum signal) to a higher frequency.

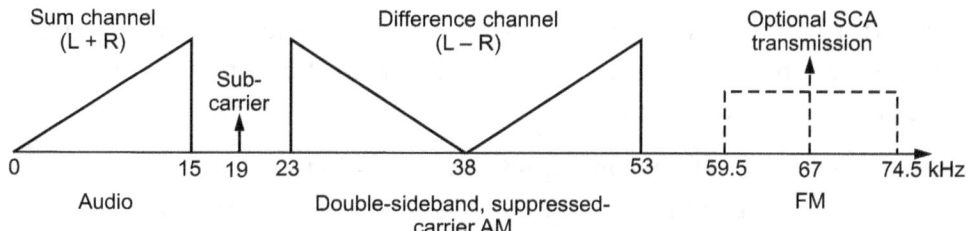

Fig. 2.23: Spectrum of stereo FM multiplex modulating signal (with optional SCA)

- In this case, as in other multiplexing, a form of single sideband suppressed carrier (SSBSC) is used, with the signals to be multiplexed up being modulated onto a subcarrier at a high audio or supersonic frequency.

- However, there is a snag here, which makes this form of multiplexing different from the more common ones.

- The problem is that the lowest audio frequency is 50 Hz, much lower than the normal minimum of 300 Hz encountered in communications voice channels.

- This makes it difficult to suppress the unwanted sideband without affecting the wanted one; pilot carrier extraction in the receiver is equally difficult.

- Some form of carrier must be transmitted, to ensure that the receiver has a stable reference frequency for demodulation; otherwise, distortion of the difference signal will result.

- The two problems are solved in similar ways. In the first place, the difference signal is applied to a balanced modulator which suppresses the carrier.

- Both sidebands are then used as modulating signals and duly transmitted, whereas normally one might expect one of them to be removed prior to transmission.

- Since the subcarrier frequency is 38 kHz, the sidebands produced by the difference signal occupy the frequency range from 23 to 53 kHz.

- It is seen that they do not interfere with the sum signal, which occupies the range of 50 Hz to 15 kHz.

- The reason that the 38–kHz subcarrier is generated by a 19–kHz oscillator whose frequency is then doubled may now be explained.

- Indeed, this is the trick used to avoid the difficulty of having to extract the pilot carrier from among the close sideband frequencies in the receiver.

- As shown in the block diagram (Fig.2.22), the output of the 19–kHz subcarrier generator is added to the sum and difference signals in the output adder preceding the modulator.

- It should be noted that the subcarrier is inserted at a level of 10 percent, which is both adequate and not so large as to take undue power from the sum and difference signals (or to cause ovemodulation).

- The frequency of 19 kHz fits neatly into the space between the top of the sum signal and the bottom of the difference signal. It is far enough from each of them so that no difficulty is encountered in the receiver.

- The FM stereo multiplex system described here is the one used in the United States, and is in accordance with the standards established by the Federal Communications Commission (FCC) in 1961.

- Stereo FM has by now spread to broadcasting in most other parts of the world, where the systems in use are either identical or quite similar to the above.

- A Subsidiary Communications Authorization (SCA) signal may also be transmitted in the U.S. stereo multiplex system.

- It is the remaining signal feeding in to the output adder. It is shown dashed in the diagram because it is not always present.

- Some stations provide SCA as a second, medium quality transmission, used as background music in stores, restaurants and other similar settings.

- SCA uses a subcarrier at 67 kHz, modulated to a depth of ±7.5 kHz by the audio signal.

- The frequency band thus occupied ranges from 59.5 to 74.5 kHz and fits sufficiently above the difference signal as not to interfere with it.

- The overall frequency allocation within the modulating signal of an FM stereo multiplex transmission with SCA is shown in Fig.2.23.

- The amplitude of the sum and difference signals must be reduced (generally by 10 percent) in the presence of SCA; otherwise, overmodulation of the main carrier could result.

2.6 GENERATION OF FREQUENCY MODULATION

- For the design of a frequency modulator, we need a device that produces an output signal whose instantaneous frequency is sensitive to variations in the amplitude of an input signal in a linear manner.

- There are two basic methods of generating frequency–modulated waves, one direct and the other indirect.

2.6.1 Direct Method

- The direct method uses a sinusoidal oscillator, with one of the reactive elements (e.g., capacitive element) in the tank circuit of the oscillator being directly controllable by the message signal.

- In conceptual terms, the direct method is therefore straightforward to implement.

- Moreover, it is capable of providing large frequency deviations. However, a serious limitation of the direct method is the tendency for the carrier frequency to drift, which is usually unacceptable for commercial radio applications. To overcome this limitation, frequency stabilization of the FM generator is required, which is realized through the use of feedback around the oscillator.

- Although the oscillator may itself be simple to build, the use of frequency stabilization adds system complexity to the design of the frequency modulator.

2.6.2 Indirect Method: Armstrong Modulator

- In the indirect method, on the other hand, the message signal is first used to produce a narrow–band FM, which is followed by frequency multiplication to increase the frequency deviation to the desired level.

- In this second method, the carrier–frequency stability problem is alleviated by using a highly stable oscillator (e.g., crystal oscillator) in the narrowband FM generation; this modulation scheme is called the Armstrong wide–band frequency modulator, in recognition of its inventor.

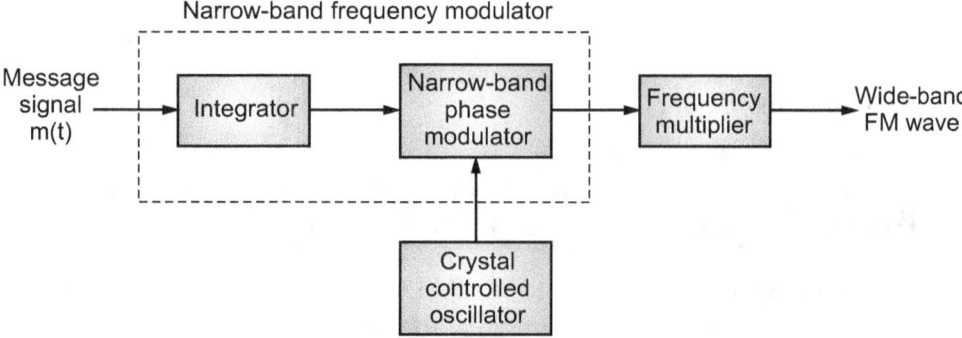

Fig. 2.24: Block diagram of the indirect method of generating a wide–band FM wave.

- A simplified block diagram of this indirect FM system is shown in Fig. 2.24. The message signal is first integrated and then used to phase–modulate a crystal–controlled oscillator; the use of crystal control provides frequency stability.

- In order to minimize the distortion inherent in the phase modulator, the maximum phase deviation or modulation index is purposely kept small, thereby resulting in a narrow–band FM wave.

- The narrow–band FM wave is next multiplied in frequency by means of a frequency multiplier so as to produce the desired wide–band FM wave.

- A frequency multiplier consists of a memoryless nonlinear device followed by a bandpass filter, as shown in Fig. 2.25.

- The implication of the nonlinear device being memoryless is that it has no energy–storage elements.

- The input–output relation of such a device may be expressed in the general form

$$v(t) = a_1 s(t) + a_2 s^2(t) + \ldots + a_n s^n(t)$$

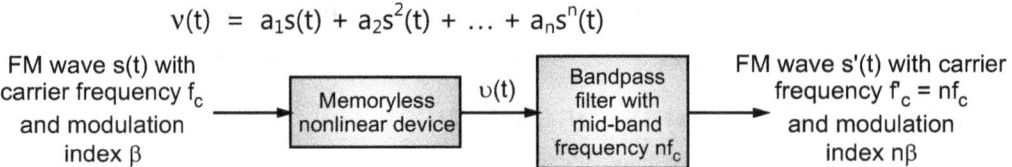

Fig. 2.25: Block diagram of frequency multiplier.

Where a_1, a_2, ..., a_n are coefficients determined by the operating point of the device, and n is the highest order of nonlinearity.

In other words, the memoryless nonlinear device is an nth power–law device.

The input s(t) is an FM wave defined by

$$S(t) = A_c \cos 2\pi f c t + 2\pi k f \int_0^t m(T)\, dT$$

Where the instantaneous frequency is

$$f_i(t) = f_c + k_f m(t)$$

2.7 FREQUENCY SPECTRUM OF THE FM WAVE

- When a comparable stage was reached with AM theory, it was possible to tell at a glance what frequencies were present in the modulated wave.

- Unfortunately, the situation is far more complex, mathematically speaking, for FM.

- The solution involves the use of Bessel functions.

$$v = A\{J_0(m_f) \sin \omega_c t$$

$$+ J1(m_f) [\sin (\omega_c + \omega_m)t - \sin (\omega_c - \omega_m)t]$$

$$+ J2(m_f) [\sin (\omega_c + 2\,\omega_m)t + \sin (\omega_c - 2\,\omega_m)t]$$

$$+ J3(m_f) [\sin (\omega_c + 3\,\omega_m)t - \sin (\omega_c - 3\,\omega_m)t]$$

$$+ J4(m_f) [\sin (\omega_c + 4\,\omega_m)t + \sin (\omega_c - 4\,\omega_m)t] \cdots \}$$

It can be shown that the output consists of a carrier and an apparently infinite number of pairs of sidebands, each preceded by J coefficients. These are Bessel functions.

Here they happen to be of the first kind and of the order denoted by the subscript, with the argument $m_f J_n(m_f)$ may be shown to be a solution of an equation of the form

$$(m_f)^2 \frac{d^2y}{dm_f^2} + m_f \frac{dy}{dm_f} + (m_f^2 - n^2)y = 0$$

This solution, i.e., the formula for the Bessel function, is

$$J_n(m_f) = \left(\frac{m_f}{2}\right)^2 \left[\frac{1}{n!} - \frac{(m_f/2)^2}{1!\,(n+1)!} + \frac{(m_f/2)^4}{2!(n+2)!} - \frac{(m_f/2)^6}{3!(n+1)!} + \cdots\right]$$

- In order to evaluate the value of a given pair of sidebands or the value of the carrier, it is necessary to know the value of the corresponding Bessel function.

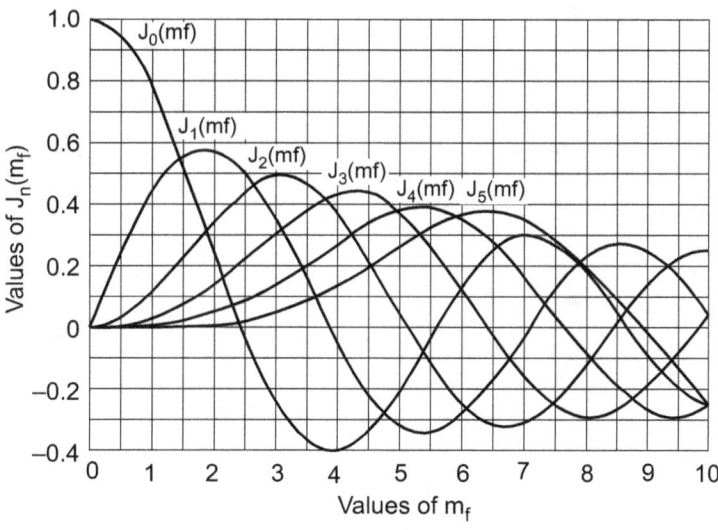

Fig. 2.26: Bessel Functions

EXERCISE

1. What is amplitude modulation? Discuss any two amplitude modulation techniques.

2. Explain in detail amplitude modulation techniques.

3. How amplitude modulated signal is generated?

4. Explain the generation of amplitude modulated signal.

5. Explain the term frequency spectrum w.r.t. amplitude modulation.

6. Explain the theory of angle modulation and its techniques.

7. Write a short note on practical issues in frequency modulation.

8. Explain the generation frequency modulation.

9. Explain the term frequency spectrum w.r.t. frequency modulation.

PULSE AND DIGITAL MODULATION TECHNIQUES

PULSE MODULATION TECHNIQUES

- Pulse modulation technique's intention is to transfer a narrowband analog signal over an analog baseband channel as a two-level signal by modulating a pulse wave.

- Some pulse modulation schemes also allow the narrowband analog signal to be transferred as a digital signal with a fixed bit rate, which can be transferred over an primary digital transmission system.

3.1 PULSE ANALOG MODULATION TECHNIQUES

3.1.1 Pulse-Amplitude Modulation (PAM)

- In pulse amplitude modulation, the amplitude of regular interval of periodic pulses or electromagnetic pulses is varied in proposition to the sample of modulating signal or message signal.

- This is an analog type of modulation. In the pulse amplitude modulation, the message signal is sampled at regular periodic or time intervals and this each sample is made proportional to the magnitude of the message signal.

- These sample pulses can be transmitted directly using wired media or we can use a carrier signal for transmitting through wireless.

- There are two types of sampling techniques for transmitting messages using pulse amplitude modulation, they are

1. FLAT TOP PAM: The amplitude of each pulse is directly proportional to immediate modulating signal amplitude at the time of pulse occurrence and then keeps the amplitude of the pulse for the rest of the half cycle.

2. Natural PAM: The amplitude of each pulse is directly proportional to the immediate modulating signal amplitude at the time of pulse occurrence and then follows the amplitude of the modulating signal for the rest of the half cycle.

- Flat top PAM is the best for transmission because we can easily remove the noise and we can also easily recognize the noise.

- When we compare the difference between the flat top PAM and natural PAM, flat top PAM principle of sampling uses sample and hold circuit.

- In natural principle of sampling, noise interference is minimum. But in flat top PAM noise interference is maximum.

- Flat top PAM and natural PAM are practical and sampling rate satisfies the sampling criteria.

- There are two types of pulse amplitude modulation based on signal polarity

  (i) Single polarity pulse amplitude modulation

  (ii) Double polarity pulse amplitude modulation

- In single polarity pulse amplitude modulation, there is fixed level of DC bias added to the message signal or modulating signal, so the output of modulating signal is always positive.

- In the double polarity pulse amplitude modulation, the output of modulating signal will have both positive and negative ends.

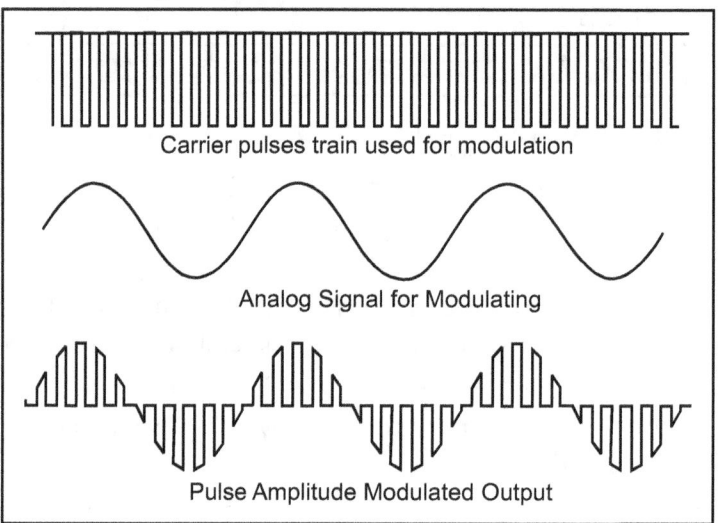

Fig. 3.1: Pulse Amplitude Modulation

Advantages of Pulse Amplitude Modulation (PAM)

- It is the simple process for both modulation and demodulation techniques.

- No complex circuitry is required for both transmission and reception. Transmitter and receiver circuitry is simple and easy to construct.

- PAM can generate other pulse modulation signals and can carry the message or information at same time.

Disadvantages of Pulse Amplitude Modulation (PAM)

- Bandwidth should be large for transmitting the pulse amplitude modulation signal. Due to Nyquist criteria high bandwidth is required.

- The frequency varies according to the modulating signal or message signal. Due to these variations in the signal frequency, interferences will be there. So noise will be great.

- For PAM, noise immunity is less when compared to other modulation techniques.

- Pulse amplitude signal varies, so power required for transmission will be more, peak power is also, even at receiving more power is required to receive the pulse amplitude signal.

Applications of Pulse Amplitude Modulation (PAM)

- It is mainly used in Ethernet which is type of computer network communication, we know that we can use Ethernet for connecting two systems and transfer data between the systems. Pulse amplitude modulation is used for Ethernet communications.

- It is also used for photo biology which is a study of photosynthesis.

- Used as electronic driver for LED lighting.

- Used in many micro controllers for generating the control signals etc.

3.1.2 Pulse-Width Modulation (PWM)

- It is a type of analog modulation. In pulse width modulation or pulse duration modulation, the width of the pulse carrier is varied in accordance with the sample values of message signal or modulating signal or modulating voltage.

- In pulse width modulation, the amplitude is made constant and width of pulse and position of pulse is made proportional to the amplitude of the signal.

- We can vary the pulse width in three ways
  - ➢ By keeping the leading edge constant and vary the pulse width with respect to leading edge
  - ➢ By keeping the tailing constant.
  - ➢ By keeping the center of the pulse constant.

- We can generate pulse width using different circuitry. In practical, we use 555 Timer which is the best way for generating the pulse width modulation signals.

- By configuring the 555 timer as monostable or astable multivibrator, we can generate the PWM signals.

- We can use PIC, 8051, AVR, ARM, etc. microcontrollers to generate the PWM signals. PWM signal generation has n number of ways.

- In demodulation, we need PWM detector and its related circuitry for demodulating the PWM signal.

Advantages of Pulse Width Modulation (PWM)

- As like pulse position modulation, noise interference is less due to amplitude has been made constant.

- Signal can be separated very easily at demodulation and noise can also be separated easily.

- Synchronization between transmitter and receiver is not required unlike pulse position modulation.

Disadvantages of Pulse Width Modulation (PWM)

- Power will be variable because of varying in width of pulse. Transmitter can handle the power even for maximum width of the pulse.

- Bandwidth should be large to use in communication, should be huge even when compared to the pulse amplitude modulation.

Applications of Pulse Width Modulation (PWM)

- PWM is used in telecommunication systems.

- PWM can be used to control the amount of power delivered to a load without incurring the losses. So, this can be used in power delivering systems.

- Audio effects and amplifications purposes also used.

- PWM signals are used to control the speed of the robot by controlling the motors.

- PWM is also used in robotics.

- Embedded applications.

- Analog and digital applications etc.

3.1.3 Pulse-Density Modulation (PDM)

- Pulse-density modulation, or PDM, is a form of modulation used to represent an analog signal with a binary signal.

- In a PDM signal, specific amplitude values are not encoded into code words of pulses of different weight as they would be in pulse-code modulation (PCM).

- Instead, it is the relative density of the pulses that corresponds to the analog signal's amplitude. The output of a 1-bit DAC is the same as the PDM encoding of the signal.

- Pulse-width modulation (PWM) is a special case of PDM where the switching frequency is fixed and all the pulses corresponding to one sample are contiguous in the digital signal.

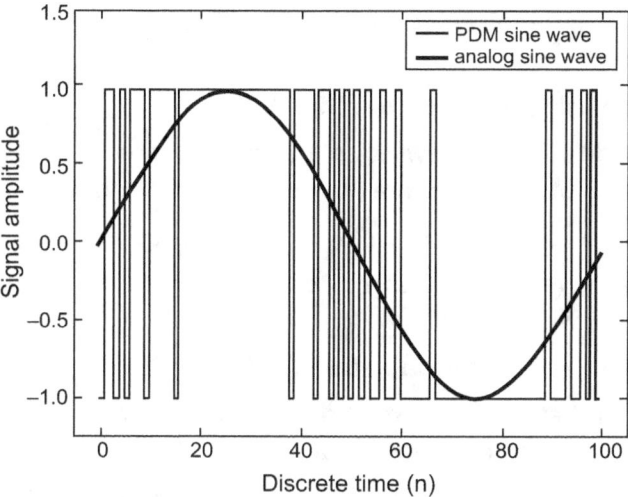

Fig. 3.2 : Pulse Density Modulation

Applications of Pulse Density Modulation (PDM)

• PDM is the encoding used in Sony's Super Audio CD (SACD) format, under the name Direct Stream Digital.

• Some systems transmit PDM stereo audio over a single data wire. The rising edge of the master clock indicates a bit from the left channel, while the falling edge of the master clock indicates a bit from the right channel

3.1.4 Pulse-Position Modulation (PPM)

• In the pulse position modulation, the position of each pulse in a signal by taking the reference signal is varied according to the sample value of message or modulating signal instantaneously.

• In the pulse position modulation, width and amplitude is kept constant. It is a technique that uses pulses of the same breath and height but is displaced in time from some base position according to the amplitude of the signal at the time of sampling.

• The position of the pulse is 1:1 which is propositional to the width of the pulse and also propositional to the instantaneous amplitude of sampled modulating signal.

• The position of pulse position modulation is easy when compared to other modulation. It requires pulse width generator and monostable multivibrator.

• Pulse width generator is used for generating pulse width modulation signal which will help to trigger the monostable multivibrator, here trial edge of the PWM signal is used for triggering the monostable multivibrator.

• After triggering the monostable multivibrator, PWM signal is converted into pulse position modulation signal.

- For demodulation, it requires reference pulse generator, flip-flop and pulse width modulation demodulator.

Advantages of Pulse Position Modulation (PPM)

- Pulse position modulation has low noise interference when compared to PAM because amplitude and width of the pulses are made constant during modulation.

- Noise removal and separation is very easy in pulse position modulation.

- Power usage is also very low when compared to other modulations due to constant pulse amplitude and width.

Disadvantages of Pulse Position Modulation (PPM)

- The synchronization between transmitter and receiver is required, which is not possible for every time and we need dedicated channel for it.

- Large bandwidth is required for transmission same as pulse amplitude modulation.

- Special equipments are required in this type of modulations.

Applications of Pulse Position Modulation (PPM)

- Used in non-coherent detection where a receiver does not need any Phase lock loop for tracking the phase of the carrier.

- Used in radio frequency (RF) communication.

- Also used in contactless smart card, high frequency, RFID (radio frequency ID) tags and etc.

3.2 SAMPLING

- There are two types of signal exist, continuous time signal and discrete time signals.

- Thus instead of having large number of continuous time signal we prefer processing of discrete signal.

- Thus conversion of continuous to discrete time signal is required. This phenomenon is obtained by fundamental mathematical tool known as Sampling Theorem.

- Sampling is the process of converting analog signal into a discrete signal or making an analog or continuous signal to occur at a particular interval of time, this phenomenon is known as sampling.

Sampling Theorem

- Sampling theorem states that a band limited signal having no frequency components higher than f_m hertz can be sampled if its sampling frequency is equal to or greater than Nyquist rate.

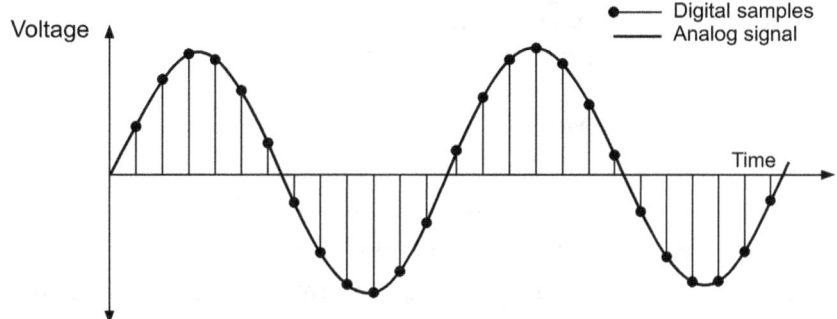

Fig. 3.3: Analog Signal Representation

Sampling Techniques

There are basically three types of Sampling techniques, namely

1. Natural Sampling
2. Flat top Sampling
3. Ideal Sampling

1. Natural Sampling

*   In Natural Sampling method pulse have finite width equal to τ.

*   Sampling is done in accord with the carrier signal and that signal is digital in nature.

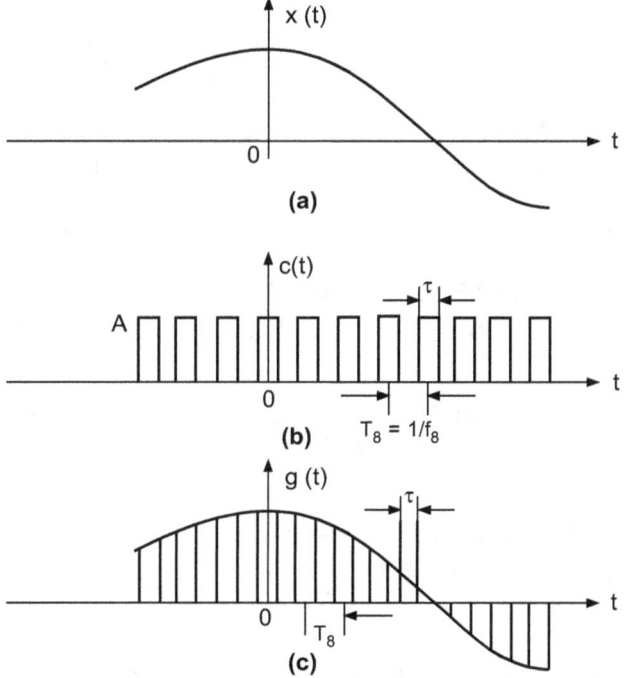

Fig. 3.4: Natural Sampled Waveform

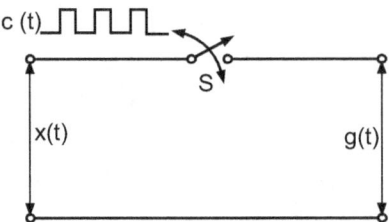

Fig. 3.5: Functional Diagram of Natural Sampler

- With the help of functional diagram of a Natural sampler, a sampled signal g(t) is obtained by multiplication of sampling function c(t) and the input signal x(t).

- Spectrum of Natural Sampled Signal is given by:

$$G(f) = A\tau/ T_s .[\Sigma \sin c(n f_s.\tau) X(f-n f_s)]$$

2. Flat Top Sampling

- Flat top sampling is same as natural sampling i.e practical in nature. In comparison to natural sampling flat top sampling can be easily obtained.

- In this sampling techniques, the top of the samples remains constant and is equal to the immediate value of the message signal x(t) at the start of sampling process.

- Sample and hold circuits are used in this type of sampling.

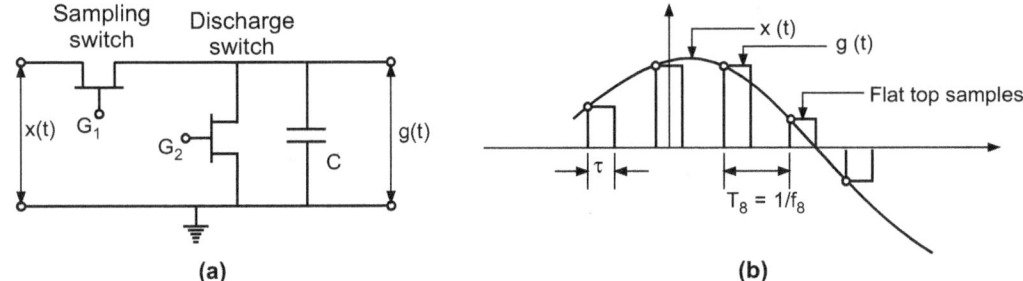

Fig. 3.6: Block Diagram and Waveform

- Figure 3.6(a), shows functional diagram of a sample hold circuit which is used to generate flat top samples.

- Figure 3.6(b), shows the general waveform of the flat top samples. It can be observed that only starting edge of the pulse represent the instantaneous value of the message signal x(t).

- Spectrum of Flat top Sampled Signal is given by:

$$G(f) = f_s .[\Sigma X(f-n f_s). H(f)]$$

3. Ideal Sampling

- Ideal Sampling is also known as instantaneous sampling or impulse Sampling.

- Train of impulse is used as a carrier signal for ideal sampling.

- In this sampling technique the sampling function is a train of impulses and the principle used is known as multiplication principle.

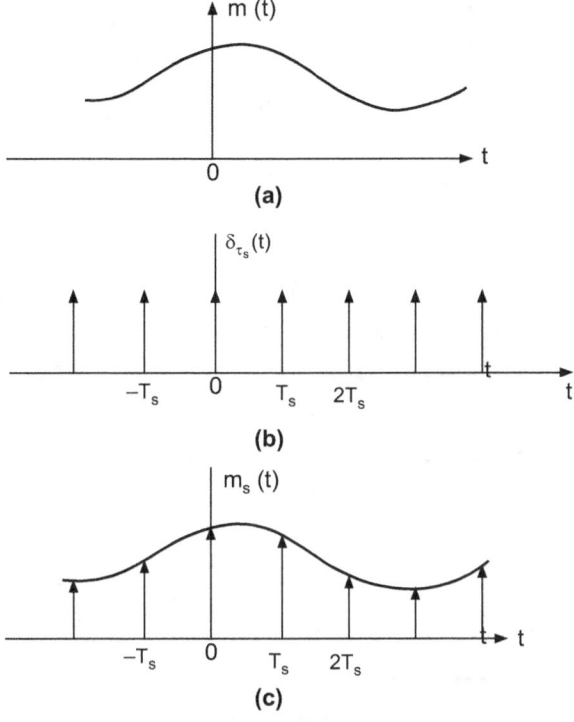

Fig. 3.7: Ideal Sampling Wave form

3.3 PULSE DIGITAL MODULATION TECHNIQUES

3.3.1 Pulse Code Modulation (PCM)

- Pulse code modulation is a method that is used to convert an analog signal into a digital signal, so that modified analog signal can be transmitted through the digital communication network.

- PCM is in binary form, so there will be only two possible states high and low (0 and 1). We can also get back our analog signal by demodulation.

- There are three steps in Pulse Code Modulation process i.e. Sampling, Quantization, and Coding.

- In sampling we are using PAM sampler that is Pulse Amplitude Modulation Sampler which converts continuous amplitude signal into Discrete-time- continuous signal (PAM pulses).

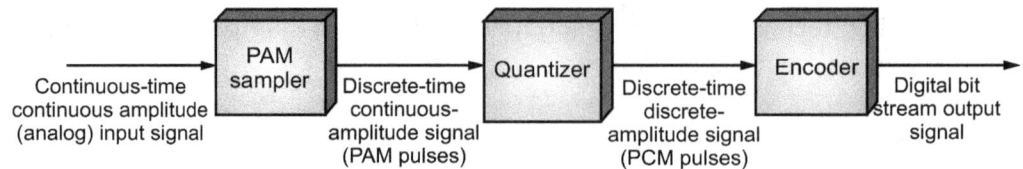

Fig. 3.8: Block diagram of PCM

What is a Pulse Code Modulation?

- To get a pulse code modulated waveform from an analog waveform at the transmitter end (source) of a communications circuit, the amplitude of the analog signal samples at regular time intervals.

- The sampling rate or number of samples per second is several times the maximum frequency. The message signal converted into binary form will be usually in the number of levels which is always to a power of 2. This process is called quantization.

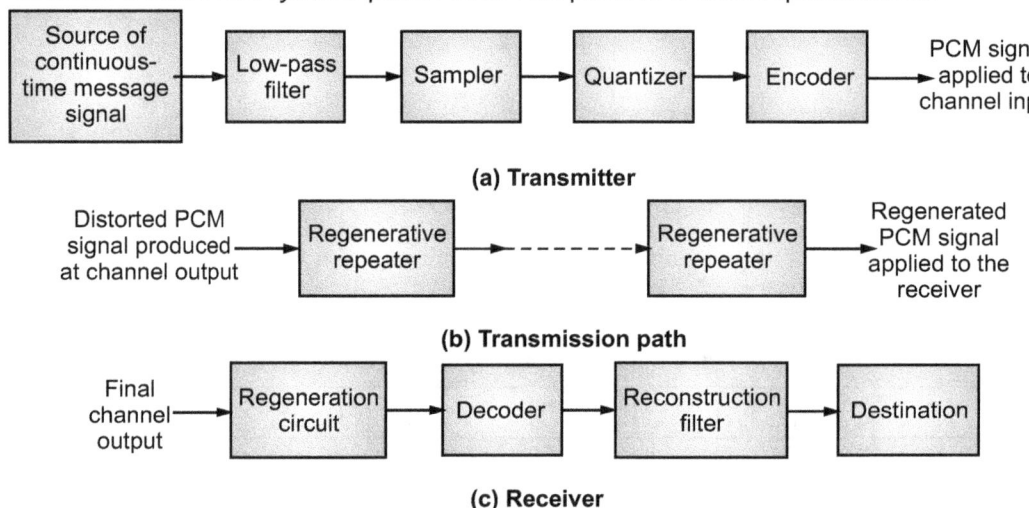

Fig. 3.9: Basic elements of PCM system

- At the receiver end, a pulse code demodulator decodes the binary signal back into pulses with same quantum levels as those in the modulator.

- By further processes we can restore the original analog waveform.

Pulse Code Modulation Theory

- The above block diagram describes the whole process of PCM.

- The source of continuous time message signal is passed through a low pass filter and then sampling, Quantization, Encoding will be done.

Sampling

- Sampling is a process of measuring the amplitude of a continuous-time signal at discrete instants, converts the continuous signal into a discrete signal. For example, conversion of a sound wave to a sequence of samples.

- The Sample is a value or set of values at a point in time or it can be spaced. Sampler extract samples of a continuous signal, it is a subsystem ideal sampler produces samples which are equivalent to the instantaneous value of the continuous signal at the specified various points.

- The Sampling process generates flat- top Pulse Amplitude Modulated (PAM) signal.

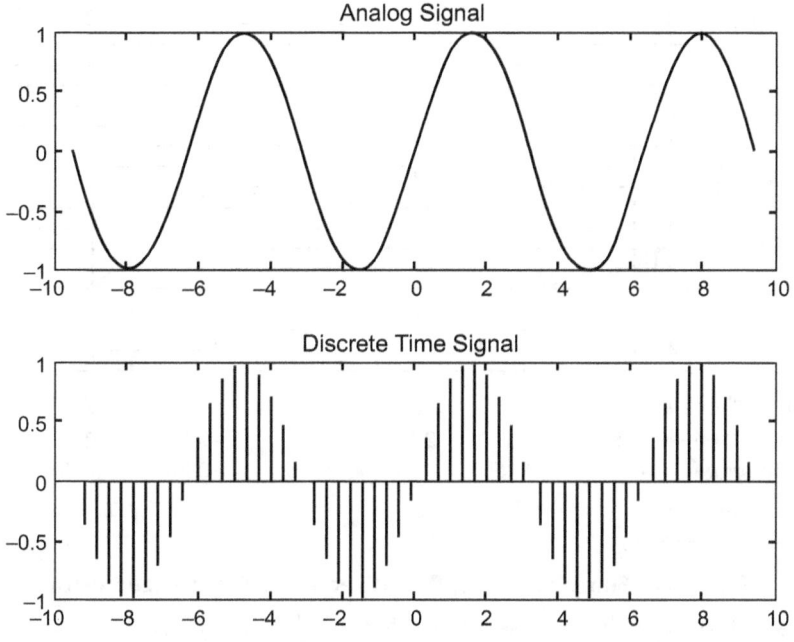

Fig. 3.10: Analog and sampled signal

- Sampling frequency, F_s is the number of average samples per second also known as Sampling rate.

- According to the Nyquist Theorem sampling rate should be at least 2 times the upper cutoff frequency. Sampling frequency, $F_s >= 2*f_{max}$ to avoid Aliasing Effect.

- If the sampling frequency is very higher than the Nyquist rate it become Oversampling, theoretically a bandwidth limited signal can be reconstructed if sampled at above the Nyquist rate.

- If the sampling frequency is less than the Nyquist rate it will become under sampling.

- Basically two types of techniques are used for the sampling process. Those are Natural Sampling and Flat- top Sampling.

Quantization

Quantization is basically a process of approximation. This is also like rounding off procedure i.e., if the sampled voltage level is 3.45 then rounding off value = 3.5. If sampled voltage level is 5.78 then rounding off value = 5.8.

Thus, quantizer converts the sampled signal level into an approximated quantized voltage level, which is nearest to the predecided standard voltage level.

These nearest predecided standard voltage levels are called as "quantization levels".

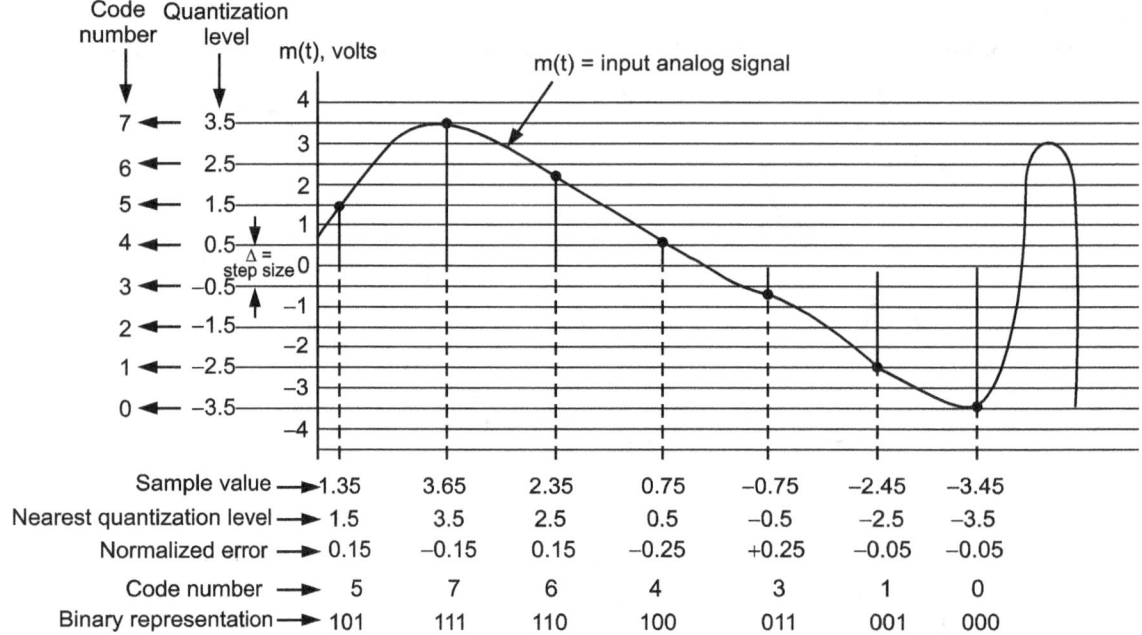

Fig. 3.11 : Sampled value, Quantized level, Normalized error

Code number and Binary code representation for the given signal

Here we assume that the original analog signal has amplitudes between Emin and Emax. Here the signal voltage is instantaneous.

In Fig. 3.11, Emax = 4 V and Emin = −4 V. This entire range has been divided into 'L' equal intervals each having equal size = Δ.

Hence, step size = Δ = Emax − EminL

Here, in Fig. 3.11,　　　L = 8

$$Emax = 4V$$

$$Emin = -4V$$

At the centre of these steps the quantization levels are located as shown.

The difference between quantized level and sampled value is known as :

* Normalized error.
* or Quantization error.
* or Quantization noise.

Quantization error should be as small as possible. Thus, maximum quantization error QE is always −Δ/2 ≤ QE ≤ Δ/2.

Thus, to minimize the quantization error, we must reduce step size.

Step size can be reduced by increasing the number of quantization levels.

Thus, if we use 3 bit PCM, then quantization levels will be 2N = 23 = 8 = L = Levels.

 If N = 4 bit i.e., 4 bit PCM, then

Quantization levels   =L = 2N = 24 = 16 levels.

To increase quantization levels, number of bits are increased and hence bit rate in PCM increases, hence bandwidth requirement of the channel increases.

In audio communication, normally we use 8-bit PCM, hence 28 = 256 levels. In video communication, the number of levels are in thousands.

Thus, if number of levels are more then bandwidth required increases.

If number of levels are less then quantization error increases.

Hence, compromise is done always, while selecting number of levels.

Signal to noise ratio is given as,

   SNRdB = 6.02 × Nb + 1.76 dB

   where, Nb=Number of bits/sample

There are two types of quantizers :

   (i)   Uniform quantizer.

   (ii) Non-uniform quantizer.

In uniform quantizer the representation levels or quantized levels are uniformly spaced.

In non-uniform quantizer the representation levels or quantized levels are spaced non-uniformly.

Coding

- The encoder encodes the quantized samples. Each quantized sample is encoded into an 8-bit code word by using A-law in the encoding process.

- Bit 1 is the most significant bit (MSB), it represents the polarity of the sample. "1" represents positive polarity and "0" represents negative polarity.

- Bit 2,3 and 4 will defines the location of sample value. These three bits together form linear curve for low level negative or positive samples.

- Bit 5, 6, 7 and 8 are the least significant bits (LSB) it represents one of the segments quantized value. Each segment is divided into 16 quantum levels.

Adaptive Differential Pulse Code Modulation (ADPCM)

- ADPCM is achieved by adapting the quantizing levels to analog signal characteristics.

- We can estimate the values with preceding sample values. Error estimation is done as same as in DPCM.

- In 32Kbps ADPCM method difference between predicted value and sample value is coded with 4 bits, so that we'll get 15 quantum levels.
- In this method data rate is half of the conventional PCM.

Pulse Code Demodulation

- Pulse Code Demodulation will be doing the same modulation process in reverse. Demodulation starts with decoding process, during transmission the PCM signal will effected by the noise interference.
- So, before the PCM signal sends into the PCM demodulator, we have to recover the signal into the original level for that we are using a comparator.
- The PCM signal is a series pulse wave signal, but for demodulation we need wave to be parallel.
- By using a serial to parallel converter the series pulse wave signal will be converted into a parallel digital signal.
- After that the signal will pass through n-bits decoder, it should be a Digital to Analog converter. Decoder recovers the original quantization values of the digital signal.
- This quantization value also includes a lot of high frequency harmonics with original audio signals.

Pulse Code Modulation Advantages

- Analog signal can be transmitted over a high- speed digital communication system.
- Probability of occurring error will reduce by the use of appropriate coding methods.
- PCM is used in Telkom system, digital audio recording, digitized video special effects, digital video, voice mail.
- PCM is also used in Radio control units as transmitter and also receiver for remote controlled cars, boats, planes.
- The PCM signal is more resistant to interference than normal signal.

3.3.2 Delta Modulation (DM)

- The basic disadvantage of the PCM system is complexity. Transmitter as well as Receiver has complex processing steps in PCM system.
- Another A to D conversion techniques are :
  - ➢ DM (Delta Modulation).
  - ➢ ADM (Adaptive Delta Modulation).
- In PCM, every sampled value is quantized and every quantized level gives you binary bit stream output whereas, in DM, instead of code words or bit stream, bits are sent one after the another.

- The **DM Modulator** block diagram is as shown in Fig. 3.12.

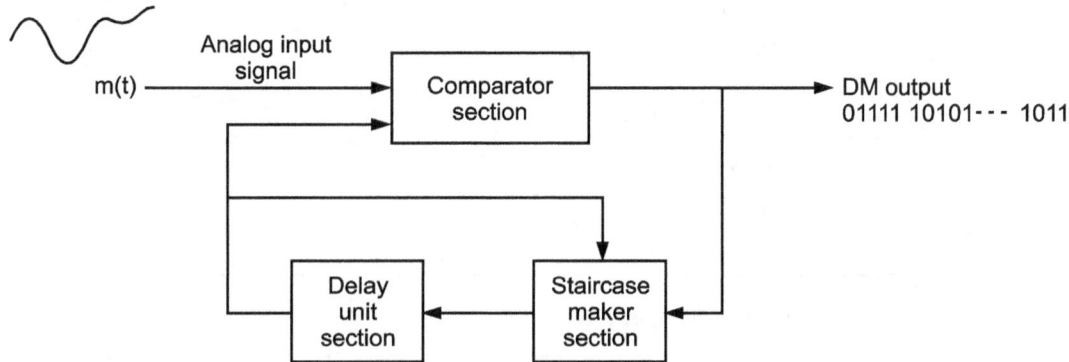

Fig. 3.12: DM Modulator Block Diagram

- The **DM Demodulator** block diagram is as shown in Fig. 3.13.

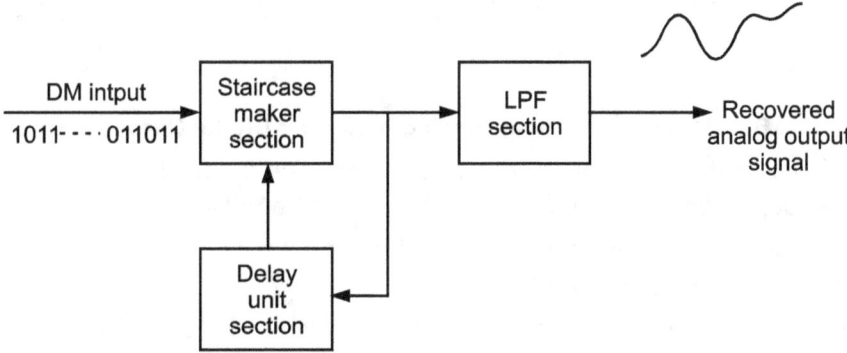

Fig. 3.13: DM Demodulator Block Diagram

- In delta modulation process, it checks and records the small negative and positive changes known as 'δ'.

- Input signal m(t) is approximated to step signal by the delta modulator system, represented as D(t).

- This step size is always fixed. The negative changes are $-\delta$ and +ve changes are known as 'δ'.

- The difference between m(t) and D(t) is positive then, approximate or D(t) signal is increased by one step i.e., 'δ' and thus, '1' is transmitted.

- The difference between m(t) and D(t) is negative then, approximate or D(t) signal is decreased by one step i.e. 'δ' and thus '0' is transmitted.

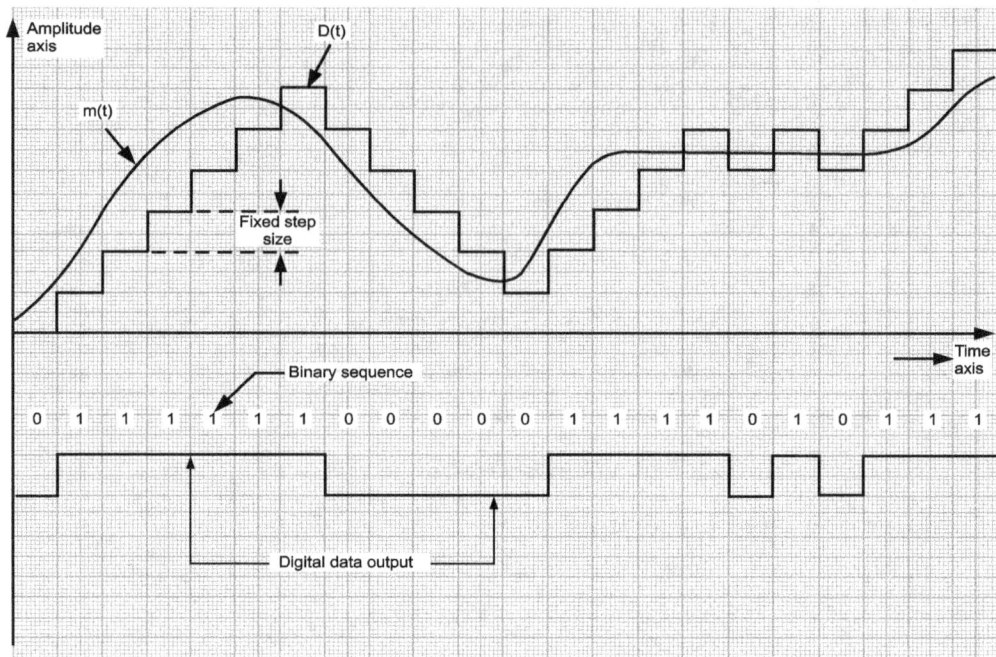

Fig. 3.14: DM (Delta Modulation), Analog Input and Digital Output Waveform

- Thus, in delta modulation, for every sample, only one binary bit i.e. either '1' or '0' is transmitted depending upon difference between m(t) and D(t).

- In other words, if the amplitude of the analog signal is larger, then the next bit in the digital data is '1', otherwise it is '0'.

- Also, delay unit section is required to hold the staircase function for a period between two comparisons we have discussed.

- In DM demodulator, digital data bit stream is applied to staircase maker section.

- Staircase maker section and Delay unit section creates the analog signal, which is not smooth in nature.

- Thus, final required analog signal which is smooth in nature, is available at the output of low-pass-filter section.

Advantages of DM

- Delta modulator gives only one bit for every sample. Hence, bit rate as well as channel bandwidth requirement is less.

- Simplest transmitter and receiver circuitry reduces the cost.

Disadvantages of DM

- There are two distortions occurring in DM.

- Slope overload distortion.

- Granular noise distortion (Hunting effect).

- These distortions are as shown in Fig. 3.15.

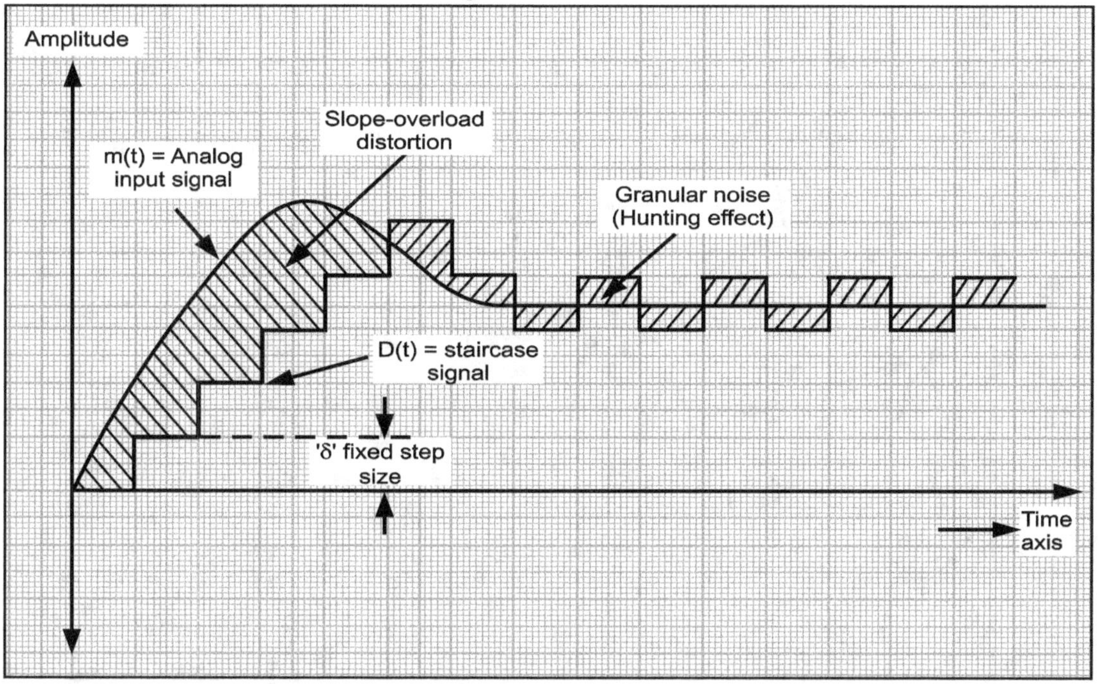

Fig. 3.15: Slope Overload and Granular Noise Distortions in DM

- If the rise rate of input signal m(t) is high, then staircase signal can not approximate it or predict it because step size 'δ' is fixed and small for staircase signal D(t) to follow the analog signal m(t).

- Due to which there is large error between m(t) and D(t) signal. This large error is known as slope overload distortion.

- To reduce this slope overload error, step size should be increased when slope or rising rate of analog signal m(t) is high. This can be achieved with new technique known as Adaptive Delta Modulation.

- Thus, in ADM (Adaptive Delta Modulation), the value of step size 'δ' changes according to the amplitude of the input analog signal m(t).

- If analog input signal m(t) is flat in nature and step size of D(t) is having high 'δ' (step size), then staircase signal D(t) keeps on oscillating by ± δ around the signal. This difference or error between m(t) and D(t) is known as granular noise and this effect of oscillating by ± δ around the signal is known as hunting effect.

- To reduce the granular noise, ADM (Adaptive Delta Modulation) technique is used, which reduces step size 'δ' when signal m(t) becomes flat in nature.

- Finally, ADM technique uses variable step size to overcome slope-overload noise and granular noise.

- The waveform of ADM technique to reduce slope-overload noise and granular noise is as shown in Fig. 3.16.

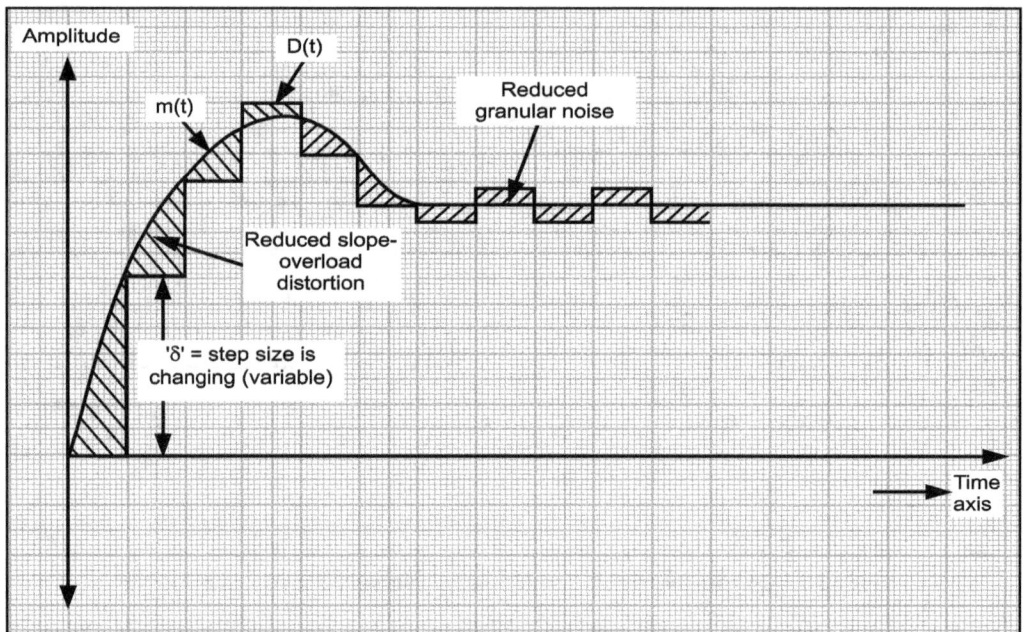

Fig. 3.16: ADM (Reduced Slope-Overload Noise and Granular Noise)

Thus, following are the advantages of ADM :

- SNR is better than DM.

- Bandwidth utilization is better than DM.

- Dynamic range is better than DM.

3.3.3 Differential Pulse Code Modulation (DPCM)

- Differential pulse code modulation (DPCM) is a procedure of converting an analog into a digital signal in which an analog signal is sampled and then the difference between the actual sample value and its predicted value (predicted value is based on previous sample or samples) is quantized and then encoded forming a digital value.

- DPCM code words represent differences between samples unlike PCM where code words represented a sample value.

- Basic concept of DPCM - coding a difference, is based on the fact that most source signals show significant correlation between successive samples so encoding uses redundancy in sample values which implies lower bit rate.

- Realization of basic concept is based on a technique in which we have to predict current sample value based upon previous samples (or sample) and we have to encode the difference between actual value of sample and predicted value (the difference between samples can be interpreted as prediction error).

- Because it's necessary to predict sample value DPCM is form of predictive coding.

- DPCM compression depends on the prediction technique, well-conducted prediction techniques lead to good compression rates, in other cases DPCM could mean expansion comparing to regular PCM encoding.

3.4 AVERAGE INFORMATION

- The theory of information was founded by Claude E. Shannon in 1930. In brief, the information, I, obtained when an event occurs with probability p(i), where i is an index ranging from 1 to n, is

$$I = - \log[p(i)]; (\text{ minus the logarithm of } p(i)).$$

- Further, if the sum of all p(i) equals 1, such that the set of p(i) represent a probability density function(PDF), then the entropy or disorder, H, may be defined for any PDF as

$$H = - \text{sum } p(i) \log[p(i)]; i = 1, 2, 3, â€¦, n.$$

- As is also well known, this is per definition the average of the negative logarithms over the PDF, which may also be called Average Information.

- Thus **Average Information** is equivalent to entropy or disorder.

3.5 ENTROPY

- In information theory, systems are modeled by a transmitter, channel, and receiver. The transmitter transmits messages that are sent through the channel. The channel changes the message during transmission. The receiver attempts to convey which message was sent.

- Entropy is the expected value (average) of the information contained in each message. 'Messages' can be modeled by any flow of information.

- Generally, entropy refers to disorder or uncertainty. Entropy is a measure of the "disorder" of a system

- Shannon entropy provides an absolute limit on the best possible average length of lossless encoding or compression of an information source.

- Entropy is a measure of unpredictability or uncertainty of information content.

Examples of entropy:

- A campfire is an example of entropy. The solid wood burns and becomes ash, smoke and gases, all of which are more disordered than the solid fuel.

- Ice melting, salt or sugar dissolving, making popcorn and boiling water for tea are processes with increasing entropy in your kitchen.

- When you clean your room, it doesn't stay neat on its own. Unless you do work each day to keep things picked up, your shoes find their way out of the closet to the side of your bed, the jewelry, coins, and beauty products on your dresser get all jumbled up, your laundry pile grows every time you try to decide which outfit to wear and the bed covers are all scrambled.

3.6 INFORMATION RATE

- The information rate is represented by R and it is given as,

  Information Rate : $R = rH$

  Here R is the information rate.

  H is the Entropy or average information

  r is the rate at which messages are generated.

Information rate R is represented in average number of bits of information per second.

  It is calculated as follows:

$$R = (r \text{ in messages / second}) * (H \text{ in bits / messages})$$
$$= \text{bits / second}$$

3.7 SOURCE CODING

- One of the problems in communication system is the effective representation of data generated by a discrete source. The process by which this representation is completed is called source encoding.

- The device that performs the representation of data is called a source encoder.

- For the source encoder to be effective, we require knowledge of the statistics of the source.

- In particular, if some source symbols are known to be more probable than others, then we may exploit this feature in the generation of a source code by assigning short code words to frequent source symbols, and long code words to rare source symbols. We refer to such a source code as a variable-length code.

- The Morse code is an example of a variable-length code. In the Morse code, the letters of the alphabet and numerals are encoded into streams of marks and spaces, denoted as dots "." and dashes "-", respectively.

- There are two functional necessities in the development of an efficient source encoder are:

  ➢ The code words produced by the encoder are in binary form.

➢ The source code is generally decodable, so that the original source sequence can be reconstructed perfectly from the encoded binary sequence.

• Source coding does not change or alter the source entropy, i.e. the average number of information bits per source symbol. In this sense source entropy is a fundamental property of the source.

• Source coding alters the entropy of the source coded symbols.

• It may also reduce variations in the information rate from the source and avoid symbol 'surges' which could overload the channel when the message sequence contains many high probability symbols.

3.7.1 Shanon-Fano Coding

• Shannon–Fano coding name is given because of inventors of this technique i.e. Claude Shannon and Robert Fano. It is a technique for constructing a prefix code based on a set of symbols and their probabilities (estimated or measured).

Basic Technique

• In Shannon–Fano coding, the symbols are arranged in order from most probable to least probable, and then divided into two sets whose total probabilities are as close as possible to being equal.

• All symbols then have the first digits of their codes assigned; symbols in the first set receive "0" and symbols in the second set receive "1".

• As long as any sets with more than one member remain, the same process is repeated on those sets, to determine successive digits of their codes.

• When a set has been reduced to one symbol this means the symbol's code is complete and will not form the prefix of any other symbol's code.

• The algorithm produces fairly efficient variable-length encodings; when the two smaller sets produced by a partitioning are in fact of equal probability, the one bit of information used to distinguish them is used most efficiently.

• Unfortunately, Shannon–Fano does not always produce optimal prefix codes; the set of probabilities {0.35, 0.17, 0.17, 0.16, 0.15} is an example of one that will be assigned non-optimal codes by Shannon–Fano coding.

Shannon–Fano Algorithm

• A Shannon–Fano tree is built according to a specification designed to define an effective code table. The actual algorithm is simple:

• First thing, for a given list of symbols, create a corresponding list of probabilities or frequency counts so that each symbol's relative frequency of occurrence is known.

• Sort the lists of symbols according to frequency, with the most frequently occurring symbols at the left and the least common at the right.

- Divide the list into two parts, with the total frequency counts of the left part being as close to the total of the right as possible.

- The left part of the list is assigned the binary digit 0, and the right part is assigned the digit 1. This means that the codes for the symbols in the first part will all start with 0, and the codes in the second part will all start with 1.

- Recursively apply the steps 3 and 4 to each of the two halves, subdividing groups and adding bits to the codes until each symbol has become a corresponding code leaf on the tree.

Example

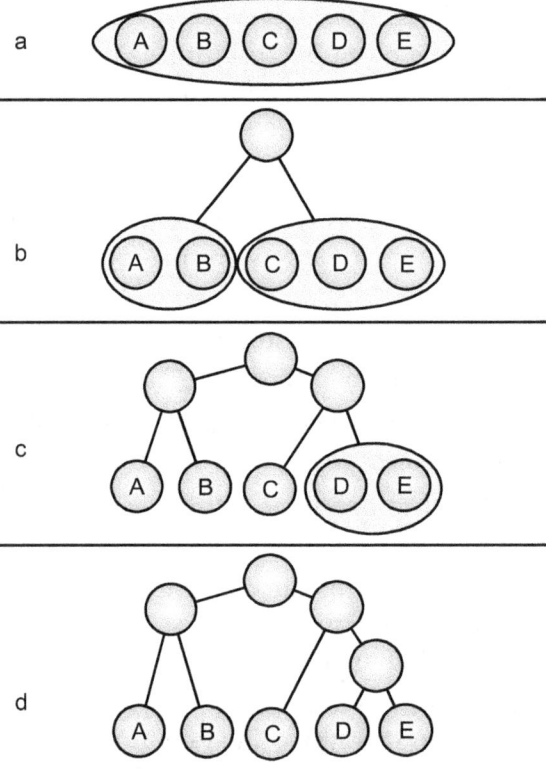

Fig. 3.17: Shannon–Fano Algorithm

The example shows the construction of the Shannon code for a small alphabet. The five symbols which can be coded have the following frequency:

Symbol	A	B	C	D	E
Count	15	7	6	6	5
Probabilities	0.38461538	0.17948718	0.15384615	0.15384615	0.12820513

- All symbols are sorted by frequency, from left to right (**shown in Figure a**). Putting the dividing line between symbols B and C results in a total of 22 in the left group and a total of 17 in the right group. This minimizes the difference in totals between the two groups.

- With this division, A and B will each have a code that starts with a 0 bit, and the C, D, and E codes will all start with a 1, as shown in Figure b.

- Subsequently, the left half of the tree gets a new division between A and B, which puts A on a leaf with code 00 and B on a leaf with code 01.

- After four division procedures, a tree of codes results. In the final tree, the three symbols with the highest frequencies have all been assigned 2-bit codes, and two symbols with lower counts have 3-bit codes as shown table below:

Symbol	A	B	C	D	E
Code	00	01	10	110	111

- Results in 2 bits for A, B and C and per 3 bits for D and E an average bit number of

$$\frac{2 \text{ bits} \cdot (15 + 7 + 6) + 3 \text{ bits} \cdot (6 + 5)}{39 \text{ symbols}} \approx 2.28 \text{ bits per symbol}$$

3.7.2 Huffman Coding

- The Shannon–Fano algorithm doesn't always generate an optimal code. In 1952, David A. Huffman gave a different algorithm that always produces an optimal tree for any given symbol weights (probabilities).

- While the Shannon–Fano tree is created from the root to the leaves, the Huffman algorithm works in the opposite direction, from the leaves to the root.
  - ➢ Create a leaf node for each symbol and add it to a priority queue, using its frequency of occurrence as the priority.
  - ➢ While there is more than one node in the queue:

- Remove the two nodes of lowest probability or frequency from the queue

- Prepend 0 and 1 respectively to any code already assigned to these nodes

- Create a new internal node with these two nodes as children and with probability equal to the sum of the two nodes' probabilities.

- Add the new node to the queue.

The remaining node is the root node and the tree is complete.

Example

Using the same frequencies as for the Shannon–Fano example above, viz:

Symbol	A	B	C	D	E
Count	15	7	6	6	5
Probabilities	0.38461538	0.17948718	0.15384615	0.15384615	0.12820513

- In this case D & E have the lowest frequencies and so are allocated 0 and 1 respectively and grouped together with a combined probability of 0.28205128.

- The lowest pair B and C so they're allocated 0 and 1 and grouped together with a combined probability of 0.33333333.

- This leaves BC and DE now with the lowest probabilities so 0 and 1 are prepended to their codes and they are combined.

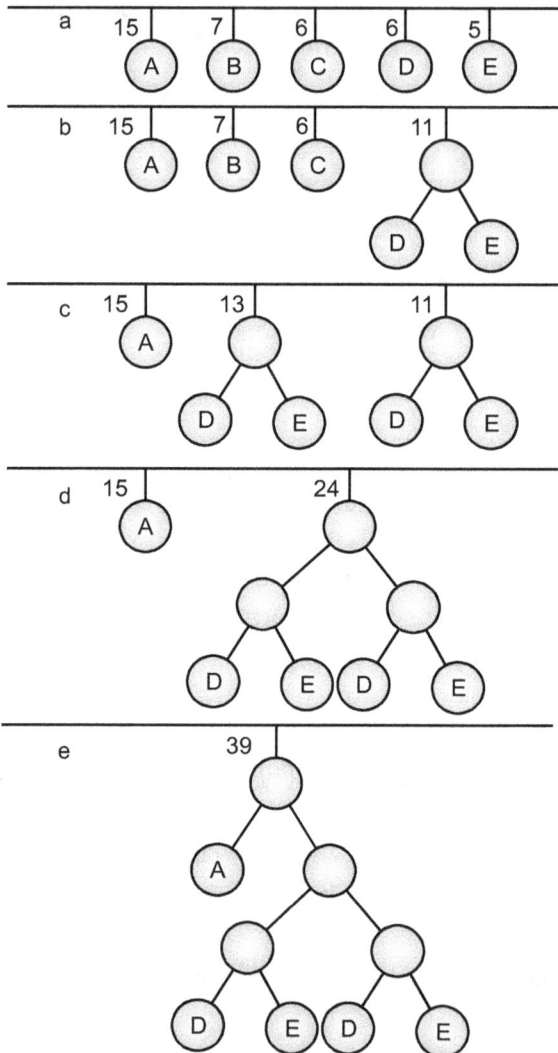

Fig. 3.18: Huffman Algorithm

- This then leaves just A and BCDE, which have 0 and 1 prepended respectively and are then combined. This leaves us with a single node and our algorithm is complete.

- The code lengths for the different characters this time are 1 bit for A and 3 bits for all other characters.

Symbol	A	B	C	D	E
Code	0	100	101	110	111

- Results in 1 bit for A and per 3 bits for B, C, D and E an average bit number of

$$\frac{1 \text{ bit} \cdot 15 + 3 \text{ bits} \cdot (7 + 6 + 6 + 5)}{39 \text{ symbols}} \approx 2.23 \text{ bits per symbol}$$

3.7.3 Limpel-Ziv Coding

- A code that might be more efficient to use statistical interdependence of the letters in the alphabet along with their individual probabilities of occurrences is the Lempel-ziv algorithm. This algorithm belongs to the class of universal source coding algorithms.

- The logic behind Lempel-ziv universal coding is as follows:

- The compression of an arbitrary binary sequence is possible by coding a series of zeros and ones as some previous such string (prefix string) + one new bit.

- The new string formed by such parsing becomes a potential prefix, string for future strings.

- These variables are called phrases (sub sequences). The phrases are listed in a dictionary or code book which stores the existing phrases and their locations.

- In encoding a new phrase be specified the location of the existing phrase in the code book and append the new letter.

- Lempel-Ziv coding represents a departure from the classic view of a code as a mapping from a fixed set of source messages (letters, symbols or words) to a fixed set of code words.

- The Lempel-Ziv algorithm consists of a rule for parsing strings of symbols from a finite alphabet into substrings, or words, whose lengths do not exceed a prescribed integer L(1); and a coding scheme which maps these substrings sequentially into uniquely decipherable code words of fixed length L(2).

- The strings are selected so that they have very nearly equal probability of occurrence. As a result, frequently-occurring symbols are grouped into longer strings while infrequent symbols appear in short strings.

- This strategy is effective at exploiting redundancy due to symbol frequency, character repetition, and high-usage patterns.

- Table 3.1 shows a small Lempel-Ziv code table. Low-frequency letters such as Z are assigned individually to fixed-length code words (in this case, 12 bit binary numbers represented in base ten for readability).

- Frequently-occurring symbols, such as blank (represented by _) and zero, appear in long strings. Effective compression is achieved when a long string is replaced by a single 12-bit code.

The Lempel-Ziv method specifies fixed-length code words. The size of the table and the maximum source message length are determined by the length of the code words.

Table 3.1: Lempel-Ziv Code Table

Symbol string	Code
A	1
T	2
AN	3
TH	4
THE	5
AND	6
AD	7
–	8
–	9
–	10
0	11
00	12
000	13
0000	14
Z	15
###	4095

Digital-To-Digital Conversion

- In Data Communication, a line code (also called digital baseband modulation) is a code chosen for use within a communication system for baseband transmission purposes.

- Line coding is often used for digital data transport. Here in this section we can represent the digital data by using digital signals. The conversion involves three techniques like Line coding, block coding and scrambling.

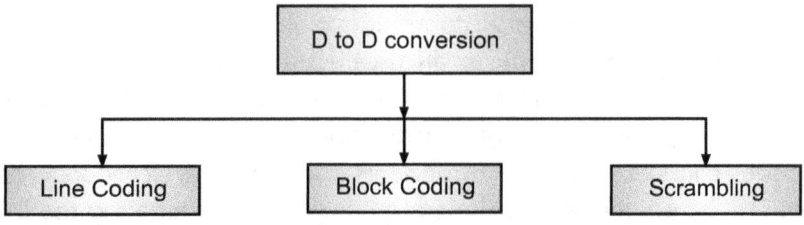

3.8 LINE CODING

Line Coding Fundamental Theory

- Line coding consists of representing the digital signal to be transported by an amplitude and time-discrete signal that is optimally tuned for the specific properties of the physical channel (and of the receiving equipment). The waveform pattern of voltage or current used to represent the 1s and 0s of a digital signal on a transmission link is called line encoding. The common types of line encoding are unipolar, polar, bipolar and Manchester encoding.

- For reliable clock recovery at the receiver, one usually imposes a maximum runlength constraint on the generated channel sequence, i.e. the maximum number of consecutive ones or zeros is bounded to a reasonable number. A clock period is recovered by observing transitions in the received sequence, so that a maximum runlength guarantees such clock recovery, while sequences without such a constraint could seriously hamper the detection quality.

- After line coding, the signal is put through a "physical channel", either a "transmission medium" or "data storage medium". Sometimes the characteristics of two very different-seeming channels are similar enough that the same line code is used for them. The most common physical channels are :

- The line-coded signal can directly be put on a transmission line, in the form of variations of the voltage or current (often using differential signaling).

- The line-coded signal (the "baseband signal") undergoes further pulse shaping (to reduce its frequency bandwidth) and then modulated (to shift its frequency bandwidth) to create the "RF signal" that can be sent through free space.

- The line-coded signal can be used to turn on and off a light in Free Space Optics, most commonly infrared remote control.

- The line-coded signal can be printed on paper to create a bar-code.

- The line-coded signal can be converted to magnetized spots on a hard drive or tape drive.

- The line-coded signal can be converted to pits on optical disc.

- Unfortunately, most long-distance communication channels cannot transport a DC component. The DC component is also called the disparity, the bias, or the DC coefficient. The simplest possible line code is called unipolar because it has an unbounded DC component which gives too many errors on such systems.

- Most line codes eliminate the DC components such codes are called DC balanced, zero-DC, zero-bias or DC equalized etc. There are two ways of eliminating the DC component:

- Use a constant-weight code: In other words, design each transmitted code word such that every code word that contains some positive or negative levels also contains enough of the opposite levels, such that the average level over each code word is zero. For example, Manchester code and Interleaved 2 of 5.

- Use a paired disparity code: In other words, design the receiver such that every code word that averages to a negative level is paired with another code word that averages to a positive level. Design the receiver so that either code word of the pair decodes to the same data bits. Design the transmitter to keep track of the running DC buildup, and always pick the code word that pushes the DC level back towards zero. For example, AMI, 8B10B, 4B3T, etc.

- Line coding should make it possible for the receiver to synchronize itself to the phase of the received signal. If the synchronization is not ideal, then the signal to be decoded will not have optimal differences (in amplitude) between the various digits or symbols used in the line code. This will increase the error probability in the received data.

- It is also preferred for the line code to have a structure that will enable error detection.

- Note that the line-coded signal and a signal produced at a terminal may differ, thus requiring translation.

- A line code will typically reflect technical requirements of the transmission medium, such as optical fiber or shielded twisted pair. These requirements are unique for each medium, because each one has different behavior related to interference, distortion, capacitance and loss of amplitude.

- Each of the various line formats has a particular advantage and disadvantage. It is not possible to select one, which will meet all needs. The format may be selected to meet one or more of the following criteria :

- Minimize transmission hardware
- Facilitate synchronization
- Ease error detection and correction
- Minimize spectral content
- Eliminate a DC component.

Line Coding Technical Theory

- Digital data is converted into digital signal in line coding.
- Digital data can be voice, video, image, text or numbers which are stored as a bit sequence in digital storage.

• Typical line coding and line decoding mechanism is as shown in Fig. 3.19.

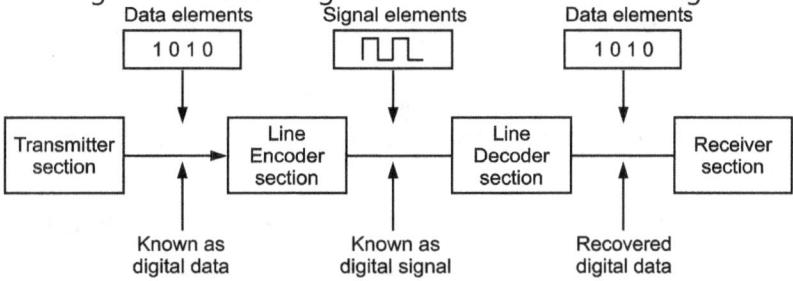

Fig. 3.19: Data Elements and Signal Elements inLine Encoding and Line Decoding Mechanism

• Thus, the block schematics clearly explain that data elements are being carried and signal elements are the carriers.

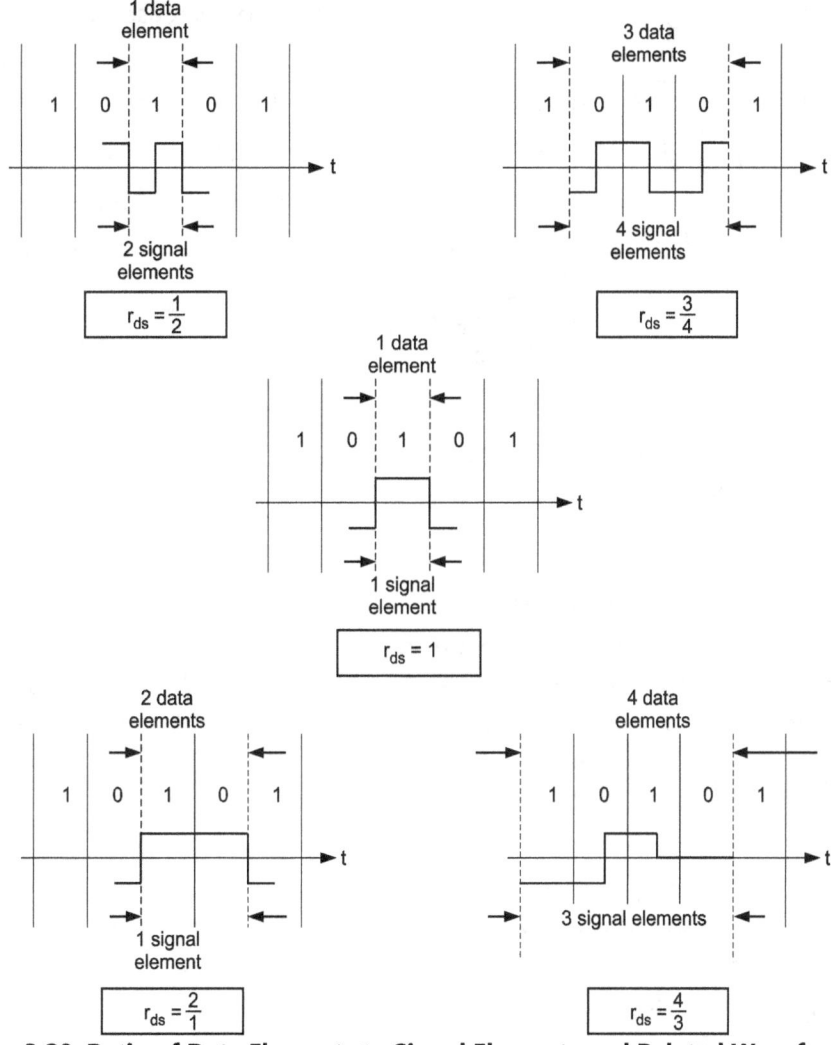

Fig. 3.20: Ratio of Data Elements to Signal Elements and Related Waveforms

The ratio r_{ds} is given as, r_{ds} = Data elements / Signal elements

Thus, for different values of r_{ds}, Fig. 3.20 clearly indicates the waveform.

The different values of r_{ds} are :

r_{ds} = 1, r_{ds} = 1 / 2 , r_{ds} = 2, r_{ds} = 3 / 4 and r_{ds} = 4 / 3 .

- Thus, data rate can be defined as, the number of data elements sent in 1s. The unit of data rate is bps.

- Signal rate can be defined as, the number of signal elements sent in 1s. The unit of signal rate is baud.

- Sometimes data rate is called as bit rate and signal rate is called as pulse rate or modulation rate or also baud rate.

- The final target or goal in data communication is to increase the data rate while decreasing the signal rate.

Thus, increase in data rate increases the speed of transmission.

Thus, decrease in signal rate decreases the bandwidth requirement.

- And we know that bandwidth spectrum is limited, hence expected thing is data rate should be high with limited signaling rate.

$$\boxed{S \ = \ \frac{C}{r_{ds}} \times N} \ \text{bauds}$$

where,   S = Signal rate

                N = Data rate

                C = Case factor

              r_{ds} = Data elements / Signal elements

- We have also seen that actual bandwidth of a digital signal is infinite, but the effective bandwidth is finite (Thus, in effective bandwidth, the upper frequency component with negligible amplitudes can be ignored. Hence, called as effective bandwidth).

Thus,   Bandwidth = $C \times N \times \dfrac{1}{r_{ds}}$

∴ $\boxed{B_{min} \ = \ C \times N \times \dfrac{1}{r_{ds}}}$

∴ $\boxed{N_{max} \ = \ \dfrac{1}{C} \times B \times r_{ds}}$

- Finally, compare this N_{max} with Nyquist formula.

$$\therefore \quad \boxed{N_{max} \; = \; \frac{1}{C} \times B \times r_{ds} \; = \; 2B \times \log_2 (L)}$$

Baseline Wandering : Receiver calculates average received signal power while decoding the line codes. This average is known as baseline. If '0' and '1' string is long then drifting in baseline is possible, which is called as **baseline wandering.** Due to which decoding becomes difficult and incorrect. Good line codes should prevent the baseline wandering.

DC Component : Telephone lines cannot pass frequencies below 210 Hz, so in line codes, if digital level '0' or '1' is constant for long time, which generates low frequencies around zero. This DC component saturate the core of coupling transformers in communication path.

Self Synchronization : Transmitter and receiver clock should be matched otherwise, data error occurs or misinterpreting of data is possible. In self synchronization the timing information is added along with data.

Thus, good line codes must have built-in error detection and correction capabilities. Also, it should have good immunity to noise and interference. But more level line code is complex in nature and it is costly.

3.9 LINE CODING SCHEMES

There are basically five categories of line coding schemes like

- Unipolar
- Polar
- Bipolar
- Multilevel
- Multi-transition.

Let's study one by one in detail.

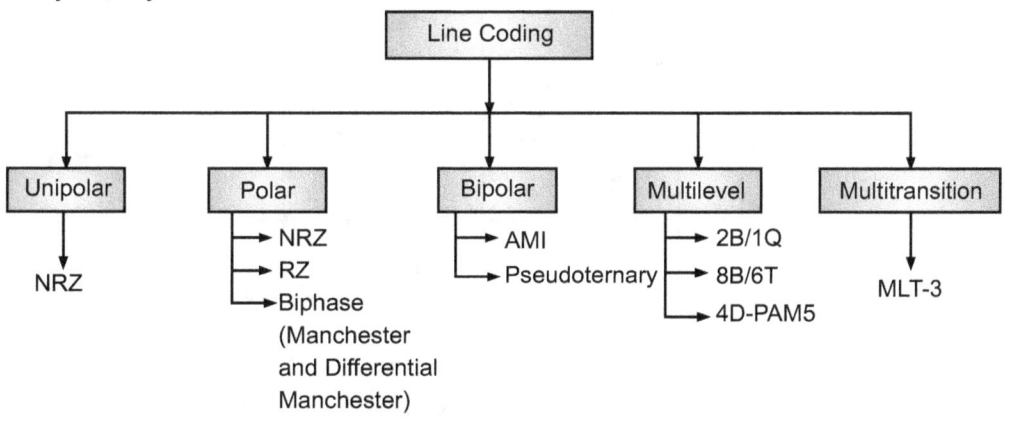

Fig. 3.21: Line coding schemes

3.9.1 Unipolar Scheme / NRZ (Non-Return-to-Zero)

- In unipolar line coding scheme, all voltage levels or signal levels are on one side of the time axis. The signal level can be below or above of time axis.

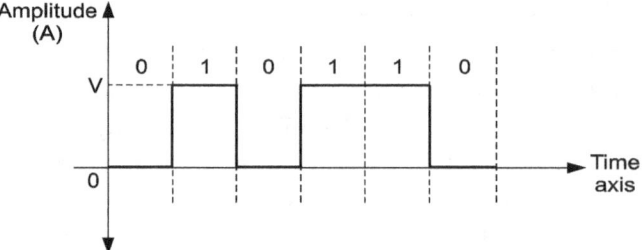

Fig. 3.22: NRZ (unipolar) Waveform

- Positive voltage defines bit '1' and zero voltage defines bit '0'.
- Here signal does not return to zero at the middle of the bit, hence called as NRZ (Non-Return-to-Zero).

- Normalized power is given as $\frac{1}{2}(V)^2 + \frac{1}{2}(0)^2 = \frac{1}{2}V^2$

i.e. Normalized power required to send 1 bit/unit line resistance is double as compared to polar NRZ. Hence NRZ unipolar scheme is costly.

3.9.2 Polar Schemes [NRZ-L, NRZ-I, RZ]

1. Polar NRZ (NRZ-L and NRZ-I)

It uses two levels of voltage amplitude.

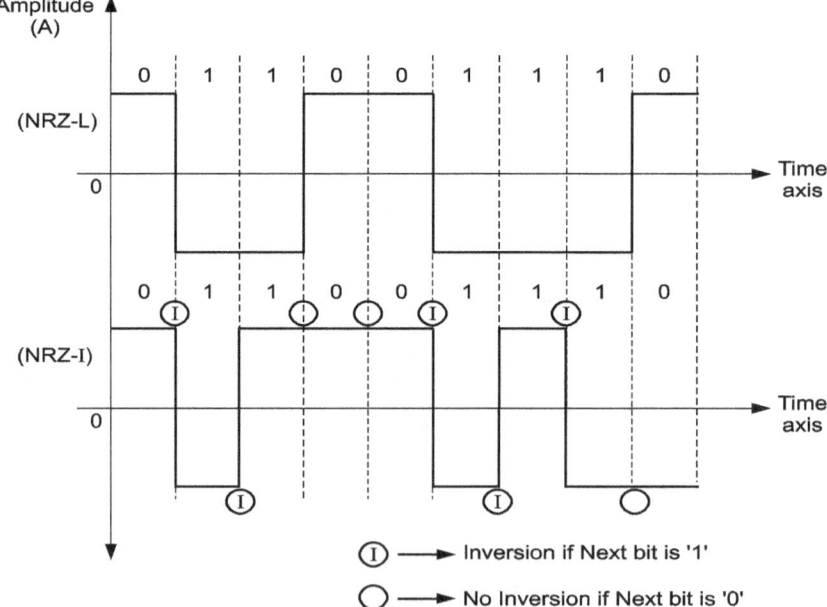

$\bigcirc\!\!\!I$ ⟶ Inversion if Next bit is '1'

$\bigcirc$ ⟶ No Inversion if Next bit is '0'

Fig. 3.23: NRZ-L and NRZ-I Waveforms

NRZ-L stands for NRZ-level and NRZ-I stands for NRZ-Invert.

In NRZ-L, the level of voltage determines the value of the bit.

In NRZ-I, the change or lack of change in the level of voltage determines the value of bit, if there is no change the bit is '0' and if there is change the bit is '1'.

The NRZ-L and NRZ-I comparison is as given:

NRZ-L	NRZ-I
1. Baseline wandering problem is severe in NRZ-L.	1. It is less as compared to NRZ-L.
2. The average signal power is less if long sequence of '0' or '1' is present.	2. This problem occurs only for a long sequence of '0'.
3. Synchronization problem exists and it is severe in NRZ-L.	3. Synchronization problem exists and it is less as compared to NRZ-L.
4. NRZ-L gives more problem if there is a sudden change of polarity in the system.	4. NRZ-I does not have this problem.
5. Average signal rate $(S_{avg}) = \dfrac{N}{2}$ bauds.	5. Average signal rate $(S_{avg}) = \dfrac{N}{2}$ bauds.
6. DC component carrying high level of energy, gives DC component problem.	6. DC component carrying high level of energy, gives DC component problem.
7. Normalized bandwidth graph is as shown below : **Fig. 3.24 (a) : NRZ-L bandwidth curve** for $\left[r = 1, S_{avg} = \dfrac{N}{2} \right]$	7. Normalized bandwidth graph is as shown below : **Fig. 3.24 (b) : NRZ-I bandwidth curve** for $\left[r = 1, S_{avg} = \dfrac{N}{2} \right]$

2. RZ (Return to Zero) Scheme

Synchronization problems are solved in RZ scheme. Receiver understands start and end of next bit.

In NRZ-L and NRZ-I, receiver does not understand the start and end of next bit.

RZ uses three values

- Positive
- Zero
- Negative.

In RZ, the signal does not change between the bits but it changes during the bits.

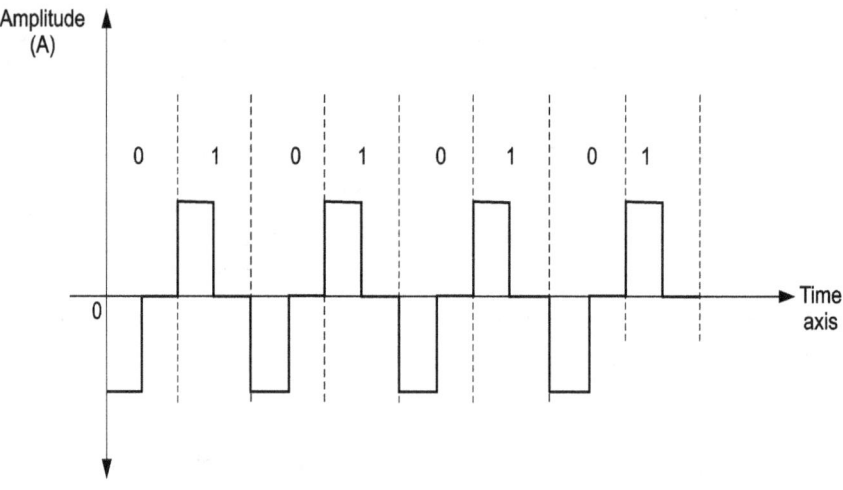

Fig. 3.25: RZ Waveform

Thus, in RZ, signal goes to zero in the middle of each bit. It does not change until the beginning of the next bit (0 or 1 bit).

In RZ, it occupies two signal changes to encode a bit and hence has more signaling rate and hence occupies more bandwidth as shown in Fig. 3.25.

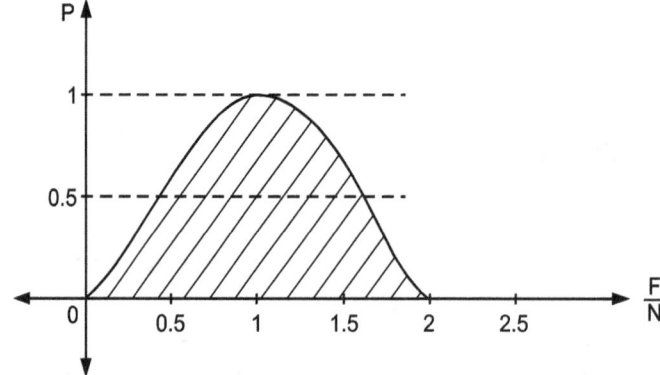

Fig. 3.26: Normalized bandwidth of RZ $\left[\text{for } r = \dfrac{1}{2}, S_{avg} = N \right]$

- Also RZ gives more problem if there is sudden change of polarity in the system (i.e. '0' will be accepted as '1' and vice versa).

- In RZ, there is no DC component problem.
- RZ system is complex because three levels are used.
- Thus, due to all these problems, RZ is not used.

3. Biphase Line Coding

- To overcome these problems, RZ has been replaced by the Manchester and differential Manchester methods.

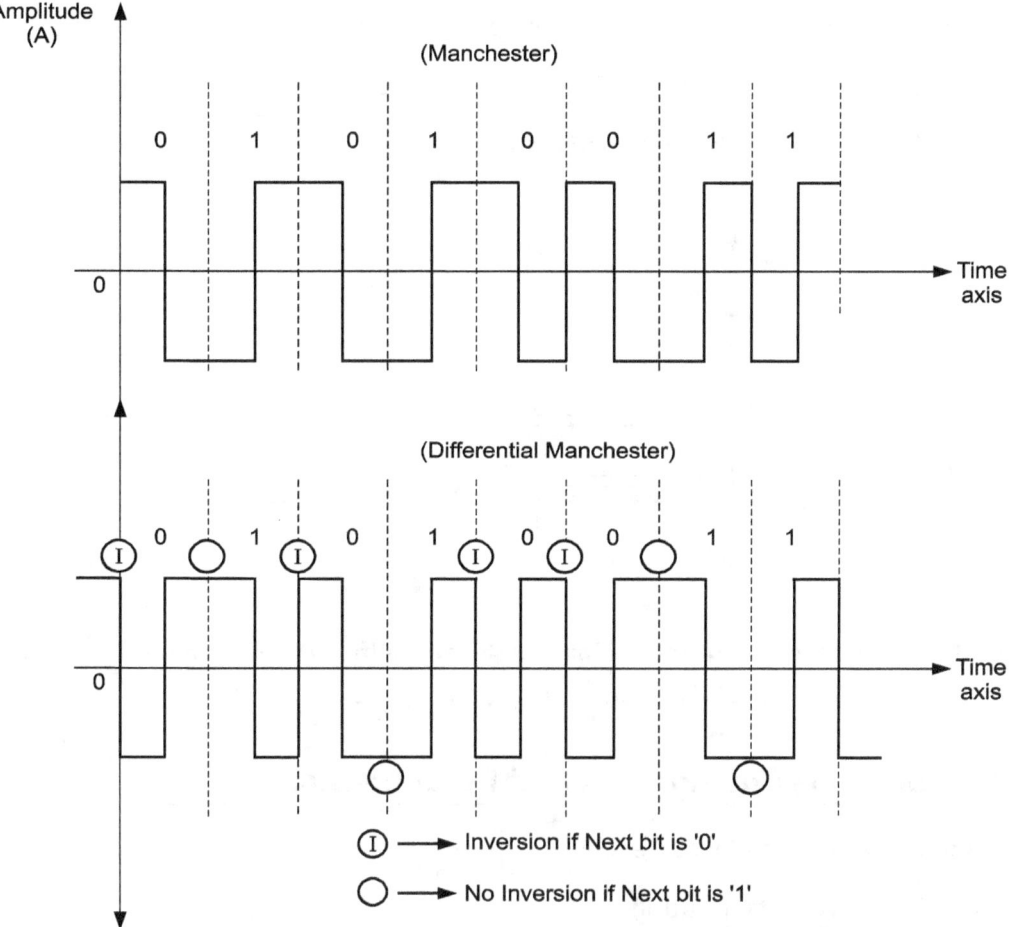

Fig. 3.27: Manchester and Differential Manchester Line Coding

- The idea of transition at the middle of the bit in RZ and NRZ (L) are combined to give Manchester line coding technique.
- Differential Manchester scheme = RZ scheme + NRZ (I) scheme
- The transition at the middle of the bit in RZ and NRZ (I) idea are combined to give differential Manchester line coding technique.

- Manchester and differential Manchester line coding waveforms are shown in Fig. 3.27.

- Manchester method overcomes the problem of NRZ-L and differential Manchester method overcomes the problem of NRZ-I line coding techniques.

Advantages of Manchester and differential Manchester method

- No baseline wandering.

- Absence of DC component (each bit has positive and negative voltage contribution).

Disadvantage of Manchester and differential Manchester method

Bandwidth required $= 2 \times$ NRZ bandwidth.

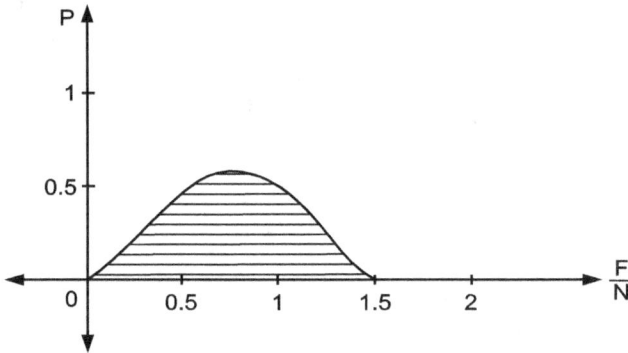

Fig. 3.28: Normalized Bandwidth of Manchester and Differential Manchester Line Coding Techniques $\left[\text{for } r = \dfrac{1}{2} , \text{ S}_{avg} = N \right]$

3.9.3 Bipolar Line Coding (AMI and Pseudoternary)

AMI stands for Alternate Mark Inversion.

Binary '0' $\rightarrow$ Zero volts (Neutral).

Binary '1' $\rightarrow$ Alternate positive and negative voltages.

In Pseudoternary,

Binary '1' $\rightarrow$ Zero volts (Neutral).

Binary '0' $\rightarrow$ Alternate positive and negative voltages.

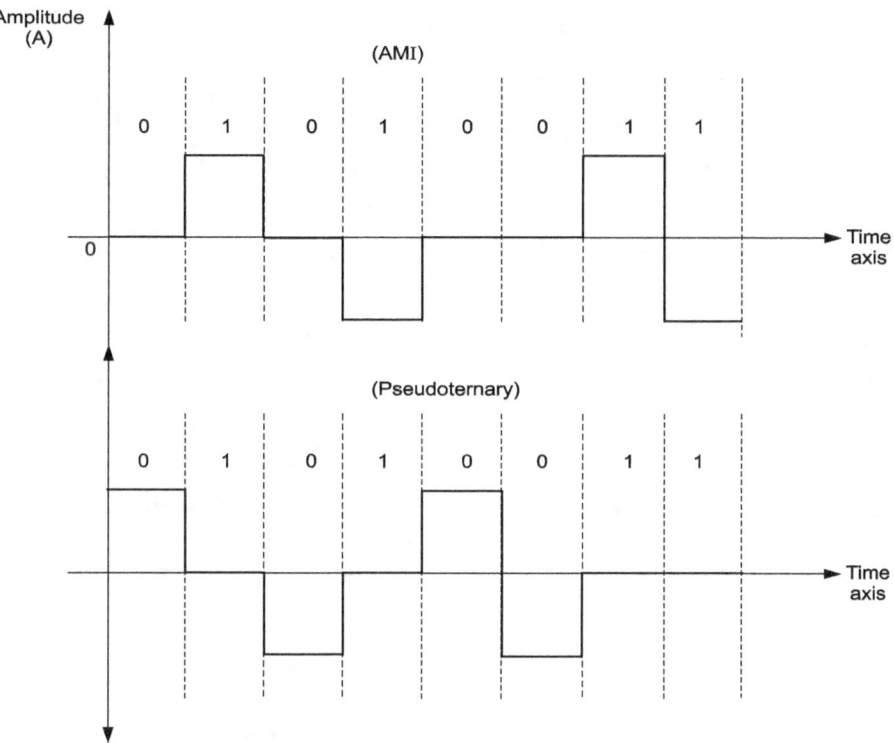

Fig. 3.29: AMI and Pseudoternary Line Coding Techniques

Typical normalized bandwidth curve for bipolar line coding method is shown in Fig. 3.30.

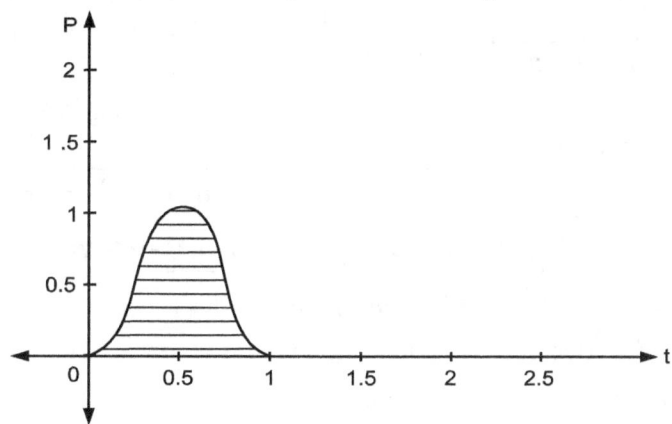

Fig. 3.30: Normalized Bandwidth for Bipolar Line Coding $\left[\text{for } r = 1 \text{ and } S_{avg} = \dfrac{N}{2} \right]$

In AMI, long stream of '0' and in Pseudoternary, long stream of '1' cannot produce DC components because these are neutral zero voltages, which cannot create DC components.

AMI is commonly used in long-distance communication applications.

AMI has synchronization problems in communication.

Comparison between Bipolar and Polar NRZ :

Bipolar Method	Polar NRZ
Bipolar method was developed as alternative to NRZ.	Polar NRZ method was developed as alternative to unipolar NRZ.
Bipolar signal rate = Polar NRZ signal rate.	Same as Bipolar.
It has no DC component problem for long '0' and '1' data.	It has DC component problem for long '0' and '1' data.
Bipolar methods has most of its energy concentrated around frequency = $\frac{N}{2}$.	NRZ method has most of its energy concentrated near zero frequency, so unsuitable for transmission.
Normalized bandwidth curve is as shown in Fig. 3.12 (a).	Normalized bandwidth curve is as shown in Fig. 3.12 (b).
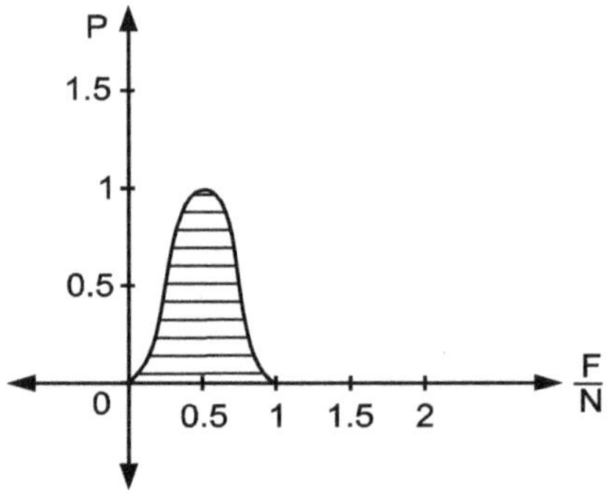 Fig. 3.31 (a)	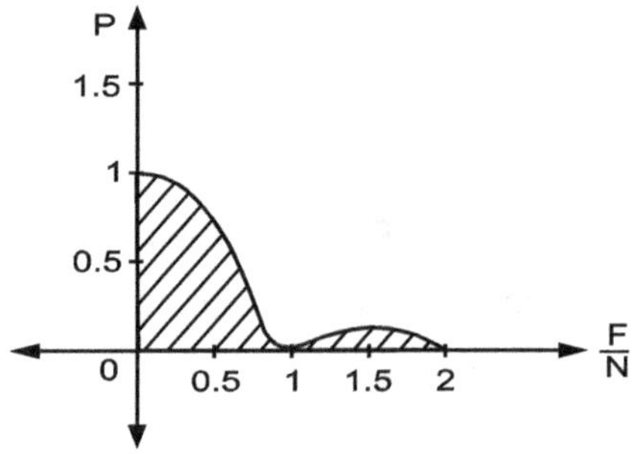 Fig. 3.31 (b)
It has synchronization problems.	It has synchronization problems.

3.9.4 Multilevel Line Coding [2B/1Q, 8B/6T, 4D-PAM5]

Multilevel line coding techniques has following advantages :

Increase in data speed or decrease in required bandwidth.

Prevents baseline wandering to provide synchronization.

Error detection possible.

For this coding the designers have classified these types as **mBnL**.

where,   m = Length of binary pattern

                B = Binary data

                n = Length of the signal pattern

L = Number of levels in signalling

L = 2 → Binary

L = 3 → Ternary

L = 4 → Quaternary

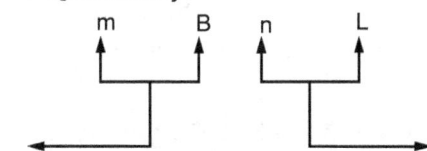

Defines data pattern Defines signal pattern

- In **mBnL** method, a pattern of 'm' data elements is encoded as a pattern of 'n' signal elements in which 2m < Ln. Because data encoding is not possible if 2m > Ln, as some of the data patterns cannot be encoded.

1. 2B1Q Coding

- 2B1Q stands for two binary, one quaternary method.

- It uses data patterns size = 2 and encodes the 2 bit patterns as one signal element belonging to a four-level signal.

- The 2B1Q (two binary, one quaternary) line encoding scheme was intended to be used by the ISDN DSL and SDSL applications.

- This code is a four-level line code in which two binary bits (2B) represent one quaternary symbol (1Q).

- The 2B1Q line coding was seen as a major enhancement over the original T1 line coding, because 2B1Q encoded two bits per signal change instead of just one per change.

2B1Q Coding Rules

- 2B1Q is a 4-level code. It takes two 2-level bits and converts them into one 4-level baud (quat) as indicated in Table 3.2.

- This conversion effectively doubles the period of the symbol. Since the period is inversely proportional to frequency (i.e., f=1/T) the frequency on the line is reduced. With every advantage there is always drawback and the 2B1Q is no exception.

- A 4-level code results in reduced distance between decision levels, thus increasing the required SNR for a given performance level (BER). However, the baud rate reduction and narrower bandwidth result in performance gains which outweigh this drawback.

- The important elements of the transmit quat are its sign, and its amplitude. The values assigned to the levels are set so that there is equal spacing between the four levels.

- Levels can be chosen to be +1, +0.33, -0.33 and -1. In order to eliminate the decimals, we will choose the four levels to be +3, +1, -1, and -3. The 2B1Q conversion table is shown in Table 3.2.

- The first bit of the dibit is called the "sign-bit". If it is 0, the output quat will have a negative sign. If the first bit is 1, then the output quat will have a positive sign.

- The second bit of the dibit is called the amplitude bit, and it determines the magnitude of the output quat. If it is 0, then the output level has an amplitude of 3.

- If the second bit of the dibit is 1, then the output amplitude is 1. This provides for a very simple means of encoding a binary bit stream into a 4-level code. An example of 2B1Q coding is shown in Fig. 3.32.

Table 3.2: 2B1Q Coding Rules

Dibit	Output Quat
10	+3
11	+1
01	−1
00	−3

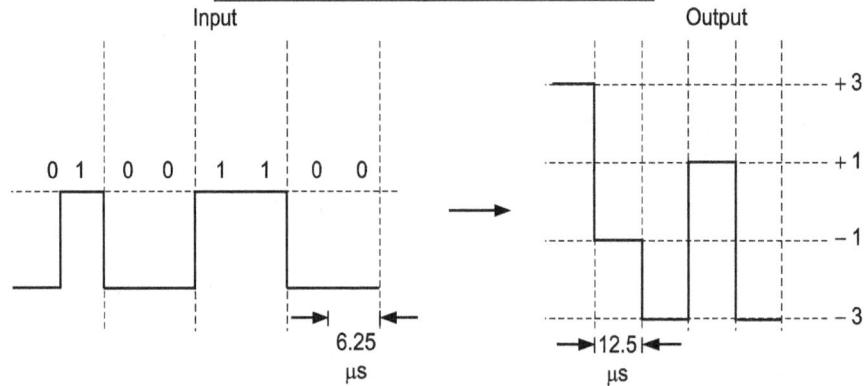

2-Level, Binary Data, 160 kbit/s   4-Level, Quaternary Data, 80 kbaud/s

Fig. 3.32: 2B1Q Line Coding Example, 2 Binary, 1 Quaternary

2. 8B6T Coding

Some Encoding schemes for Ethernets are :

    10Mbps Ethernet (*Manchester encoding*).

    100baseTX (*MLT-3*, 2 pair cat5, 4B5B).

    100BaseFX (*NRZ-I*, 2 pair fiber, 4B5B).

    100BaseT4 (3 level 1V, 0V, & -1V, 4 pair cat 3, *8B/6T*).

    Token Ring (*Differential Manchester*).

- 100Base-T4 is designed to produce a 100 Mbps data rate over lower-quality voice grade, or Category 3, cable. The advantage of this is that in many existing buildings, there is an abundance of voice-grade cabling and very little else. Thus, if this cabling can be used, installation costs are minimized.

- With present technology, a data rate of 100 Mbps over one or two Category 3 pairs is impractical. Instead, 100Base-T4 specifies that the data stream to be transmitted is divided into three separate data streams. Four twisted pairs are used.

- Data are transmitted using three pairs and received using three pairs. Thus, two of the pairs must be configured for bidirectional transmission.

- As with 100Base-X, a simple NRZ encoding scheme is not used for 100Base-T4. This would require a signaling rate of 33 Mbps on each twisted pair and does not provide synchronization.

- Instead, a ternary signaling scheme known as 8B6T is used. With ternary signaling, each signal element can take on one of three values-positive voltage, negative voltage, or zero voltage.

- A pure ternary code is one in which the full information-carrying capacity of the ternary signal is exploited. However, pure ternary is not attractive for the   same reason for which pure binary (NRZ) code is rejected the lack of synchronization.

- The 8B6T code is designed to approach the efficiency of ternary and overcome this disadvantage.

- With 8B6T, the data to be transmitted is handled in 8-bit blocks. Each block of 8 bits is mapped into a code group of 6 ternary symbols. The stream of code groups is then transmitted in round-robin fashion across the three output channels.

- In 8B6T line encoding technique,

  The data to be transmitted are handled in 8-bit blocks.

  Each block of 8 bits is mapped into a code group of 6 ternary symbols.

  The stream of code groups is then transmitted in round-robin fashion across the three output channels.

  Thus, the ternary transmission rate on each output channel is

  $(6/8) \times 33.333 = 25$ Mbaud.

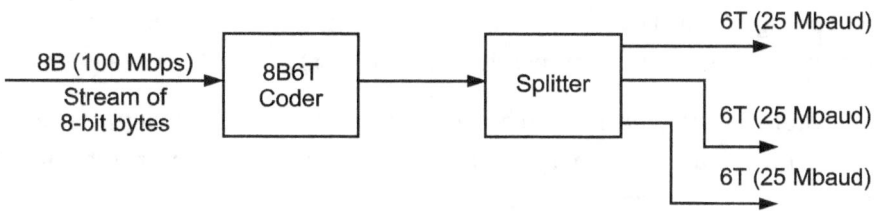

Fig. 3.33: Transmission Scheme

3.   The 4D-PAM5 Line Coding

- 4D-PAM5 **encoding** is a four-dimensional, five-level pulse amplitude modulation.

- This is a way of encoding bits on copper wires to get a 1 GB per second transfer rate when the maximum rate of a single wire is 125 MHz. This is done by employing a multilevel amplitude signal.

- A five-level signal, called pulse amplitude modulation 5, is used.

- This works in a similar manner to MLT-3 except the levels are −2V, −1V, 0V and 2V.

- The transmitted signal on each wire is a five-level pulse modulation symbol.

- Four symbols transmitted simultaneously on the four pairs of wire forms the 4D-PAM5 code group that represents an 8-bit frame octet.

- The symbols to be transmitted are selected from a four-dimensional (4D) code group of five-level symbols.

- Because there are four separate pairs being used for transmission and reception of data, there are 625 possible codes to choose from when using all four pairs. Therefore, all 8 bits can be transferred using only one 4D-PAM5 symbol.

- The data signals have distinct and measurable amplitude and phases, allowing more data bits per cycle.

- This type of encoding is used by Gigabit Ethernet, whereby 1000 Mbps is squeezed into 125 MHz signals.

- The electronics are more complex and the technology is more susceptible to noise.

- Actually, only four levels are used for data; the 0V level is used to recover the transmitted signal from high noise. This fifth level of coding is used for error detection and correction.

3.9.5 MLT-3 Line Coding

- MLT-3 encoding (Multi-Level Transmit) is a line code (a signalling method used in a telecommunication system for transmission purposes) that uses three voltage levels.

- An MLT-3 interface emits less electromagnetic interference and requires less bandwidth than most other binary or ternary interfaces that operate at the same bit rate, such as Manchester code or Alternate Mark Inversion.

- MLT-3 cycles through the voltage levels −1, 0, +1, and 0. It moves to the next state to transmit a 1 bit, and stays in the same state to transmit a 0 bit.

- Similar to simple NRZ encoding, MLT-3 has a coding efficiency of 1 bit/baud, however it requires four transitions (baud) to complete a full cycle (from low-to-middle, middle-to-high, high-to-middle, middle-to-low).

- Thus, the maximum fundamental frequency is reduced to one fourth of the baud rate. This makes signal transmission more amenable to copper wires.

- MLT-3 was first introduced by Cisco Systems as a coding scheme for FDDI copper interconnects (TP-PMD).

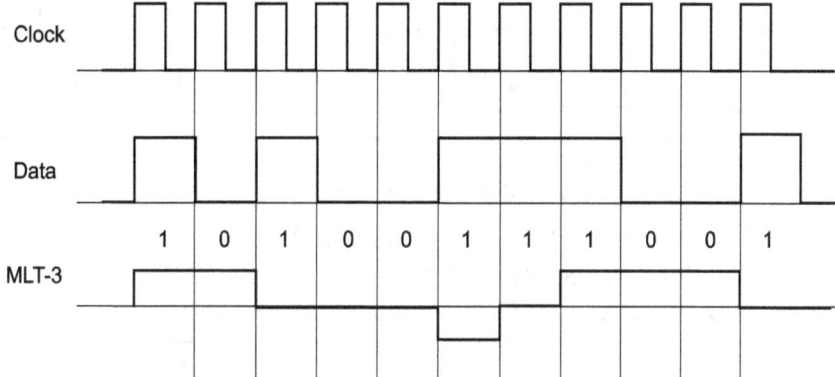

Fig. 3.34: Example of MLT-3 Encoding (Light-colored lines indicate two previous states)

- Ethernet LANs use digital signals to share data among network devices. 10Base-T uses Manchester encoding to transmit the signal : transition occurs in the middle of each bit period. Two levels represent one bit.

- A low to high transition in the middle of the bit represents a '1'. A high to low transition in the middle of the bit represents a '0'. There is no DC component. It uses positive/negative voltages.

- 100-BaseTX uses 4B/5B encoding, where each 4-bit nibbles is being transferred, encoded as 5-bit symbols. The signaling model is a three level multi-level technique called MLT-3.

Table 3.3: Ethernet Encoding and Signaling

	10Base-T	100Base-TX
Data rate	10 Mbps	100 Mbps
Encoding	Manchester	4B/5B
Signaling	5V, differential	MLT-3
Cable	Cat. 3 UTP	Cat. 5 UTP

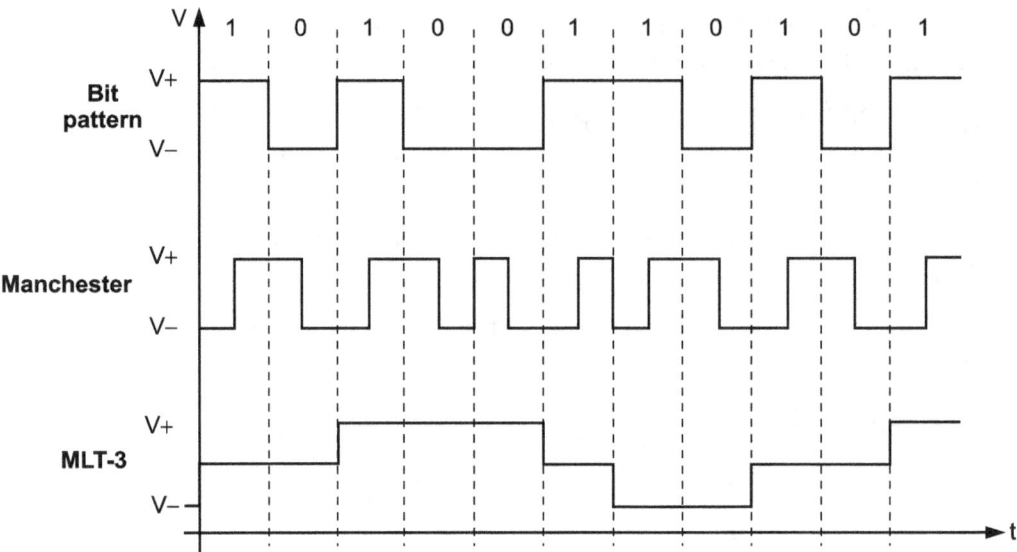

Fig. 3.35: Ethernet Encoding Schemes

• It is also used by FDDI and TP-PMD to obtain 100 Mbps out of a 31.25 MHz signal. Where TP-PMD stands for Twisted Pair-Physical layer, Medium Dependent (TP-PMD) and FDDI stands for Fiber Distributed Data Interface backbone network.

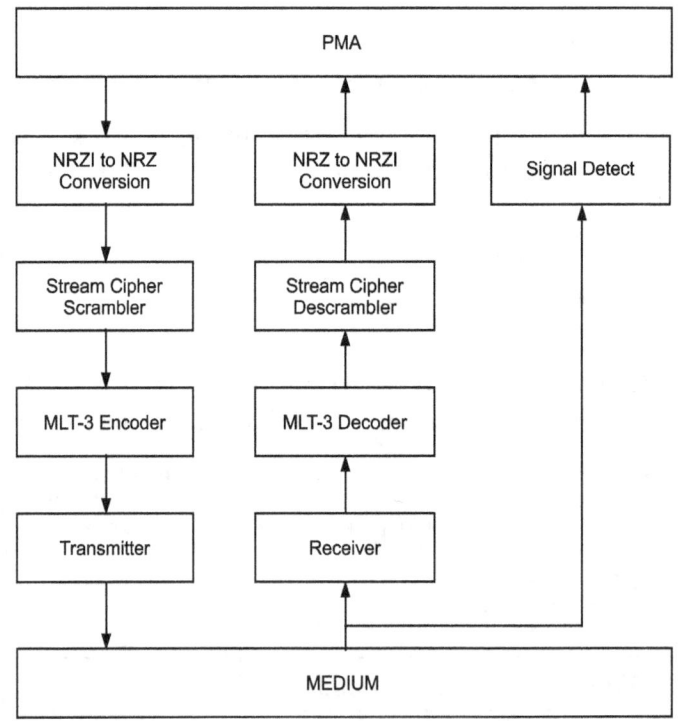

Fig. 3.36: TP-PMD Block Diagram (PMA Physical Medium Attachment)

- The mechanism chosen to overcome signaling rate issues is Multi-Level Transmit 3 (MLT-3). This is a tri-polar encoding mechanism based on three different signal levels. Its purpose within TP-PMD is to encode the data in such a manner that the signaling rate is reduced with the emissions that radiate from the cable.

- MLT-3 encoding is essentially very simple, operating with a positive signal level, a negative one and a zero level. It does however require a binary input rather than the normal NRZI encoded signal normally passed from the PHY.

- Therefore, an NRZI decoder is placed within the PMD to produce a binary output suitable for MLT-3.

- The transition between levels is what differentiates between a binary 1_2 and 0_2. In addition to the ability to transition between three signal levels, a counter is required.

- This can be a single bit counter as it is only necessary to determine between odd and even.

The rules for encoding are :

- The transmitter can only transition between adjacent signal states i.e. from positive to zero, zero to negative, zero to positive. A transition from negative to positive is not allowed.

- A transition only takes place when a 1_2 is transmitted. No transition takes place when a 0_2 is transmitted.

- If a 1_2 is transmitted, the signal will transition from its current state to an adjacent state, i.e. from positive to zero, negative to zero.

- If the current state is zero and a transition is required then it will be positive if the counter is even or negative if the counter is odd.

- The counter is incremented when the zero state is left.

- These rules are demonstrated in Fig. 3.34, which shows a example of MLT-3 encoding. The receiver function is opposite to that described above, with the decoded MLT-3 signal being passed through an NRZI encoder before being handed to the PHY.

- The benefit produced by this system is the much reduced signaling rate, down from 125 MHz on fiber to 31.25 MHz over copper.

- This produces much lower radiated emissions allowing the technology to stay well within published guidelines.

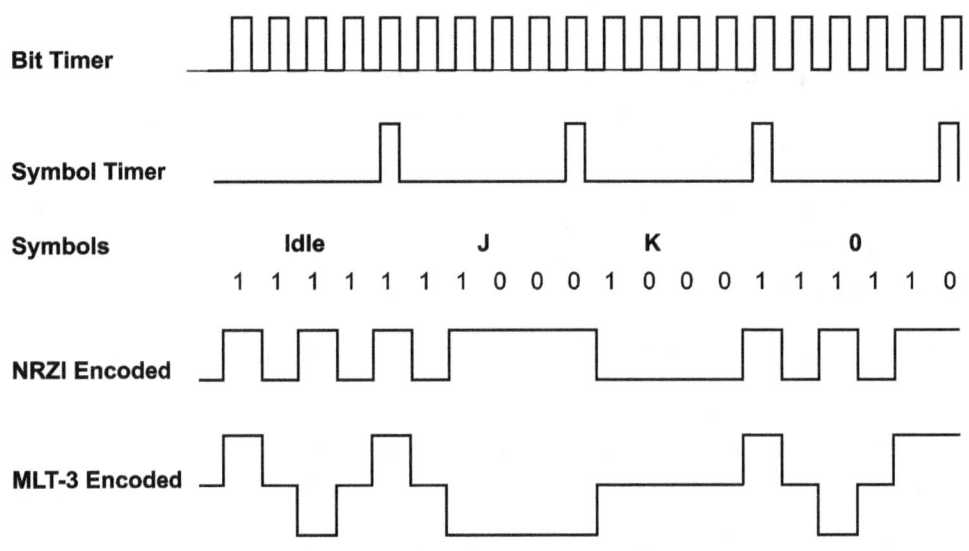

Fig. 3.37: Sample MLT-3 Encoding

Summary of Line coding

Common Line Codes	
Signal	**Comments**
NRZ-L	Non-return to zero level. This is the standard positive logic signal format used in digital circuits. 1 forces a high level 0 forces a low level
NRZ-M	Non-return to zero mark. 1 forces a transition 0 does nothing
NRZ-S	Non-return to zero space. 1 does nothing 0 forces a transition
RZ	Return to zero. 1 goes high for half the bit period 0 does nothing
Common Line Codes :	
Signal	Comments
Biphase-L	Manchester. Two consecutive bits of the same type force a transition at the beginning of a bit period. 1 forces a negative transition in the middle of the bit 0 forces a positive transition in the middle of the bit

conti.

Biphase-M	There is always a transition at the beginning of a bit period.
	1 forces a transition in the middle of the bit.
	0 does nothing.
Biphase-S	There is always a transition at the beginning of a bit period.
	1 does nothing
	0 forces a transition in the middle of the bit.
Differential Manchester	There is always a transition in the middle of a bit period.
	1 does nothing
	0 forces a transition at the beginning of the bit
Bipolar	The positive and negative pulses are alternate.
	1 forces a positive or negative pulse for half the bit period.
	0 does nothing.

Common Line Codes

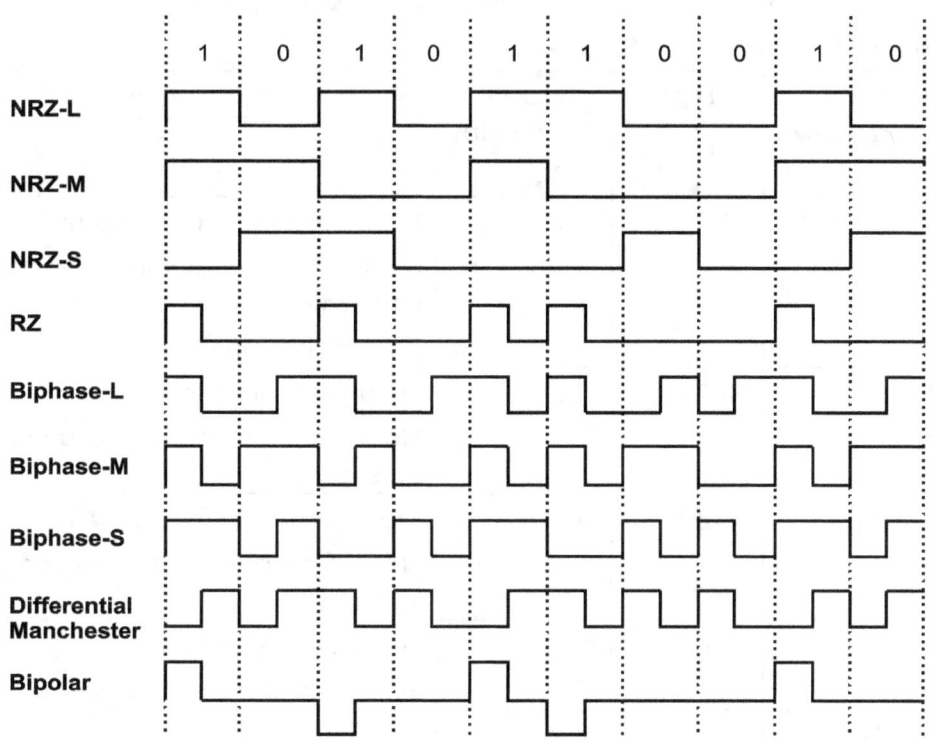

Fig. 3.38: Common Line Codes at a Glance

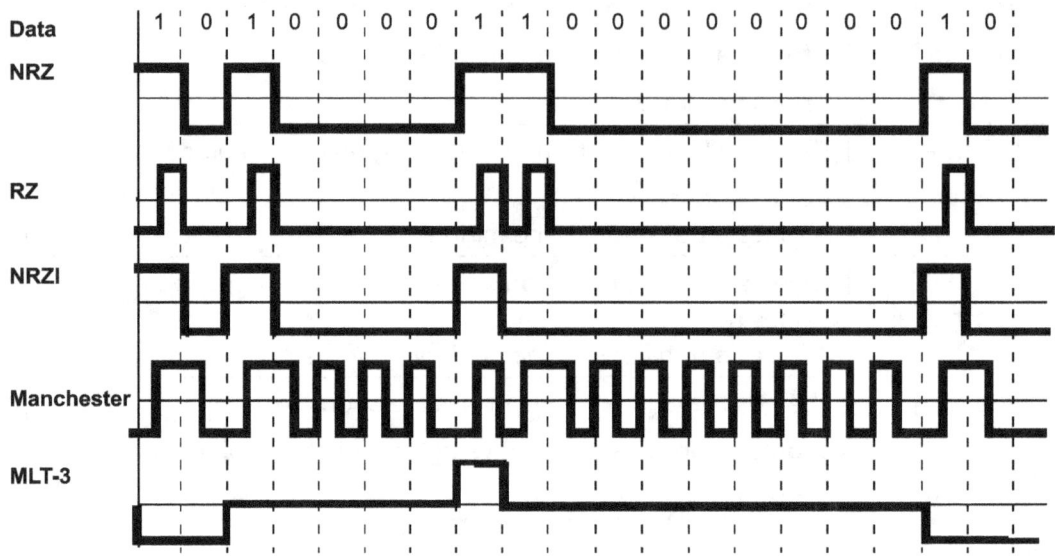

Fig. 3.39: Symbol Encoding Schemes used in Ethernet

Comparison of Line Coding Techniques

Sr. No.	Main Technique	Type	Average Bandwidth B_{avg} =	Characteristics
1.	Unipolar Line coding	NRZ	N/2	DC component effect present. No self synchronization for long 0 & 1 bit streams. Implementation is costly.
2.	Polar Line coding	NRZ-L	N/2	DC component effect present. No self synchronization for long 0 & 1 bit streams.
		NRZ-I	N/2	DC component effect present. No self synchronization for long 0 bit streams.
		Biphase	N	DC component effect absent. Self synchronization is achieved.
3.	Bipolar Line coding	AMI	N/2	DC component effect present. No self synchronization for long 0 bit streams.

conti.

4.	Multilevel Line coding	2B1Q	N/4	No self synchronization for long same double bits.
		8B6T	3N/4	DC component effect absent. Self synchronization is achieved.
		4D-PAM5	N/8	DC component effect absent. Self synchronization is achieved.
5.	Multiline Line coding	MLT-3	N/3	DC component effect absent. No self synchronization for long 0 bit streams.

3.10 BLOCK CODING

- The performance of previous line codes studied is not adequate in advanced data communication applications.

- We need redundancy to ensure the synchronization between transmitter and receiver.

- We also need to incorporate the error detection mechanism, hence, new block coding concept comes into picture.

- Block coding is indicated as mB/nB coding.

    In block coding, each m-bit group is replaced with n-bit group.

    Examples of block coding are :

    ➢ 4B/5B.

    ➢ 8B/10B.

- In 4B/5B, (/) slash indicates block coding, whereas 8B6T is example of multilevel coding.

- Block coding includes the following three steps.

    ➢ Division step.

    ➢ Substitution step.

    ➢ Combination step.

- In the division step, sequences of bits are divided into the groups of m-bits in block encoding.

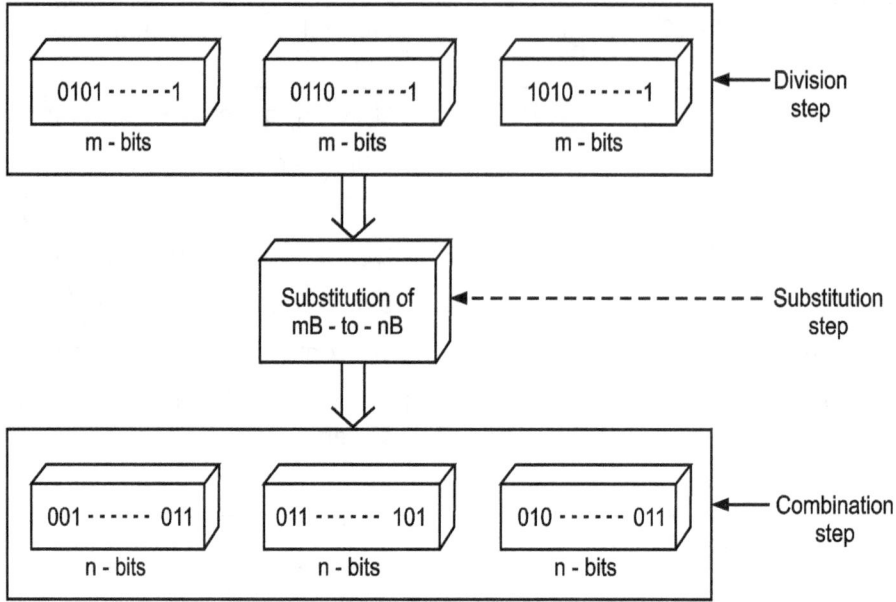

Fig. 3.40: Basic Block Encoding Steps

- For example in 4B/5B, the bit sequence is divided into 4-bit groups, in block encoding.

- In the substitution step, we substitute m-bit group for n-bit group, in block encoding.

- For example, in 4B/5B, we substitute 4-bit code for a 5-bit group in block encoding.

- In last or final step i.e. combination step, n-bit groups are combined together to form a block encoded stream output.

3.10.1 4B/5B Block Coding

This 4B/5B technique was designed to be used in combination with NRZ-I line coding technique.

In NRZ-I, there are two problems :

- DC component effect.

- Self synchronization problem for long stream of '0's.

Also in NRZ, average bandwidth $B_{avg} = \dfrac{N}{2}$, i.e. it has good signaling rate (i.e. $\dfrac{1}{2}$ of Biphase coding).

The solution over self-synchronization problem for long stream of '0's is to change the bit stream prior to encoding with NRZ-I, so that long bit stream of '0's will be cancelled.

Thus, maximum number of consecutive '0's will be three only.

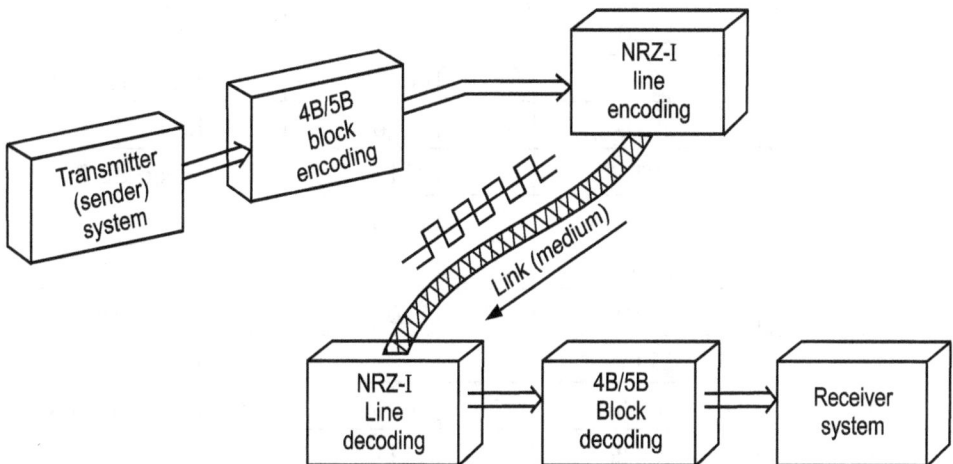

**Fig. 3.41: 4B/5B Block Coding + NRZ-I Line Coding to
improve Self-Synchronization and DC Component Effect**

Depending on the standard or specification of interest, there may be several 4B/5B characters left unused.

The presence of any of the "unused" characters in the data stream can be used as an indication that there is a fault somewhere in the link.

Therefore, the unused characters can actually be used to detect errors in the data stream.

The use of only 16 of the possible 32 groups of 5 bits means that 4B/5B allows some errors to be detected as the error may change the group of 5 bits into one of the 16 unused groups and thus invalid combinations.

4B/5B is used in the following standards :

- 00BASE-TX standard defined by IEEE 802.3u in 1995.

- ADI (Multichannel Audio Digital Interface)

Table 3.4: Encoding table of 4B/5B

Name	4B	5B	Description
0	0000	11110	hex data 0
1	0001	01001	hex data 1
2	0010	10100	hex data 2
3	0011	10101	hex data 3
4	0100	01010	hex data 4
5	0101	01011	hex data 5
6	0110	01110	hex data 6
7	0111	01111	hex data 7

Conti.

8	1000	10010	hex data 8
9	1001	10011	hex data 9
A	1010	10110	hex data A
B	1011	10111	hex data B
C	1100	11010	hex data C
D	1101	11011	hex data D
E	1110	11100	hex data E
F	1111	11101	hex data F
Q	-NONE-	00000	Quiet (signal lost)
I	-NONE-	11111	Idle
J	-NONE-	11000	Start #1
K	-NONE-	10001	Start #2
T	-NONE-	01101	End
R	-NONE-	00111	Reset
S	-NONE-	11001	Set
H	-NONE-	00100	Halt

- Note that normal data symbols begin with at most one 0 bit and end with at most two, so there can be most three 0 bits in a row.

- Control symbols used in combinations that also preserve this rule. Thus, 4B/5B encoding is a (0,3) RLL code.

- FDDI and 100BASE-TX begin frames with a JK pair. FDDI ends frames with a TT pair, while 100BASE-TX uses a TR pair.

- The following character sets are sometimes referred to as command characters.

Table 3.5: Control characters

Control Character	5B symbols	Purpose
JK	11000 10001	Sync, Start delimiter
II	11111 11111	Not Used
TT	01101 01101	FDDI end delimiter
TS	01101 11001	Not Used
IH	11111 00100	SAL
TR	01101 00111	100BASE-TX end delimiter
SR	11001 00111	Not Used

Conti.

SS	11001 11001	Not Used
HH	00100 00100	HDLC0
HI	00100 11111	HDLC1
HQ	00100 00000	HDLC2
RR	00111 00111	HDLC3
RS	00111 11001	HDLC4
QH	00000 00100	HDLC5
QI	00000 11111	HDLC6
QQ	00000 00000	HDLC7

(HDLC = High-Level Data Link Control)

(FDDI = Fiber Distributed Data Interface)

- Despite this 4B/5B does not guarantee at least one transition for each bit period, however there are enough transitions to allow the clock signal to be recovered.

- Unfortunately the use of 5 bits to represent 4 bits does mean that the bandwidth needed to transmit the data is increased by 25%.

- Substitution in 4B/5B block coding is as shown in Fig. 3.42.

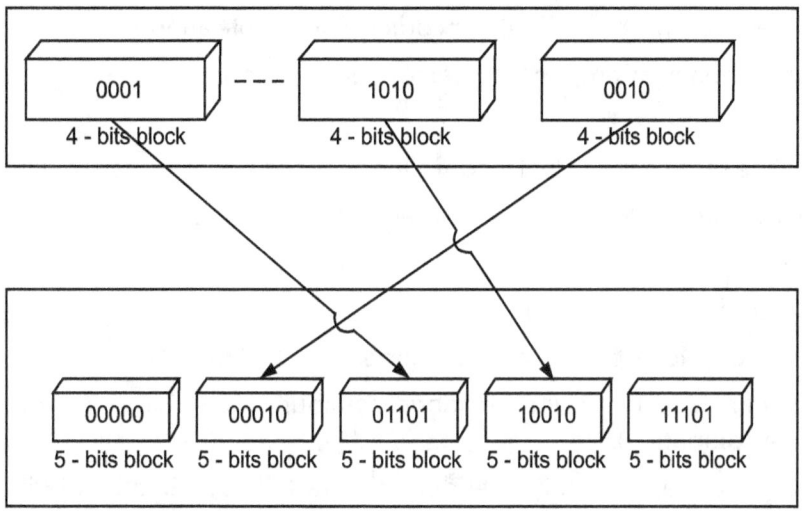

Fig. 3.42: 4B/5B Substitution Process

3.10.2 The 8B/10B Block Coding

- The 8B/10B code is known as 8-Binary/10-Binary block coding technique.

- The 4B/5B is similar to 8B/10B, except that a group of 8 bits of data is substituted by a 10 bit code.

- It has greater error detection capability than 4B/5B block coding technique.
- The 8B/10B is combination of 5B/6B and 3B/4B.

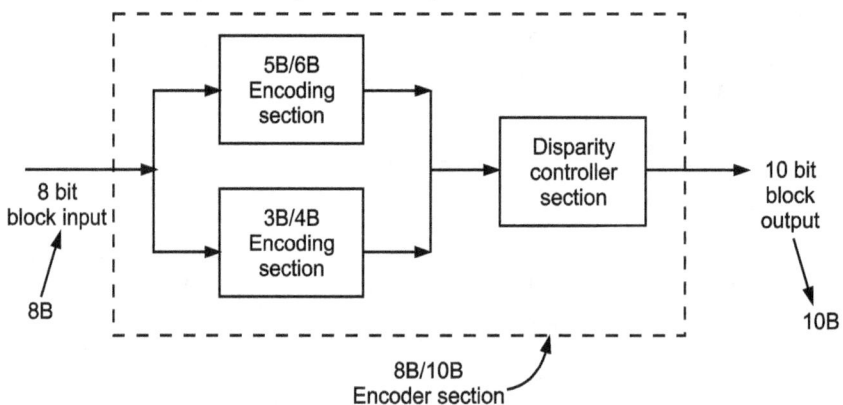

Fig. 3.43: The 8B/10B Block Coding Method

- Disparity controller section minimizes/removes DC component effect due to long streams of consecutive '0' or '1's.
- Thus, 8B/10B encoding also has better self-synchronization capacity as compared to 4B/5B block encoding.

Technologies that uses 8b/10b

Following are the areas in which 8b/10b encoding finds application

- PCI Express (Peripheral Component Interconnect Express).
- IEEE 1394b.
- Serial ATA (The serial ATA, or SATA computer bus, is a storage interface).
- SAS (Serial Attached SCSI) (Small Computer System Interface).
- Fiber Channel.
- SSA (Serial Storage Architecture).
- Gigabit Ethernet (except for the twisted pair based 1000Base-T).
- InfiniBand (InfiniBand is a switched fabric communication link primarily used in high-performance computing).
- XAUI (XAUI is a standard for extending the XGMII (10 Gigabit Media Independent Interface) between the MAC and PHY layer of 10 Gigabit Ethernet (10GbE). XAUI is pronounced "zowie", a concatenation of the roman numeral X, meaning ten, and the initials of "Attachment Unit Interface".
- Serial RapidIO (The RapidIO architecture is a high-performance packet-switched, interconnect technology for interconnecting chips on a circuit board, and also circuit boards to each other using a backplane.)

- DVI (Digital Visual Interface) and HDMI (Transition Minimized Differential Signaling) (High-Definition Multimedia Interface).
- DVB (Asynchronous Serial Interface (ASI)) (Digital Video Broadcasting).
- DisplayPort Main Link.
- HyperTransport.
- Common Public Radio Interface (CPRI).
- USB 3.0.

Digital Audio Applications

Encoding has a heavy use in digital audio applications which use this modulation scheme :

- Digital Audio Tape.
- Digital Compact Cassette (DCC).
- A differing but related scheme is used for audio CDs and CD-ROMs
- Compact Disc Eight-to-Fourteen Modulation.

3.11 SCRAMBLING

Properties of Biphase line codes are :

- No DC component.
- Self-synchronization capacity.
- High bandwidth requirement.
- Biphase technique can be used in LAN environment of short distance communication.
- It cannot be used for long distance communication because of their wide bandwidth requirement.
- DC component problem does not allow combination of block coding + NRZ coding. Also synchronization problems for long stream of '0' occur.
- To avoid synchronization problems, we can use Bipolar AMI for long distance.
- But scrambling can give you synchronization that substitutes long '0' level pulses with a combination of other levels.

Thus, part of AMI can be modified to include scrambling as shown in Fig. 3.44.

There are two scrambling techniques :

- 8ZS.
- DB3.

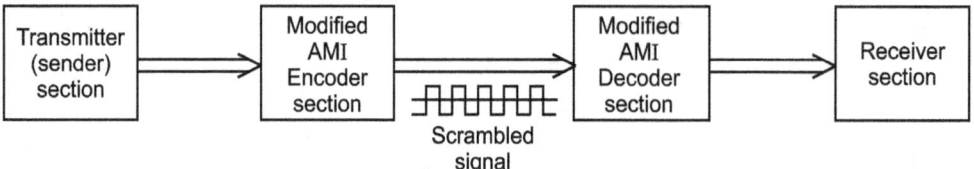

Fig. 3.44: Modified AMI – Scrambling Technique

3.11.1 Bipolar with 8-zeros Substitution (B8ZS) Signal Encoding

The bipolar-AMI encoding supplemented with a scrambling scheme, which uses two code violations to ensure synchronization in runs of 0's.

Replace '00000000' with '000+−0−+', if the preceding voltage pulse was positive.

Replace '00000000' with '000−+0+−', if the preceding voltage pulse was not positive.

The amount of data remains unchanged.

The spectrum graph shows that there is no dc component, with most of the energy concentrating in a relative sharp spectrum, making the encoding suitable for high-rate transmissions.

Used mainly in North America.

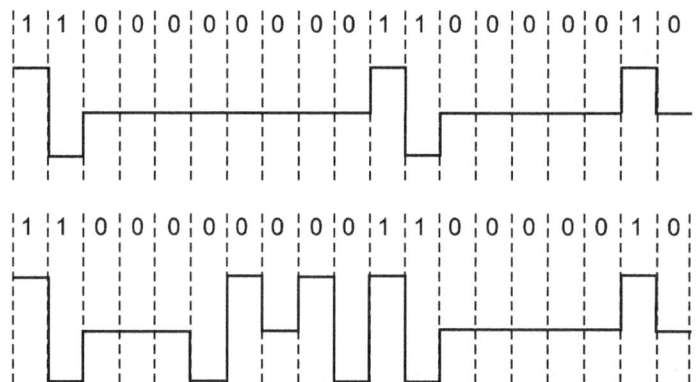

Fig. 3.45: Bipolar with 8-zeros Substitution (B8ZS) Signal Encoding

Following Data for B8ZS Encoding is Very Important

- B8ZS is an abbreviation for bipolar with eight-zeros substitution, which is a method of line coding used in the T-carrier system which allows full 64 kbps per channel, though it does not allow for Clear Channel Capability (CCC - 64 kbps) in and of itself.

- The service would still have to be point-to-point (P2P) and not switched throughout digital switching network.

- The standard is to use B8ZS as the line encoding option when providing P2P circuits and services.

- The older AMI scheme was implemented in channel cards that always robbed a bit for signaling regardless if the service on that channel was switched or P2P. B8ZS cards can be optioned not to rob that bit.

- On a T1, ones are sent by applying voltage to the wire, where a zero is sent by having no voltage on the wire. Sending excessive zeros in a row could cause receiving equipment to lose synchronization with sending equipment, so it is important that such a pattern is not sent.

- The original standard of line coding, Alternate Mark Inversion, specifies that there are three states of the line, no voltage is a zero, positive voltage is a one (or mark), and negative voltage is also a one (or mark).

- Because of the inversion of the voltage for each "mark," or one, sent, the receiving equipment can easily determine the data rate of the line and not lose synchronization.

- B8ZS builds upon this, by using violations of this rule to replace a pattern of eight zeros in a row.

Original signal :							
0	0	0	0	0	0	0	0
B8ZS encoded signal (V = Bipolar violation)							
0	0	0	V	1	0	V	1
Signal Polarity (assuming that the previous mark was negative)							
0	0	0	–	+	0	+	–

B8ZS is used in the North American hierarchy at the T1 rate. When European E1 was developed much later than T1, it was then common knowledge that forcing 'ones' into a DS0 would corrupt data. E1 uses another method called High Density Bipolar Three (HDB3) code.

3.11.2 High-Density Bipolar 3-Zeros (HDB3) Signal Encoding

The bipolar-AMI encoding is supplemented with the following substitution scheme for '0000' runs.

Used in Europe and Japan.

Successive violations are of alternate polarity to avoid dc component.

Number of bipolar pulses (ones) since last substitution		
Polarity of preceding pulse	odd	even
–	000–	+00+
+	000+	–00–

The HDB3 signal encoding is shown in Fig. 3.46.

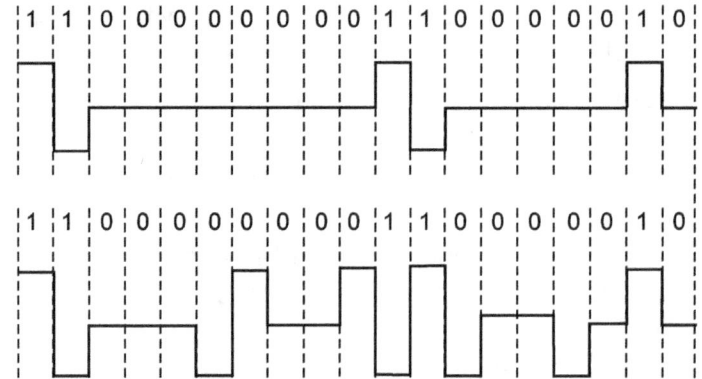

Fig. 3.46: High-Density Bipolar 3-Zeros (HDB3) Signal Encoding

- Based on the AMI code (alternating the levels of voltage when transmitting "1"), this limits the maximum number of consecutive zeros transmitted to three.

- The basic idea consists of replacing series of four bits that are equal to "0" with a code word "000V" or "B00V", where "V" is a pulse that violates the AMI law of alternate polarity and is rectangular or some other shape. The rules for using "000V" or "B00V" are as follows :

- "B00V" is used when up to the previous pulse, the coded signal presents a DC component that is not null (the number of positive pulses is not compensated for by the number of negative pulses).

- "000V" is used under the same conditions as above when up to the previous pulse the DC component is null.

- The pulse "B" ("B" for balancing), which respects the AMI alternancy rule, has positive or negative polarity, ensuring that two successive V pulses will have different polarity.

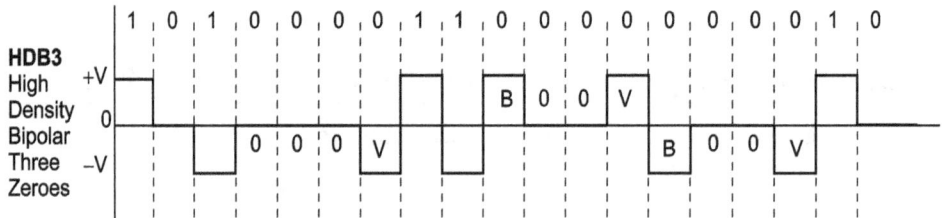

Fig. 3.47: The HDB3 Coding Waveforms

The HDB3 Code has the Following Characteristics

- The timing information is preserved by embedding it in the line signal even when long sequences of zeros are transmitted, which allows the clock to be recovered properly on reception.

- The DC component of a signal that is coded in HDB3 is null.

3.12 AMPLITUDE SHIFT KEYING (ASK)

• In ASK technique, amplitude of sine wave carrier signal is varied to create signal elements by keeping frequency and phase of carrier signal unchanged (or constant).

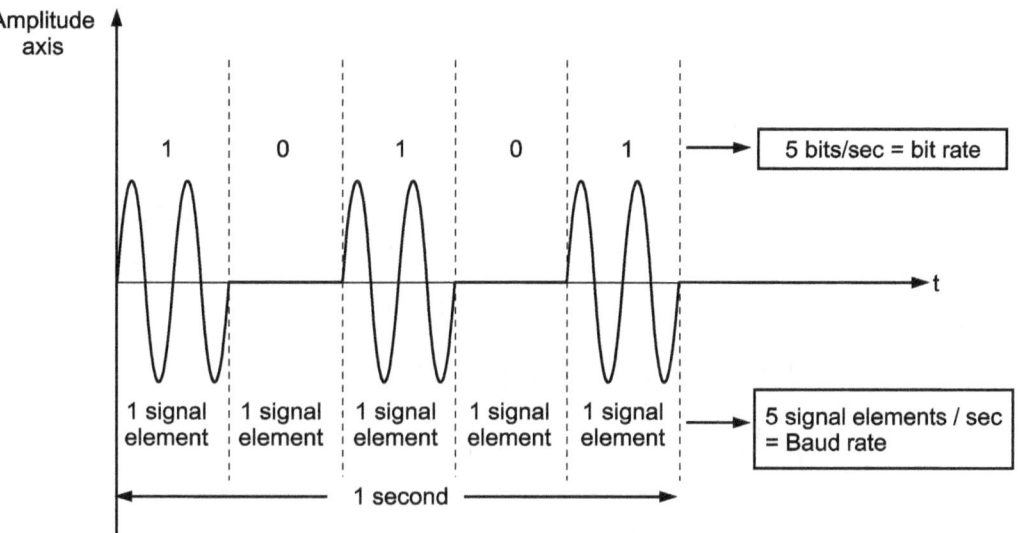

Fig. 3.48: ASK Digital to Analog Conversion

Bandwidth calculation for ASK technique is given by formula

B.W. = (1 + D) × S

Where, S = Signal rate

D = Factor which depends upon modulation and filtering process

Practical implementation of ASK system is done with the help of multiplier unit as shown in Fig. 3.49.

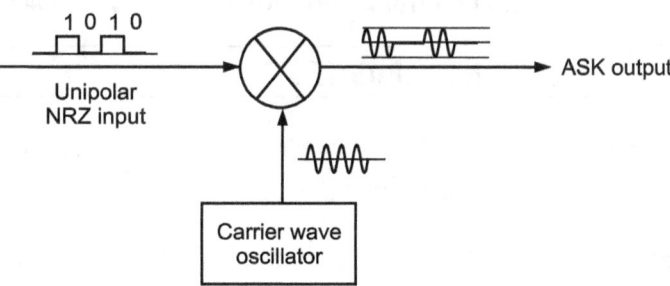

Fig.3.49: ASK generation using multiplier

The typical waveform for ASK generation is as shown in Fig. 4.50.

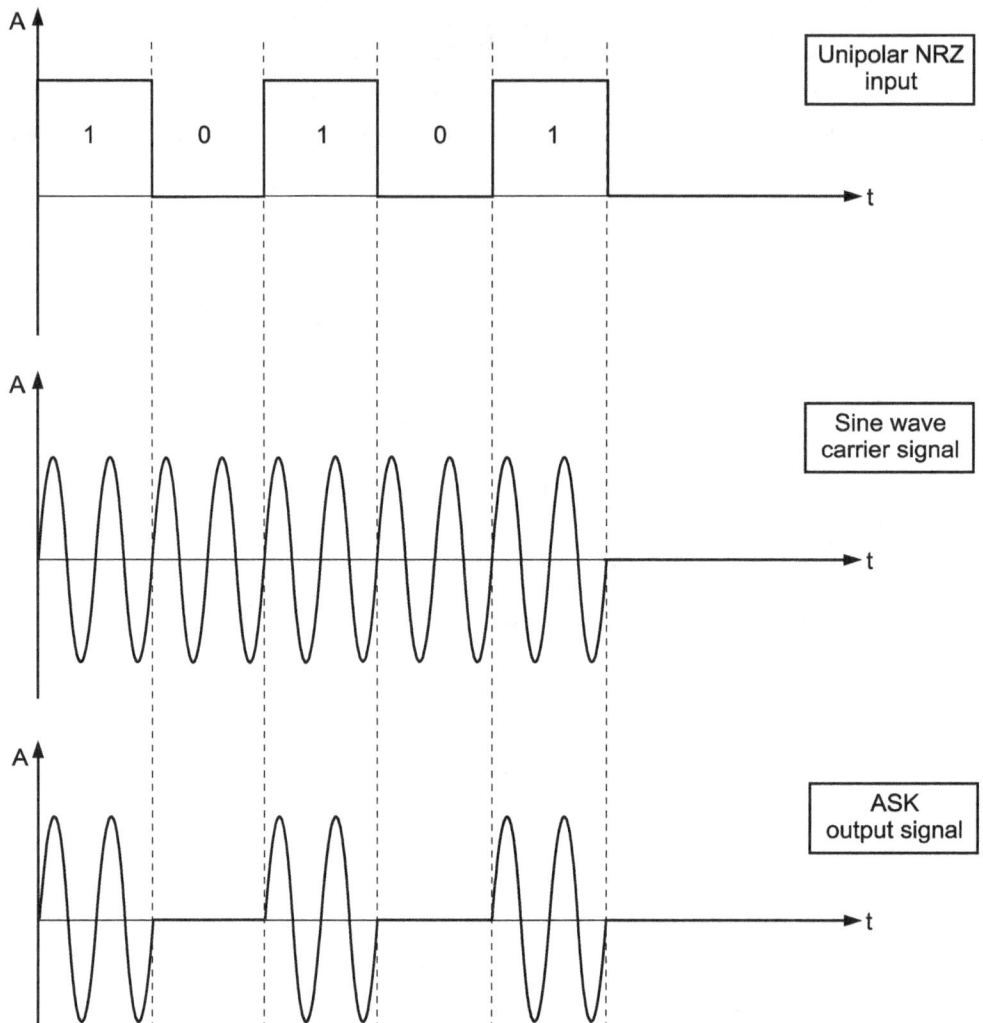

Fig. 3.50: ASK Generation from Unipolar NRZ and Sine Wave Signal

3.13 FREQUENCY SHIFT KEYING (FSK)

In FSK technique, frequency of sine wave carrier signal is varied to create signal elements by keeping amplitude and phase of carrier signal unchanged (or constant).

Here, two carrier frequencies are selected for '0' and '1' input, i.e. f_1 and f_2 respectively.

Bandwidth calculation for FSK technique is given by formula,

$$\text{B.W.} = (1 + D) \times S + 2\Delta f$$

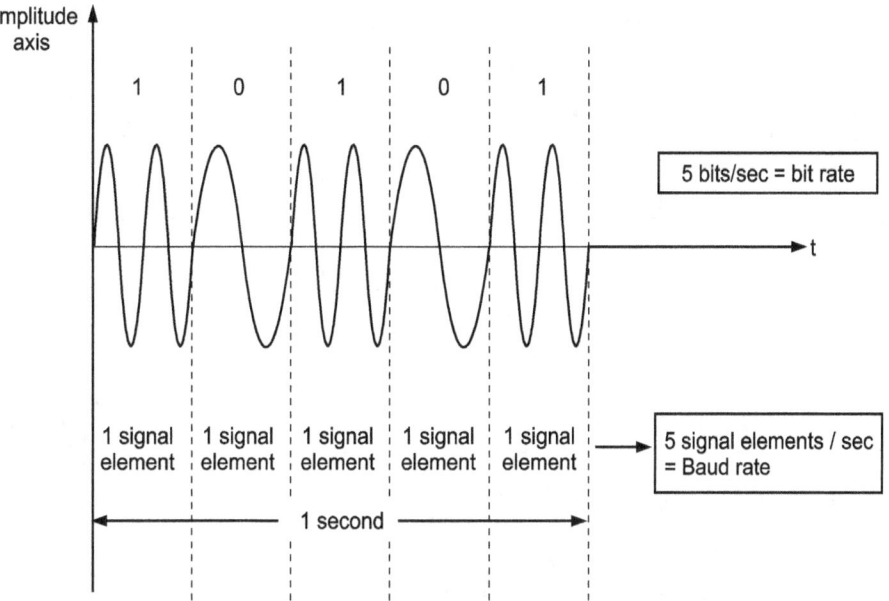

Fig. 3.51: FSK Digital to Analog Conversion

Where, S = Signal rate

      D = Factor which depends upon modulation and filtering process

Here in above formula required $2\Delta f$ is calculated from Fig.3.52

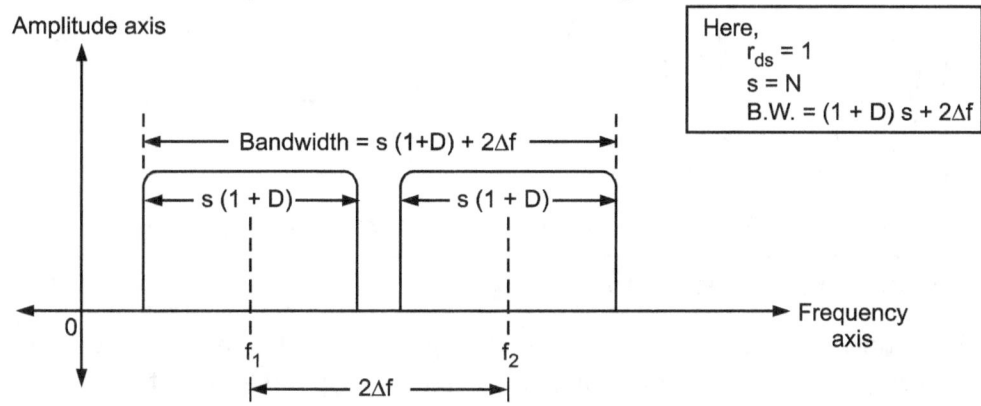

Fig. 3.52: $2\Delta f$ calculation using f_1 and f_2 (or difference between f_1 and f_2)

Practical implementation of FSK system is done with the help of VCO (Voltage Controlled Oscillator) section.

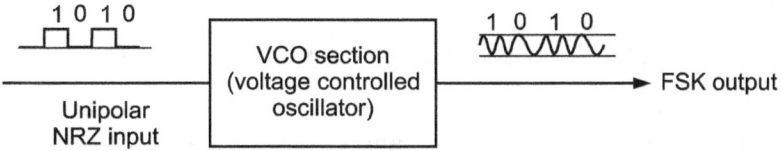

Fig. 3.53: FSK Generation using VCO (Voltage Controlled Oscillator)

The typical waveform for FSK generation is as shown in Fig.3.54.

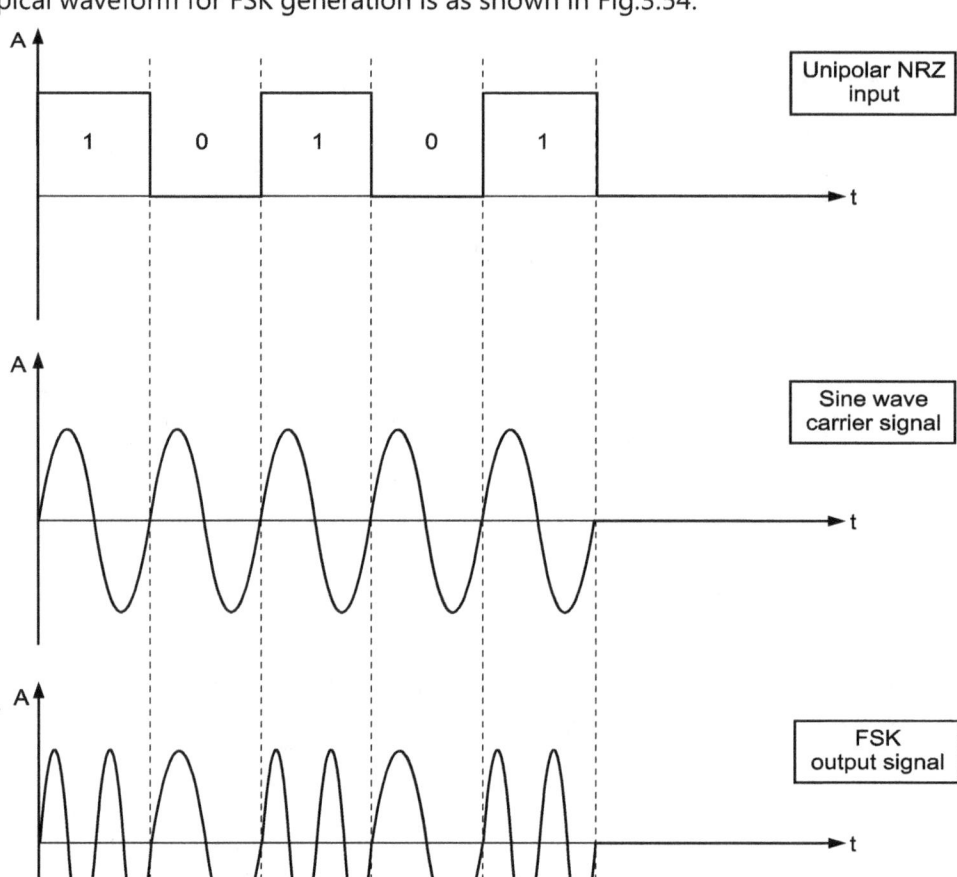

Fig. 3.54: FSK Generation from Unipolar NRZ and Sine Wave Signal

3.14 PHASE SHIFT KEYING (PSK)

- In PSK technique, phase of sine wave carrier signal is varied to create signal elements by keeping amplitude and frequency of carrier signal unchanged (or constant).

- PSK technique is widely used as compared to ASK and FSK.

- In PSK, we have only two signal elements, one with $\theta1$ = Phase = 0° and other with $\theta2$ = Phase = 180°.

- PSK is better than ASK, because PSK is less susceptible to noise than ASK (or PSK is highly immune to noise).

- PSK is better than FSK, because FSK requires two frequencies f1 and f2 whereas PSK requires one frequency only.

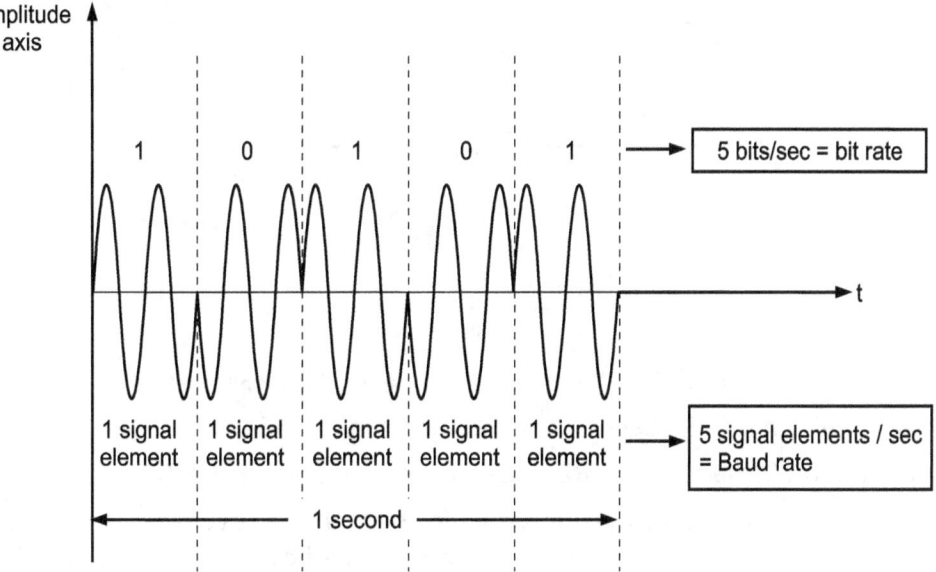

Fig. 3.55: PSK Digital to Analog Conversion

Bandwidth calculation for PSK technique is given by formula,

$$B.W. = (1 + D) \times S$$

Where, S = Signal rate

D = Factor which depends upon modulation and filtering process.

Bandwidth of PSK system is given as,

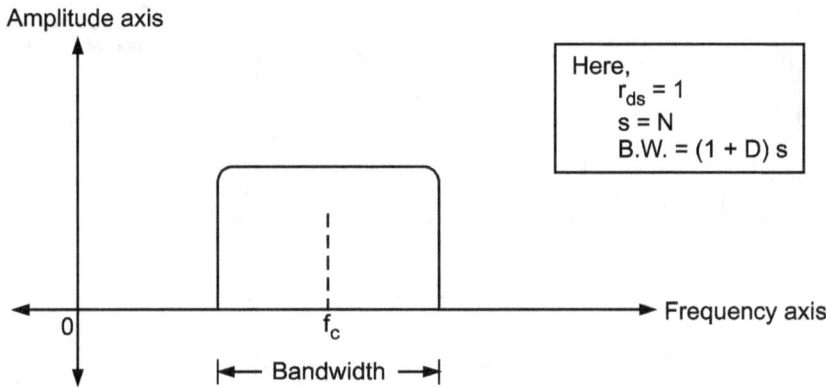

Fig. 3.56: Bandwidth Spectrum for PSK

Practical implementation of PSK system is done with the help of multiplier and carrier oscillator section.

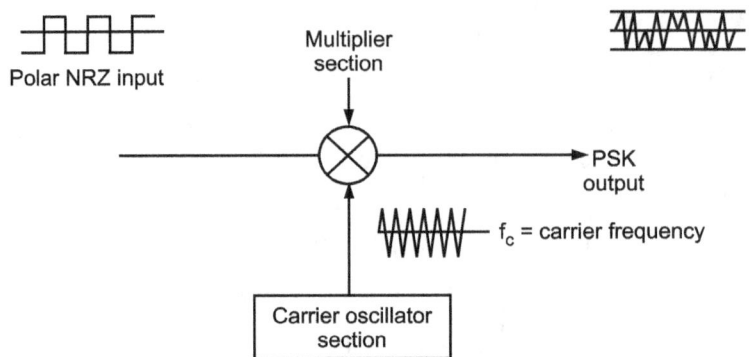

Fig. 3.57: PSK Generation using Multiplier Section

The typical waveform for PSK generation is as shown in Fig. 3.58.

As compared to BASK, here polar NRZ is used instead of unipolar NRZ.

Polar NRZ signal is multiplied by carrier signal fc, the '1' bit (+ve voltage) is represented by a phase starting at 0° and bit '0' (−ve voltage) is represented by a phase starting at 180°.

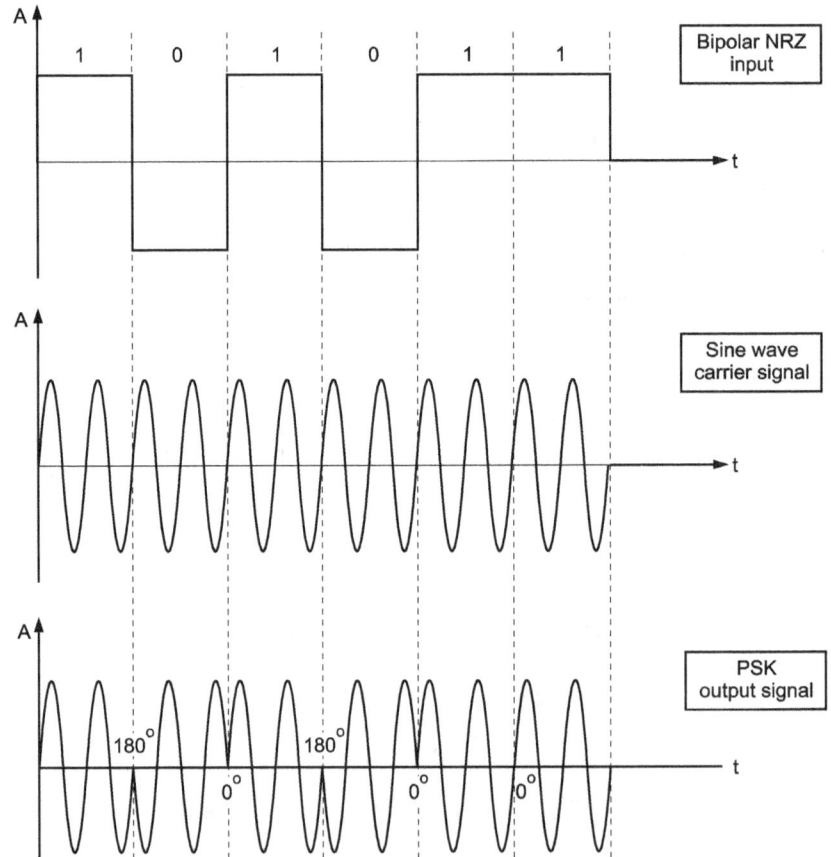

Fig. 3.58: PSK Generation from Bipolar NRZ and Sine Wave Signal

3.15 QUADRATURE AMPLITUDE MODULATION (QAM)

In Binary PSK system, Bit rate is limited due to small difference in phase of two different signal elements.

- In BASK, BFSK or BPSK, only one characteristic of the carrier is changed.

- QAM system is a combination of ASK and PSK.

- The different varieties of QAM systems are as shown below.

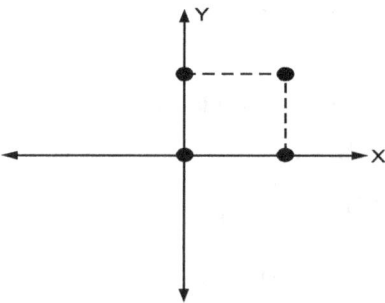

Fig. 3.59: 4-QAM using Unipolar NRZ Signal to Modulate each Carrier

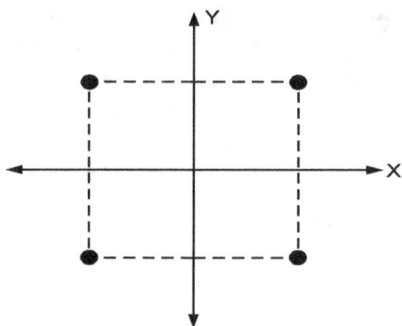

Fig3.60: 4-QAM using Polar NRZ Signal to Modulate each Carrier

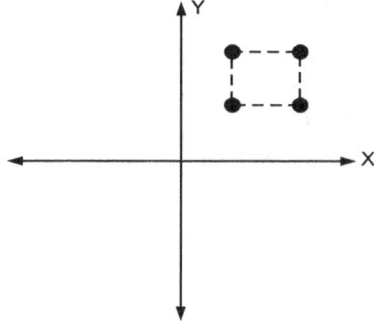

Fig. 3.61: 4-QAM in which Signal with

Two Positive Levels is used to Modulate each of the Two Carriers

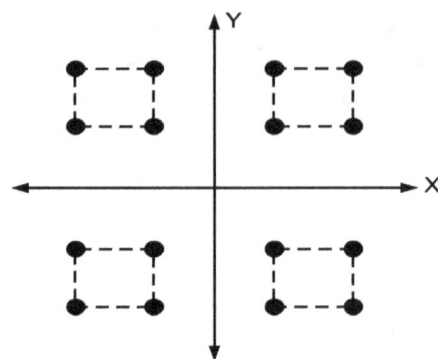

Fig. 3.62: 16-QAM Signal with Eight levels, Four Positive and Four Negative

Bandwidth requirement in QAM system is,

$$\text{B.W. of QAM} = \text{B.W. of ASK} = \text{B.W. of PSK}$$

Also QAM has all advantages of PSK over ASK system.

QAM system is very useful in data networks like modem equipments etc.

ANALOG-TO-ANALOG CONVERSION

3.16 AMPLITUDE MODULATION

In amplitude modulation method following signals play the role:

Information signal or modulating signal (having low frequency and denoted by f_m).

The carrier signal (having high frequency and denoted by f_c).

Just recall the equation of carrier wave

$$X = A \sin(\omega t + \phi)$$

In amplitude modulation, the amplitude of a carrier signal is varied by the modulating signal.

Practically, the process of changing the amplitude of the carrier wave according to the intensity (amplitude) of the modulating signal is called as Amplitude Modulation.

So, in amplitude modulation,

$$X = A \sin(\omega t + \phi)$$

A = Amplitude of carrier is varied by the modulating signal as shown in Fig. 3.63.

The above waveform is the time domain representation of the AM signal. Here only amplitude of carrier wave is varied or modified keeping its frequency and phase unchanged.

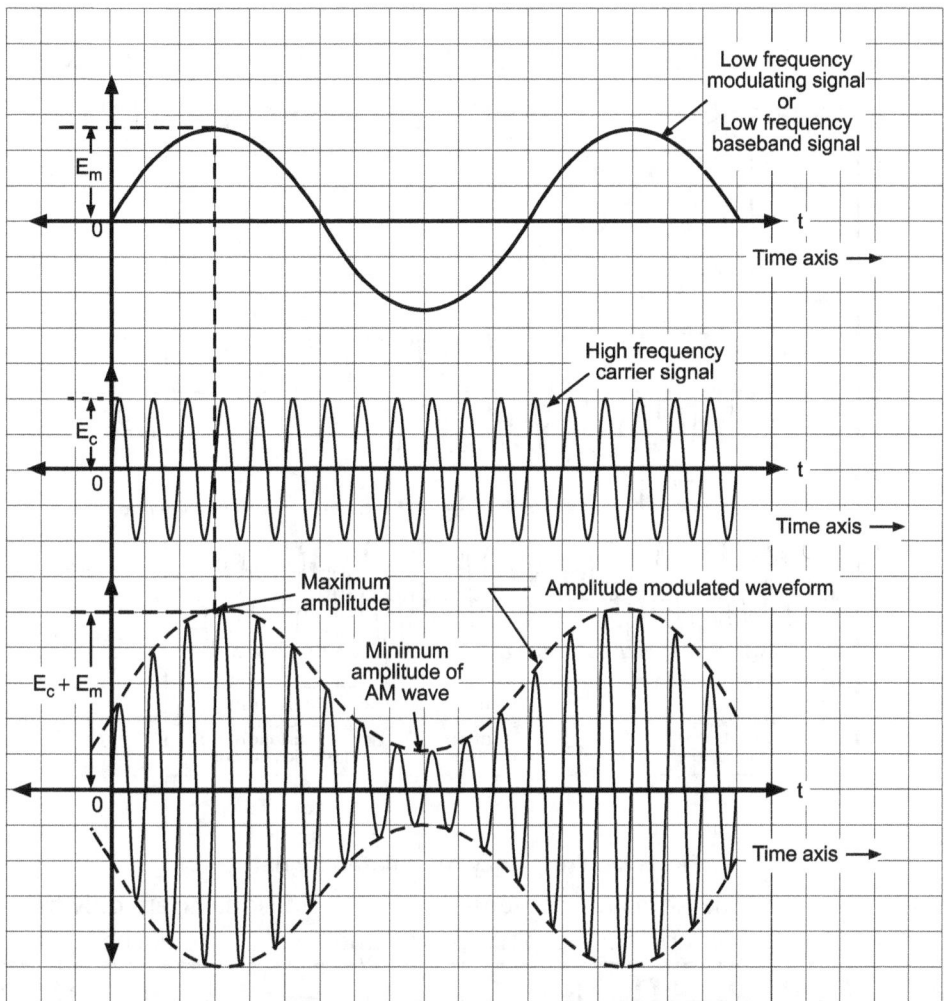

Fig. 3.63: Amplitude Modulated Signal

3.17 FREQUENCY MODULATION

In frequency modulation method following signals play the role:

Information signal or modulating signal (has low frequency and denoted by f_m).

The carrier signal (has high frequency and denoted by f_c).

In frequency modulation the frequency of a carrier signal is varied by the modulating signal. Practically, the process of changing the frequency of the carrier wave according to the intensity (amplitude) of the modulating signal is called as frequency modulation. So in frequency modulation,

$$X = A \sin(\omega t + \phi) \text{ equation of carrier wave}$$

$$\omega = 2\pi f$$

f = Frequency of carrier is varied by the modulating signal as shown in Fig. 3.64.

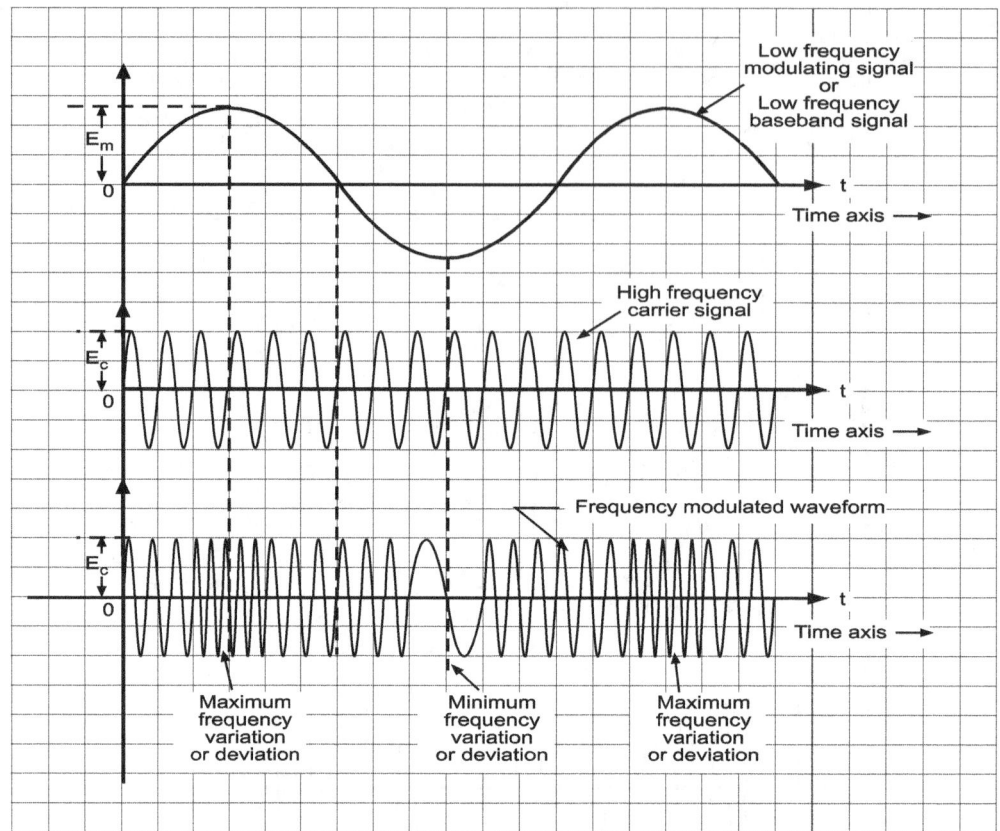

Fig. 3.64: Frequency Modulated Signal

Above waveform is the time domain representation of the FM signal. Here only frequency of the carrier wave is varied or modified keeping its amplitude and phase unchanged.

3.18 PHASE MODULATION

In phase modulation method following signals play the role:

Information signal or modulating signal (has low frequency and denoted by f_m).

The carrier signal (has high frequency and denoted by f_c).

In phase modulation, the phase of a carrier signal is varied by the modulating signal.

Practically, the process of changing the phase of the carrier wave according to the intensity (amplitude) of the modulating signal is called as phase modulation. Greater is the amplitude of the modulating signal, greater is the phase shift and vice versa.

$$X = A \sin(\omega t + \phi) \text{ equation of carrier wave}$$

ϕ = Phase of the carrier is varied by the modulating signal as shown in Fig. 3.65

The waveform in Fig. 3.65 is the time domain representation of the PM signal. Here the amplitude of the carrier wave is unchanged.

Following processes occur in phase modulation.

- Here positive amplitude of modulating signal produces a lagging phase shift.

- Negative amplitude of modulating signal produces a leading phase shift.

- Thus positive amplitude of modulating signal causes lagging phase shift in carrier causes effective stretching of carrier signal causes reduction in carrier frequency or carrier frequency reduces.

- Negative amplitude of modulating signal causes leading phase shift in carrier causes effective compressing of carrier signal causes increase in carrier frequency or carrier frequency increases.

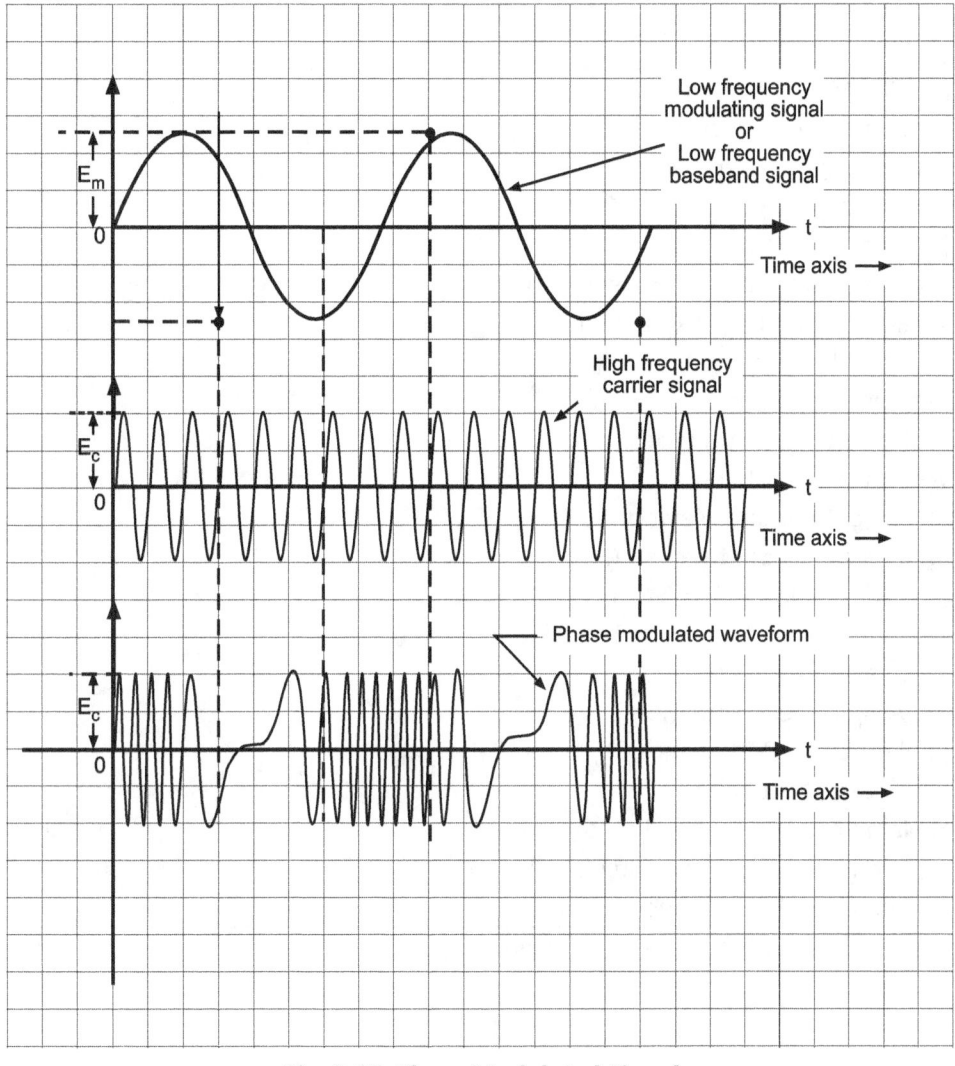

Fig. 3.65: Phase Modulated Signal

EXERCISE

1. What is pulse modulation? Explain in detail pulse modulation techniques.
2. Write a short note on
   (i) PAM   (ii) PWM
   (iii) PDM   (iv) PPM
3. Explain pulse amplitude modulation with its types.
4. What is sampling? Explain sampling theorem.
5. Which are the pulse digital modulation techniques?
6. Write a short note on
   (i)   PCM
   (ii) DM
   (iii) PCDM
7. Write a short note on
   (i)   Average Information
   (ii) Entropy
   (iii) Information rate
8. What is source coding? Explain source coding techniques.
9. What is line coding? Explain line coding schemes.
10. What is block coding?
11. What is scrambling?
12. Explain block coding types.
14. Write a short note on
   (i)   Amplitude Shift Keying (ASK)
   (ii) Frequency Shift Keying (FSK)
   (iii) Phase Shift Keying (PSK)
   (iv) Quadrature Amplitude Modulation (QAM)
15. Write a short note on
   (i)   Amplitude Modulation
   (ii) Frequency Modulation
   (iii) Phase Modulation
16. Explain Shanon-Fano coding technique.
17. Explain Huffman source coding technique.
18. Explain Limpel-Ziv coding technique.

Unit IV

ERROR CONTROL CODING AND DATA LINK CONTROL

We will discuss some terminologies used in electronic communication system.

4.1 ERROR DETECTION AND CORRECTION

4.1.1 Introduction

- Physical layer takes care of transmitting information over a communication channel.

- Information transmitted may be affected by noise or distortion caused in the channel.

- Hence, the transmission over communication channel is not reliable.

- The data transfer is also affected by delay and has finite rate of transmission. This reduces the efficiency of transmission.

- Data link layer is designed to take care of these problems i.e. data link layer improves reliability and efficiency of channel.

- We can also say that the services provided by physical layer are not reliable.

- Hence, we require some layer above physical layer which can take care of these problems. The layer above physical layer is Data Link Layer (DLL).

Following are some of the functions of a data link layer.

- **Error Control :** Physical layer is error prone. The errors introduced in the channel need to be corrected.

- **Flow Control :** There might be mismatch in the transmission rate of sender and the rate at which receiver receives. This mismatch must be taken care of.

- **Addressing :** In the network where there are multiple terminals, whom to send the data has to be specified.

- **Frame Synchronization :** In physical layer, information is in the form of bits. These bits are grouped in blocks of frames at data link layer. In order to identify beginning and end of frames, some identification mark is put before and/or after each frame.

- **Link Management :** In order to manage co-ordination and co-operation among terminals in the network, initiation, maintenance and termination of link is required to be done properly. These procedures are handled by data link layer. The control signals required for this purpose use the same channels on which data is exchanged. Hence, identification of control and data information is another task of data link layer.

- **Services Provided to Network Layer :** Data link layer provides services to the layer above it viz. network layer. The basic service is transferring packets from network layer on source machine to network layer on destination machine as shown in Fig. 4.1.

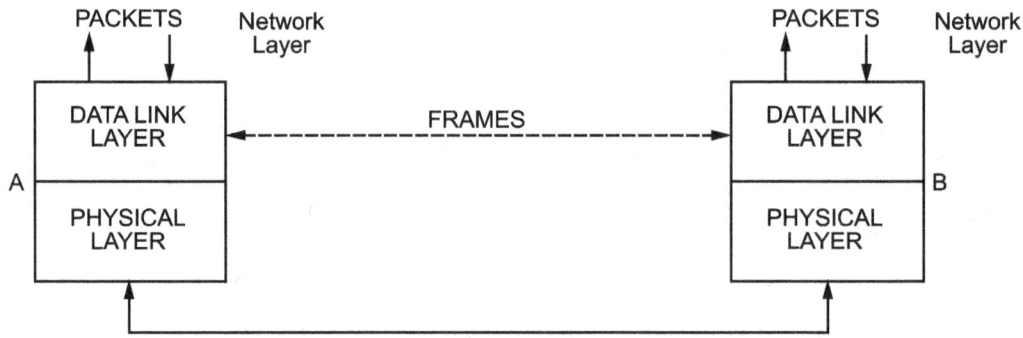

Fig. 4.1 : Service provided to network layer

The service model describes the service provided by a protocol.

There are two categories of service models :

- Connection-oriented service.
- Connectionless service.

In connection-oriented service, connection is established between the peer entities first and then data transfer begins. There will be connection setup, data transfer and connection release procedure required to be carried out.

Connectionless services do not require a connection setup procedure. Information blocks are transmitted using address information in each Protocol Data Unit (PDU).

Acknowledged connectionless services provide acknowledgement for each PDU so that data transfer is reliable.

Unacknowledged connectionless services do not provide acknowledgement for each PDU. This is also called best effort service. In such case, network layer has to provide reliable service i.e. acknowledged service.

The service model specifies the Quality of Service (QoS). It includes expected performance level in transfer of information. Examples of some QoS parameters are :

- Probability of error.
- Probability of loss.
- Transfer delay.

4.2 ERROR DETECTION AND CORRECTION

Whenever bits flow from one point to another, they are subjected to unpredictable changes, because of interference. This interference can change the shape of signals. In a single bit error a0 is changed to a1 or a1 to a0. In a burst error, multiple bits are changed. For example, 1/100s burst of impulse noise on a transmission with a data rate of 1200 bps might change all or some of the 12 bits of information.

*   **Single Bit Error :** It means that only 1 bit of a given data unit (as a byte, character or packet) is changed from 1 to 0 or 0 to 1.

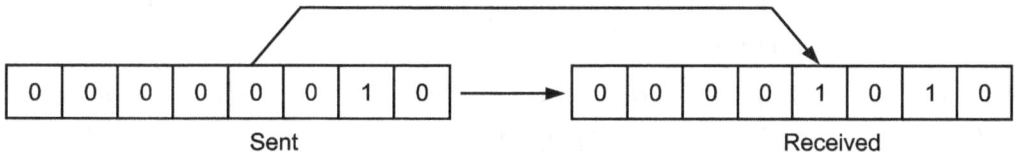

Fig. 4.2

Fig. 4.2 shows the effect of single bit error on a data unit. To understand the impact of change, imagine that each group of 8 bits is an ASCII character with a0 bit added to the left. In Fig. 4.2, 00000010 (ASCII/STX) was sent, meaning start of text but 00001010 (ASCII LF) was received, meaning line feed.

Single bit errors are the least likely type of errors in serial data transmission. To understand imagine data sent at 1 Mbps. This means that each bit lasts only 1/1,000,000s or 1 µs. For single bit error to occur, the noise must have a duration of only 1 µs, which is very rare. Noise normally lasts much longer than this.

*   **Burst Error :** The term means that 2 or more bits in the data unit have changed from 1 to 0 or from 0 to 1.

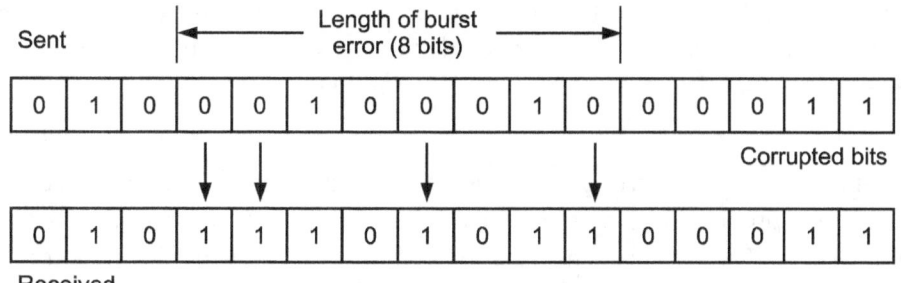

Fig. 4.3

In this case 0100010001000011 was sent, but 0101110101100011 was received. A burst error does not necessarily mean that the errors occur in consecutive bits. The length of the burst is measured from the first corrupted bit to the last corrupted bit. Some bits in between may not have been corrupted.

A burst error is more likely to occur than a single bit error. The duration of noise is normally longer than the duration of 1 bit, this means when noise affects data, it affects a set of bits. The number of bits affected depends on the data rate and duration of noise. For example, if we are sending data at 1 kbps, a noise of 1/100s can affect 10 bits, if we are sending data at 1 Mbps, the same noise can affect 10,000 bits.

Redundancy :

The main concept in detecting errors is redundancy. To detect errors we need to send some extra bits with our data. These redundant bits are added by sender and removed by the receiver. Their presence allows the receiver to detect corrupted bits.

Detection Versus Correction :

The correction of error is more difficult than detection. In error detection, we are looking only to see if any error has occurred. The answer is a simple yes or no. We are not even interested in the number of errors. A single bit error is the same for us as a burst error.

In error correction, we need to know the exact number of bits that are corrupted and more importantly, their location in the message. The number of errors and the size of the message are important factors. If we need to correct one single error in an 8-bit data unit. We need to consider eight possible error locations. If we need to correct two errors in data unit of the same size, we need to consider 28 possibilities. You can imagine the receiver's difficulty in finding 10 errors in data unit of 1000 bits.

Forward Error Correction Versus Retransmission :

There are two main methods of error correction. Forward error correction is the process in which the receiver tries to guess the message by using redundant bits. This is possible, as we see later, if the number of errors is small.

Correction by retransmission is a technique in which the receiver detects the occurrence of an error and asks the sender to resend the message. Resending is repeated until a message arrives that the receiver believes in error-free.

Coding :

Redundancy is achieved through various coding schemes. The sender adds redundant bits through a process that creates a relationship between the redundant bits and the actual data bits. The receiver checks the relationship between the two sets of bits to detect the errors. The ratio of redundant bits to the data bits and the robustness of the process are important factors in any coding scheme.

We can divide coding schemes into two broad categories :

- Block coding.
- Convolution coding.

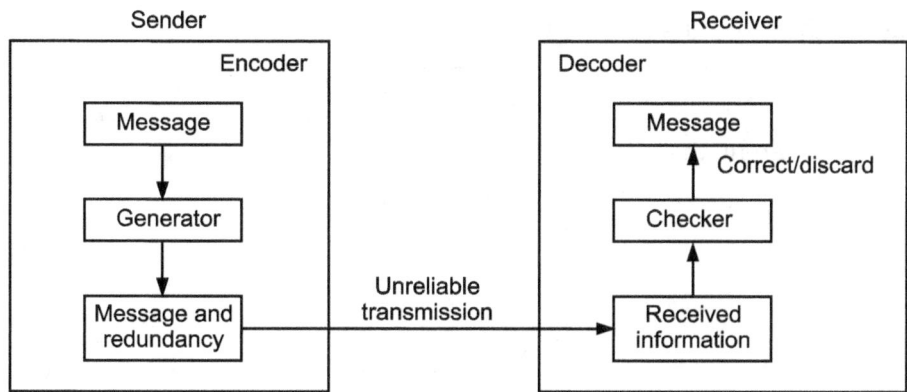

Fig. 4.4 : The Structure of Encoder and Decoder

Modular Arithmetic :

In modular arithmetic we use only limited range of integers. We define an upper limit, called modulus N. We use only the integers 0 to N – 1, inclusive. This is modulo-N arithmetic.

For example, if the modulus is 12, we use only the integers 0 to 11, inclusive. An example of modulo arithmetic is our clock system. It is based on modulo 12 arithmetic, substituting the number 12 for 0.

In a modulo-N system, if a number is greater than N, it is divided by N and the remainder is the result. If it is negative, as many Ns as needed are added to make it positive.

Consider our clock system again, if we start job at 11 a.m. and the job takes 5 hrs., we can say that the job is to be finished at 16.00 if we are in the military, or we can say that it will be finished at 4 p.m. (the remainder of 16/12 is 4).

Addition and subtraction in modulo arithmetic are simple. There is no carry when you add two digits in a column. There is no carry when you subtract one digit from another in column.

Modulo-2 Arithmetic :

In this arithmetic, the modulus N is 2. We can use only 0 and 1. Operations in this arithmetic are very simple. The following shows how we can add or subtract 2 bits.

Adding : $0 + 0 = 0$ $0 + 1 = 1$ $1 + 0 = 1$ $1 + 1 = 0$

Subtracting : $0 – 0 = 0$ $0 – 1 = 1$ $1 – 0 = 1$ $1 – 1 = 0$

Notice particularly that addition and subtraction give the same results. In this arithmetic we use the XOR operation for both addition and subtraction. The result of an XOR operation is 0 if two bits are same, the result is 1 if two bits are different. Fig. 4.4 shows the operation :

XORing of two single bits or two words.

$$0 + 0 = 0 \quad 1 + 1 = 0$$

- Two bits are the same, the result is 0.

$$0 + 1 = 1 \quad 1 + 0 = 1$$

- Two bits are different, the result is 1.

$$
\begin{array}{r}
1\ 0\ 1\ 1\ 0 \\
+\ 1\ 1\ 1\ 0 \\
\underline{0} \\
0\ 1\ 0\ 1\ 0
\end{array}
$$

- Result of XORing two patterns.

Other Modulo Arithmetic :

We use modulo-N arithmetic through the book. The principle is the same. We use numbers between 0 and N − 1. If the modulus is not 2, addition and subtraction are distinct. If we get a negative result, we add enough multiples of N to make it positive.

4.3 BLOCK CODING

- A digital communication system must have higher data rate, minimum signal power, reliable transmission and minimum bandwidth requirement.

- The channel over which the transmission takes place is usually noisy and it will have limited bandwidth.

- If we have to keep the signal power minimum the signal to noise ratio will be lower. This will lead to increase in error probability (p_e), as it depends on E_b/N_0 ratio. Hence, reliability of the system suffers.

- Hence, in order to improve reliability for given E_b/N_0 ratio, we can use error control coding techniques.

- Error control coding techniques can correct errors, so that messages which are likely to go wrong in a noisy channel can be retrieved correctly at the receiver end.

- This is also known as Forward Error Correction (FEC).

- For a fixed value of error probability, it is also possible to reduce E_b/N_0 ratio (signal power) using error control coding.

- Since this technique tries to overcome channel noise, it is also called **channel coding.**

- The error correcting codes are generated by adding redundancy to original message before transmitting it on a noisy channel. The channel encoder block in the transmitter does this as shown in Fig. 4.5.

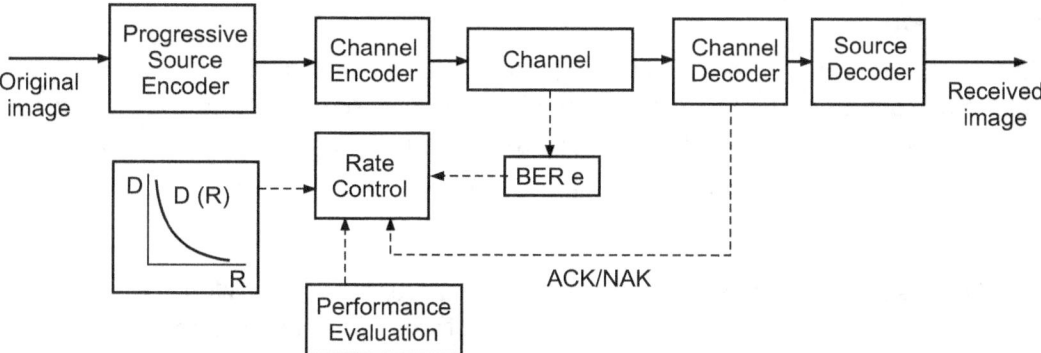

Fig. 4.5 : Channel Coding in Communication System

- At the receiver we can recover the original message if the errors are within the limit as per the design of code. The channel decoder block does this recovery.

- A good error control coding technique should have

  ➢ Better error correcting capability.

  ➢ Faster and efficient method of coding and decoding.

  ➢ Maximum transfer of information in bit/sec. (or less overheads).

- If we try to increase error correcting capability, information rate will reduce and coding and decoding will also be slower. Complexity of design increases in order to achieve better coding technique. The addition of redundancy also increases the bandwidth requirement. Thus, reliability is at the cost of bandwidth and system complexity.

- Reliability can be increased by designing error detecting systems. In these systems, we add redundancy at the transmitter end in the message. The code is then transmitted. At the receiver end we will detect whether the code received is correct or not. If not, we request the transmitter to retransmit the code. The overheads required in this case are lower than that of FEC. This technique is called Automatic Repeat Request (ARQ).

- There are number of error correcting codes. They are classified as :

  ➢ Block codes.

  ➢ Convolutional codes.

- In block codes a block of k-bit message is encoded into n bits by adding n–k redundant bits.

- Convolutional codes are generated using a sliding window where, incoming message slides forward in the window. The window length is usually small and output code consists of encoder output corresponding to the message bits in the window.

- The memory requirement for linear block code encoder is more than convolutional code.

Basic Definitions

In digital communication, we use binary symbols (I/O) for transmission of message hence, we will be using the word bits instead of symbols in our discussion. But correct and general word should be symbols as a message may generate more than two types of symbols.

Let us first discuss some frequently used terms with coding.

- **Word :** It is a sequence of symbols.

e.g. Suppose we have a message consisting of 1010, then it is called a **message word.** Similarly, there will be code corresponding to this message called as **codeword.**

- **Code :** It is a set of vectors called as codewords or code vectors.

- **Parity Bits :** The bits which are added to the message bits are called parity bits.

- **Systematic Code :** Code in which codewords consists of message bits and parity bits separately is called systematic code.

- **Block Codes :** These are fixed length codewords generated from a block of message words.

- **Block Code Specification :** The block code is specified in terms of number of code bits and number of message bits. If there are k bits in the message word and n bits are generated to form codeword, the block code is called (n, k) block code.

- **Code Rate :** For an (n, k) block code the code rate is defined as the ratio of message bits and code bits (k/n). Code rate is always less than one.

- **Parity Check Codes :** These are simplest possible block codes. These codes are generated by adding one bit to the message bits. They can be even parity check codes or odd parity check codes. Even parity check codes add 1 to message if number of 1's in message are odd and 0 if number of 1's in message are even.

e.g.

Message	Code	Parity bit
100101	1001011	
110101	1101010	

Similarly,

Odd Parity Check Codes

Message	Code	Parity bit
010011	0100110	
010001	0100011	

If single error occurs in these codewords, it can be detected at the receiver end.

- **Weight of a Codeword :** The number of non-zero symbols in a codeword is called weight of the codeword.

  e.g.

Codeword	Weight
10101	3
11110	4

- **Hamming Distance :** It is a number of symbols in which two codewords differ.

  e.g.

  $$c_1 = 10101$$

  $$c_2 = 11010$$

  Hamming distance between c_1 and c_2 is 4, denoted as $d(c_1, c_2) = 4$.

- Minimum hamming distance between any two codewords of a code is called minimum hamming distance of that code. It is denoted as d_{min}.

- **A linear code :** It is a code which has following properties.

  ➢ The sum of any two codewords in the code will yield another codeword of that code.

  ➢ There is always all-zero codeword.

  ➢ The minimum hamming distance between any two codewords is equal to minimum weight of any non-zero codeword.

SOLVED EXAMPLES

Example 4.1 : Consider the following code.

$$C = \{000, 111\}$$

Solution :

It consists of the two codewords.

Weight of 000 is 0

Weight of 111 is 3.

Hamming distance between two codewords = 3.

Minimum hamming distance of the code = 3.

It is a linear code since addition of the two codewords yield one of the codewords 111.

Example 4.2 : Consider a code.

$$C = \{000, 010, 001, 111\}$$

Codeword	Weight
000	0
010	1
001	1
111	3

Solution :

Minimum hamming distance = 1

It is not a linear code as addition of 001 and 010 does not yield valid codeword i.e. 011 is not a valid codeword of this code.

- **Minimum hamming distance (d_{min}) : Minimum Hamming distance** of a linear code is equal to minimum weight of the non-zero codewords in that code.

    Consider a code C = {000, 010, 101, 111}

Codeword	Weight
000	0
010	1
101	2
111	3

Since, minimum weight of non-zero code is 1.

Minimum hamming distance d_{min} = 1.

4.4 LINEAR BLOCK CODES

Consider an (n, k) block code in which there are k message bits (or symbols) and code bits (or symbols).

Let the code bits be,

$$C = (c_1, c_2, c_3, ... c_n) \qquad ... (4.1)$$

Let the message bits be,

$$d = (d_1, d_2, d_3, ... d_k) \qquad ... (4.2)$$

For general case, n bits of code C are generated by linear combinations of k message bits. This is called non-systematic code.

For a special case,

If $\qquad c_1 = d_1 \quad c_2 = d_2 ... c_k = d_k$

and c_{k+1} to c_n are generated from linear combinations of $d_1, d_2, ... d_k$ then the code is called systematic code. First k bits are message bits and (n – k) parity bits added to the message.

As we have seen in earlier section, any code C is a subspace of $GF(q^n)$ and any set of basic vectors S can be used to generate code space C = <S> by linear combinations of basis vectors. Hence, m can put all basic vectors in a matrix which is called generator matrix (G). This matrix is used to generate the codewords of C. If we have to generate the codewords of length n from k message bits we will need the generator matrix of the order $k \times n$. Hence, we should have k basic vectors in the generator matrix. The code is generated by,

$$C = d \times G \qquad \qquad \qquad \text{... (4.3)}$$

Now, if we have to generate systematic code we should have relationship between c and d as below :

$$c_1 = d_1$$
$$c_2 = d_2$$
$$c_3 = d_3$$
$$\vdots$$
$$\vdots$$
$$c_k = d_k$$
$$c_{k+1} = p_{11} \cdot d_1 \oplus p_{21} \cdot d_2 \oplus ... \oplus p_{k1} \cdot d_k$$
$$c_{k+2} = p_{12} \cdot d_1 \oplus p_{22} \cdot d_2 \oplus ... \oplus p_{k2} \cdot d_k$$
$$\vdots$$
$$\vdots$$
$$c_n = p_{1n-k} \cdot d_1 \oplus p_{2n-k} \cdot d_2 \oplus ... \oplus p_{kn-k} d_k \qquad \qquad \text{... (4.4)}$$

Hence the generator matrix will be,

$$G = \begin{bmatrix} 1 & 0 & 0 & ... & 0 & p_{11} & p_{12} & p_{1n-k} \\ 0 & 1 & 0 & ... & 0 & p_{21} & p_{22} & p_{2n-k} \\ \vdots & \vdots & \vdots & & \vdots & & & \\ \vdots & \vdots & \vdots & & \vdots & & & \\ 0 & 0 & 0 & ... & 1 & p_{k1} & p_{k2} & p_{kn-k} \end{bmatrix} \qquad \text{... (4.5)}$$

Thus, generator matrix G consists of two parts Identity matrix I_k and Parity   matrix P.

Order of I_k is $k \times k$.

Order of P is $k \times n - k$.

i.e. $$G = [I_k \quad P] \qquad \qquad \qquad \text{... (4.6)}$$

The generator matrix provides a concise and efficient way of representing linear block code i.e. a code can be written as,

$$C = dG \qquad\qquad ... (4.7)$$

Thus, we need not store all codewords corresponding to all messages but we can generate them with the help of generator matrix which stores only few codewords.

Example 4.3 : Generate all codewords of (7, 4) Linear Block Codes (LBC) for following generator matrix.

$$G = (I_k, P) \quad \begin{bmatrix} 1 & 0 & 0 & 0 & 1 & 1 & 0 \\ 0 & 1 & 0 & 0 & 0 & 1 & 1 \\ 0 & 0 & 1 & 0 & 1 & 1 & 1 \\ 0 & 0 & 0 & 1 & 1 & 0 & 1 \end{bmatrix} \qquad ... (4.8)$$

Solution :

We know that,

$$C = dG$$

Here, n = 7, k = 4.

Hence, there will be $2^k = 2^4 = 16$.

To generate code we take each message word and multiply with G.

e.g. For message word d = [1 0 1 0]

$$C = [1\,0\,1\,0] \times \begin{bmatrix} 1 & 0 & 0 & 0 & 1 & 1 & 0 \\ 0 & 1 & 0 & 0 & 0 & 1 & 1 \\ 0 & 0 & 1 & 0 & 1 & 1 & 1 \\ 0 & 0 & 0 & 1 & 1 & 0 & 1 \end{bmatrix} \qquad ... (4.9)$$

$[1 \cdot 1 \oplus 0 \cdot 0 \oplus 1 \cdot 0 \oplus 0 \cdot 0 \quad = \quad 1$

$1 \cdot 0 \oplus 0 \cdot 1 \oplus 1 \cdot 0 \oplus 0 \cdot 0 \quad = \quad 0$

$1 \cdot 0 \oplus 0 \cdot 0 \oplus 1 \cdot 1 \oplus 0 \cdot 0 \quad = \quad 1$

$1 \cdot 0 \oplus 0 \cdot 0 \oplus 1 \cdot 0 \oplus 0 \cdot 1 \quad = \quad 0$

$1 \cdot 1 \oplus 0 \cdot 1 \oplus 1 \cdot 1 \oplus 0 \cdot 0 \quad = \quad 0$

$1 \cdot 1 \oplus 0 \cdot 1 \oplus 1 \cdot 1 \oplus 1 \cdot 0 \quad = \quad 0$

$1 \cdot 0 \oplus 0 \cdot 1 \oplus 1 \cdot 1 \oplus 0 \cdot 1 \quad = \quad 1]$

$\qquad\qquad\qquad = \quad [1\,0\,1\,0\,0\,0\,1]$

Similarly, we can generate code for all message words which are given below.

Message Word	Code Word
0 0 0 0	0 0 0 0 0 0 0
0 0 0 1	0 0 0 1 1 0 1
0 0 1 0	0 0 1 0 1 1 1
0 0 1 1	0 0 1 1 0 1 0
0 1 0 0	0 1 0 0 0 1 1
0 1 0 1	0 1 0 1 1 1 0
0 1 1 0	0 1 1 0 1 0 0
0 1 1 1	0 1 1 1 0 0 1
1 0 0 0	1 0 0 0 1 1 0
1 0 0 1	1 0 0 1 0 1 1
1 0 1 0	1 0 1 0 0 0 1
1 0 1 1	1 0 1 1 1 0 0
1 1 0 0	1 1 0 0 1 0 1
1 1 0 1	1 1 0 1 0 0 0
1 1 1 0	1 1 1 0 0 1 0
1 1 1 1	1 1 1 1 1 1 1

From given generator matrix we can write code bits in a code word as,

$$c_1 = d_1$$

$$c_2 = d_2$$

$$c_3 = d_3$$

$$c_4 = d_4$$

$$c_5 = d_1 \oplus d_3 \oplus d_4$$

$$c_6 = d_1 \oplus d_2 \oplus d_3$$

$$c_7 = d_2 \oplus d_3 + d_4 \qquad \qquad \text{... (4.10)}$$

Hence, the generator circuit for above code is shown below.

Message Word	Code Word
0 0 0 0	0 0 0 0 0 0 0
0 0 0 1	0 0 0 1 1 0 1
0 0 1 0	0 0 1 0 1 1 1
0 0 1 1	0 0 1 1 0 1 0
0 1 0 0	0 1 0 0 0 1 1
0 1 0 1	0 1 0 1 1 1 0
0 1 1 0	0 1 1 0 1 0 0
0 1 1 1	0 1 1 1 0 0 1
1 0 0 0	1 0 0 0 1 1 0
1 0 0 1	1 0 0 1 0 1 1
1 0 1 0	1 0 1 0 0 0 1
1 0 1 1	1 0 1 1 1 0 0
1 1 0 0	1 1 0 0 1 0 1
1 1 0 1	1 1 0 1 0 0 0
1 1 1 0	1 1 1 0 0 1 0
1 1 1 1	1 1 1 1 1 1 1

Parity Check Matrix

We have seen that generator matrix is used to generate codewords from message words. These codewords will be transmitted through a noisy channel. At the receiver end we have to validate these codewords i.e. they are to be checked whether they are correctly received or not. If not the codewords should be corrected with the help of redundant bits that we have added at the transmitter end. For this, consider a matrix H called parity check matrix which is given by,

$$H = [P_T \quad I_{n-k}]_{n-k \times n} \qquad \qquad ... (4.11)$$

i.e. H consists of two parts. Transpose of parity matrix whose order will be $n - k \times k$ and identity matrix whose order will be $(n - k) \times (n - k)$.

It can be verified for any codeword C.

$$CH^T = 0 \qquad \qquad ... (4.12)$$

i.e. if we multiply any codeword with transpose of parity check matrix H result will be zero-vector.

Thus, the received codeword at the receiver is multiplied with H^T and we get zero vector if the codeword is correctly received. But if multiplication results into non-zero codeword, there will be error in the received codeword.

Substitute $C = dG$ in equation (4.12),

$$d\,G\,H^T = 0$$

Thus, for equation (4.12) to hold true we should have,

$$G\,H^T = 0$$

Now consider, $G = [I_k \ P]$

and $H = [P^T \ I_{n-k}]$

$$G^T = \begin{bmatrix} I_k \\ P^T \end{bmatrix}$$

$\therefore$ $H\,G^T = [P^T \ I_{n-k}] \begin{bmatrix} I_k \\ P^T \end{bmatrix}$

$$= P^T \oplus P^T$$

$$= 0$$

$\therefore$ $G\,H^T = 0$

The process of coding and detection is shown in Fig. 4.6.

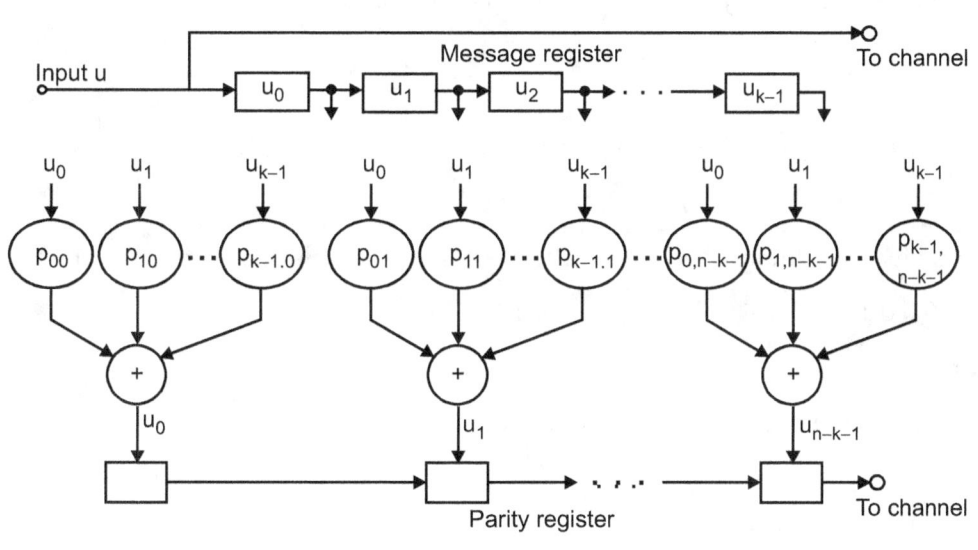

(i) Coding

```
                                         Parity
               LSB                       (VRC)
        H   0  0  0  1  0  0  1  0
        e   1  0  1  0  0  1  1  0
        I   0  0  1  1  0  1  1  0
        P   0  0  0  0  1  1  1  1
        !   1  0  0  0  0  1  0  0
      LRC   0  0  0  1  0  0  1
```

(a) Correct LRC sent

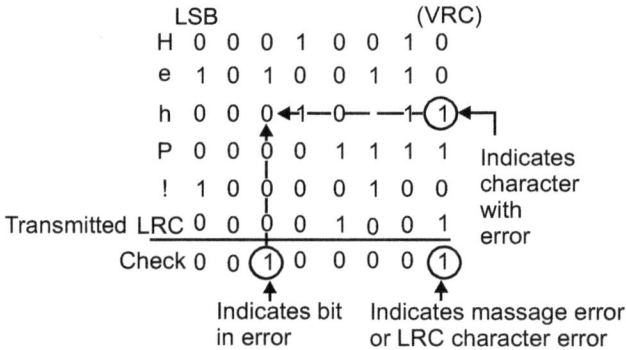

(b) Receive message with error

(ii) Detection

Fig. 4.6

Example 4.4 : Consider a generator matrix given in example 4.3.

$$G = \begin{bmatrix} 1 & 0 & 0 & 0 & 1 & 1 & 0 \\ 0 & 1 & 0 & 0 & 0 & 1 & 1 \\ 0 & 0 & 1 & 0 & 1 & 1 & 1 \\ 0 & 0 & 0 & 1 & 1 & 0 & 1 \end{bmatrix}$$

Find parity check matrix and check whether following codewords are valid or not.

(i) 1 0 0 0 1 1 0   (ii) 0 1 0 1 0 1 1

Solution :

The given generator matrix is of the order 4×7.

Hence, $n = 7$

      $k = 4$

The parity matrix in the generator is,

$$P = \begin{bmatrix} 1 & 1 & 0 \\ 0 & 1 & 1 \\ 1 & 1 & 1 \\ 1 & 0 & 1 \end{bmatrix}$$

Now parity check matrix is given by,

$$H = [P^T \; I_{n-k}]$$

$$= \begin{bmatrix} 1 & 0 & 1 & 1 & 1 & 0 & 0 \\ 1 & 1 & 1 & 0 & 0 & 1 & 0 \\ 0 & 1 & 1 & 1 & 0 & 0 & 1 \end{bmatrix}$$

$$\therefore \qquad H^T = \begin{bmatrix} 1 & 1 & 0 \\ 0 & 1 & 1 \\ 1 & 1 & 1 \\ 1 & 0 & 1 \\ 1 & 0 & 0 \\ 0 & 1 & 0 \\ 0 & 0 & 1 \end{bmatrix}$$

To check whether given codewords are valid or not we find CH^T.

(i)   Given : $C = [1\ 0\ 0\ 0\ 1\ 1\ 0]$

$$\therefore \qquad CH^T = [1\ 0\ 0\ 0\ 1\ 1\ 0] \begin{bmatrix} 1 & 1 & 0 \\ 0 & 1 & 1 \\ 1 & 1 & 1 \\ 1 & 0 & 1 \\ 1 & 0 & 0 \\ 0 & 1 & 0 \\ 0 & 0 & 1 \end{bmatrix}$$

$$= [0\ 0\ 0]$$

Hence, given codeword is valid.

(ii) $C = [0\ 1\ 0\ 1\ 0\ 1\ 1]$

$$\therefore \qquad CH^T = [0\ 1\ 0\ 1\ 0\ 1\ 1] \begin{bmatrix} 1 & 1 & 0 \\ 0 & 1 & 1 \\ 1 & 1 & 1 \\ 1 & 0 & 1 \\ 1 & 0 & 0 \\ 0 & 1 & 0 \\ 0 & 0 & 1 \end{bmatrix}$$

$$= [1\ 0\ 1]$$

Hence, given codeword is invalid.

Minimum Distance and H^T

- Hamming distance between two codewords is the number of positions in which their symbols differ.

- Hamming weight is number of non-zero elements in the codewords.

- The minimum distance d_{min} of a linear block code is the smallest distance between any pair of code vectors in the code.

- From the closure property of linear block codes the sum (or difference) of two codewords is another codeword.

- Minimum distance of a linear block code is the smallest hamming weight of the non-zero codeword in the code.

- Parity check matrix H and in turn generator matrix G are also related to minimum distance d_{min} of a code.

- Since $CH^T = 0$, the number of 1's in code vector C should be such that, corresponding rows of H^T add to zero i.e. corresponding columns of parity check matrix H must add to zero.

Consider the H^T discussed in earlier example.

$$H^T = \begin{bmatrix} 1 & 1 & 0 \\ 0 & 1 & 1 \\ 1 & 1 & 1 \\ 1 & 0 & 1 \\ 1 & 0 & 0 \\ 0 & 1 & 0 \\ 0 & 0 & 1 \end{bmatrix}$$

Now consider a valid code vector.

$$C = [1\,0\,0\,0\,1\,1\,0]$$

There are three non-zero elements at positions 1, 5 and 6 and the sum of 1st, 5th and 6th row of H^T is,

$$\begin{bmatrix} 1 \\ 1 \\ 0 \end{bmatrix} + \begin{bmatrix} 1 \\ 0 \\ 0 \end{bmatrix} + \begin{bmatrix} 0 \\ 1 \\ 0 \end{bmatrix} = \begin{bmatrix} 0 \\ 0 \\ 0 \end{bmatrix}$$

- The number of non-zero elements in the code is 3. If you check other codewords in the (7, 4) code discussed earlier, the minimum number of   non-zero elements is 3 which is nothing but minimum weight of that code and it is also minimum hamming distance.

- Hence, the minimum distance of linear block code (d_{min}) is equal to

  minimum number of rows of H^T (or columns of H) whose sum is equal to zero vector.

Decoding of a Linear Block Code

Decoding is a process of detecting and correcting errors when messages in the form of codewords are transmitted on a noisy channel. The important question here is how many errors can we detect and correct. It will depend on the design of the code. The number of errors the code can correct or detect errors is called error correcting or detecting capability of that code.

A code contains certain number of codewords which are at some distance from each other which is specified in terms of hamming distance.

e.g. Consider the following code.

Message Word	Code Word
0	0 0 0
1	1 1 1

There are two codewords in the code whose hamming distance is 3.

When one of the codewords is transmitted the noise or distortion is likely to change some bits. e.g. when 0 0 0 is transmitted we might receive 0 0 1. As long as one codeword is not transformed into another codewords we can detect whether there was error in transmission or not. Thus, the number of errors that can be detected depends on minimum hamming distance of the code, as it is the minimum distance between any two codewords.

i.e. if a code has hamming distance d_{min} the number of errors that can be detected is,

$$\boxed{t_d \le d_{min} - 1} \qquad \text{... (4.13)}$$

The number of errors that can be corrected also depends on minimum hamming distance. When a codeword is received with error we have to find which codeword was actually transmitted ? Obviously, the codeword nearest to the valid codewords will be the answer. But then the received codeword might be at same hamming distance from two or more valid codewords. Hence, it is not possible to correct the code with this criteria. Also, if more errors occur, the received codeword will go near to another valid codeword which was not transmitted.

e.g. If 0 0 0 is transmitted and 0 1 0 is received we can make decision in favour of 0 0 0 as 0 1 0 is nearer to 0 0 0 than 1 1 1. But if 0 0 0 is transmitted and 0 1 1 is received we will make decision in favour of 1 1 1 as 0 1 1 is nearer to 1 1 1 than 0 0 0 which is not correct. Hence, this code cannot correct two errors. For error correction capability any two codewords in the code should be separated such that the number of errors (t_c) should result into a received word which is closest to original codeword and away from all other codewords. The condition for this is,

$$\boxed{t_c \leq \frac{d_{min} - 1}{2}}$$ ... (4.14)

This can be well understood using pictorial view. We can consider the codewords to be placed in spheres separated from each other. The sphere are of radius t_c, where, t_c is number of errors that can be corrected. If t_c errors occur in code c_1/c_2, the new codeword will be within their spheres and remain nearer to the valid codeword. Hence, the minimum hamming distance has to be greater than $2t_c + 1$. If we consider the code C = {0 0 0, 1 1 1}, the codewords will be placed from other possible distortions as below on the vertices of a cube. If (0 0 0) is transmitted and (0 0 1) is received we find 0 0 1 is near to 0 0 0 than   (1 1 1). Hence, we can make the correction in favour of (0 0 0). But if (0 0 0) is transmitted and (0 1 1) is received we find (0 1 1) is nearer to (1 1 1) than (0 0 0), hence we cannot correct the two errors here. Thus, this code has error correcting capability of 1 error. This can be verified from the formula also. The code has d_{min} = 3.

$$\therefore \qquad t_c \leq \frac{d_{min} - 1}{2}$$

$$\leq \frac{3 - 1}{2}$$

$$\leq 1$$

Note that, if 0 1 1 is received when 0 0 0 was transmitted, decision will be made in favour of 1 1 1, even though it is incorrect. Here, we assume that probability of occurrence of 2 errors is far less than that of 1 error.

Example 4.5 : Find the error correcting capability of code generated in example 4.5.

Solution :

Code Word	Hamming Weight
0 0 0 0 0 0 0	0
0 0 0 1 1 0 1	3
0 0 1 0 1 1 1	4
0 0 1 1 0 1 0	4
0 1 0 0 0 1 1	3
0 1 0 1 1 1 0	4
0 1 1 0 1 0 0	3
0 1 1 1 0 0 1	4
1 0 0 0 1 1 0	3
1 0 0 1 0 1 1	4
1 0 1 0 0 0 1	3
1 0 1 1 1 0 0	4
1 1 0 0 1 0 1	4
1 1 0 1 0 0 0	3
1 1 1 0 0 1 0	4
1 1 1 1 1 1 1	7

Since minimum weight of the non-zero codewords is 3.

$$d_{min} = 3$$

∴   Error correcting capability

$$t_c \leq \frac{d_{min} - 1}{2}$$

$$t_c \leq \frac{3 - 1}{2}$$

$$t_c \leq 1$$

If the code is such that there is ambiguity in deciding closest codeword, then it is called incomplete decoder. A complete decoder can decode every received word even if there are not more than t_c errors. They will make a good guess about the codeword.

There will be limit on maximum distance, on the code which will be,

$$d_{max} \leq n - k + 1 \qquad \qquad \text{... (4.15)}$$

where, k is number of message bits.

n is number of code bits.

This is called Singleton Bound.

Syndrome Decoding

Minimum hamming distance d_{min} of a code decides error correcting capability of a code. Now, let us see how these errors can be corrected.

The generator matrix (G) is used at the transmitter to generate the code corresponding to message. The parity check matrix can be used to decode the received codeword.

- Let r be the received code vector.

- This code vector may or may not differ from transmitted code vector C.

- Let there be another vector e which will be called error vector defining the corresponding error pattern.

  Hence, $r = C \oplus e$ ... (4.16)

If there is no error, e will be having all zero symbols. If there are some errors, then there will be that many number of 1's in the corresponding location.

  i.e. $e_i = \begin{cases} 1 & \text{If an error has occurred in the } i^{th} \text{ location} \\ 0 & \text{Otherwise} \end{cases}$ ... (4.17)

The received code vector is multiplied with H^T to get syndrome vector. As we see if received codeword is same as transmitted codeword, this multiplication will result into 0 as $CH^T = 0$.

Since the received code vector is $1 \times n$ and H^T is of the order $n \times n - k$.

The syndrome vector will have $n - k$ bits.

  Thus, $S = r H^T$ ... (4.18)

  If $r = C$, S will have all 0 vector.

  If $r \neq C$ $S = r H^T$

                $= (C \oplus e) H^T$

                $= C \cdot H^T \oplus e H^T$

                $= e H^T$ ... (4.19)

  Thus, the syndrome depends on error pattern e.

Another property of the syndrome is that all error patterns that differ by a codeword have the same syndrome. Let us look into this.

  Let there be k message bits.

  Hence, there will be 2^k codewords $C_1, C_2, C_3, \ldots C_{2^k}$.

  Let there be some error pattern e which will also have 2^{k-1} distinct vectors $e_1, e_2, \ldots e_{2^k}$.

  $\therefore$ $e_i = e \oplus C_i$ ... (4.20)

  Set of vectors $\{e_1, e_2, e_3, \ldots e_{2^k}\}$ is called coset of the code. There will be 2^{n-k} possible cosets of an (n, k) block code.

Now, $e_i \cdot H^T = (e \oplus C_i) H^T$

$$= e H^T \oplus C_i H^T$$

$$= e H^T = S \qquad\qquad\qquad ... (4.21)$$

Thus, each coset of the code is characterised by unique syndrome.

The vector having minimum weight in the coset is called coset leader.

A standard array is constructed using these coset leaders.

In the first row all valid codewords are written starting with all-zero codewords.

In the second row we write vector e_2 which is not in first row as coset leader and then write the cosets $e_2 + c$ below each valid code vector. We continue this till all the cosets are listed.

e.g. $C = \{0\,0\,0, 1\,1\,1\}$

Standard Array :

Syndrome	Coset Leaders	n-tupes
0 0	0 0 0	1 1 1
1 1	1 0 0	0 1 1
1 0	0 1 0	1 0 1
0 1	0 0 1	1 1 0

The 0 0 / 1 1 1 row is marked ← Code vectors. The lower three rows are bracketed as Single errors.

The decoding procedure for a linear block code will be as below.

*   Compute $S = r H^T$, where, r is received code.

*   Identify the error pattern i.e. coset leader corresponding to the syndrome. Let it be e.

*   Compute code vector.

$$C = r \oplus e$$

Example 4.6 : Decoding procedure for (7, 4) block code whose generator matrix is given in example 4.4.

$$G = \begin{bmatrix} 1 & 0 & 0 & 0 & 1 & 1 & 0 \\ 0 & 1 & 0 & 0 & 0 & 1 & 1 \\ 0 & 0 & 1 & 0 & 1 & 1 & 1 \\ 0 & 0 & 0 & 1 & 1 & 0 & 1 \end{bmatrix}$$

Also find the corrected codewords for following received words.

(i) 1 0 0 0 1 1 0   (ii) 0 1 0 1 0 1 1   (iii) 0 0 0 1 1 0 0

Solution :

Step I :

The given code has error correcting capability of 1. Hence, there will be $2^{n-k} = 2^3 = 8$ single error patterns.

Step II :

The parity check matrix is given by,

$$H = [P^T \ I_{n-k}]$$

$$= \begin{bmatrix} 1 & 0 & 1 & 1 & 1 & 0 & 0 \\ 1 & 1 & 1 & 0 & 0 & 1 & 0 \\ 0 & 1 & 1 & 1 & 0 & 0 & 1 \end{bmatrix}$$

$$\therefore \qquad H^T = \begin{bmatrix} 1 & 1 & 0 \\ 0 & 1 & 1 \\ 1 & 1 & 1 \\ 1 & 0 & 1 \\ 1 & 0 & 0 \\ 0 & 1 & 0 \\ 0 & 0 & 1 \end{bmatrix}$$

Step III :

We find syndrome vectors corresponding to each error pattern using,

$$S = e \, H^T$$

e.g. for error pattern 0 0 0 0 0 0 1 the syndrome will be,

$$S = [0 0 0 0 0 0 1] \begin{bmatrix} 1 & 1 & 0 \\ 0 & 1 & 1 \\ 1 & 1 & 1 \\ 1 & 0 & 1 \\ 1 & 0 & 0 \\ 0 & 1 & 0 \\ 0 & 0 & 1 \end{bmatrix}$$

$$= [0\ 0\ 1]$$

Following table gives all syndrome with their error patterns.

Error Pattern	Syndrome
0 0 0 0 0 0 0	0 0 0
1 0 0 0 0 0 0	1 1 0
0 1 0 0 0 0 0	0 1 1
0 0 1 0 0 0 0	1 1 1
0 0 0 1 0 0 0	1 0 1
0 0 0 0 1 0 0	1 0 0
0 0 0 0 0 1 0	0 1 0
0 0 0 0 0 0 1	0 0 1

Note : If you observe above syndrome they are nothing but matrix H^T itself.

Thus, if there is single error in i^{th} bit, the syndrome will be i^{th} row of H^T.

Step IV :

Once above table is ready we can now correct the errors in the received codewords.

(i) $r = [1\,0\,0\,0\,1\,1\,0]$

$\therefore$ $S = r\,H^T$

                        $= [0\;0\;0]$

Hence, there is no error.

$\therefore$ Corrected codeword

                        $C = r$

(ii) $r = [0\,1\,0\,1\,0\,1\,1]$

                        $S = r\,H^T$

                        $= [1\;0\;1]$

Corresponding error pattern from above table,

                        $e = 0\,0\,0\,1\,0\,0\,0$ [Error in 4th bit]

$\therefore$ Corrected codeword

                        $C = r \oplus e$

                        $= [0\,1\,0\,1\,0\,1\,1] \oplus [0\,0\,0\,1\,0\,0\,0]$

                        $= [0\,1\,0\,0\,0\,1\,1]$

(iii) $r = [0\,0\,0\,1\,1\,0\,0]$

                        $S = r\,H^T$

                        $= [0\;0\;1]$

∴ Error pattern is,

$$e = [0\,0\,0\,0\,0\,0\,1]$$

∴ Corrected codeword

$$C = r \oplus e$$
$$= [0\,0\,0\,1\,1\,0\,0] + [0\,0\,0\,0\,0\,0\,1]$$
$$= [0\,0\,0\,1\,1\,0\,1]$$

4.5 CYCLIC CODES

Cyclic codes are subclass of linear block codes. Generator matrix is used for generating linear block codes. Hence, for higher order codes we have to use large memory requirements and circuit becomes complex. Cyclic codes are linear block codes with an additional constraint. Cyclic codes are very easy to encode. Cyclic codes possess a well defined mathematical structure which makes them efficient in decoding.

Thus, cyclic codes are simple for implementation which is an important feature of cyclic code.

A binary code is said to be cyclic if it satisfies following two fundamental properties.

*   **Linearity :** The sum of any two codewords in a cyclic code is also a valid codeword.

*   **Cyclic Property :** A cyclic shift of bits in a codeword gives rise to another valid codeword.

    As per the cyclic property if $(c_1, c_2, c_3, \dots c_n)$ is a codeword, then,

$$(c_2, c_3, \dots c_n, c_1)$$
$$(c_3\ c_4, \dots c_n, c_1, c_2)$$
$$\vdots$$
$$\vdots$$
$$(c_n, c_1, c_2, \dots c_{n-2}, c_{n-1})$$

are all codewords in that code.

Example 4.7 :   C = {0 0 0 0, 0 1 0 1, 1 0 1 0, 1 1 1 1} is a cyclic code.

As this code satisfies both linearity property and cyclic property.

Example 4.8 : C = {0 0 0, 0 1 0, 0 0 1, 1 0 0, 1 1 1} is not cyclic code. It satisfies cyclic property but does not satisfy linearity property.

Polynomials

Cyclic code can be represented in polynomial form. e.g. given a codeword of code C,

$$c_1, c_2, c_3, \dots c_n$$

We can write it as,

$$c(x) = c_1 x^{n-1} + c_2 x^{n-2} + c_3 x^{n-3} + \ldots + c_{n-1} x + c_n \qquad \ldots (4.22)$$

In general, if $a_1, a_2, a_3, \ldots a_n$ are elements of GF(q) then a polynomial of these sequence of elements is expressed as,

$$p(x) = a_1 x^{n-1} + a_2 x^{n-2} + a_3 x^{n-3} + \ldots + a_{n-1} x + a_n \qquad \ldots (4.23)$$

➤ If q = 2, coefficients $a_1, a_2, \ldots$ will be 1 or 0.

➤ a_1 is called leading coefficient.

➤ n − 1 is called degree of polynomial.

➤ If a_1 is unity, it is called monic polynomial.

➤ Let p[x] represent a set of polynomials in x with coefficients in GF(q). It is called a ring e.g. c[x] will be a set of polynomials of all valid codewords.

These polynomials satisfy first seven of eight properties that define a field.

e.g. addition or multiplication of two polynomials will result into coefficients in GF(q) only.

Consider 2 polynomials.

$$a(x) = x + 1$$
$$b(x) = x^3 + x + 1 \text{ defined over GF(2)}$$

Then,

$$
\begin{aligned}
a(x) + b(x) &= (x \oplus 1) \oplus (x^3 \oplus x \oplus 1) \\
&= x^3 \oplus [x \oplus x] \oplus [1 \oplus 1] \\
&= x^3 \oplus [1 \oplus 1] x \oplus [1 \oplus 1] \\
&= x^3 + 0x + 0 \\
&= x^3
\end{aligned}
$$

$$
\begin{aligned}
a(x) \cdot b(x) &= (x^3 \oplus x \oplus 1) \cdot (x \oplus 1) \\
&= x^3 \cdot x \oplus x^3 \cdot 1 \oplus x \cdot x \oplus x \cdot 1 \oplus 1 \cdot x \oplus 1 \cdot 1 \\
&= x^4 \oplus x^3 \oplus x^2 \oplus x \oplus x \oplus 1 \\
&= x^4 \oplus x^3 \oplus x^2 \oplus (1 \oplus 1) x \oplus 1 \\
&= x^4 \oplus x^3 \oplus x^2 + x + 1 \\
&= x^4 + x^3 + x^2 + 1
\end{aligned}
$$

(A) Division Algorithm for Polynomials :

Consider two polynomials a(x) and b(x).

If divide a(x) by b(x) [b(x) ≠ 0)]

we can write,

$$a(x) = q(x) b(x) + r(x) \qquad \qquad ... (4.24)$$

where, $q(x)$ is quotient.

r(x) is remainder or residue whose degree will be less than $b(x)$.

e.g.   Let $a(x) = x^4 + x^2 + 1$

$$b(x) = x + 1$$

$$x^3 + x^2 \leftarrow q(x)$$

$$x + 1 \quad \overline{\smash{)}\; x^4 + x^2 + 1}$$

$$x^4 + x^3$$

$$x^3 + x^2 + 1$$

$$x^3 + x^2$$

$$1 \leftarrow r(x)$$

Note that in GF(2), $1 - 1 = 0$ and $0 - 1 = -1 = 1$, $1 - 0 = 0$ and $0 - 0 = 0$ which is equivalent to modulo-2 addition. Hence, the subtraction is equivalent to modulo-2 addition.

$$\therefore \qquad (x^4 + x^2 + 1) = (x^3 + x^2) \cdot (x + 1) \quad + \quad 1$$

$$\qquad \qquad \downarrow \qquad \qquad \downarrow \qquad \quad \downarrow \qquad \qquad \downarrow$$

$$\qquad \qquad a(x) \qquad \quad q(x) \qquad b(x) \qquad \quad r(x)$$

A polynomial $p(x)$ in $p[x]$ is said to be reducible if $p(x) = a(x) \cdot b(x)$, where $a(x)$ and $b(x)$ are elements of $p[x]$ and degree of $a(x)$ and $b(x)$ are smaller than degree of $p(x)$.

A monic polynomial is a polynomial whose leading coefficient is one.

A monic polynomial which is irreducible and has a degree atleast one is called prime polynomial. Some examples of prime polynomials are x, $x + 1$, $x^2 + 1$, $x^2 + x + 1$, $x^3 + x^2 + 1$, $x^3 + x + 1$, etc.

(B) Representation of Cyclic Codes using Polynomials :

We have seen that a codeword can be represented using polynomial as,

$$c(x) = c_1 x^{n-1} + c_2 x^{n-2} + c_3 x^{n-3} + ... + c_{n-1} x + c_n$$

e.g. if you are given a code word C = (1 0 1 1 0), it will be written as,

$$C = (1 \qquad 0 \qquad 1 \qquad 1 \qquad 0)$$

$$\qquad \downarrow \quad \downarrow \quad \downarrow \quad \downarrow \quad \downarrow$$

$$c(x) = 1 \cdot x^4 + 0 \cdot x^3 + 1 \cdot x^2 + 1 \cdot x + 0 \cdot x$$

$$\therefore \qquad c(x) = x^4 + x^2 + x$$

We have seen that cyclic code satisfies cyclic property. We can verify that if $c(x)$ is a code polynomial corresponding to a codeword then the remainder after dividing $x^i\, c(x)$ by $x^n + 1$ also represents a valid codeword.

e.g. $\quad\quad x^i \cdot c(x) = c_1 x^n + c_2 x^{n-1} + c_3^{n-2} + \ldots + c_{n-1} x^2 + c_n x$ $\quad\quad$ ... (4.25)

Divide $x^i\, c(x)$ by $x^n + 1$ and find remainder.

c_1

$$x^n + 1 \quad\quad c_1 x^n + c_2 x^{n-1} + c_3 x^{n-2} + \ldots + c_{n-1} x^2 + c_n x$$

$$c_1 x^n + c_1$$

Remainder $\Rightarrow\ c_2 x^{n-1} + c_3 x^{n-2} + \ldots + c_{n-1} x^2 + c_n x + c_1$

The remainder represents the codeword

$$c_1 = (c_2, c_3, \ldots c_{n-1}, c_n, c_1) \quad\quad\quad\quad \text{... (4.26)}$$

which is a cyclic shifted version of orginal code word C. Similarly, you can verify that remainder after divisor of $x^2 c(x)$ and $x^n + 1$ will give rise to another cyclic shifted codeword.

In general,

$$\mathrm{Rem}\left[\frac{x^i \cdot c(x)}{x^n + 1}\right] = c_{i+1}\, x^{n-1} + c_{i+2}\, x^{n-2} + \ldots + c_n\, x^i + c_1\, x^{i-1} + \ldots c_i \quad\quad \text{... (4.27)}$$

It is denoted as $c^i(x)$.

i.e. $\quad\quad\quad c^{(i)}(x) = x^i\, c(x) \bmod (x^n + 1)$ $\quad\quad\quad\quad$ ... (4.28)

[Mod is a remainder after division operation].

A Method for Generating Cyclic Code

Theorem :

Cyclic code polynomial $c(x)$ can be generated using data polynomial $d(x)$ of degree $k - 1$ and a generator polynomial $g(x)$ of degree $n - k$ as,

$$c(x) = d(x) \cdot g(x) \quad\quad\quad\quad \text{... (4.29)}$$

where, $g(x)$ is $(n - k)^{th}$ order factor of $x^n + 1$.

Proof :

Let $d(x)$ represent data polynomial of k message bits $d_1, d_2, d_3, \ldots d_k$ as,

$$d(x) = d_1 x^{k-1} + d_2 x^{k-2} + d_3 x^{k-3} + \ldots + d_{k-1} x + d_k \quad\quad \text{... (4.30)}$$

Now, consider the polynomial.

$$c(x) = d(x) \cdot g(x)$$

$\therefore\quad\quad\quad c(x) \quad = \quad d_1 x^{k-1} g(x) + d_2 x^{k-2} g(x) + \ldots + d_k\, g(x) \quad\quad \text{... (4.31)}$

Since g(x) is $(n-k)^{th}$ order polynomial, c(x) will be of degree n − 1 or less. i.e. degree of c(x) will be atmost n − 1.

Now, we have to prove that this code is cyclic.

Let,

$$c(x) = c_1 x^{n-1} + c_2 x^{n-2} + ... + c_n$$

$$x\, c(x) = c_1 x^n + c_2 x^{n-1} + ... + c_n x$$

$$= (c_1 x^n + c_1) + (c_2 x^{n-1} + c_3 x^{n-2} + ... + c_n x + c_1) \qquad ... (4.32)$$

Adding $c_1 \oplus c_2$,

$$= c_1(x^n + 1) + (c_2 x^{n-1} + c_3 x^{n-2} + ... + c_n x + c_1)$$

$$= c_1(x^n + 1) + c^{(1)}(x) \qquad ... (4.33)$$

But, $x\, c(x) = x \cdot d(x)\, g(x)$ $\qquad\qquad\qquad\qquad$ ... (4.34)

Thus, from equations (4.33) and (4.34), we get,

$$x\, c(x) \cdot g(x) = c_1 (x^n + 1) + c^{(1)}(x) \qquad ... (4.35)$$

But g(x) is a factor of $(x^n + 1)$ and if equation (4.35) has to hold good, $c^{(1)}(x)$ also has to be multiple of $(x^n + 1)$. But $c^{(1)}(x)$ is a cyclic shifted version of c(x). Hence, the code c(x) generated by multiplying d(x) and g(x) is cyclic.

Example 4.9 : Find generator polynomial g(x) for a (7, 4) cyclic code and final codewords for following data words.

(i)   1 1 0 0

(ii) 1 0 1 0

(iii) 0 1 1 1

Solution :

Given :   n = 7

k = 4

The generator polynomial should be of the degree n − k = 3.

The generator polynomial should be factor of $x^7 + 1$.

$$(x^7 + 1) = (x + 1)(x^6 + x^5 + x^4 + x^3 + x^2 + x + 1)$$

$$= (x + 1)(x^6 + x^5 + x^4 + x^3 + x^3 + x^3 + x^2 + x + 1)$$

$$= (x + 1)(x^6 + x^4 + x^3 + x^5 + x^3 + x^2 + x^3 + x + 1)$$

$$= (x + 1)[x^3(x^3 + x + 1) + x^2(x^3 + x + 1) + 1(x^3 + x + 1)]$$

$$= (x + 1)(x^3 + x^2 + 1)(x^3 + x + 1)$$

We have two polynomials of order 3, one of which can be selected as generator polynomial.

Let $g(x) = x^3 + x^2 + 1$

Now, a code is generated using,

$$c(x) = d(x)\, g(x)$$

(i)   1 1 0 0

$$d(x) = x^3 + x^2$$

$\therefore$

$$c(x) = (x^3 + x^2)\,(x^3 + x^2 + 1)$$

$$= (x^6 + x^5 + x^3 + x^5 + x^4 + x^2)$$

$$= x^6 + x^4 + x^3 + x^2$$

$$= 1.x^6 + 0.x^5 + 1.x^4 + 1.x^3 + 1.x^2 + 0.x + 0.x$$

$\therefore$ $c = [1\ 0\ 1\ 1\ 1\ 0\ 0]$

(ii)   1 0 1 0

$$d(x) = x^3 + x$$

$$c(x) = (x^3 + x)\,(x^3 + x^2 + 1)$$

$$= x^6 + x^5 + x^3 + x^4 + x^3 + x$$

$$= x^6 + x^5 + x^4 + x$$

$$= 1.x^6 + 1.x^5 + 1.x^4 + 0.x^3 + 0.x^2 + 1.x + 0$$

$\therefore$ $c = [1\ 1\ 1\ 0\ 0\ 1\ 0]$

(iii) 0 0 1 1

$$d(x) = x + 1$$

$\therefore$ $c(x) = (x + 1)\,(x^3 + x^2 + 1)$

$$= x^4 + x^3 + x + x^3 + x^2 + 1$$

$$= x^4 + x^2 + x + 1$$

$$= 0.x^6 + 0.x^5 + 1.x^4 + 0.x^3 + 1.x^2 + 1.x + 1$$

$\therefore$ $c = [0\ 0\ 1\ 0\ 1\ 1\ 1]$

It can be observed from above example that the code generated is non-systematic code as message bits and parity bits are not in separate blocks.

Example 4.10 : Find generator polynomial for a (7, 3) cyclic code.

Solution :

Given : $n = 7$

                           $k = 3$

$\therefore$ The order of generator polynomial will be,

$$n - k = 4$$

$g(x)$ will factor of $x^7 + 1$.

$$
\begin{aligned}
x^7 + 1 &= (x + 1)(x^6 + x^5 + x^4 + x^3 + x^2 + 1) \\
&= (x + 1)(x^6 + x^5 + x^4 + x^3 + x^3 + x^3 + x^2 + 1) \\
&= (x + 1)[x^3(x^3 + x + 1) + x^2(x^3 + x + 1) + 1(x^3 + x + 1)] \\
&= (x + 1)(x^3 + x^2 + 1)(x^3 + x + 1) \\
&= (x^4 + x^3 + x + x^3 + x^2 + 1)(x^3 + x + 1) \\
&= (x^4 + x^2 + x + 1)(x^3 + x + 1)
\end{aligned}
$$

∴   Generator polynomial of order 4 is,

$$g(x) = x^4 + x^2 + x + 1$$

(A) Systematic Cyclic Code :

In order to encode message sequence into systematic form, it is necessary to have message bits and parity bits in separate block in the codeword.

Consider a message polynomial.

$$d(x) = d_1 x^{k-1} + d_2 x^{k-2} + \ldots + d_k \qquad \ldots (4.36)$$

Multiply above polynomial by x^{n-k}.

where, n = Number of code bits

                k = Number of message bits

∴ $x^{n-k} d(x) = d_1 x^{n-1} + d_2 x^{n-2} + \ldots + d_k x^{n-k} \qquad \ldots (4.37)$

Dividing equation (4.37) by $g(x)$, we get,

$$\frac{x^{n-k} d(x)}{g(x)} = q(x) + \frac{p(x)}{g(x)} \qquad \ldots (4.38)$$

or

$$x^{n-k} d(x) = q(x) \cdot g(x) + p(x) \qquad \ldots (4.39)$$

Adding $p(x)$ on both sides of equation (4.39), we get,

$$x^{n-k} d(x) + p(x) = q(x) \cdot g(x) \qquad \ldots (4.40)$$

$$\downarrow \qquad\qquad \downarrow \qquad\qquad \downarrow$$

Message bits   Remainder   Code
shifted by n – k   (k – 1) bits

where, $q(x)$ will be quotient after division whose order will be $k - 1$ or less, $p(x)$ is remainder after division of the order $n - k - 1$.

Since $q(x)$ is of order $k - 1$ or less and $g(x)$ of order $n - k$, $q(x) \cdot g(x)$ will be code polynomial.

$x^{n-k} d(x)$ represents $d(x)$ shifted by $n - k$ digits or the left side and since $p(x)$ is of the order $k - 1$, it represents parity bits.

Thus, procedure for generating systematic cyclic code is as below.

- Write $d(x)$ for given message bits.
- Find $x^{n-k} \cdot d(x)$.
- Divide $x^{n-k} d(x)$ by $g(x)$ and find remainder $p(x)$.
- Find $c(x) = x^{n-k} d(x) + p(x)$.
- Write codeword corresponding to $c(x)$.

Example 4.11 : Construct a systematic (7, 4) cyclic code using generator polynomial $g(x) = x^3 + x^2 + 1$ for the messages.

   (i)   1 0 1 0

   (ii)   1 0 0 0

Solution :

Given : $g(x) = x^3 + x^2 + 1$

                 $n = 7, \ k = 4$

$\therefore$ $d(x) = x^3 + x$

$\therefore$ $x^{n-k} d(x) = x^3(x^3 + x)$

              $= x^6 + x^4$

$$x^3 + x^2 + 1$$
$$x^3 + x^2 + 1 \quad\quad x^6 + x^4$$
$$x^6 + x^5 + x^3$$
$$x^5 + x^4 + x^3$$
$$x^5 + x^4 + x^2$$
$$x^3 + x^2$$
$$x^3 + x^2 + 1$$
$$1 \leftarrow p(x)$$

$\therefore$ $c(x) = x^{n-k} d(x) + p(x)$

              $= x^3(x^3 + x) + 1$

              $= x^6 + x^4 + 1$

$\therefore$ $c = [1\ 0\ 1\ 0\ 0\ 0\ 1]$

(ii)　　　　　　　　　　$d = [1\ 0\ 0\ 0]$

　　　　　　　　　　$d(x) = x^3$

　　　　　　　$x^{n-k}\, d(x) = x^3 \cdot x^3$

　　　　　　　　　　　　　$= x^6$

　　　　　　　　　　$x^3 + x^2 + x$

　　　　　　　　　　$x^3 + x^2 + 1$　　　x^6

　　　　　　　　　　$x^6 + x^5 + x^3$

　　　　　　　　　　$x^5 + x^3$

　　　　　　　　　　$x^5 + x^4 + x^2$

　　　　　　　　　　$x^4 + x^3 + x^2$

　　　　　　　　　　$x^4 + x^3 + x$

　　　　　　　$x^2 + x \leftarrow p(x)$

∴　　　　　　　$c(x) = x^{n-k}\, d(x) + p(x)$

　　　　　　　　　　　$= x^3 \cdot x^3 + x^2 + x$

　　　　　　　　　　　$= x^6 + x^2 + x$

　　　　　　　　$c = [1\ 0\ 0\ 0\ 1\ 1\ 0]$

(B) Parity Check Polynomial :

For linear block code we have seen that there is a generator matrix (G) and a parity check matrix (H) pair used at transmitter and receiver respectively.

A cyclic code can be specified by its generator polynomial g(x). There can be another polynomial called parity check polynomial h(x) such that,

$[g(x) \cdot h(x)]\ \text{mod}\ [x^n + 1] = 0$　　　　　　　　　　　　... (4.41)

　　or　　　　$g(x) \cdot h(x) = x^n + 1$　　　　　　　　　　　　... (4.42)

　　　　　　(Analogous to $GH^T = 0$)

The parity check polynomial is of the order k and is specified as,

$$h(x) = 1 + \left(\sum_{i=1}^{k-1} h_i\, x^i \right) + x^k \qquad \text{... (4.43)}$$

–Equation (4.21) shows that just like g(x), h(x) is also a factor of $x^n + 1$.

　　e.g. for (7, 4) cyclic code, let $g(x) = x^3 + x + 1$.

∴　　　　　$x^7 + 1 = (x + 1)\ (x^3 + x^2 + 1)\ (x^3 + x + 1)$

　　　　　　　　　$= (x^4 + x^2 + x + 1)\ (x^3 + x + 1)$

$$\therefore \qquad h(x) = x^4 + x^2 + x + 1$$

Decoding of Cyclic Code

The decoding process of cyclic code is same for both systematic and non-systematic cyclic codes.

Every valid codeword polynomial $c(x)$ is a multiple of $g(x)$. When this codeword is transmitted there may be some errors introduced, hence the received codeword polynomial $r(x)$ may not be same as $c(x)$.

If received codeword is same as transmitted codeword then $r(x) \bmod g(x) = 0$. Otherwise it will be non-zero polynomial. Consider $\dfrac{r(x)}{g(x)}$. It can be written as,

$$\frac{r(x)}{g(x)} = q(x) + \frac{s(x)}{g(x)} \qquad\qquad \text{... (4.44)}$$

where, $q(x)$ is quotient polynomial and $s(x)$ is remainder polynomial also called as syndrome polynomial.

Degree of $q(x)$ will be $k - 1$ and that of $s(x)$ will be $n - k - 1$.

$r(x)$ can be written in terms of $c(x)$ as,

$$r(x) = c(x) \oplus e(x) \qquad\qquad \text{... (4.45)}$$

where, $e(x)$ is an error polynomial decided by the bit error pattern in $r(x)$.

$$\therefore \qquad \frac{r(x)}{g(x)} = \frac{c(x) \oplus e(x)}{g(x)} \qquad\qquad \text{... (4.46)}$$

$$= \frac{c(x)}{g(x)} \oplus \frac{e(x)}{g(x)} \qquad\qquad \text{... (4.47)}$$

$$\therefore \text{Remainder}\left[\frac{r(x)}{g(x)}\right] = \text{Rem}\left[\frac{c(x)}{g(x)}\right] + \text{Rem}\left[\frac{c(x)}{g(x)}\right] \qquad\qquad \text{... (4.48)}$$

But Remainder after division of $c(x)$ and $g(x)$ will be zero.

$$\therefore \qquad \text{Rem}\left[\frac{r(x)}{g(x)}\right] = \text{Rem}\left[\frac{e(x)}{g(x)}\right] \qquad\qquad \text{... (4.49)}$$

Comparing equations (4.44) and (4.49), we can write,

$$s(x) = \text{Rem}\left[\frac{e(x)}{g(x)}\right] \qquad\qquad \text{... (4.50)}$$

Equation (4.50) shows that the syndrome polynomial of error polynomial $e(x)$ is same as received word polynomial.

Thus, the decoding process of a cyclic code will be as below.

If our aim is to only detect errors, then the received codeword polynomial is divided by g(x). If the remainder i.e. syndrome polynomial is zero, there will be no error and if it is non-zero then there will be error. If it is required to correct those errors, then the procedure will be,

- Prepare a table of error patterns and syndromes using relation (4.50).
- Find syndrome after diving received word polynomials r(x) and g(x).
- Select the error pattern corresponding to the syndrome.
- Add error pattern to the received codeword.

Example 4.12 : Design (3, 1) cyclic repetition code and its decoding method. Find corrected codewords for

  (i) 0 1 0

  (ii) 1 1 0

Solution :

Given : $n = 3$

$k = 1$

The generator polynomial g(x) order = $3 - 1 = 2$.

Generator polynomial should be factor of $x^3 + 1$.

Now, $(x^3 + 1) = (x + 1)(x^2 + x + 1)$

∴ $g(x) = x^2 + x + 1$

Since, $k = 1$, there will be two message words 0 and 1.

1. Coding :

(i) $d = [0]$

$$d(x) = 0$$

$$x^{n-k} d(x) = x^2 \cdot 0 = 0$$

∴ $$p(x) = 0$$

∴ $$c(x) = x^{n-k} d(x) + p(x)$$

$$= 0 + 0$$

$$= 0$$

∴ $$c = [0\ 0\ 0]$$

(ii) $d = [1]$

$$d(x) = 1$$

∴ $$x^{n-k} d(x) = x^2 \cdot 1$$

$$= x^2$$

To find p(x).

$$1$$

$$x^2 + x + 1 \qquad x^2$$

$$x^2 + x + 1$$

$$x + 1 \leftarrow p(x)$$

$$\therefore \qquad c(x) = x^{n-k} d(x) + p(x)$$

$$= x^2 + x + 1$$

$$\therefore \qquad c = [1\ 1\ 1]$$

Hence, codewords are

Message	Code
0	0 0 0
1	1 1 1

2. Decoding :

Since $d_{min} = 3$

Error correcting capability

$$t_c \leq \frac{d_{min} - 1}{2}$$

$$\leq \frac{3 - 1}{2}$$

$$\leq 1$$

$$error$$

The error patterns will be,

$$1\ 0\ 0$$

$$0\ 1\ 0$$

$$0\ 0\ 1$$

Find s(x) = e(x) mod g(x) for each error pattern.

(i)   For e = 1 0 0

$$e(x) = x^2$$

$$1$$

$$x^2 + x + 1 \qquad\qquad x^2$$

$$x^2 + x + 1$$

$$x + 1 \leftarrow s(x)$$

$$\therefore \qquad s = [1\ 1]$$

(ii) For e = 0 1 0

$$e(x) = x$$

$$0$$

$$x^2 + x + 1 \qquad\qquad x$$

$$0$$

$$x \leftarrow s(x)$$

$$\therefore \qquad s = [1\ 0]$$

(iii) For e = 0 0 1

$$e(x) = 1$$

$$0$$

$$x^2 + x + 1 \qquad 1$$

$$0$$

$$1$$

$$\therefore \qquad s = [0\ 1]$$

Hence, syndrome and error vector table will be as below.

Syndrome	Error Vector
1 0 0	1 1
0 1 0	1 0
0 0 1	0 1

Now, let us decode given received words.

(i) r = 0 1 0

$$\therefore \qquad r(x) = x$$

$$0$$

$$x^2 + x + 1 \qquad\qquad x$$

$$0$$

$$x \leftarrow s(x)$$

$$\therefore \qquad s = [1\ 0]$$

This syndrome corresponds to e = [0 1 0].

∴ Corrected codeword c = r ⊕ e

$$= [0\ 1\ 0] \oplus [0\ 1\ 0]$$
$$= [0\ 0\ 0]$$

(ii) $r = 1\ 1\ 0$

$\therefore$ $r(x) = x^2 + x$

$\qquad\qquad\qquad\qquad 1$

$\qquad\qquad x^2 + x + 1 \qquad\qquad\qquad x^2 + x$

$\qquad\qquad x^2 + x + 1$

$\qquad\qquad\quad 1 \leftarrow s(x)$

$\therefore$ $s = [0\ 1]$

This syndrome corresponds to e = $[0\ 0\ 1]$

$\therefore$ Corrected codeword c = r $\oplus$ e

$$= [1\ 1\ 0] \oplus [0\ 0\ 1]$$
$$= [1\ 1\ 1]$$

Error Detecting Codes

Error detection system consists of encoding procedure similar to error correcting codes but at the receiver end the errors are detected by using pattern checking. The system has a provision of feedback which tells the transmitter to retransmit a message in error.

The number of errors that can be detected $t_d = d_{min} - 1$, where d_{min} is minimum hamming distance of the code.

The parity check code discussed earlier is an example of error detecting codes. In case of even parity code, there are even number of 1's in the code. If the receiver detects odd number of 1's the received codeword is incorrect. This system will fail if there are even number of errors.

The effectiveness of an error detection code is measured by the probability that the system fails to detect an error. It depends on the properties of communication channel.

Following are some examples of error detecting codes.

1. **Parity Check Code :** A parity bit is added to the message such that number of 1's in the code becomes even in case of even parity and odd in case of odd parity. Errors can be detected by wanting number of 1's at the receiver end.

2. **Two-Dimensional Parity Code :** k information bits from m messages are arranged in m $\times$ k matrix form. Even parity of each row is calculated and stored in k+1th column and even parity of each of m columns is calculated and stored in m+1th row as shown in Fig. 4.8. If there are 3 or less errors anywhere in the matrix, error can be detected as

atleast one row will fail the parity check. But some patterns with 4 errors cannot be detected as shown in Fig. 4.7.

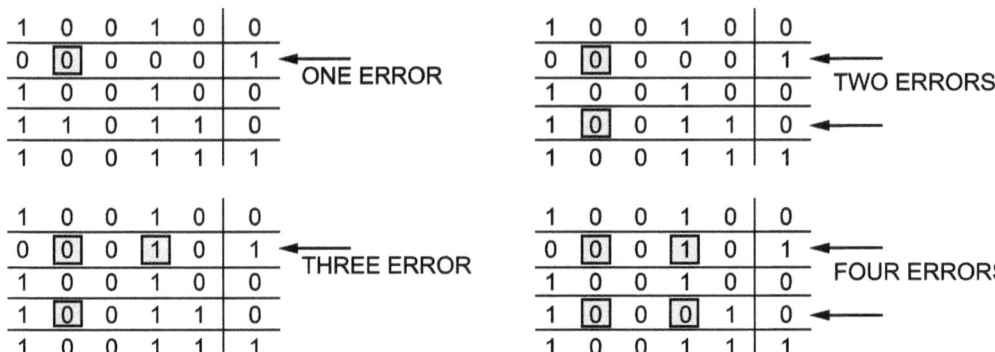

Fig. 4.7 : Two-dimensional parity code

3. Polynomial Codes :

- They are used both in error detection as well as error correction as discussed earlier.

- Polynomial codes are easy to implement using shift register.

- Cyclic Redundancy Check (CRC) codes are used to generate check bits for error detection.

- As seen earlier the message, codeword and error vectors are represented in terms of polynomials with binary coefficient.

- The codeword is generated using

$$c(x) = x^{n-k} d(x) + p(x)$$

where,

$$p(x) = \text{Rem}\left[\frac{x^{n-k} d(x)}{g(x)}\right]$$

- Detection involves finding syndrome

$$s(x) = \text{Rem}\left[\frac{r(x)}{g(x)}\right]$$

If remainder is zero, codeword is correctly received otherwise there will be error.

- Implementation of encoder and detector using shift register is already discussed.

Standardized Polynomial Codes

Three polynomials listed below are used as standard polynomials in many applications.

They are

$$CRC\text{-}12 – x^{12} + x^{11} + x^3 + x^2 + x + 1$$
$$CRC\text{-}16 – x^{16} + x^{15} + x^2 + 1$$
$$CRC\text{-}CCITT – x^{16} + x^{12} + x^5 + 1$$

Recently, CRC-8 and CRC-10 are also recommended for use in ATM networks. They are

$$CRC\text{-}8 – x^8 + x^2 + x + 1$$
$$CRC\text{-}10 – x^{10} + x^9 + x^5 + x^4 + x + 1$$

Following two polynomials are also in use.

$$CCITT\text{-}16 – x^{16} + x^{12} + x^5 + 1$$
$$CCITT\text{-}32 – x^{32} + x^{26} + x^{23} + x^{22} + x^{16} + x^{12} + x^{11} + x^{10} + x^8 + x^7 + x^5 + x^4 + x^2 + x + 1$$

Error Detecting Capability of Polynomial Codes

As seen earlier syndrome s(x) is calculated by dividing r(x) with g(x). The error pattern e(x) is given by

$$e(x) = r(x) \oplus d(x)$$
$$\therefore \quad r(x) = d(x) \oplus e(x)$$
$$\therefore \quad s(x) = \text{Rem}\left[\frac{r(x)}{g(x)}\right]$$
$$= \text{Rem}\left[\frac{d(x) + e(x)}{g(x)}\right]$$
$$= \text{Rem}\left[\frac{d(x)}{g(x)}\right] + \text{Rem}\left[\frac{e(x)}{g(x)}\right] = \text{Rem}\left[\frac{e(x)}{g(x)}\right]$$

Thus, we can formulate g(x) that will not divide the given error polynomials.

e.g.

1. **To Detect All Single Errors.**

$$e(x) = x^i \qquad\qquad 0 \le i \le n - 1$$

If g(x) has more than one term, it will not divide e(x).

2. **To Detect All Double Errors.**

$$e(x) = x^i + x^j \qquad\qquad 0 \le i \le j \le n - 1$$
$$= x^i (1 + x^{j-1})$$

As seen above, x^i is not divisible by g(x). Hence, we should ensure that $1 + x^{j-1}$ is also not divisible by g(x).

For this, g(x) should be a primitive polynomial. Primitive polynomials have the property that, if degree of primitive polynomials is N then smallest value of m for which $1 + x^m$ is divisible by the polynomial is $2^N - 1$. Since g(x) has degree n–k, it will detect all double errors if codeword has length less than or equal to $2^{n-k} - 1$.

The CRC-16 polynomial $x^{16} + x^{15} + x^2 + 1 = (x + 1) (x^{15} + x + 1)$ where, $x^{15} + x + 1$ is primitive. Hence, it can detect all double errors, if $n <= 2^{15} - 1 = 32767$.

3. To Detect all Odd Numbered Errors : If there are odd numbered errors, e(x) will have odd numbered terms. Such polynomial does not have x + 1 as a factor. Hence, by selecting (x + 1) as a factor, g(x) we can detect all odd numbered errors.

4. To Detect All Burst Errors : If a burst error of length L occurs starting from i^{th} bit position

$$e(x) = x^i b(x)$$

where, b(x) is of degree L–1 representing burst-error pattern. To detect this error, b(x) should not be divisible by g(x). For this, b(x) should have degree less than g(x)   i.e. n–k. Thus, we can detect a burst error of length less than or equal to n–k. We can also detect a burst error of length n–k+1, if error pattern does not match g(x). Even we can detect some of the burst errors of length L > n–k+1.

All the CRC polynomials contain (x + 1) as a factor. Hence they can detect all odd numbered errors, all single and double errors and all burst errors of length ≤ n – k.

4.6 CHECKSUM

- It is an error detection method used in many protocols of internet.

- It is based on the concept of redundancy.

- As the name indicates it is a method in which error is "checked" by taking "sum" of the information in bits/digits.

- For example, if we want to transmit the digits (5, 2, 8, 7) we will transmit the sum of these digits along with them as additional (redundancy) information i.e. we will transmit (5, 2, 8, 7, 22). Now, when this information is received at the receiver end we can "check" the sum of the first four digits. If it matches with 5th, the information is received correctly otherwise there will be error.

- We can have one more alternative which will make receiver's job simple. Transmit the negative of sum instead of sum so that if we add all received digits the sum will be 0.

- If you look at the information digits they will require only 4 bits for representation whereas the sum will require 5 bits and if negative sum is used we will require sign bit also. For this, we can use 1's complement arithmetic. Let us see how we can find the checksum using 1's complement arithmetic.

One's Complement Arithmetic :

In this method, a n bit number is represented in 1's complement form as below.

- If a number has more than n bits the extra leftmost bits are added to n right most bits.
- A negative number is represented by inverting all bits. e.g.

1. In 4 bit representation number, 22 will be represented in 1's complement arithmetic as below.

    NUMBER 22 is 10110

    The 5th bit which is extra is added to leftmost bit as below.

    $$0110$$
    $$+\quad 1$$
    $$0110$$

    which is 7.

    Hence, 22 is represented as 0111 or 7.

2. In 4 bit representation, the number −10 will be represented as below.

    Number 10 is 1010.

    The negative number is represented by inverting the bits.

    ∴ −10 is represented as 0101 or 5.

Another way to find the complement is subtract the number from $2^n - 1$.

In above case, 4 bit representation $2^n - 1 = 15$. Hence, −10 will be represented as 15 − 10 = 5.

Example 4.13 : Represent the following numbers using 1's complement arithmetics using 4 bits.

    (i) 36, (ii) −6, (iii) 42, (iv) −20.

Solution :

(i) 36

    Binary representation of 36 is

        100100

    More than 4 bits are added to leftmost bits

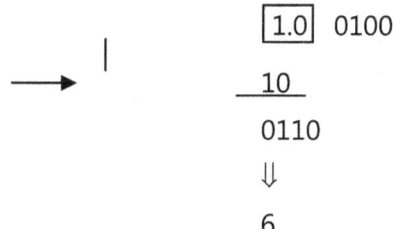

    $$\boxed{1.0}\quad 0100$$
    $$\underline{10\quad}$$
    $$0110$$
    $$\Downarrow$$
    $$6$$

(ii) −6

Binary representation of 6 is 0110.

Since negative number is represented by inverting bits.

0110

↓

1001

⇓

9

(iii) 42

Binary representation of 42 is 101010.

| 10 | 1010

⬜ 1 ─────→   10

1100

⇓

12

(iv) −20

Binary representation of 20 is 10100.

More than 4 bits. Hence wrap.

| 1 | 0100

⬜ 1 ─────→   1

0101

Invert the bits

1010

10

Now, let us find the checksum using one's complement arithmetic.

Let the transmitted digits be 5, 2, 8, 7.

The checksum will be (5 + 2 + 8 + 7) = −22.

−22 will be represented in one's complement arithmetic as below.

10110

└─→   1

0111

Inverting   1000

$\Downarrow$

8

Hence, transmitted pattern will be,

(5, 2, 8, 7, 8).

If received pattern is same and if we add

5 + 2 + 8 + 7 + 8 = 30

Now, 30 in one's complement form is as below :

30 in binary 11110

└──➤   wrap ____1

Inverting 0000

If the final result is 0, it means there is no error in the transmitted digits/numbers.

Internet Checksum :

Internet uses 16 bit checksum. The information to be transmitted i.e. message has to be represented in terms of numbers so that it can be converted into 16 bit words. The steps to be followed for computing checksum at transmitter and receiver are as below :

1. **Transmitter end :**

    •   Divide the message into 16 bit words.

    •   Initialize checksum to 0.

    •   Add words using one's complement arithmetic.

    •   Complement the sum.

2. **Receiver end :**

    •   Divide the received message (including checksum).

    •   Add words using one's complement arithmetic.

    •   Complement the sum.

    •   If result is 0, no error. Otherwise there is error.

Let us take an example. Suppose we want to find the checksum for the word "communication". This word has to be expressed in ASCII format. The ASCII values of a-z are 97 to 122 in decimal, in hex they are 61 to 7A.

ASCII value of c is   0x63

o is   0x6F

m is   0x6D

u is	0x75	
n is	0x6E	
t is	0x74	
i is	0x69	
a is	0x61	

Now we add these alongwith checksum as below :

$$
\begin{array}{llr}
 & 4\,2\,3 & \\
c \rightarrow & 0\,0\,6\,3 & \\
om \rightarrow & 6\,F\,6\,D & \\
mu \rightarrow & 6\,D\,7\,5 & \\
ni \rightarrow & 6\,E\,6\,9 & \\
ca \rightarrow & 6\,3\,6\,1 & \\
ti \rightarrow & 7\,4\,6\,9 & \\
on \rightarrow & 6\,F\,6\,E & \\
checksum \rightarrow & & \underline{2\,0\,0\,0\,0} \\
wrap & 9\,2\,D\,6 & \\
 & \underline{\qquad 2} & \\
 & 9\,2\,D\,8 & \\
Complement & & 6\,D\,2\,7 \\
\therefore\ \text{Checksum is} & 6\,D\,2\,7 & \\
\end{array}
$$

4.7 FRAMING

When the bits of information is received from physical layer, data link layer entity identifies beginning and end of block of information i.e. frames with the help of special pattern placed by the peer entity.

The frames may be fixed length or variable length. The requirements of framing methods will vary accordingly.

In case of fixed length frames, a frame consists of a single bit followed by a particular length sequence.

Variable length frames required additional information for frame identification.

For example,

- Special characters to identify beginning and end of frame.
- Starting and ending flags.

- Character counts.
- CRC Checking Methods (Checksum).

The first framing method uses ASCII characters DLE and STX at the start of each frame and DLE and ETX at the end of the frame. It is as shown in Fig. 4.8 (a), where DLE is Data Link Escape, STX is Start of Text and ETX is End of Text.

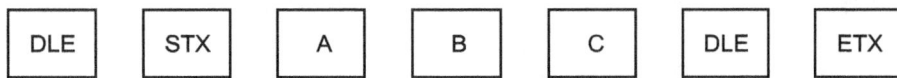

Fig. 4.8 (a) : Character Framing

But then this framing method has a problem. Consider the case where the data to be transmitted contains the character DLE STX in this case wrong identification of start of frame will be made. Similarly, if DLE ETX occur it will trigger end of frame. This problem can be solved by stuffing (adding) another DLE whenever DLE occurs in the data sequence. This technique is called **character stuffing**. The stuffed DLE can be destuffed (deleted) by receiving DLL entity. It is shown in Fig. 4.8 (b).

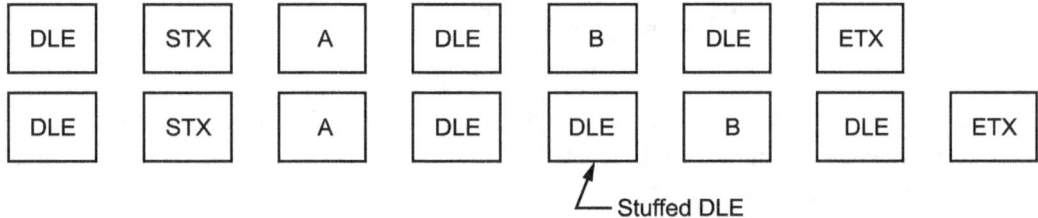

Fig. 4.8 (b) : Character Stuffing

This method is suitable only for data containing ASCII or printable characters and not for arbitrary sized characters.

The second technique which is also called as bit stuffing allows arbitrary number of bits per character. At the beginning and end of each frame a special bit pattern 01111110 called as flag is used. Here also there is a possibility that the flag bits may occur in the data. The technique used to avoid this problem is bit stuffing. Whenever there are five 1's in data sequence, 0 is stuffed and at the receiving end it is destuffed.

Bit stuffing is shown in Fig. 4.9.

ORIGINAL PATTERN : (Data)

11111111111011111101111110

AFTER BIT STUFFING :

11111 0 11111 0 110111110 1011111 010

Fig. 4.9 : Bit Stuffing

Five 1's followed by 11 will indicate an error.

If receiver looses synchronization all it has to do is scan for flag pattern.

The character count method employs count of number of characters in the frame to be placed at the beginning of each frame. The receiver will look into character count and extract those many character from the frame and hence it knows the end of frame also. Problem will come when the count is changed due to error in transmission. The synchronization will be completely lost. Even if we use checksum, there will be no way of identifying the start of next frame. Hence this method is not used much. It is shown in Fig. 4.10.

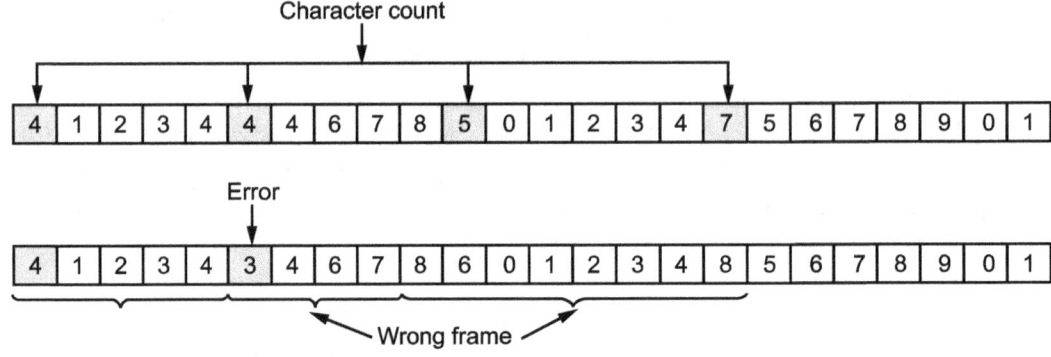

Fig. 4.10 : Character Count

In CRC based framing method, alongwith character count, CRC of count field is placed. Hence, the receiver examines four bytes at a time to see if CRC computed over first two bytes equals contents of next two bytes.

Many data link protocols use a combination of character count with other methods, for making it doubly sure that proper synchronization is achieved. For example, count of character is placed at the beginning of the frame and a flag is placed at the end of frame and may be checksum is also used. Count field is used to locate end of frame and only if appropriate flag is present at the end of frame and checksum is correct, the frame is accepted.

4.8 FLOW AND ERROR CONTROL

As pointed out earlier the two important functions of data link layer are flow control and error control.

Flow Control :

In a communication network the two communicating entities will have different speed of transmission and reception. There will be problem if sender is faster than receiver. The fast sender will swamp over the slow receiver. The "flow" of information between sender and receiver has to be "controlled". The technique used for this is called flow control technique. Also there will be time required to process incoming data at the receiver. This time required for processing is often more than the time for transmission. Incoming data must be checked and processed before they can be used. Hence, we require a buffer at the receiver to store the received data. This buffer is limited, therefore, before it becomes full the sender has to be informed to halt transmission temporarily. A set of procedures are required to be carried out to restrict the amount of data the sender can send before waiting for acknowledgement. This is called flow control.

Error Control :

When the data is transmitted it is going to be corrupted. We have seen how to tackle this problem by adding redundancy. Still the error is bound to occur. If such error occurs, the receiver can detect the errors and even correct them. What we can do is if error is detected by receiver, it can ask the sender to retransmit the data. This process is called Automatic Repeat Request (ARQ). Thus, error control is based on ARQ, which is retransmission of data.

Protocols :

The functions of data link layer viz. framing, error control and flow control are implemented in software. There are different protocols depending on the channel. For noiseless channel, there are two protocols : (i) Simplest, (ii) Stop-and-wait. For noisy channel, there are 3 protocols.

- Stop-and-wait ARQ
- Go-back-N ARQ
- Selective repeat ARQ.

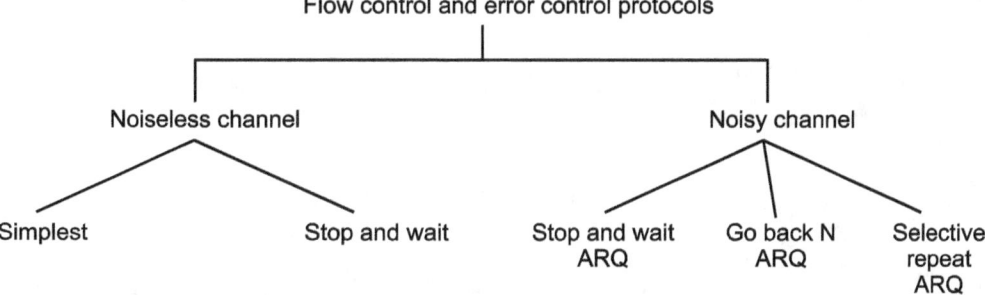

The protocols discussed here assume that the data flows only in one direction from sender to receiver. In practice, however, it is bidirectional. Hence, when the flow is bidirectional, we will be using piggybacking i.e. sending acknowledgement (positive/ negative) alongwith data if any to be sent to the other end.

4.9 NOISELESS CHANNELS

If the channel is noiseless it will not corrupt the data or there will be no loss of information during transmission. There are two protocols for noiseless channel.

- Simplest protocol which does not require flow control.
- Stop-and-wait protocol which requires flow control.

Simplest Protocol :

Since the channel is noiseless, no error is introduced, hence it does not require error control. The receiver can receive all the data transmitted to by the sender at any speed. Hence, there will be no flow control.

Transmitter station A transmits a frame to receiver B whenever the network layer hands over the packet to data link layer in transmitter A. Fig. 4.11 shows the same.

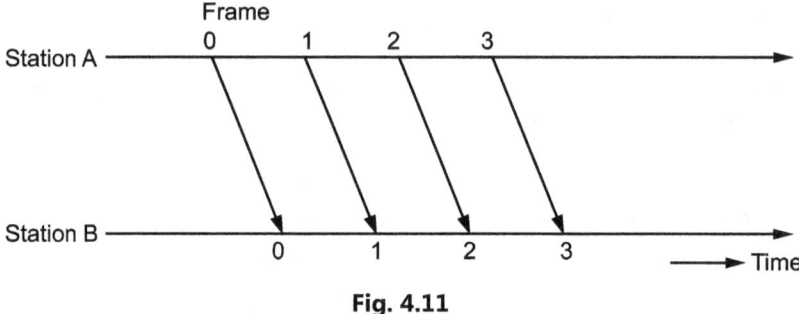

Fig. 4.11

The algorithms at transmitter and receiver will be as below :

Algorithm 4.1 : Transmitter site algorithm for Simplest Protocol

```
     start
1.  while(True)
2.  {
3.  wait_for_event( );
4.  if(Event(Request_to_send))
5.  {
6.     get_packet( )
7.     make_frame( );
8.     send_frame( );
9.  }
10. }
```

Explanation :

The algorithm runs continuously i.e. all the statements are repeated forever after the start. The tr-ansmitter DLL entity waits for the packet to be delivered by network layer, the wait_for_event( ) function does the same. If a packet comes it is accepted and DLL entity prepares frame by adding overheads (header tailer) to the packet. makeframe( ) function is used for this. The send_frame( ) function sends the frame and the DLL waits for a new packet.

Algorithm 4.2 : Receiver site algorithm for Simplest Protocol :

1. while(true)
2. {
3. wait_for_event( )
4.   if(Event (frame_arrival))
5.   {
6.   accept_frame( );
7.   extract_packet( );
8.   deliver_packet( );
9.   }
10. }

Explanation :

The algorithm runs continuously. The receiver DLL entity waits for the frame to be received from physical layer, the wait_for_event( ) function does this. When the frame arrives it is accepted. This accept_frame( ) function does this. The extract_packet( ) function extracts the packet by processing and removing overheads added by transmitter DLL entity. The deliver_packet( ) function hands over the packet to network layer. Then the receiver DLL entity waits for the new event to occur.

Stop_and_Wait Protocol :

When there is a situation in which the sender is sending data faster than the receiver can process and accept it, there will be loss of frames. We must have a feedback mechanism in this case from receiver to sender to tell the sender when to send the next frame. In case of noiseless channel, there is no error control. Hence, we have to feedback the acknowledgement whenever the frame is received as shown in Fig. 4.12.

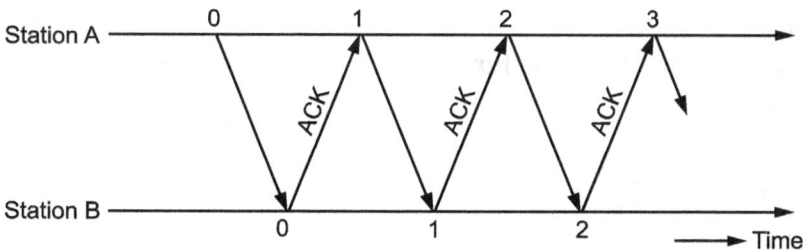

Fig. 4.12

The algorithms at transmitter and receiver will be as below :

Algorithm 4.3 : Transmitter site algorithm for stop_and_wait protocol

```
1.  ack=true
2.  while(true)
3.  {
4.      wait_for_event( );
5.      if(Event(Request_to_Send) && ack=true)
6.      {
7.        get_packet( );
8.        make_frame( );
9.        send_frame( );
10.       ack=false
11.     }
12.     wait_for_event( );
13.     if(event(ack_received))
14.     {
15.       get_ack( );
16.       ack=true;
17.     }
18. }
```

Explanation :

1. For first frame ack is set true.
2. Wait_for_event( ) waits for packet from network layer.
3. Whenever packet arrives and ack is true i.e. previous packet's acknowledgement is received get the packet, make frame and send it and wait for its acknowledgement by setting ack = false.
4. The second wait_for_event waits for acknowledgement whenever it arrives it is accepted and ack is made true.

Algorithm 4.4 : Receiver site algorithm for stop_and_wait protocol :

```
1.  while(true)
2.  {
3.      wait_for_event( );
4.      if(Event(frame_arrival))
5.      {
6.        accept_frame( );
```

```
7.      extract_packet( );
8.      deliver_packet( );
9.      send_ack( );
10.  }
11. }
```

Explanation :

1. The algorithm runs continuously.

2. Wait_for_event( ) waits for frame arrival from sender.

3. When frame arrives it is accepted, packet is extracted by processing the frame and the frame is delivered to network layer entity.

4. Acknowledgement is sent back.

4.10 NOISY CHANNELS

Noiseless channels are impossible practically. When the information is transmitted the channel is going to corrupt it and the receiver has to do error control. The three protocols that do error control are :

- Stop_and_wait ARQ.
- Go back_N ARQ.
- Selective Repeat (ARQ).

ARQ Protocols :

- Automatic repeat request is a combination of error detection and retransmission to ensure reliable data transmission.

- There are two basic types of ARQ protocols :
  - ➤ Simplex protocols.
  - ➤ Sliding window protocols.

- Simplex protocols use stop-and-wait ARQ and sliding window protocols use Go-back-N ARQ and selective repeat ARQ.

- As shown in Fig. 4.13, the data link layer transmits information frames containing header and CRC alongwith payload. The receiving DLL entity checks for errors using CRC. Accordingly, a control frame is sent back to transmitting entity which includes acknowledgement (positive/negative). If Positive Acknowledgement (ACK) is received, next frame can be transmitted. In case of Negative Acknowledgement (NAK), retransmission of previous frame (s) is made.

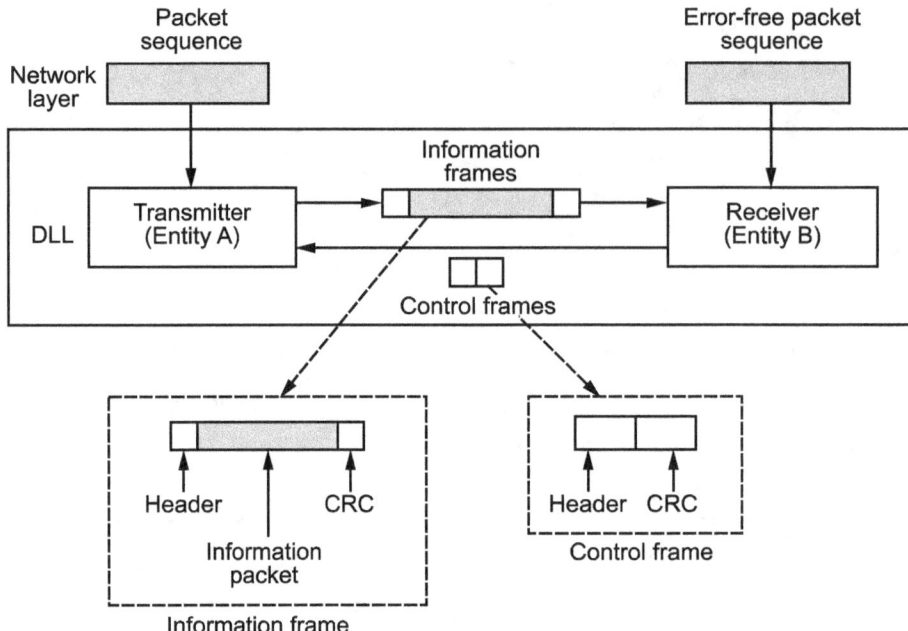

Fig. 4.13 : Frame Transmission in DLL

Stop and Wait ARQ (Simplex Protocol)

- In this technique, transmitter (A) transmits a frame to receiver (B) and waits for an acknowledgement from B.

- When acknowledgement from B is received, it transmits next frame.

- Now, consider a case where the frame is lost i.e. not received by B. B will not send an acknowledgement. A will wait and wait and wait ...... To avoid this, we can start a timer at A, corresponding to a frame. If the acknowledgement for a frame is not received within the time timer is on, we can retransmit the frame, as shown in Fig. 4.14 (a).

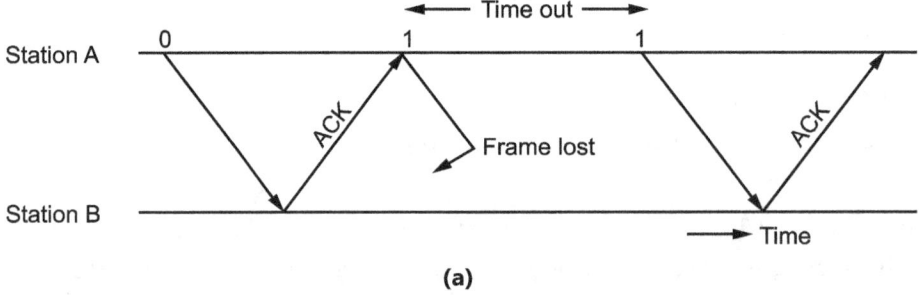

(a)

- Same thing can happen when frame is in error and B does not send acknowledgement. After A times out it will retransmit.

- There is another situation when some frame is transmitted but its acknowledgement is lost as shown in Fig. 4.14 (b).

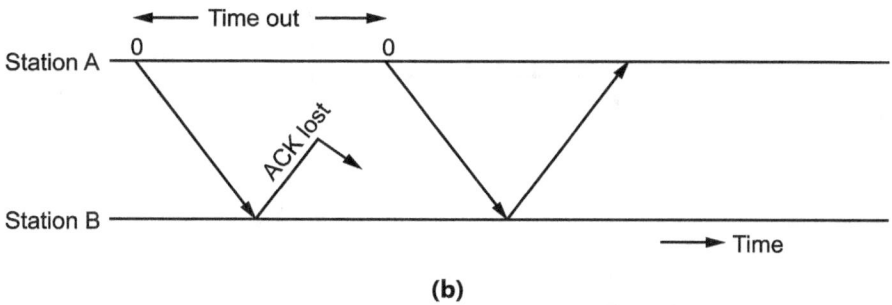

(b)

The time out will send the same frame again which will result into accepting duplicate frame at B. For this, we have to bring in the concept of sequence number to frames. In case a duplicate frame is received due to loss of Ack, it can be discarded.

• A second ambiguity will arise due to delayed acknowledgement as shown in Fig. 4.14 (c).

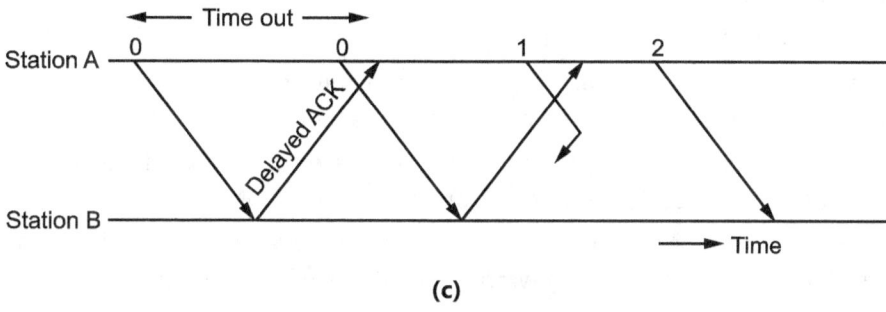

(c)

Fig. 4.14 : Stop_and_wait ARQ

As shown in figure, the acknowledgement received after frame 1 is transmitted would result into acknowledging frame 1 which is actually lost. We can give sequence number to acknowledgements so that transmitter knows the acknowledgement of which frame is received.

The acknowledgement number will be the number of next frame expected i.e. when frame 0 is received properly, we will be sending Acknowledgement number 1 as frame 1 is expected next.

Now, the next question is what should be the sequence numbers given to frame and acknowledgement. We cannot give large sequence numbers because they are going to occupy some space in frame header. Hence, sequence number should have minimum number of bits.

In stop_and_wait ARQ (simplex) protocol, one bit sequence number is sufficient. For this consider that frame 0 is transmitted and the receiver receives and sends acknowledgement number 1. Now, frame 1 is transmitted and sends acknowledgement for it since frame 0 is already received. We can use same number for next frame as shown in Fig. 4.15.

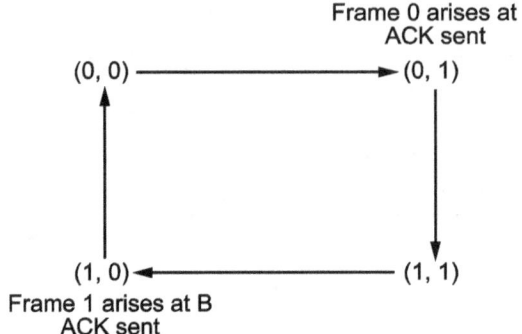

Fig. 4.15 : Sequence Number for Stop_and_Wait ARQ

This ARQ technique is used in IBM's Binary Synchronous Communication (BISYNC) protocol and XMODEM, a file transfer protocol for modems.

Sliding Window Protocol

- The stop_and_wait ARQ is inefficient.

- We can also use full-duplex transmission to transmit and receive from both sides called piggybacking i.e. we send information alongwith acknowledgement.

- The protocols known as sliding window protocols are robust in nature and perform well, inspite of garbled frames, lost frames or premature timeouts.

- In all sliding window protocols, each frame transmitted from transmitter has sequence numbers. They are part of sending window whose size is W_S (Number of frames).

- Each frame received at the receiver is kept in a buffer called receiving window. Its size is W_R (Number of frames).

- There are two sliding window protocols :
  - ➢ Go_Back_N ARQ.
  - ➢ Selective-Repeat ARQ.

Go-Back_N ARQ

- Unlike stop_and_wait ARQ, in this technique transmitter continues sending frames without waiting for acknowledgement.

- The transmitter keeps the frames which are transmitted in a buffer called sending window till its acknowledgement is received.

- Let the number of frames transmitter can keep in its buffer be W_S. It is called size of sender's window.

- The size of window is selected on the basis of delay-bandwidth product so that channel does not remain idle and efficiency is more.

- The transmitter keeps on transmitting the frames in window (buffer), till acknowledgement for the first frame in the window is received.

- When frames 0 to $W_S - 1$ are transmitted, the transmitter waits for acknowledgement of frame 0. When it is received the next frame is taken from network layer into the buffer i.e. window slides forward by one frame.

- If acknowledgement for an expected frame (i.e. first frame in the window) does not reach back and time-out occurs for the frame, all the frames in the buffer are transmitted again. Since there are $N = W_S$ frames waiting in the buffer, this technique is called Go_back_N ARQ.

- Thus, Go_back_N ARQ pipelines the processing of frames to keep the channel busy.

- Fig. 4.16 (a) shows Go_Back_N ARQ.

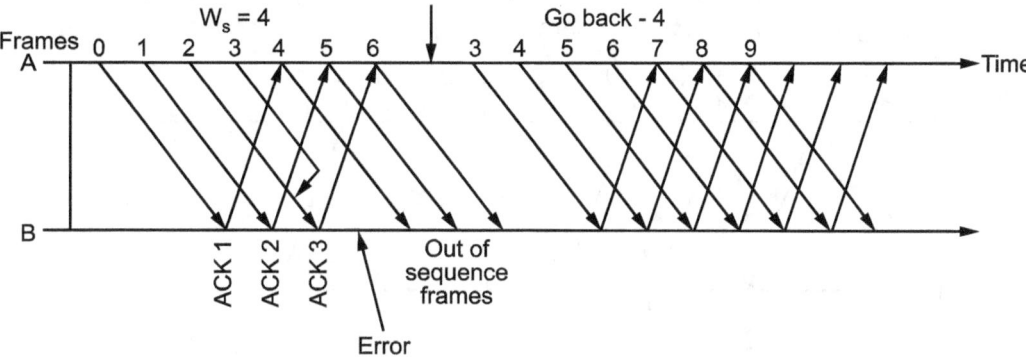

Fig. 4.16 (a)

- It can be seen that the receiver window size will be 1, since only one frame which is in order is accepted.

- Also, the expected frame number at the receiver end is always less than or equal to recently transmitted frame.

- What should be the maximum window size at the transmitter i.e. what should be value of W_S. It will depend on the number of bits used in sequence number field of the frame. So maximum window size at transmitter should be $W_S = 2^m$ i.e. if 3 bits are reserved for sequence number $W_S = 8$, but it will not ! For this consider following situation shown in Fig. 4.16 (b).

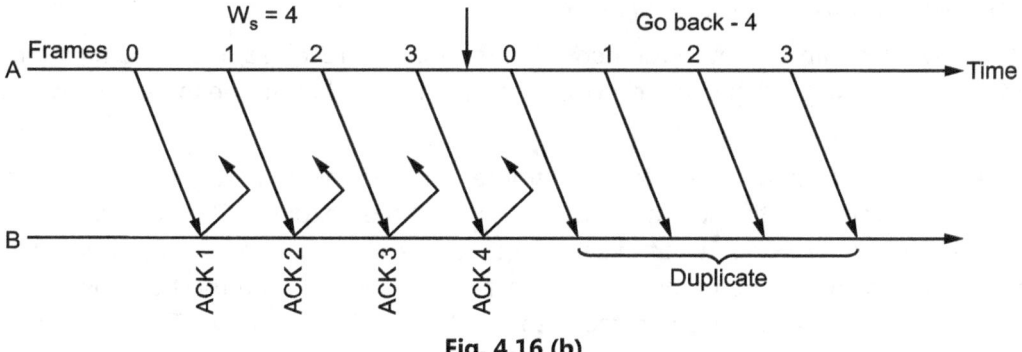

Fig. 4.16 (b)

i.e. if all the frames transmitted are acknowledged or their acknowledgement is lost. The transmitter will retransmit the frames in the buffer. The receiver will accept them as if they are new frames ! Hence, to avoid this problem, we reduce window size by 1 i.e. $W_S = 2^2 - 1 = 3$ i.e. make it Go_back_3. But the sequence number is maintained from 0 to 3. Now consider Fig. 4.16 (c), where the acknowledgements of all the received frames 0, 1, 2 are lost but the receiver is expecting frame 3. Hence, even if we transmit 0, 1, 2 again they will not be accepted as the expected sequence number does not match transmitted one. Hence, the window size should be $2^m - 1$ for Go_Back_N ARQ.

- Go_Back_N can be implemented for both ends i.e. we can send information and acknowledgement together which is called **piggybacking**. This improves the use of bandwidth. Fig. 4.16 (c) shows the scheme.

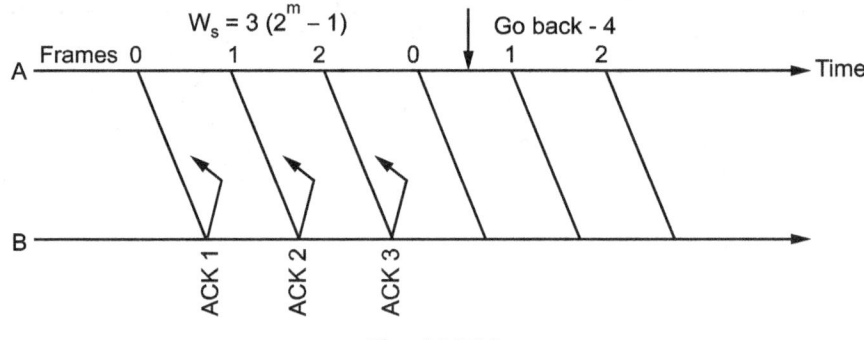

Fig. 4.16 (c)

Fig. 4.16 : Go_Back_N ARQ

Note that both transmitter and receiver need sending and receiving windows.

- Go_back_N ARQ is implemented in HDLC protocol and V-24 modem standard.

Selective Repeat ARQ

- Go_Back_N ARQ is inefficient when channels have high error rates.

- Instead of transmitting all the frames in buffer, we can transmit only the frame in error.

- For this, we have to increase the window size of receiver so that it can accept frames which are error free but out of order (not in sequence).

- Normally, when an acknowledgement for first frame is received, the transmit window is advanced. Similarly, whenever acknowledgement for the first frame in receiver window is sent it advances.

- Whenever there is error or loss of frame and no acknowledgement is sent, the transmitter retransmits the frame whenever its timer expires. The receiver whenever accepts next frame which is out of sequence now sends negative acknowledgement NAK corresponding to the frame number it is expecting. Till the time the frame is received it keeps on accumulating frames received in the receiver window. Then, it sends the acknowledgement of recently accepted frame that was in error. It is shown in Fig. 4.17 (a).

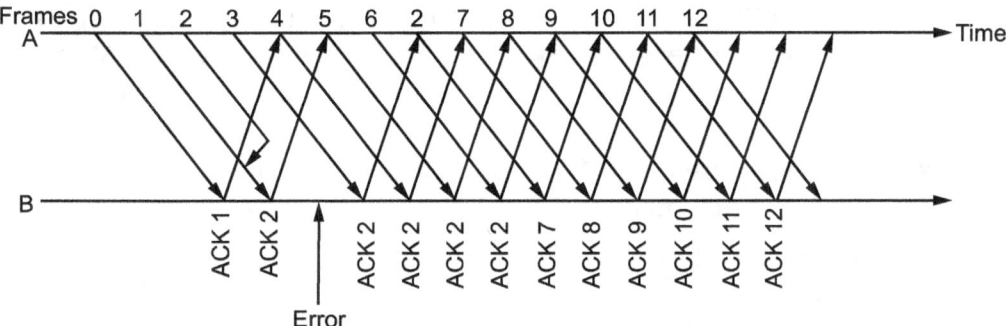

Fig. 4.17 (a)

To calculate the window size for given sequence numbering having m bits, consider the situation shown in Fig. 4.17 (b).

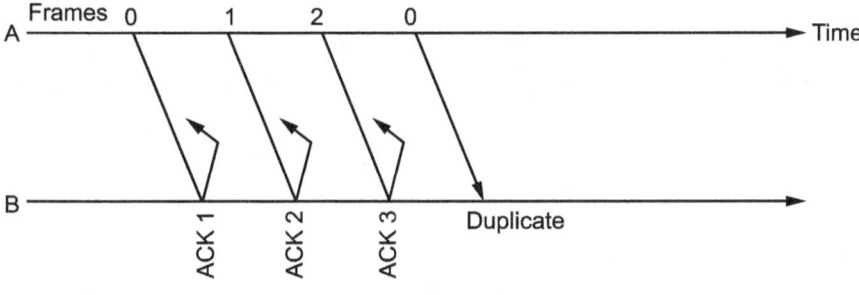

Fig. 4.17 (b)

Let us select window size for m = 2 as $W_S = 2^m - 1 = 3$. Let the frames 0, 1, 2 be in the buffer and are transmitted. They are received correctly but their acknowledgements are lost. Timer for frame 0 expires, hence is retransmitted. The receiver window is expecting frame 0 which it accepts as new frame but actually, it is duplicate !

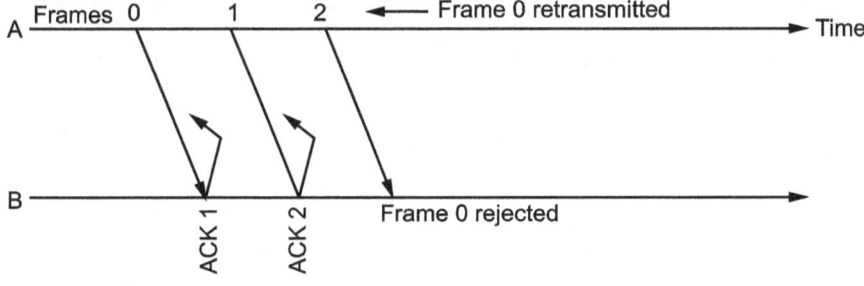

Fig. 4.17 (c)

Fig. 4.17 : Selective Repeat ARQ

Thus, the window size at transmitter and receiver are too large. Hence, we select $W_S = W_R = 2^m/2 = 2^{m-1}$. In above case, $W_S = W_R = 2^2/2 = 2$. Sequence numbers for frames will be 0, 1, 2, 3, as shown in Fig. 4.17 (c). The transmitter transmits frames 0, 1. But because of lost acknowledgements, timer for frame 0 expires. Hence, it retransmits frame 0. At the receiver we have expected frames {2, 3}. Hence, frame 0 is rejected as it is duplicate and not part of receiver window.

The selective repeat ARQ is used in TCP (Transmission Control Protocol) and SSCOP (Service Specific Connection Oriented Protocol).

Performance of ARQ Techniques

Stop_and_Wait ARQ

Let $T_F \rightarrow$ Frame time

$T_P \rightarrow$ Propagation Delay (One way)

∴ Total time taken to transmitting one frame

$$= T_F + 2T_P$$

(Neglecting acknowledgement time)

Efficiency or throughput is the ratio of time for one frame to the actual time taken to transmit the frame.

∴ $$\eta = \frac{T_F}{T_t} = \frac{T_F}{T_F + 2T_P}$$

Let R be the rate of transmission.

∴ Number of frame bits $= N_F = T_F \times R$

∴ $$\eta = \frac{\dfrac{N_F}{R}}{\dfrac{N_F}{R} + 2T_P}$$

If errors occur the frames are to be retransmitted. Let p be the error probability of frame. Let $\overline{N_r}$ be the average number of retransmissions required to transmit a frame successfully.

∴ $$\overline{N_r} = \sum_{i=1}^{\infty} i \times p \text{ (i transmissions)}$$

$$= \sum_{i=1}^{\infty} i \times p_f^{i-1} (1 - p_f)$$

$$= \frac{1}{1 - p_f}$$

∴   Efficiency of stop_and_wait ARQ,

$$\eta = \frac{T_F}{(T_F + 2T_P) \times \bar{N_r}}$$

$$= \frac{T_F}{(T_F + 2T_P)} \times \frac{1}{1 - p_f}$$

$$= \frac{T_F}{T_F + 2T_P} \times (1 - p_f)$$

Sliding Window Protocol

If there is no error, W_S frames are successfully transmitted in time $T_F + 2T_P$.

Hence, the efficiency or throughput is given by,

$$\eta = \frac{W_S \, T_F}{T_F + 2T_P}$$

If rate of transmission is R,

∴ $$T_F = \frac{N_F}{R}$$

∴ $$\eta = \frac{W_S \times \dfrac{N_F}{R}}{\dfrac{N_F}{R} + 2T_P}$$

If there is an error in the frame Go_Back_N and Select Repeat ARQ will have different throughput.

(i) Go_Back_N ARQ :

The average number of retransmissions required will be,

$$\bar{N_r} = \sum_{i=1}^{\infty} f(i) \, P_f^{i-1} \, (1 - p_f)$$

$$f(i) = 1 + (i - 1)k$$

where, k is number of frames retransmitted when error occurs.

$$\bar{N_r} = (1 - k) \sum_{i=1}^{\infty} p_f^{i-1} (1 - p_f) + k \sum_{i=1}^{\infty} i \, P_f^{i-1} (1 - p_f)$$

$$= 1 - k + \frac{k}{1 - p_f}$$

Since, $\qquad k = W_s$

$$\bar{N_r} = 1 - W_s + \frac{W_s}{(1 - p_f)}$$

$\therefore \qquad$
$$\eta = \frac{W_s\, T_F}{\bar{N_r}\,(T_F + 2T_P)}$$

$$= \frac{W_s\,(1 - p_f)}{\left(1 + \dfrac{2T_P}{T_F}\right)(1 - p_f + W_s\, p_f)}$$

(ii) Selective Repeat ARQ :

Since this case is similar to stop_and_wait ARQ, where we retransmit only one frame,

$$\bar{N_r} = \frac{1}{1 - p_f}$$

$\therefore \qquad$ Throughput $\eta = \dfrac{W_s T_F}{(T_F + 2T_P)} \times (1 - p_f)$

Flow Control

- When there is a mismatch in the speed of transmitting entity and receiving entity, data transfer will not be effective.

- Flow control is required in such case which is a function of data link layer.

- Example when there is a data transfer from high end server to a client flow control will be required.

- The ARQ techniques discussed earlier during error control can also be used for flow control viz. stop_and_wait ARQ and sliding window ARQ.

  Stop_and_Wait Flow Control

- Stop_and_wait ARQ is simplest form of flow control.

- The transmitting entity transmits a frame and waits till the acknowledgement for the frame is received. After receiving acknowledgement it sends next frame i.e. receiver tells transmitter that Yes, I am ready to receive next frame. If acknowledgement is not received the frame is retransmitted. As seen earlier, this scheme is inefficient.

Sliding Window Flow Control

- In situation where the link length is greater than frame length ($T_P >> T_F$) stop_and_wait ARQ proves to be inefficient, as line remains idle for long time.

- If multiple frames are allowed simultaneously on the link instead of one, efficiency can be improved.

- The two stations A and B allocate some buffer space for W_S frames.
- Each frame is given sequence number.
- A maintains list of sequence numbers it is allowed to send.
- B maintains list of sequence numbers it is prepared to receive.
- As shown in Fig. 4.18, the stations A and B transmit and receive information.

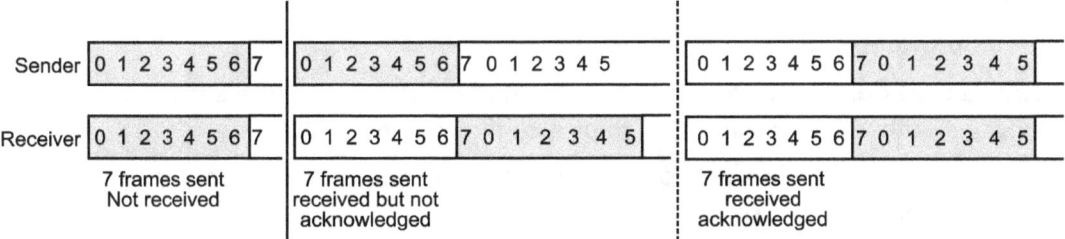

Fig. 4.18 : Sliding Window Flow Control

- The simplest procedure for flow control will be to tell sender to stop transmitting information.
- Whenever receiving station senses its buffer is getting full, it can send the stop signal to transmitting station.
- Note that receiving station is going to receive $2T_P \times R$ bits after it sends stop signal where T_P is propagation delay and R is transmitting rate.
- Sliding window protocols using ARQ techniques can also be used to provide flow control.
- The receiver's window size can be made equal to sender's window and whenever acknowledgement is received transmitter can accommodate next frame in buffer.
- Signals like Receive Ready (RR) and Receive Not Ready (RNR) can also be used.
- Receive Ready will indicate the expected frame to be received at the receiver.
- Receive Not Ready (RNR) will indicate buffer full and stop transmitting.
- A station can send both data and acknowledgement if it has both to send. It is called **piggybacking** which improves efficiency of transmission.
- A separate acknowledgement frame (RR or RNR) can be sent if station has only acknowledgement and no data to send.

4.11 HIGH LEVEL DATA LINK CONTROL (HDLC)

- It is the most widely used DLL protocol.
- It has a set of functions which provides communication service to network layer.
- HDLC supports variety of applications for which it has three types of stations, two link configurations and three data transfer modes.

Types of Stations :

- **Primary Station :** It controls operation of link. It issues commands.

- **Secondary Station :** Primary station controls it by issuing command frames transmitted by secondary station.

- **Combined Station :** It has features of both primary and secondary stations i.e. it issues both commands and response.

Types of Configuration :

- **Unbalanced Configuration :** It has one primary and one or more secondary stations. It supports both full duplex and half duplex configuration.

- **Balanced Configuration :** It consists of two combined stations supporting half duplex and full duplex transmission.

  These configurations are shown in Fig. 4.19 (a), (b) and (c).

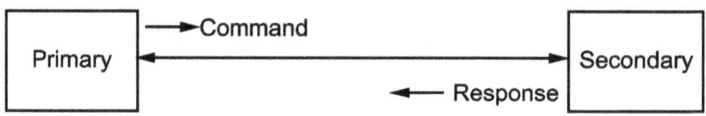

(a) Unbalanced Point-to-Point Link

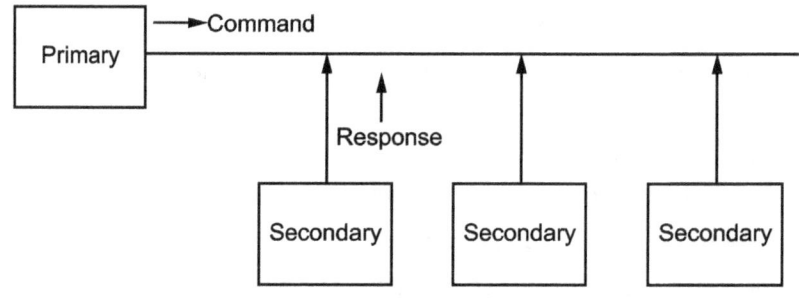

(b) Unbalanced Multidrop Link

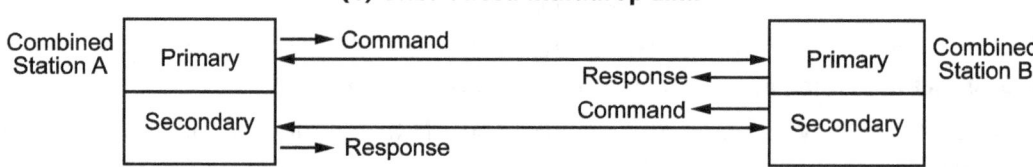

(c) Balanced Point-to-Point Link

Fig. 4.19

- **Types of Data Transfer Modes :**

  ➢ **Normal Response Mode (NRM) :** Used with unbalanced configuration. Primary can initiate data transfer to a secondary. Secondary can only transfer data in response to command from primary.

> ➤ **Asynchronous Balanced Mode (ABM) :** Used with balanced configuration. Any one of the combined station can initiate transmission without the permission of other station.

> ➤ **Asynchronous Response Mode (ARM) :** Used with unbalanced configuration secondary can initiate transmission without permission from primary. But primary has control of the link.

NRM can be used on multidrop lines and point-to-point links. ABM is most widely used. ARM is rarely used.

HDLC Frame Format

- The functionality of a protocol depends on the control fields that are defined in the header and trailer.

- The various data transfer modes are determined by the frame structure.

- Fig. 4.20 shows HDLC frame format.

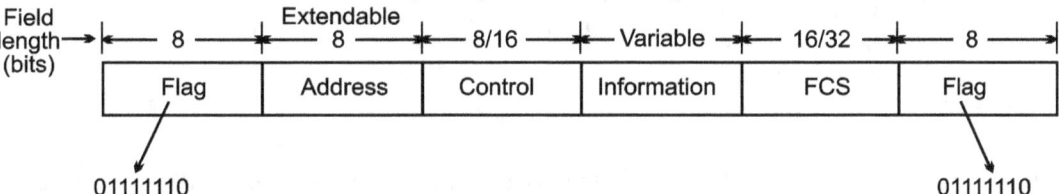

Fig. 4.20 : HDLC frame format

- Information is attached with an header consisting of flag, address and control fields and a trailer consisting of checksum and flag.

- Flag fields which are 8 bit long delimit the frame at both ends with a pattern 01111110 as discussed in Section 4.7. Bit stuffing is used to achieve data transparency.

- The addressing function of DLL is identifying the station that transmitted the frame and the station that will be receiving the frame. The address field specifies this. It is extendable over more than 8 bits in multiples. If this field is all 1's, the frame is broadcast to all secondaries.

- There are three types of control fields to identify three types of frames.

  - **Information frame (I-frame)** has 0 in the first bit of control field.

  - **Supervisory frame (S-frame)** has 10 in first two bits of control field.

  - **Unnumbered frame (U-frame)** has 11 in first two bits of control field.

Error control and flow control functions of DLL are provided by I-frame and S-frame. The three frame fields are shown in Fig. 4.21.

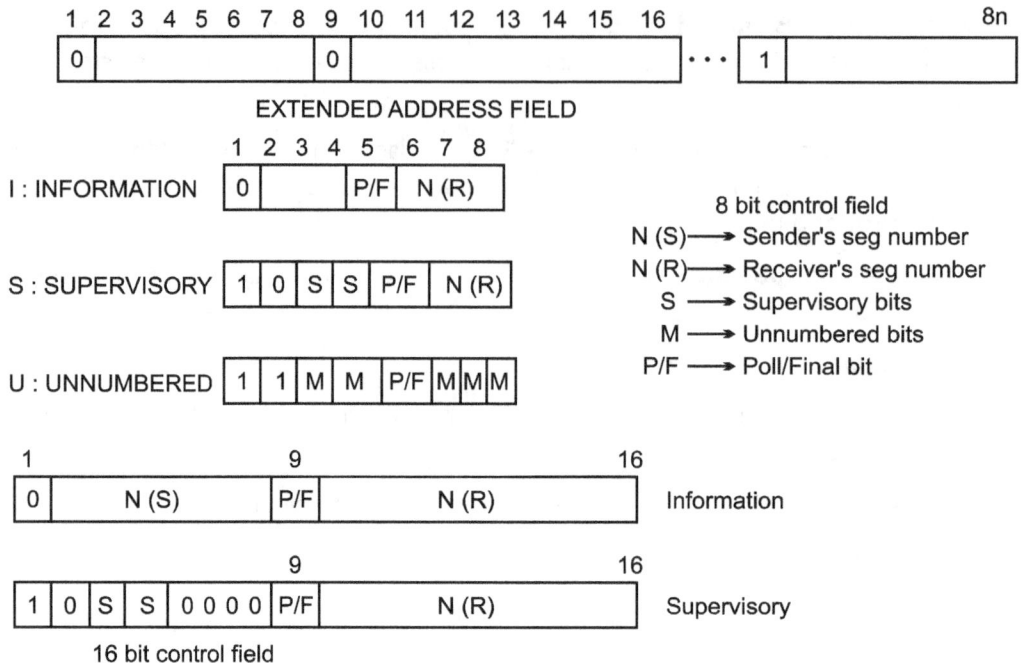

Fig. 4.21

Information field consists of 3 bit sequence number N(S) and N(R) of sender and acknowledgement number of receiver respectively (piggybacked). All frames have a P/F bit. Its uses depend on situation. In command frames it is called P bit and is set to 1 whenever a response frame is expected (Polled) from peer entity. In response frames it is called F bit and is set to 1 to indicate that the frame is response to a command frame (Poll). The length of information frame can be variable.

There are four types of supervisory frames decided by S-field.

If SS = 00. It is receive ready (RR) which acknowledges received frames in absence of piggybacking.

If SS = 01. It is reject frame indicating negative acknowledgement and transmitter should go back and transmit frames N(R) onward.

SS = 10 means receive not ready (RNR). Buffer full condition.

SS = 11 indicates selective reject, where N(R) is frame to be retransmitted.

- Combination of I-frame and S-frame allows HDLC to implement ARQ techniques.

- The unnumbered frames implement number of control functions.

  The M bits decide the function.

They are as below.

- **Set Asynchronous Balanced Mode (SABM) :** To set up asynchronous balanced mode connection.

- Set Normal Response Mode (SNRM) : To set up normal response mode.

- **Disconnect (DISC) :** Indicates station wishes to disconnect connection.

- **Unnumbered Acknowledgement (UA) :** Acknowledges frames during call set up.

- **Frame Reject (FRMR) :** Reject unacceptable frame.

- The information field contains sequence of bits in multiples of octets. Length of F-field is variable.

- Frame Check Sequence (FCS) field consists of error detecting code calculated from frame bits except flag fields. It has 16 bit CRC CCITT code.

Operation of HDLC

Let us now see how HDLC operates.

Connection Establishment and Release :

- Station A sends SAMB (Set Asynchronous Balanced Mode) frame indicating that it wants to establish a new connection.

- Station B sends unnumbered acknowledgement if it is ready to proceed. Otherwise it will REJECT the request by sending RNR frame.

- Whenever station wants to release connection it sends DISC frame and other station sends unnumbered acknowledgement. It is shown in Fig. 4.22.

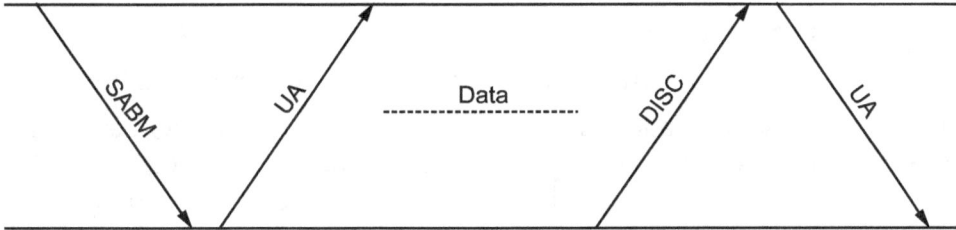

Fig. 4.22 : HDLC Connection Establishment and Release

Exchange of Frames using Normal Response Mode :

Assuming that connection is established between station A as primary and stations B and C as secondary, exchange of frames is shown in Fig. 4.23.

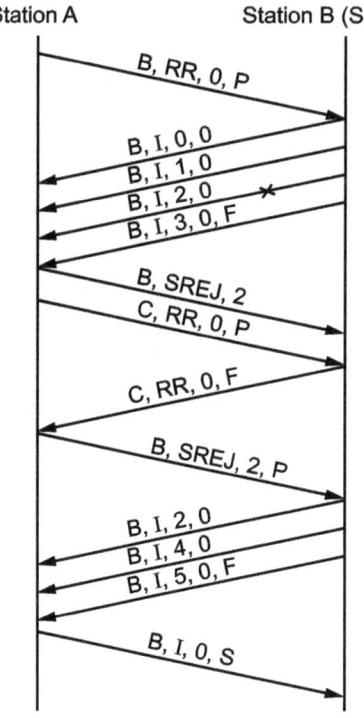

Fig. 4.23 : Exchange of Frames using NRM

- Station A polls B with N(R) = 0. Station B responds by sending frames 0, 1, 2, 3, with F bits set in last frame.

- Station A sends rejection of frame 2 and polls station C, which responds with receive ready frame.

- Station A again sends request to transmit frame 2 to B with poll bit set. Station B responds by sending frames 2, 4, 5 with F bit set in last frame.

- Station A sends information frame piggybacking acknowledgement of 5.

    Exchange of frames using Asynchronous Balanced Mode (Refer Fig. 4.24).

    Address field consists of address of receiving station, if it is information frame and address of transmitting station, if it is command frame or a response frame. Whenever frame is in error a REJ frame is send indicating number of bad frame so that transmitting station resends all the frames starting from that frame (Go_back_N) as is seen in case frame 1 rejected by station B.

    Information frame consists of N(S) and N(R), where N(S) is transmitted frame number and N(R) is expected frame number i.e. piggyback acknowledgement. In case station does not have information frame to send it sends RR frame with acknowledgement of previously received frame.

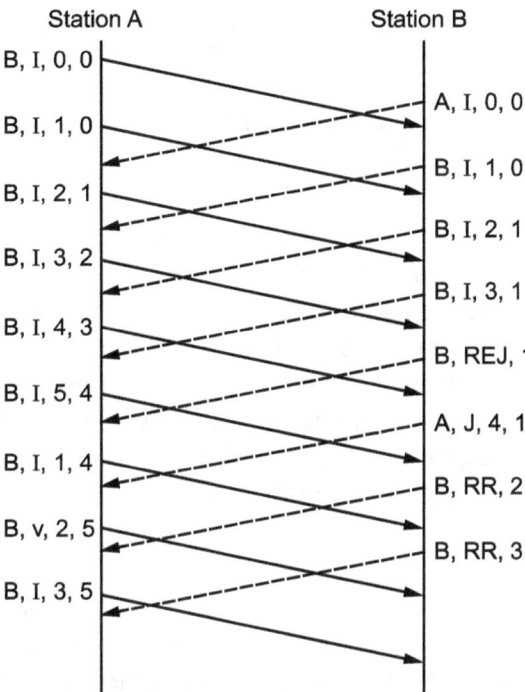

Fig. 4.24 : Exchange of Frames using ABM

4.12 POINT-TO-POINT PROTOCOL (PPP)

Introduction

The *Point-to-Point Protocol (PPP)* originally emerged as an encapsulation protocol for transporting IP traffic over point-to-point links. PPP also established a standard for the assignment and management of IP addresses, asynchronous (start/stop) and bit-oriented synchronous encapsulation, network protocol multiplexing, link configuration, link quality testing, error detection, and option negotiation for such capabilities as network layer address negotiation and data-compression negotiation. PPP supports these functions by providing an extensible Link Control Protocol (LCP) and a family of Network Control Protocols (NCPs) to negotiate optional configuration parameters and facilities. In addition to IP, PPP supports other protocols, including Novell's Internetwork Packet Exchange (IPX) and DECnet.

PPP Components :

PPP provides a method for transmitting datagrams over serial point-to-point links. PPP contains three main components :

- A method for encapsulating datagrams over serial links. PPP uses the High-Level Data Link Control (HDLC) protocol as a basis for encapsulating datagrams over point-to-point links.

- An extensible LCP to establish, configure, and test the data link connection.

- A family of NCPs for establishing and configuring different network layer protocols. PPP is designed to allow the simultaneous use of multiple network layer protocols.

General Operation :

To establish communications over a point-to-point link, the originating PPP first sends LCP frames to configure and (optionally) test the data link. After the link has been established and optional facilities have been negotiated as needed by the LCP, the originating PPP sends NCP frames to choose and configure one or more network layer protocols. When each of the chosen network layer protocols has been configured, packets from each network layer protocol can be sent over the link. The link will remain configured for communications until explicit LCP or NCP frames close the link, or until some external event occurs (for example, an inactivity timer expires or a user intervenes).

Physical Layer Requirements :

PPP is capable of operating across any DTE/DCE interface. Examples include EIA/TIA-232-C (formerly RS-232-C), EIA/TIA-422 (formerly RS-422), EIA/TIA-423 (formerly RS-423), and International Telecommunication Union Telecommunication Standardization Sector (ITU-T) (formerly CCITT) V.35. The only absolute requirement imposed by PPP is the provision of a duplex circuit, either dedicated or switched, that can operate in either an asynchronous or synchronous bit-serial mode, transparent to PPP link layer frames. PPP does not impose any restrictions regarding transmission rate other than those imposed by the particular DTE/DCE interface in use.

PPP Link Layer :

PPP uses the principles, terminology, and frame structure of the International Organization for Standardization (ISO) HDLC procedures (ISO 3309-1979), as modified by ISO 3309 :1984/PDAD1 "Addendum 1 : Start/Stop Transmission." ISO 3309-1979 specifies the HDLC frame structure for use in synchronous environments. ISO 3309 : 1984/PDAD1 specifies proposed modifications to ISO 3309-1979 to allow its use in asynchronous environments. The PPP control procedures use the definitions and control field encodings standardized in ISO 4335-1979 and ISO 4335-1979/Addendum 1-1979. The PPP frame format appears as shown in Fig. 4.25.

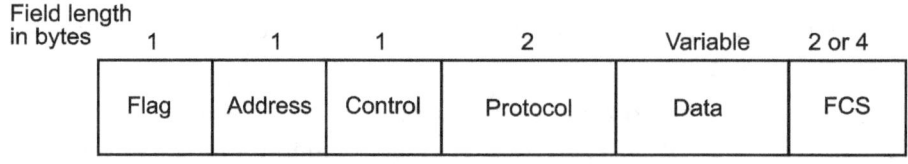

Fig. 4.25 : Six Fields make up the PPP Frame

The following descriptions summarize the PPP frame fields illustrated in Fig. 4.25.

- **Flag** : A single byte that indicates the beginning or end of a frame. The flag field consists of the binary sequence 01111110.

- **Address** : A single byte that contains the binary sequence 11111111, the standard broadcast address. PPP does not assign individual station addresses.

- **Control** : A single byte that contains the binary sequence 00000011, which calls for transmission of user data in an unsequenced frame. A connectionless link service similar to that of Logical Link Control (LLC) Type 1 is provided.

- **Protocol** : Two bytes that identify the protocol encapsulated in the information field of the frame. The most up-to-date values of the protocol field are specified in the most recent Assigned Numbers Request For Comments (RFC).

- **Data** : Zero or more bytes that contain the datagram for the protocol specified in the protocol field. The end of the information field is found by locating the closing flag sequence and allowing 2 bytes for the FCS field. The default maximum length of the information field is 1,500 bytes. By prior agreement, consenting PPP implementations can use other values for the maximum information field length.

- **Frame check sequence (FCS)** : Normally 16 bits (2 bytes). By prior agreement, consenting PPP implementations can use a 32-bit (4-byte) FCS for improved error detection.

The LCP can negotiate modifications to the standard PPP frame structure. Modified frames, however, always will be clearly distinguishable from standard frames.

PPP Link-Control Protocol :

The PPP LCP provides a method of establishing, configuring, maintaining, and terminating the point-to-point connection. LCP goes through four distinct phases.

First, link establishment and configuration negotiation occur. Before any network layer datagrams (for example, IP) can be exchanged, LCP first must open the connection and negotiate configuration parameters. This phase is complete when a configuration-acknowledgment frame has been both sent and received.

This is followed by link quality determination. LCP allows an optional link quality determination phase following the link-establishment and configuration-negotiation phase. In this phase, the link is tested to determine whether the link quality is sufficient to bring up network layer protocols. This phase is optional. LCP can delay transmission of network layer protocol information until this phase is complete.

At this point, network layer protocol configuration negotiation occurs. After LCP has finished the link quality determination phase, network layer protocols can be configured separately by the appropriate NCP and can be brought up and taken down at any time. If LCP closes the link, it informs the network layer protocols so that they can take appropriate action.

Finally, link termination occurs. LCP can terminate the link at any time. This usually is done at the request of a user but can happen because of a physical event, such as the loss of carrier or the expiration of an idle-period timer.

Three classes of LCP frames exist. Link-establishment frames are used to establish and configure a link. Link-termination frames are used to terminate a link, and link-maintenance frames are used to manage and debug a link.

These frames are used to accomplish the work of each of the LCP phases.

Example 4.14 : Let $g(x) = x^3 + x + 1$. Consider the information sequence 1001.

(i)   Find the codeword corresponding to the information sequence given.

(ii) Suppose that the codeword has a transmission error in the first bit. What will be the syndrome generated at the receiver ?

Solution :

Given :
$$g(x) = x^3 + x + 1$$
$$d = [1\ 0\ 0\ 1]$$
$$d(x) = x^3 + 1$$

Here, $n - k = 3$
$$k = 4$$
$$\therefore \quad n = 7$$

(i)   Assuming systematic code generation.
$$c(x) = x^{n-k}\, d(x) + p(x)$$

where,
$$p(x) = \text{Rem}\left[\frac{x^{n-k}\, d(x)}{g(x)}\right]$$

$$\begin{array}{r} x^3 + x \\ \hline x^3 + x + 1 \overline{)\ x^6 + x^3} \\ x^6 + x^4 + x^3 \end{array}$$

$$x^4$$

$$x^4 - x^2 + x$$

$$x^2 + x$$

$\therefore$ $\quad p(x) = x^2 + 1$

$\therefore$ $\quad c(x) = x^3 (x^3 + 1) + x^2 + 1$

$$= x^6 + x^3 + x^2 + 1$$

$$= [1\,0\,0\,1\,1\,0\,1]$$

(ii) If error is there in first bit,

Error pattern e $= [1\,0\,0\,0\,0\,0\,0]$

$\therefore$ $\quad e(x) = x^6$

Now, syndrome

$$s(x) = \text{Rem}\left[\frac{r(x)}{g(x)}\right] = \text{Rem}\left[\frac{e(x)}{g(x)}\right]$$

$$x^3 + x + 1$$

$$x^3 + x + 1$$

$$x^6$$

$$x^6 + x^4 + x^3$$

$$x^4 + x^3$$

$$x^4 + x^2 + x$$

$$x^3 + x^2 + x$$

$$x^2 + x + 1$$

$$x^2 + 1$$

$\therefore$ $\quad s = [1\,0\,1]$

Example 4.15 : To provide more reliability than single parity bit can give, an error detecting coding scheme uses one parity bit for checking all the odd numbered bits and a second parity for all even numbered bit. What is the hamming distance of this code ?

Solution :

If 1 parity bit is provided for odd numbered bits and 1 parity for even numbered bits, two changes in odd or even numbered positions will generate a valid codeword. Hence, hamming distance = 2.

e.g. Let message be 1010.

Code will be 101000.

If two errors occur in 1st and 3rd position codeword will be 000000 which is valid codeword as it satisfies parity condition.

$\therefore$ The hamming distance between these codewords is 2.

Example 4.16 : A bit stream 10011101 is transmitted using the standard CRC method. The generator polynomial is $x^3 + 1$. Show the actual bit string transmitted. Suppose the third bit from left is inverted during transmission. Show that this error is detected at the receiver's end.

Solution :

Given : $d = [1\ 0\ 0\ 1\ 1\ 1\ 0\ 1]$

$g(x) = x^3 + 1$

$\therefore$ $d(x) = x^7 + x^4 + x^3 + x^2 + 1$

$x - k = 3 \qquad k = 8$

$\therefore$ $x = 11$

(i) $x^{n-k}\, d(x) = x^3\, (x^7 + x^4 + x^3 + x^2 + 1)$

$= x^{10} + x^7 + x^6 + x^5 + x^3$

$$
\begin{array}{r}
x^7 + x^3 + x^2 \\
x^3 + 1\ \overline{)\ x^{10} + x^7 + x^6 + x^4 + x^3} \\
\underline{x^{10} + x^7} \\
x^6 + x^4 + x^3 \\
\underline{x^6 + x^3} \\
x^5 \\
x^5 + x^2
\end{array}
$$

$x^2 = p(x)$

$\therefore$ $c(x) = x^{n-k}\, d(x) + p(x)$

$= x^{30} + x^7 + x^6 + x^5 + x^3 + x^2$

$= [1\ 0\ 0\ 1\ 1\ 1\ 0\ 1\ 1\ 0\ 0]$

(ii)   c = [1 0 0 1 1 1 0 1 1 0 0]

Third bit is inverted.

∴   r = [1 0 1 1 1 1 0 1 1 0 0]

$$r(x) = x^{10} + x^8 + x^7 + x^6 + x^5 + x^3 + x^2$$

$$x^7 + x^5 + x^3$$

$$x^3 + 1 \quad x^{10} + x^8 + x^7 + x^6 + x^5 + x^3 + x^2$$

$$x^{10} + x^7$$

$$x^8 + x^6 + x^5 + x^3 + x^2$$

$$x^8 + x^5$$

$$x^6 + x^3 + x^2$$

$$x^6 + x^3$$

$$x^2$$

∴ $s(x) = x^2$

∴   s = [1 0 0]

Since syndrome in non-zero above error is detected.

Example 4.17 :

If you are given the following bit sequence of HDLC frame, identify various fields.

0111111001111110   10100011   01100010

0111000011000011   01010101   10101011

0111111001111110

Solution :

An HDLC frame has following format

8 bit	8 bit	8 bit	Variable	16 bit	8 bit
Flag	Address	Control	Information	FCS	Flag

There are two flag fields at the start and end.

Start Flag   01111110

Flag   01111110

Address   10100011

Control	01100010		
Information	01110000	11000011	01010101
FCS	01010101	10101011	
Flag	01111110		
End Flag	01111110		

Example 4.18 : Consider a 64 kbps geostationary satellite channel is used to send 512 byte data frames in one direction, with very short acknowledgement coming back the other way. What is maximum throughput for window size of 1, 7, 15 and 127 ? (Sliding window protocol is used).

Solution :

Given :   R = 64 kbps = 64000 bits/sec

Frame size = 512 byte = 4096 bits

$$\text{Frame time, } T_F = \frac{\text{Frame size}}{\text{Rate}} = \frac{4096}{64000} = 64 \times 10^{-3} \text{ sec} = 64 \text{ ms}$$

Round trip propagation delay.

$$2T_P = 540 \text{ ms}$$

Throughput is given by,

$$\eta = \frac{W_S T_F}{T_F + 2T_P}$$

(i) $W_S = 1$

$$\eta = \frac{1 \times 64}{64 + 540} = 0.1059$$

i.e. throughput is 10.59%

(ii)

$$\eta = \frac{7 \times 64}{64 + 540} = 0.7413$$

i.e. throughput is 74.13%

(iii) $W_S = 15$

Here, $W_S \geq \frac{2T_P}{T_F} + 1$

$\therefore$ $\qquad\qquad$ $\eta = 1$

i.e. throughput is 100%.

(iv) $\qquad\qquad$ $W_S = 127$

Here also,

$$W_S \geq \frac{2T_P}{T_F} + 1$$

$\therefore$ $\qquad\qquad$ $\eta = 1$

i.e. throughput is 100%.

[i.e. when window size $W_S \geq \dfrac{2T_P}{T_F} + 1$, sender keeps on sending the frames and does not remain idle at any time].

Example 4.19 : A 4 Mbps token ring has a token holding timer value of 10 m/sec. What is the longest frame that can be sent on this ring ?

Solution :

Given : $\qquad$ R = 4 Mbps = 4×10^6 bits/sec.

Token holding time = 10×10^{-3} sec.

$\therefore$ Number of bits that can be transmitted in 10 msec.

$\qquad\qquad$ = $4 \times 10^6 \times 10 \times 10^{-3}$

$\qquad\qquad$ = 40000 bits

$\qquad\qquad$ = 5000 bytes

Hence, longest frame is 5000 bytes including overheads. Data portion will be slightly less than this.

Example 4.20 : Consider the use of 1000 bit frames on a 1 Mbps satellite channel. What is the maximum links utilization for

(i) Stop and Wait ARQ

(ii) Continuous ARQ with Windowsize 7.

(iii) Continuous ARQ with Windowsize 127.

(iv) Continuous ARQ with Windowsize 255.

Solution :

Given : Frame size = 1000 bits

$\qquad\qquad$ Bit rate = 1×10^6 bits/sec.

$\therefore$ $\qquad\qquad$ $T_F = \dfrac{1000}{1 \times 10^6} = 1 \times 10^{-3}$ = 1 msec.

For satellite channel,

$$T_P = 270 \text{ ms.}$$

(i) Stop-and-Wait ARQ :

$$\text{Utilization} = U = \frac{1}{1 + 2\dfrac{T_P}{T_F}}$$

$$= \frac{1}{1 + 2 \times \dfrac{270}{1}}$$

$$= 0.0018 \text{ i.e. } 0.18\%$$

(ii) For Continuous ARQ (Sliding Window) :

$$\text{Utilization} = U = \frac{W_S}{1 + 2 \times \dfrac{T_P}{T_F}}$$

$$W_S = 7$$

$\therefore$

$$U = 7 \times \frac{1}{541}$$

$$= 0.0129$$

i.e. 1.29%

(iii)

$$W_S = 127$$

$$U = \frac{127}{541}$$

$$= 0.2343$$

i.e. 23.43%

(iv)

$$W_S = 255$$

$$U = \frac{255}{541}$$

$$= 0.4713 \text{ i.e. } 47.13\%$$

Example 4.21 : A channel has a bit rate of 4 kbps and propagation delay 20 ms. For what range of frame size does stop-and-wait ARQ gives throughput $\geq 50\%$?

Solution :

Given : $R = 4 \text{ kbps}$

$$= 4 \times 10^3 \text{ bits/sec}$$

$$T_P = ?$$

$$\eta \geq 50\%$$

For stop-and-wait ARQ,

$$\eta = \frac{1}{1 + \dfrac{2T_P}{T_F}}$$

$$\therefore \qquad \frac{1}{1 + \dfrac{2T_P}{T_F}} \geq \frac{1}{2}$$

$$\therefore \qquad \frac{1}{1 + \dfrac{2 \times 20}{T_F}} \geq \frac{1}{2}$$

$$\frac{T_F}{T_F + 40} \geq \frac{1}{2}$$

$$2T_F \geq T_F + 40$$

$$T_F \geq 40$$

$$T_F \geq 40 \text{ ms}$$

$$\therefore \qquad \text{Frame size} = R \times T_F$$

$$= \frac{4 \times 10^3}{10^3} \times 40 \times 10^{-3}$$

$$= 160 \text{ bits}$$

$$\therefore \qquad \text{Frame size} \geq 160 \text{ bits}$$

$$\geq 20 \text{ bytes}$$

Example 4.22 : Draw sender and receiver windows for a system using Go-back N ARQ and selective repeat ARQ.

(a) Frame 0 is sent; frame 0 is acknowledged.

(b) Frame 1 and 2 are sent; frame 1 and 2 are acknowledged.

(c) Frames 3, 4 and 5 are sent NAK 4 is received.

(d) Frames 4, 5, 6, 7 are sent frames 4 through 7 are acknowledged.

Solution :

(i)   Go-back N ARQ

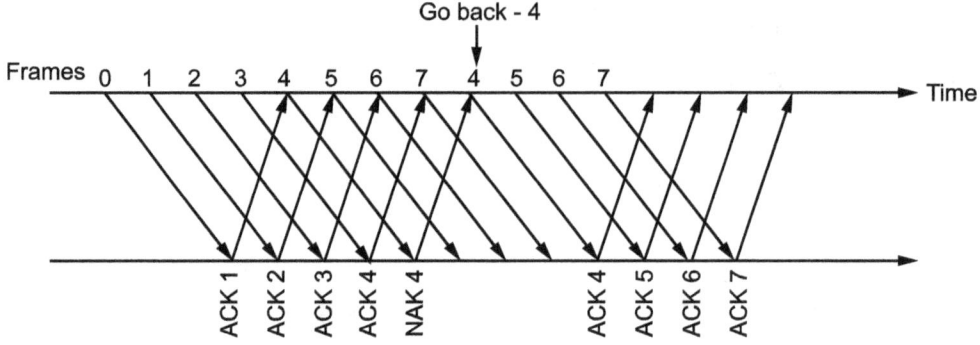

Fig. 4.26 (a)

(ii) Selective Repeat ARQ

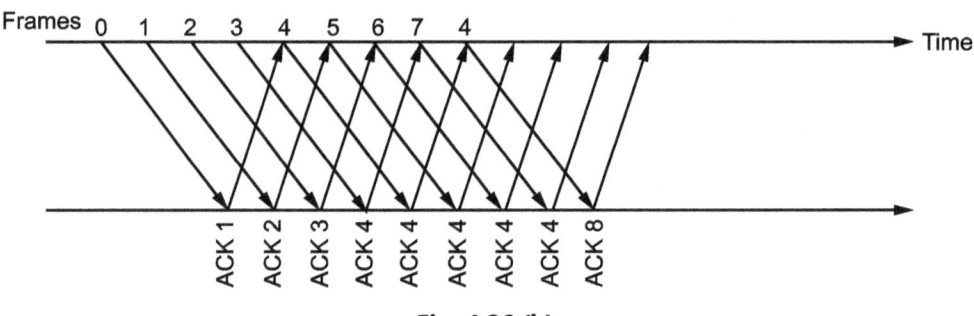

Fig. 4.26 (b)

Example 4.23 : Computer A uses stop-and-wait ARQ protocol to send packets to computer B. Distance between A and B is 4000 km. How long does it take for computer A to send out a packet of size 1000 byte if throughput is 100000 kbps ? How much time the computer is idle ? (Assume propagation speed to be speed of light).

Solution :

Given :

$$d = 4000 \text{ km}$$

$$N_F = 1000 \text{ byte} = 8000 \text{ bits}$$

$$v = 3 \times 10^8 \text{ m/s}$$

$$T_F = ?$$

$\therefore$ Propagation delay $T_P = \dfrac{4000 \times 10^3}{3 \times 10^8} = \dfrac{4}{3} \times 10^{-2}$

$$s = 0.0133 \text{ s}$$

Throughput for stop and wait ARQ is

(i) Here throughput means rate at which data is coming out of station A.

$\therefore$ Time token to transmit one packet is,

$$T_F = \frac{8000}{100000 \times 10^3}$$

$$= 8 \times 10^{-6}$$

(ii)   Idle time $= 2T_P - T_F$

$$= 0.01333 \times 2 - 8 \times 10^{-5}$$

$$= 0.026658663$$

Example 4.24 : Calculate the maximum link utilization efficiency for stop-and-wait flow control mechanism if the frame size is 2400 bits, bit rate is 4800 bps and distance between the devices is 2000 km. Speed of propagation be 2×10^8 m/s.

Solution :

Frame transmission time $T_F = \dfrac{2400}{4800} = 0.5$

Propagation time $T_P = \dfrac{d}{v} = \dfrac{2000 \times 10^3}{2 \times 10^8} = 0.01$ s

Link utilization is throughput

$$\eta = \frac{T_F}{T_F + 2T_P}$$

$$= \frac{0.5}{0.5 + 0.01 \times 2}$$

$$= 96.15\%$$

EXERCISE

1. Explain different types of errors that can occur in transmission of bits.

2. What are functions of data link layer ?

3. What is error control ? How it is achieved ?

4. Explain error correction and detection.

5. What are linear block codes ? Explain.

6. What are cyclic codes ? Explain.

7. What is hamming distance ? Explain with example.

8. What is generator matrix in LBC ? How it is created and used ?

9. What is generator polynomial in cyclic codes ?

10. How is systematic cyclic code generated ?

11. What is checksum ? Explain with example.

12. What is framing ? What are different types of framing ?

13. What is flow control in DLL ? Explain.

14. Explain :

    (i) Simplest Protocol,

    (ii) Stop_and_wait protocol.

15. What are ARQ protocols ? Explain.

16. What is stop_and_wait ARQ ?

17. What is Go_back_N ARQ ?

18. What is selective_repeat ARQ ?

19. Give frame format of HDLC protocol. Explain each field.

20. Give frame format of PPP protocol. Explain each field.

MULTIPLEXING AND MULTIPLE ACCESS

5.1 INTRODUCTION TO MULTIPLEXING

Various Definitions of Multiplexing :

- Multiplexing is a set of techniques that allows the simultaneous transmission of multiple signals across a single transmission link.

- Multiplexing is the transmission of multiple data communication sessions over a common wire or medium.

- Multiplexing is the process to combine multiple signals (analog or digital) for transmission over a single line or media. A common type of multiplexing combines several low speed signals for transmission over a single high speed connection.

- Multiplexing is a technique for sending more than one information signal at a time over a single communication path (e.g. medium, circuit or channel).

Thus, multiplexing is loosely referred to many into one as shown in Fig. 5.1.

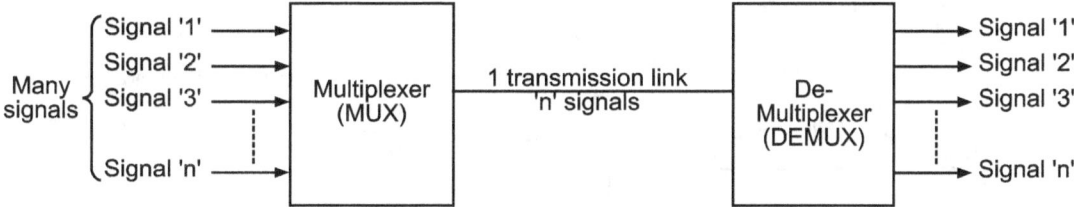

Fig. 5.1 : Multiplexer and demultiplexer

The reverse procedure of multiplexing is called as demultiplexing referred to as one into many. Whenever the transmission capacity of a medium linking two devices is greater than the transmission needs of the devices, the transmission link can be shared in order to maximize the utilization of the link. For example, one cable can carry hundred channels of TV in cable TV system.

Types of Multiplexing : There are two basic techniques : (1) Frequency division multiplexing (FDM) and (2) Time division multiplexing (TDM).

Generally, FDM is used for analog signal multiplexing and TDM is used for digital signal multiplexing. The classification of multiplexing techniques can be given as :

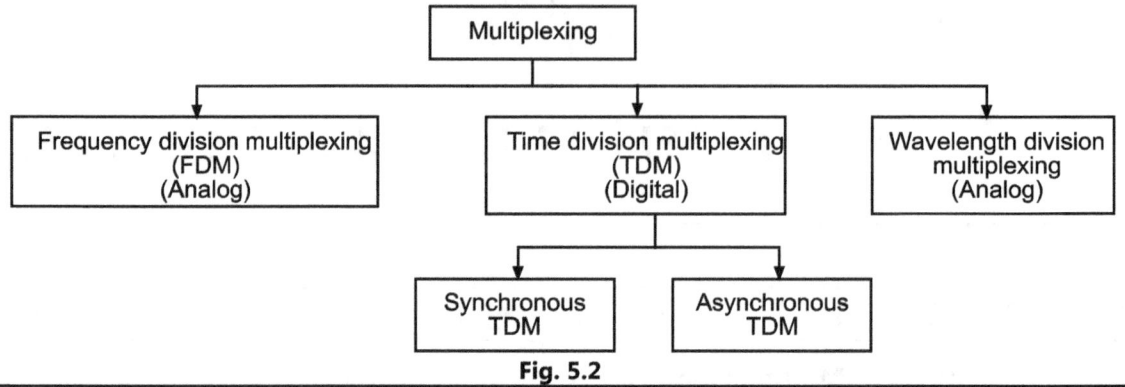

Fig. 5.2

5.2 FREQUENCY DIVISION MULTIPLEXING (FDM)

In FDM, total bandwidth available to the system is divided into several frequency sub-bands on one transmission line. The signals to be transmitted simultaneously will modulate a separate carrier. The modulation method can be AM, FM, PM, SSB (single sideband technique) or VSB (vestigial sideband technique) etc. Then different modulated signals are added using the simple adder circuit. Thus this added signal acts as multiplexed signal and then transmitted over a single or common transmission line as shown in Fig. 5.3.

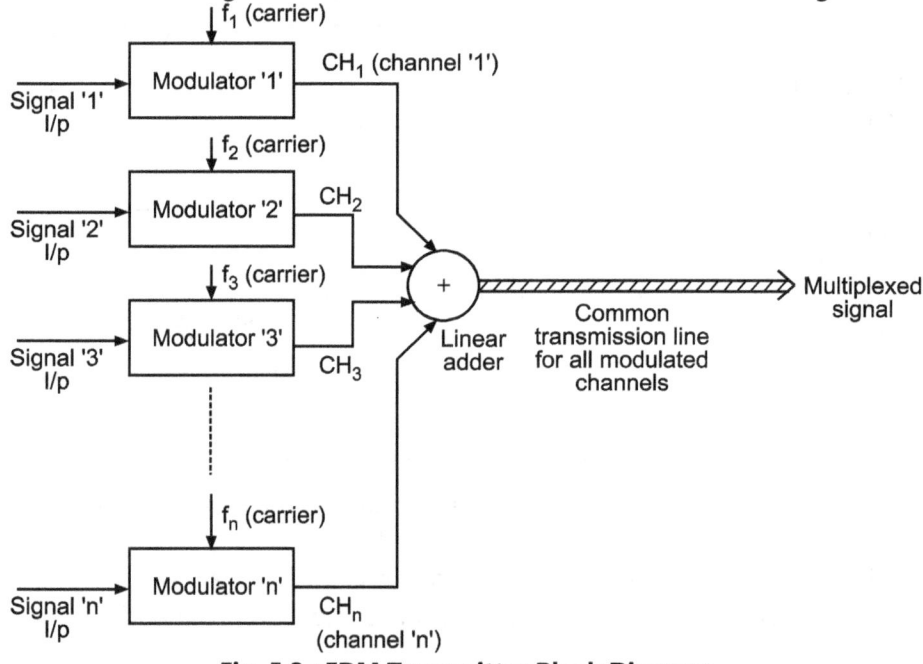

Fig. 5.3 : FDM Transmitter Block Diagram

The operation of FDM transmitter is as follows :

- Signal 1 is going to modulate carrier 1 and channel 1 will be available. Signal 2 is going to modulate carrier 2 and channel 2 will be available. Each modulated channel will be having specific bandwidth.

- Algebraic addition of different channels are done in the linear adder circuit. Thus multiplexed signal is available and transmitted on a common transmission line.
- Thus every channel will have specific frequency band. There is always guard band separating these channels. This is an unused band of frequencies. This band reduces the overlapping of frequencies and effect of "cross talk" that may occur between different channels.
- Frequency spectrum for FDM signal in frequency domain is as shown in Fig. 5.4.

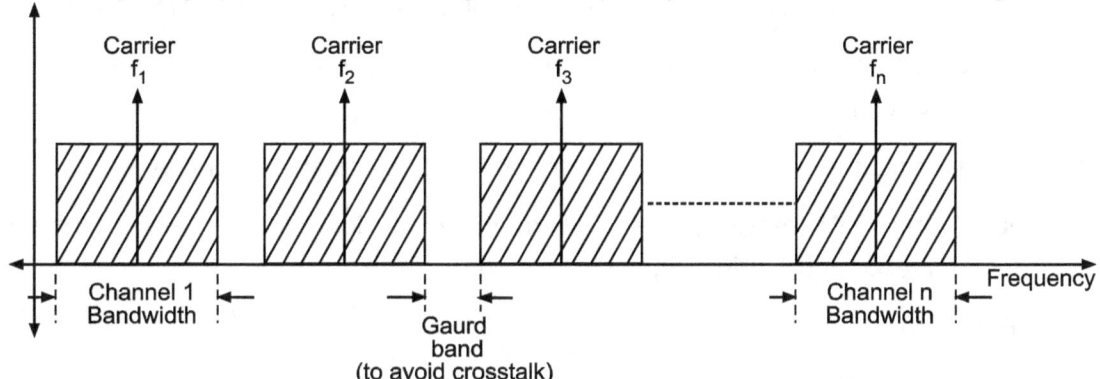

Fig. 5.4 : Frequency Spectrum of FDM Signal (in frequency domain)

FDM Receiver :

In FDM receiver, the multiplexed signal is given to the first stage from common transmission line as shown in Fig. 5.5.

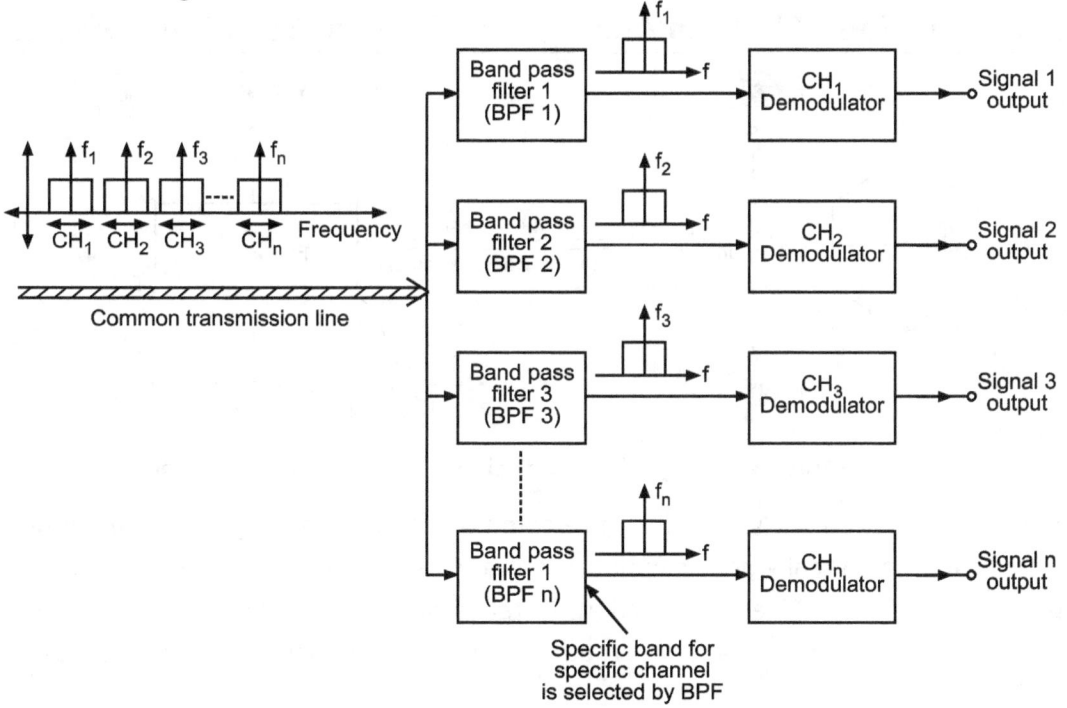

Fig. 5.5 : FDM Receiver Block Diagram

The operation of FDM receiver is as follows :

- Channel 1 is filtered out using BPF_1. Channel 2 is filtered out using BPF_2.   Cut-off frequencies of band pass filters are sharp enough to avoid the overlapping or mixing of adjacent channels.

- BPF_1 output is given to CH_1 demodulator. BPF_2 output is given to CH_2 demodulator. Thus demodulator output will be original signal 1 and signal 2 respectively.

- Thus centre frequency of each band pass filter is corresponding to the carrier of respective channel.

- Thus each filter will pass only its own channel and rejects the other channels.

- Thus, using FDM receiver, the FDM multiplexed signal in frequency domain is demultiplexed and original signal is recovered.

FDM Applications :

- Radio broadcast
- TV broadcast
- Mobile Radio
- Fiber optic channel communication
- Wireless communication
- Analog telephony

5.2.1 Application of FDM in Analog Telephony or Telephone System

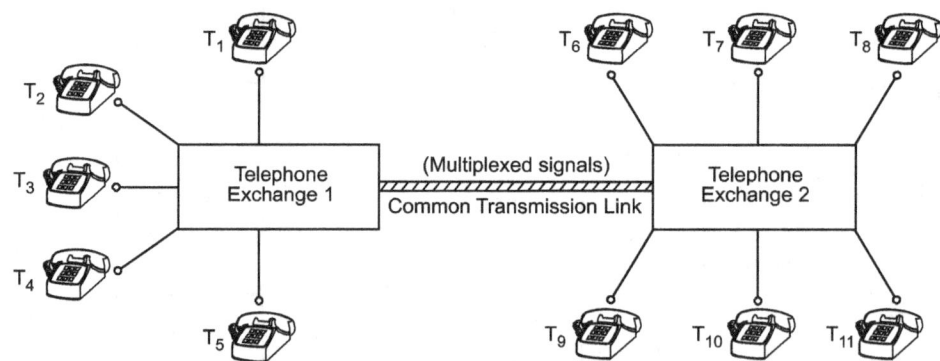

Fig. 5.6 : Multiplexed Signal Transmission Across Telephone Exchange

Telephone system is basically used for voice communication. The range of voice frequency is 300 Hz to 3400 Hz. In real world telephone communication, each telephone is connected to the telephone exchange. These connections of telephones to the telephone exchange follow the star topology. In this connection layout, the telephone exchange is at centre position as shown in Fig. 5.6.

At telephone exchange, these voice channels modulate different sub-carriers. These modulated sub-bands are then added together. There are several levels of multiplexing as shown in Table 5.1.

Table 5.1 : Levels of Multiplexing Process

Levels	Groups (Service)	Multiplexed channels	Total voice channels
Level (1)	1 Basic group	12 Voice channels	12
Level (2)	1 Super group	5 Basic groups	60
Level (3)	1 Master group	10 Super groups	600
Level (4)	1 Jumbo group	6 Master groups	3600

Though the voice frequency range given is 300 to 3400 Hz, considering guard band, the frequency band for one voice channel is 4 kHz. Accordingly, the bandwidth for Basic group, Super group, Master group and Jumbo group is calculated and shown.

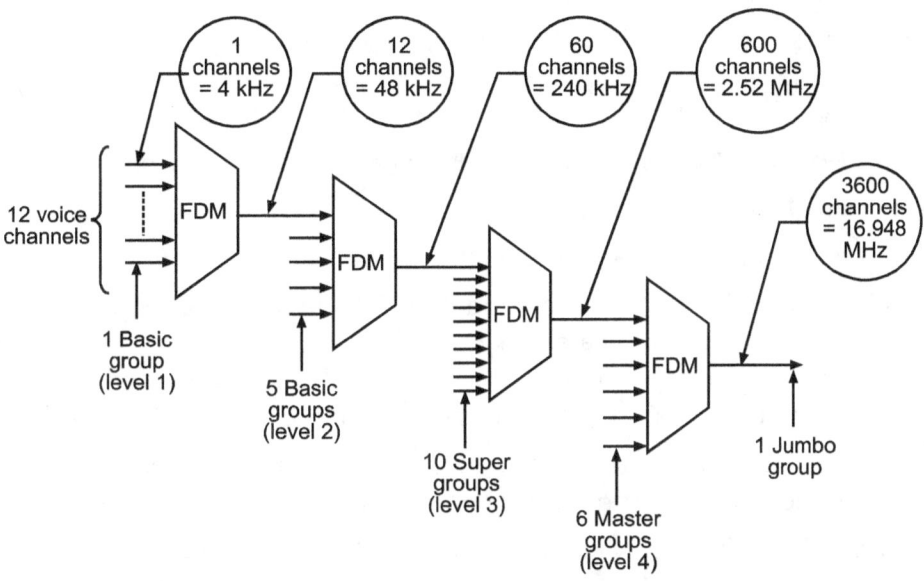

Fig. 5.7 : Levels of Multiplexing Process

At telephone exchange, these voice channels modulate different sub-carriers. These modulated sub-carriers are then added together as shown in Fig. 5.8. This modulation at telephone exchange is given for basic group only.

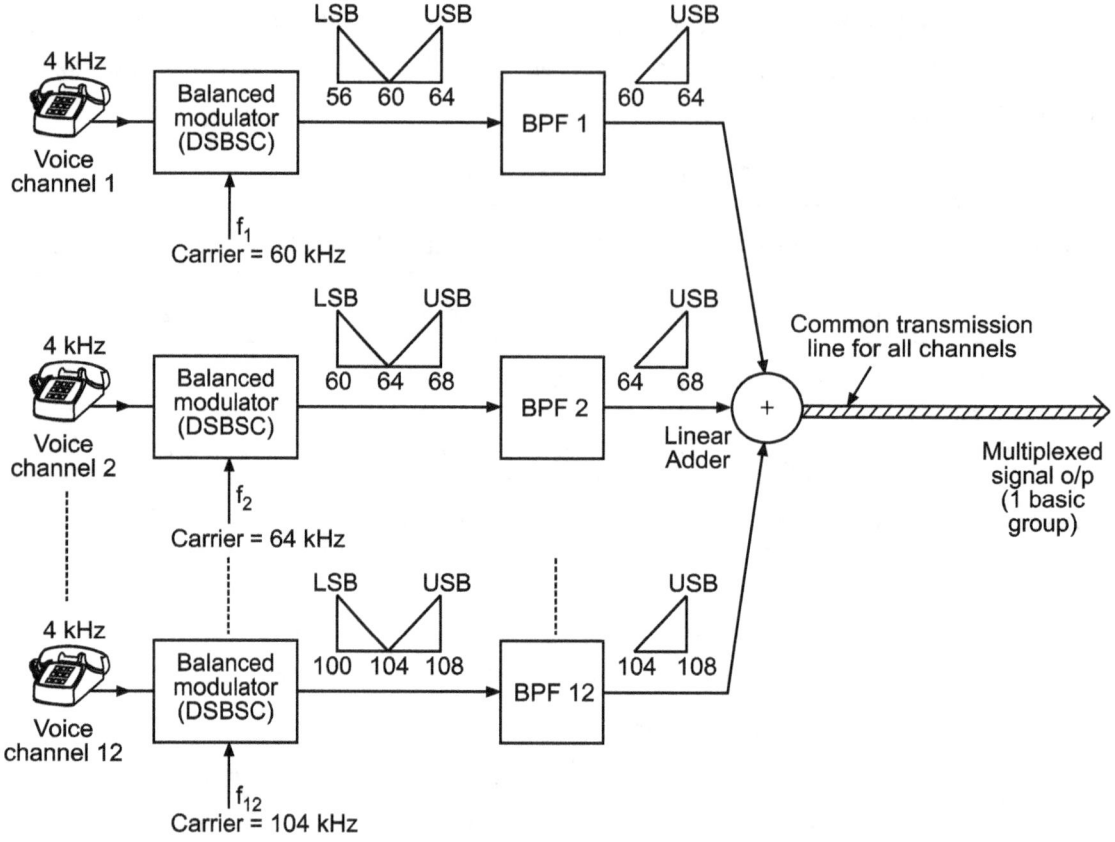

Fig. 5.8 : FDM Transmitter for 1 Basic group (12 Voice channels)

Operation of FDM Transmitter is as Follows :

- In this system, 12 voice channels of 4 kHz bandwidth each are used.

- 12 voice channels are used to modulate 12 different carrier frequencies. Voice channel 1 is used to modulate 60 kHz carrier frequency. Voice channel 2 is used to modulate 64 kHz carrier frequency. And voice channel 12 is used to modulate 104 kHz carrier frequency. Carrier frequencies are spaced at 4 kHz from each other.

- SSB modulation technique is used to save the bandwidth and power output of balanced modulator having lower sideband as well as upper sideband.

- Using bandpass filter only upper sideband (USB) is selected. These sidebands are added using a linear adder. This added signal is nothing but the multiplexed signal output of 1 basic group i.e. 12 voice channels.

Thus this multiplexed signal is used as one input to a super group which is already shown in levels of multiplexing in Fig. 5.7. Lets see the spectrum for the 12 voice channels which are multiplexed in frequency domain.

The frequency spectrum for multiplexed 12 voice channels is shown in Fig. 5.9.

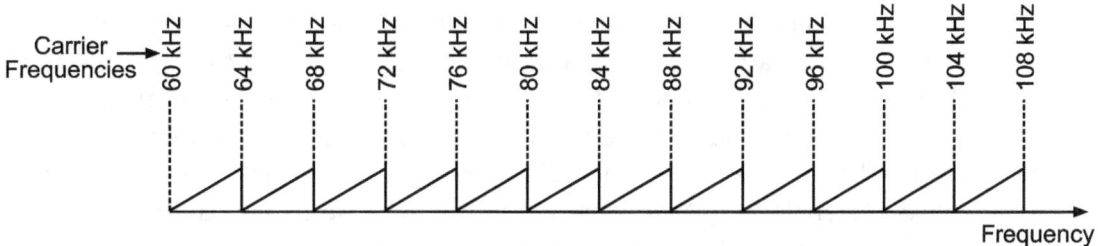

Fig. 5.9 : Frequency Spectrum for Frequency Division Multiplexed 12 Voice Channels

Lets see the FDM receiver for 1 basic group which is shown in Fig. 5.10.

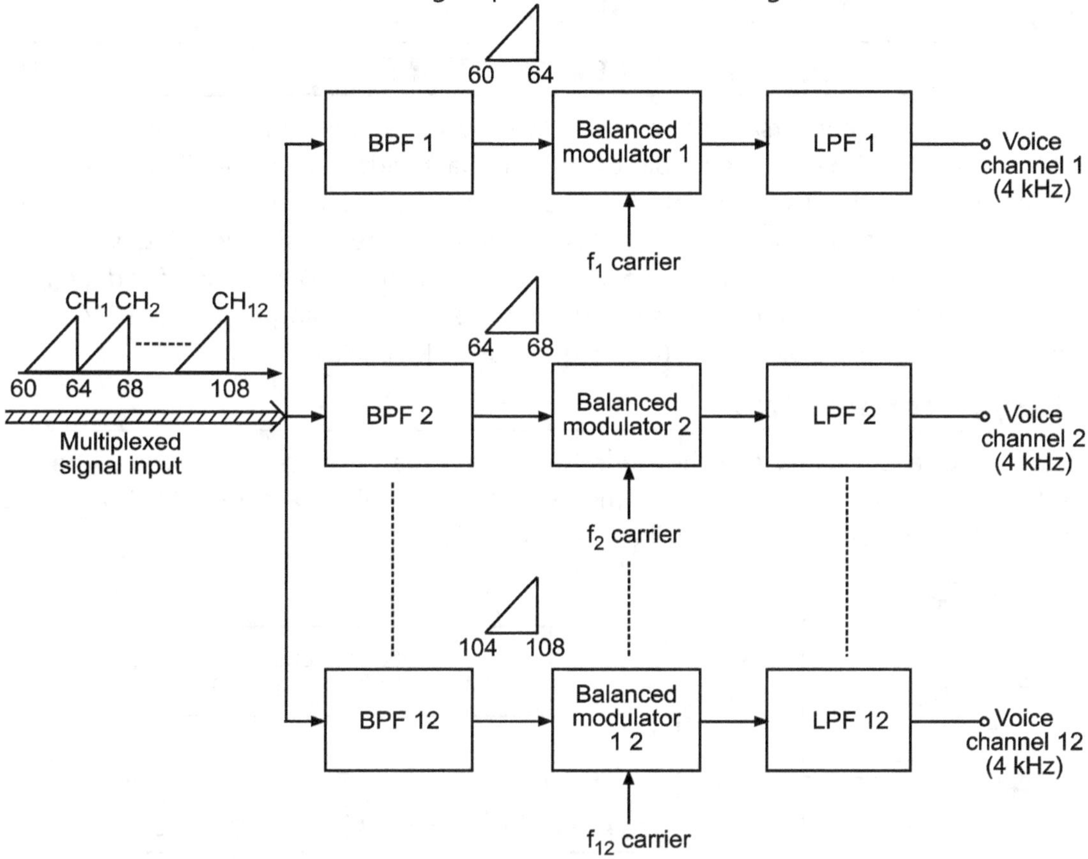

Fig. 5.10 : FDM Receiver (Demultiplexing of Signal)

Operation of the FDM Receiver is as Follows :

- This FDM receiver unit is known as demultiplexer.
- Band pass filters are used to separate the basic group signals which are multiplexed.
- BPF_1 is used to select the 1st multiplexed channel, BPF_2 is used to select the 2nd multiplexed channel and likewise BPF_{12} is used to select the 12th multiplexed channel.
- Balanced modulator is acting as SSB demodulator. Thus demodulated signal is filtered by low pass filter, which is nothing but original voice channel of 4 kHz.

Thus FDM system for multiplexing ordinary telephone calls is widely used. It is purely analog system that is based on repeated amplitude modulation. SSB is one of the type of AM. FDM system is used in a telephone exchange office to transmit phone calls to another telephone exchange office, where the phone calls are demultiplexed by filtering and demodulation. The pilot signals are used at the receiving end to generate carriers of the correct frequencies. Thus demultiplexed signals are then further distributed, some of them are possibly multiplexed again to be transmitted to another exchange office.

The system is obviously one-directional, while phone calls are two-directional. Therefore those systems are used in pairs, one system for each direction.

5.3 TIME DIVISION MULTIPLEXING (TDM)

TDM allows multiple conversations to take place by the sharing of medium or channel in **time**. A channel is allocated the whole of the line bandwidth for a specific period of time. This means each sub-carrier is allocated a time slot. Time division multiplexing is a technique where a short time sample of each channel is inserted into the multiplexed data stream. Each channel is sampled in turn, and then the sequence is repeated. TDM is used for digital signal multiplexing only. It cannot be used to multiplex the analog signals. TDM can be implemented in two ways as follows (i) Synchronous TDM, (ii) Asynchronous TDM.

5.3.1 Synchronous TDM

The multiplexer allocates exactly the same time slot to each device at all times, whether or not a device has anything to transmit. Time slot 1, for example, is assigned to device 1 alone and cannot be used by any other device as shown in Fig. 5.11.

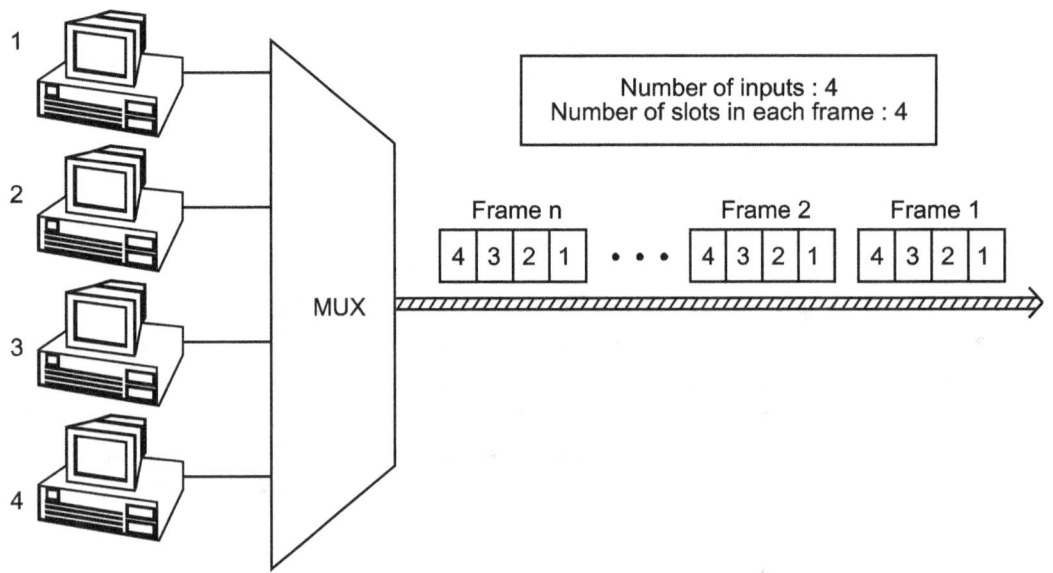

Fig. 5.11 : Basic Synchronous TDM System

In Fig. 5.11, a frame consists of one complete cycle of time slots. Thus the number of slots in a frame is equal to the number of inputs.

Multiplexing and demultiplexing processes in synchronous TDM system are clearly shown in Fig. 5.12 (a) and (b).

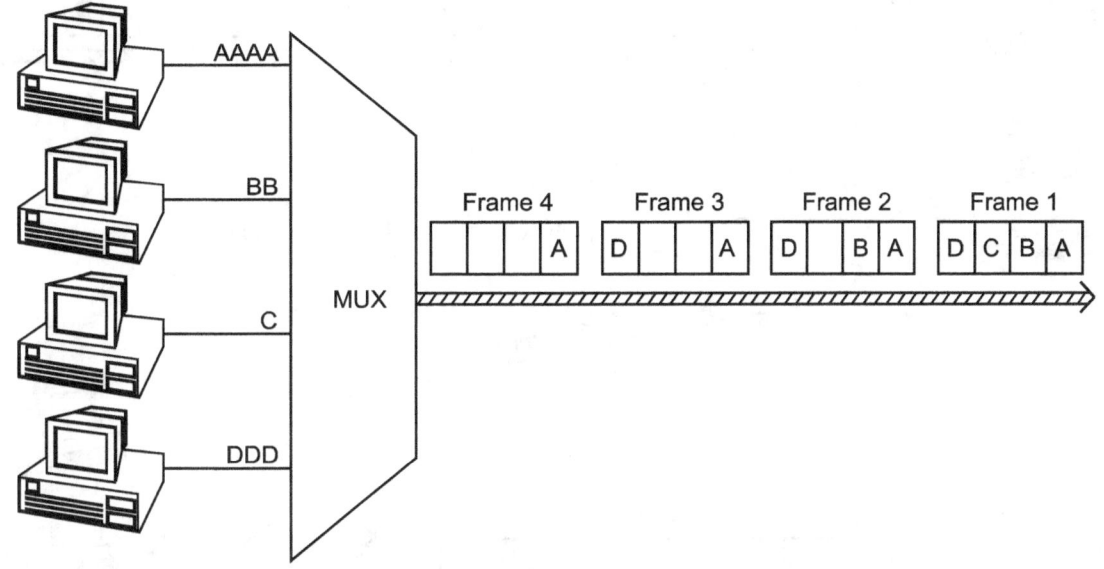

(a) Synchronous TDM (Multiplexing Process)

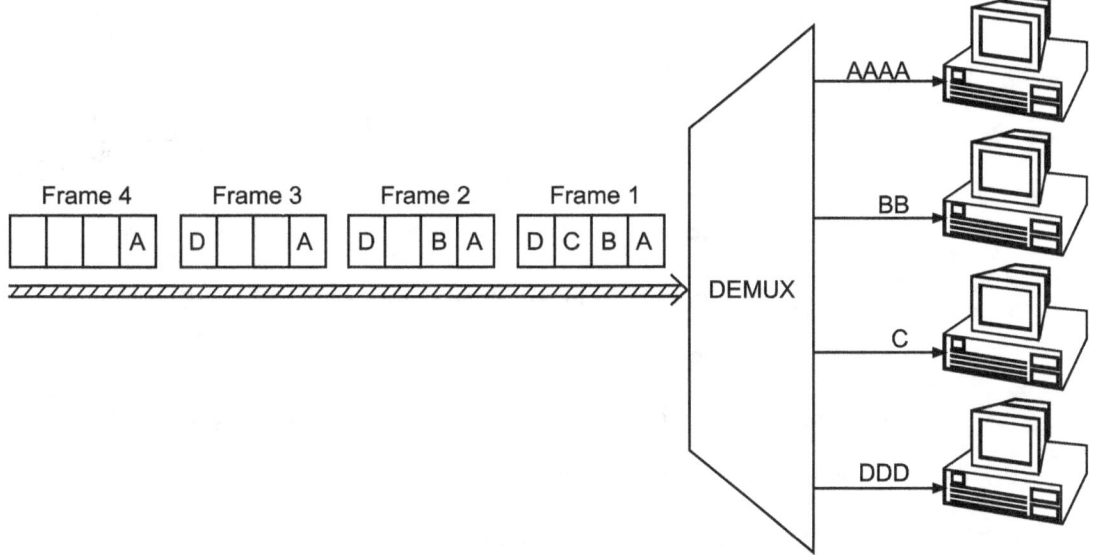

(b) Synchronous TDM (Demultiplexing Process)

Fig. 5.12

Synchronous TDM (Multiplexing and Demultiplexing) system can also be explained with Fig. 5.13 (a) and (b).

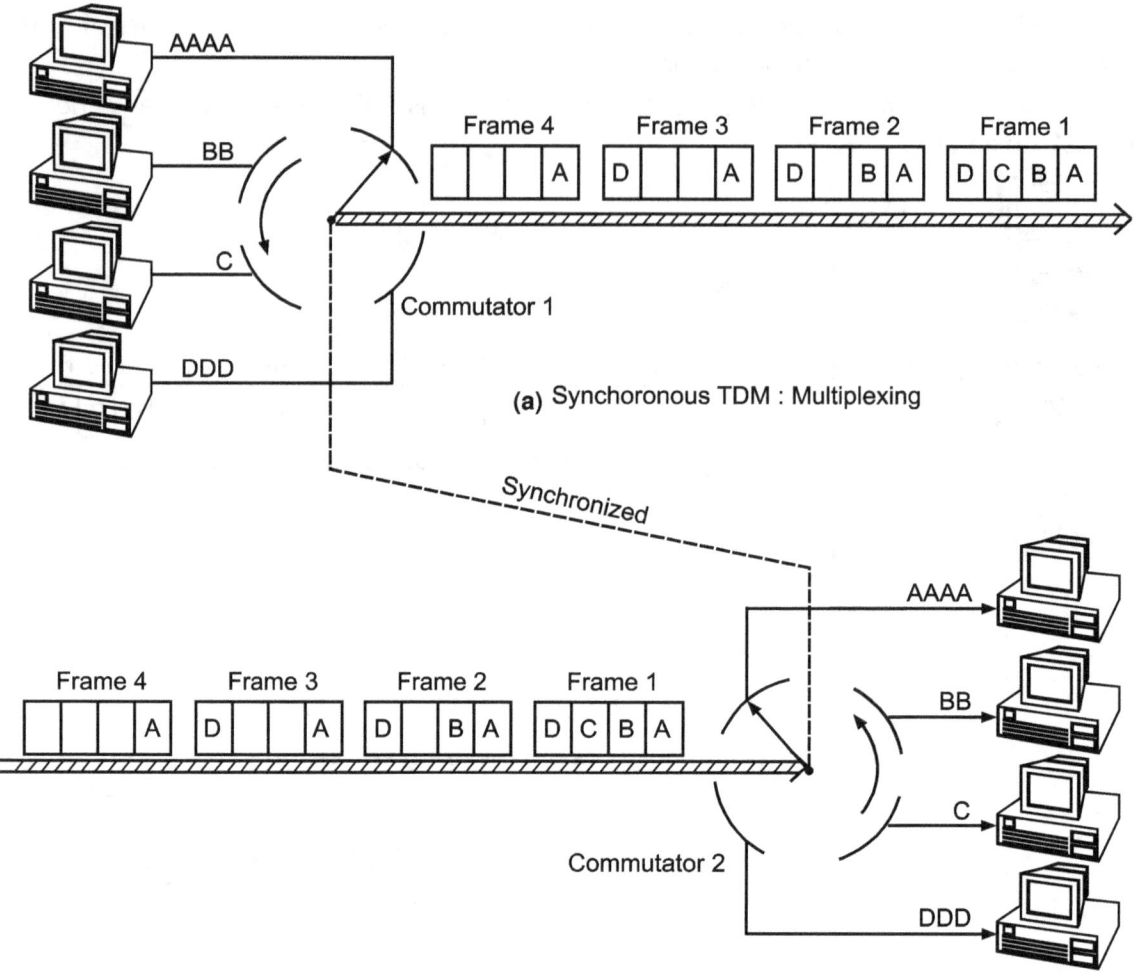

(b) Synchronous TDM : Demultiplexing

Fig. 5.13 : Synchronous TDM (Multiplexing and Demultiplexing)

[Showing MUX as commutator]

Commutator : Single pole rotating switch (Mechanical or electronic)

In synchronous TDM systems, the following points are important :

- Both transmitter and receiver must be synchronized.

- This synchronization causes fixed cycle of operation.

- The channel is divided into time slots and each user is allocated a slot - whether it is empty or not.

- The slots are rotated among the attached users.

- Access to channel is granted at specific time slots.

5.3.2 Asynchronous TDM (or Statistical Time Division Multiplexing)

In asynchronous TDM, each slot in a frame is not dedicated to the fixed device. Each slot contains an index of the device to be sent to and a message. Thus, the number of slots in a frame can be allocated for an input device. This technique allows a number of lower speed input lines to be multiplexed to a single higher speed line (transmission link) as shown in Fig. 5.13.

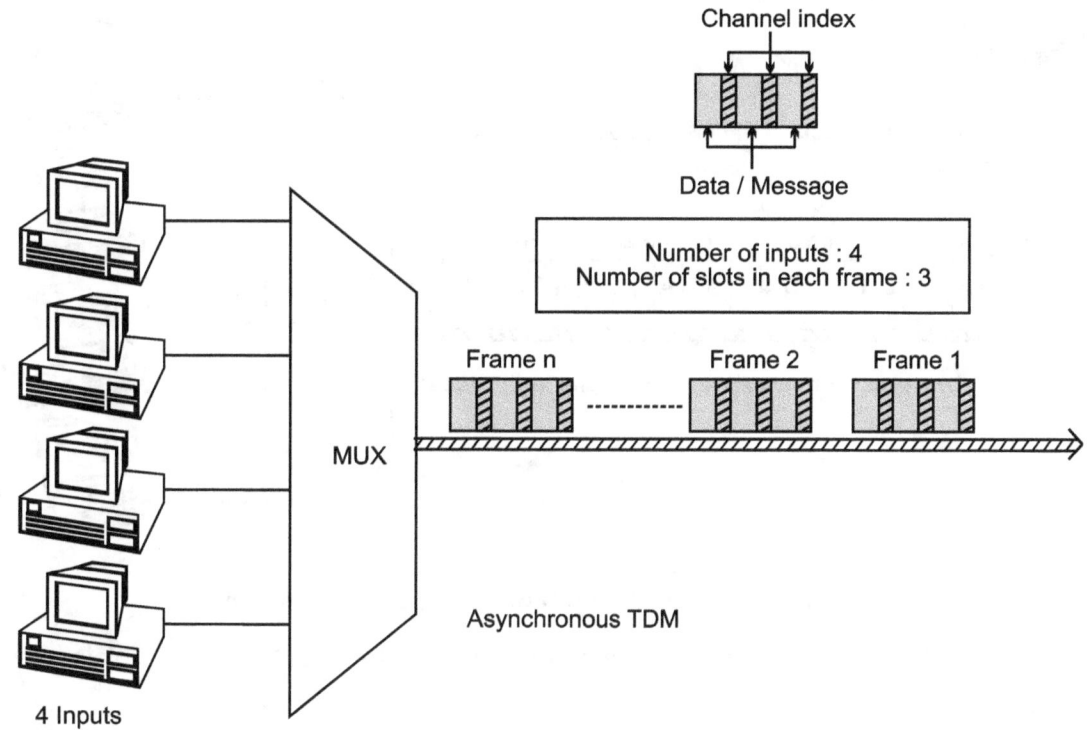

Fig. 5.14 : Basic Asynchronous TDM System

In Fig. 5.14 a frame contains a fixed number of time slots. Each slot has an index of which device to receive.

Multiplexing and demultiplexing processes in asynchronous TDM system are clearly shown in Fig. 5.15.

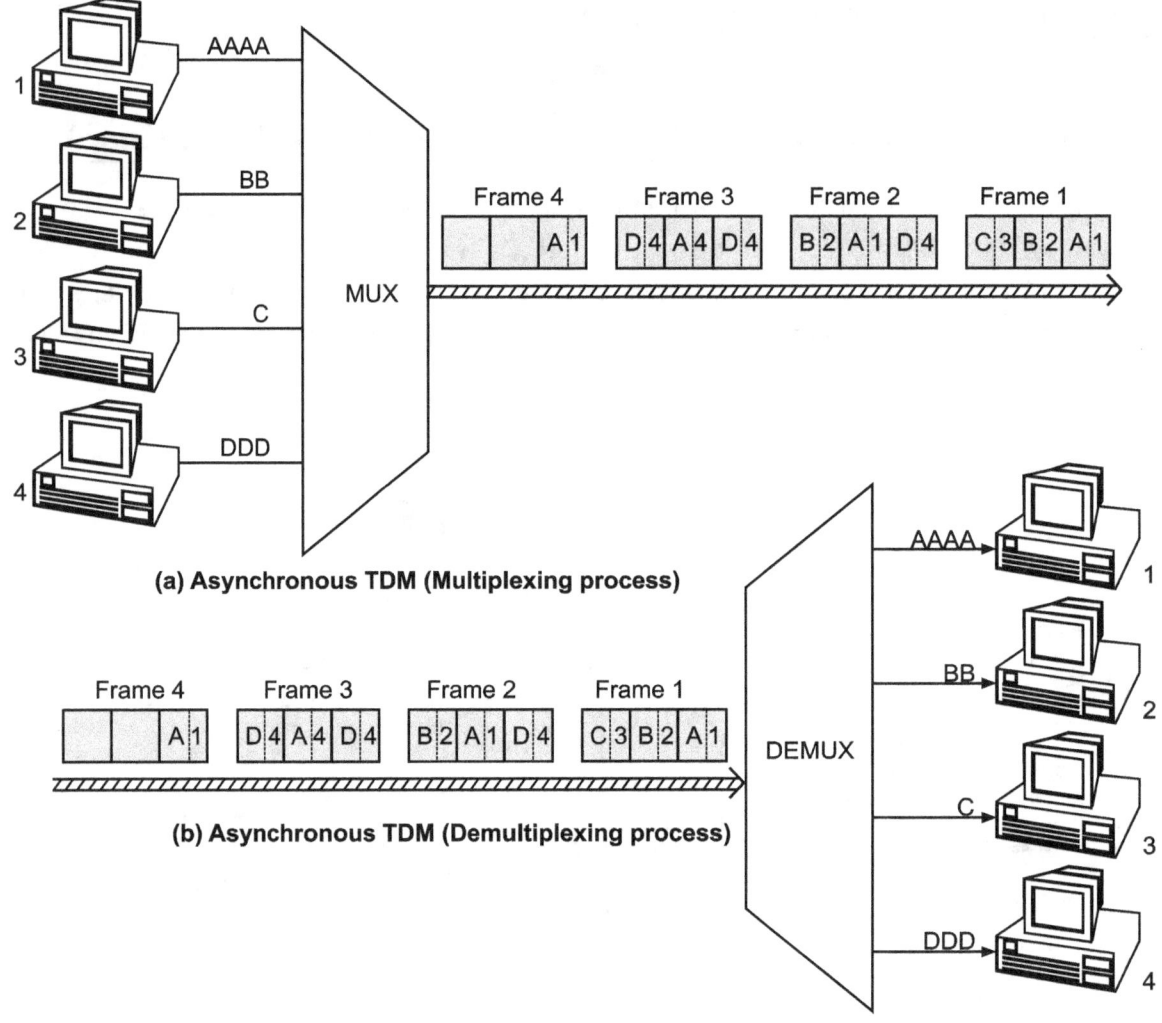

Fig. 5.15 : Asynchronous TDM (Multiplexing and Demultiplexing)

Asynchronous TDM (multiplexing and demultiplexing) system can also be explained with Fig. 5.16.

In asynchronous TDM systems, following points are important :

- Time slots are allocated on demand instead of a fixed cycle.

- Allows unused slots to be allocated to active users. The devices wanting to transmit must request a slot, which is granted for the duration of the transmission.

- Many devices can be connected and provide more efficient use of the available bandwidth.

- This system performs best with bursty sources. (i.e. not continuously sending).

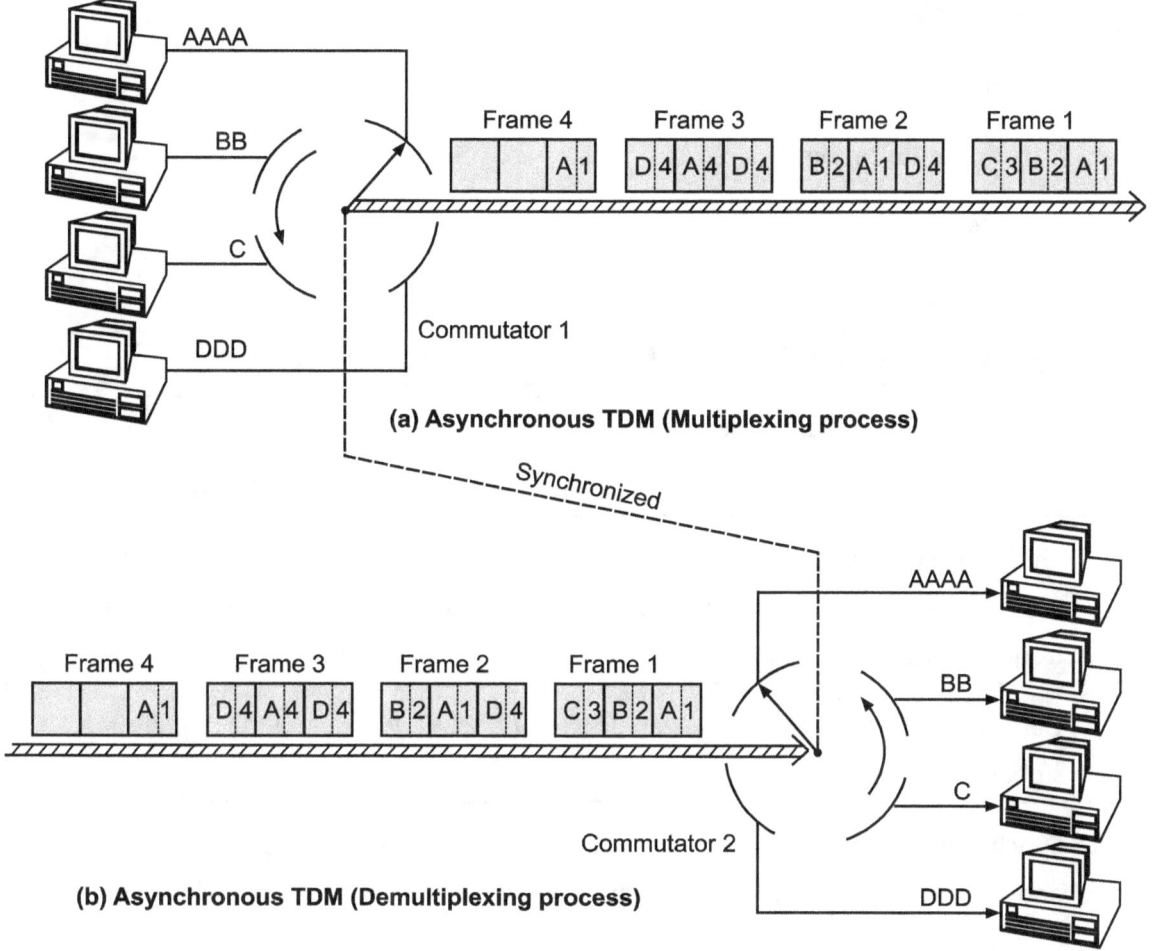

(a) Asynchronous TDM (Multiplexing process)

(b) Asynchronous TDM (Demultiplexing process)

Fig. 5.16 : Asynchronous TDM (Multiplexing and Demultiplexing)

[Showing MUX as commutator]

Commutator : Single pole rotating switch (Mechanical or electronic)

- Thus asynchronous TDM system provides some advanced capabilities like :

  ➢ Data compression

  ➢ Line priority

  ➢ Mixed speed lines

  ➢ Automatic speed detection, etc.

Applications of TDM :

- Digital Telephony

- Data communication

- Satellite access

- Cellular radio.

5.4 COMPARISON OF FDM AND TDM TECHNIQUES

Sr. No.	FDM	TDM
1.	The signals, which are to be multiplexed, occupy different slots in frequency domain.	The signals, which are to be multiplexed, are send by dividing time domain slots, in which one slot for each signal is given.
2.	Generally FDM is used for analog signals.	Generally TDM is used for digital data.
3.	Synchronization between transmitter and receiver is not required for proper operation.	Synchronization between transmitter and receiver is must for proper operation.
4.	Circuit complexity is more in FDM system.	Circuit for transmitter and receiver is not complex.
5.	A problem of cross talk (or frequency overlapping) exists in the FDM system. This is due to BPF characteristics used in the circuit.	In TDM, there is no problem of crosstalk.
6.	FDM requires modulators, filters (LPF and BPF), adders and demodulators for their operation.	TDM requires a commutator which is one pole fast rotating mechanical or electronic switch.

Conti.

7.	Applications of FDM :	Applications of TDM :
	• Radio broadcast	• Data communication
	• TV broadcast	• Satellite access
	• Mobile radio	• Cellular radio
	• Fiber optic channel communication	• Digital telephony
	• Wireless communication	
	• Analog telephony	

5.5   WAVELENGTH DIVISION MULTIPLEXING (WDM)

• WDM is a FDM (frequency division multiplexing) technique for fiber optic cable in which multiple optical signal channels are carried across a single strand of fiber at different wavelengths of light.

• These channels are also called *lambda circuits*. Think of each wavelength as a different colour of light in the infrared range that can carry data.

• With the exponential growth in communication, caused mainly by the wide acceptance of the Internet, many carriers are finding that their estimates of fiber needs have been highly underestimated.

• Although most cables include many spare fibers when installed, this growth has used many of them and new capacity is needed.

Three methods exist for expanding capacity :

  • Installing more cables,
  • Increasing system bit rate to multiplex more signals or
  • Wavelength Division Multiplexing.

• Installing more cables will be the preferred method in many cases, especially in metropolitan areas, since fiber has become incredibly inexpensive and installation methods more efficient (like mass fusion splicing).

• But if conduit space is not available or major construction is necessary, this may not be the most cost effective.

• Increasing system bit rate may not prove cost effective either.

• The third alternative, Wavelength Division Multiplexing (WDM), has proven more cost effective in many instances.

• It not only allows using current electronics and current fibers, but also simply shares fibers by transmitting different channels at different wavelengths (colours) of light.

• Systems, that already use fiber optic amplifiers as repeaters, also do not require upgrading for most WDM systems.

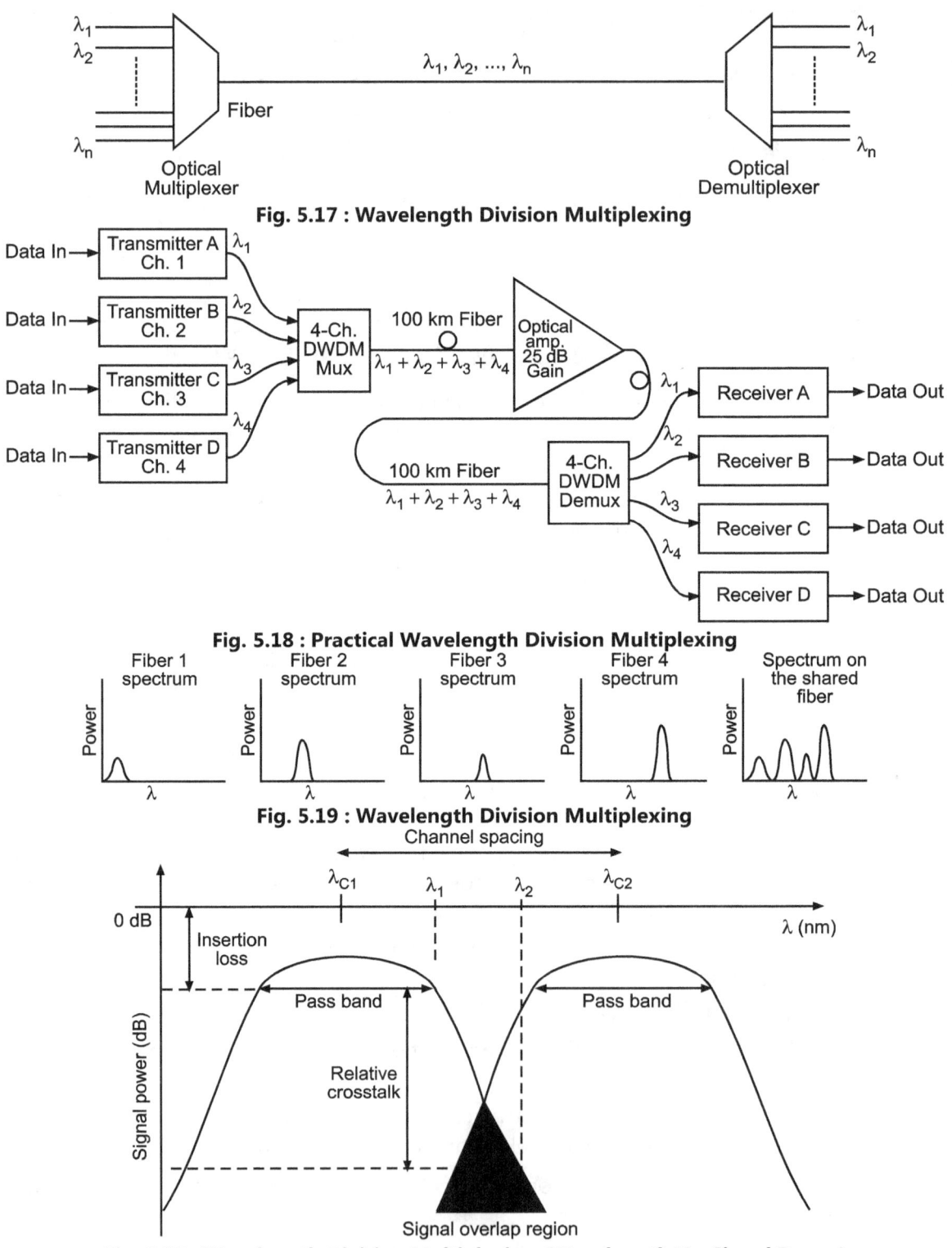

Fig. 5.17 : Wavelength Division Multiplexing

Fig. 5.18 : Practical Wavelength Division Multiplexing

Fig. 5.19 : Wavelength Division Multiplexing

Fig. 5.20 : Wavelength Division Multiplexing (Wavelength Vs. Signal Power)

5.5.1 Advantages of WDM like Full Utilization of Fiber Bandwidth

- Because WDM allows the large bandwidth of the optical fiber to be more fully utilized, optical fiber becomes more than a simple 1 : 1 replacement for copper wires (one channel per fiber).

- Optical multiplexing enables an N : 1 capability (N channels per fiber, where each channel may operate at the full electronic limit, allowing multi-gigabit per second aggregate data rates).

- In addition, WDM technology offers network planners considerable flexibility in which the optical channels are both bit-rate and data-format independent.

5.5.2 Three Categories of Wavelength Division Multiplexing

- **WDM (Wavelength Division Multiplexing) :** Two to four wavelengths per fiber. The original WDM systems were dual-channel 1310/1550 nm systems.

- **CWDM (Coarse Wavelength Division Multiplexing) :** From 4 to 8 wavelengths per fiber, sometimes more. Designed for short to medium-haul networks (regional and metropolitan area).

- **DWDM (Dense Wavelength Division Multiplexing) :** A typical DWDM system supports 8 or more wavelengths. Emerging systems support hundreds of wavelengths.

5.5.3 Applications of WDM

- Two obvious applications are already in use, submarine cables and extending the lifetime of cables where all fibers are being used.

- For submarine cables, DWDM enhances the capacity without adding fibers, which create larger cables and bulkier and more complicated repeaters.

- Adding service in areas, where cables are now full, is another good application.

- But this technology may also reduce the cost on all land-based long distance communication links and new technology may lead to totally new network architectures.

5.6 SPREAD SPECTRUM SYSTEM

- In multiplexing, the main goal is to achieve efficiency, by combining several channels into one.

- In spreading, the main goal is privacy and antijamming. Thus, we expand the bandwidth of channel to insert redundancy.

- Spread spectrum technique is designed specially for wireless applications like wireless LANs and wireless WANs.

- In RF communication, following are the problems :

- In military communication, the information has to be secured. It can be hacked by intruder or unauthorized person if secured environment is not established.

- Intruder or enemy can "Jam" the transmission. Hence, the communication will be disturbed between sender and receiver.

- These problems can be solved by using "spread spectrum" technique of modulation.

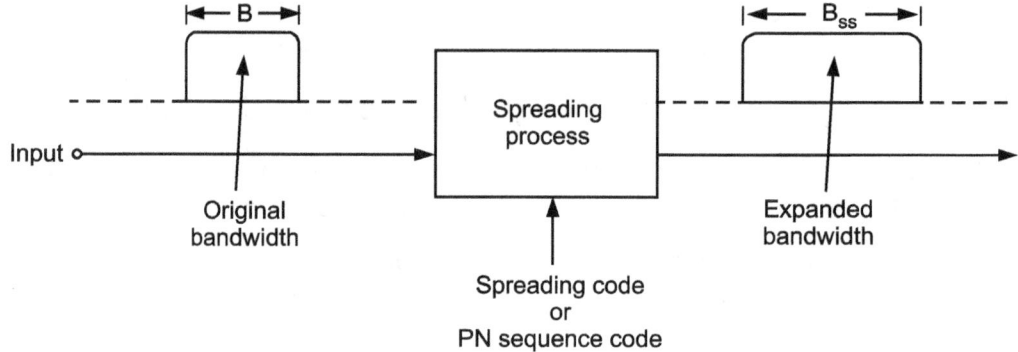

Fig. 5.21 : Typical Spread Spectrum Process

5.6.1 Difference between Spread Spectrum Signal and Normal Signal

- Spread spectrum signal occupies larger bandwidth (wideband) as compared to normal signal (which is narrowband signal).

- Spreading technique is used at transmission, whereas dispreading technique is used at receiver end.

- Spread spectrum signal is "pseudo random" in nature. That's why it appears like "random noise". So intruder or enemy can not recover the original data with normal receiver and thus secured environment is created.

- Spread spectrum transmitters use similar transmit power levels to narrowband transmitters, but because spread spectrum signals are so wide, they can be transmitted at much lower spectral power density (measured in watts per hertz), than narrowband transmitters.

- Since spread spectrum (SS) is transmitted with low power, but wide bandwidth, SS and narrowband signals can occupy the same band with little to no interference.

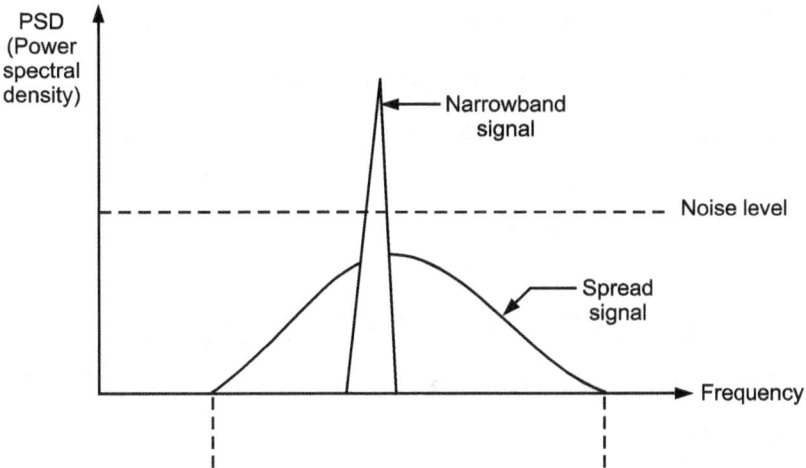

Fig. 5.22 : Spread Spectrum compared to Narrowband Signal

- Thus, to qualify as SS signal, two criteria should be met :

The transmitted signal bandwidth is much greater than the information bandwidth.

- Some function, other than the information being transmitted, is being employed to determine the resultant transmitted bandwidth.

- Most SS systems transmit a radio frequency signal bandwidth as wide as 20 to 254 times the bandwidth being sent. Some SS systems have employed radio frequency bandwidths 1000 times their information bandwidth.

5.6.2 Typical Spread Spectrum Communication

- Typical spread spectrum communication system is as shown in Fig. 5.23.

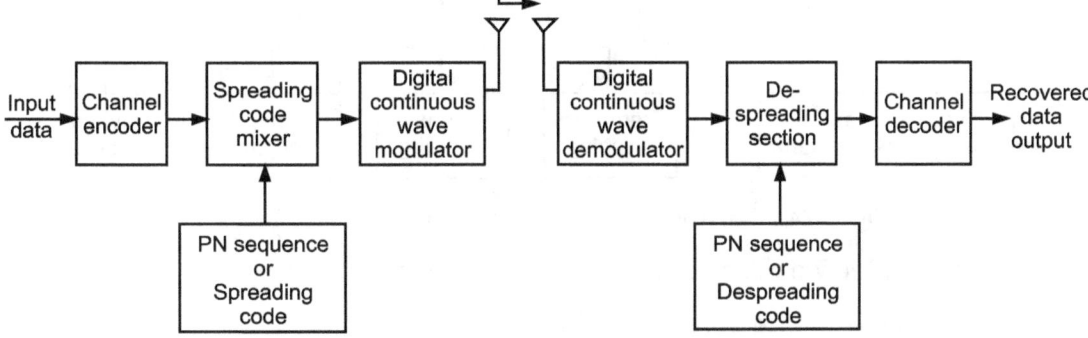

Fig. 5.23 : Typical Spread Spectrum Communication System

- Input data is applied to the channel encoder to take care of transmission errors.

- Encoded data and PN sequence signals are applied to spreading code mixer. PN sequence "spreads" the signal randomly over a wideband.

- Spreaded resultant code is modulated by the digital continuous wave modulation technique like BPSK etc. for final transmission.

- Radiated signal from transmitter is received at receiver end.

- Initially the digital continuous wave demodulation process is done.

- Demodulated signals are applied to dispreading section where same PN sequence pattern which works in synchronization with transmitter is applied.

- The dispreaded data available from dispreading section is finally given to channel decoder to recover the original data required.

5.6.3 Classification of Spread Spectrum Techniques

- Spread spectrum modulation techniques are broadly classified into two categories :

    - Averaging type technique.

    - Avoidance type technique.

- In averaging type technique, the interference is reduced by averaging it over a long period.

- In avoidance type technique, the interference is reduced by making the signal to avoid the interference over a large fraction of time.

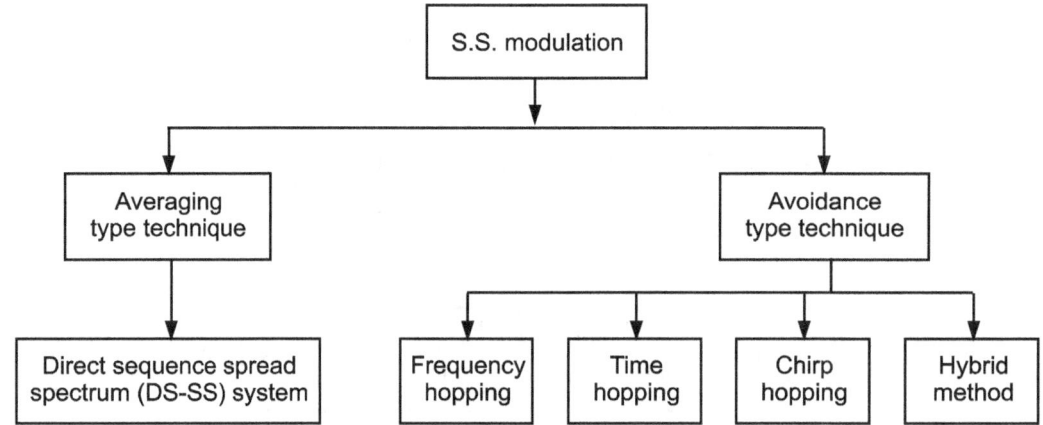

Fig. 5.24 : Classification of Spread Spectrum Techniques

- Here in this chapter, we will discuss only two techniques :

    (i)   DSSS (Direct Sequence Spread Spectrum).

    (ii) FHSS (Frequency Hopping Spread Spectrum).

5.7 FHSS (FREQUENCY HOPPING SPREAD SPECTRUM)

- In FHSS 'M' are used for different carrier frequencies that are modulated by the input modulating signal or source information signal.

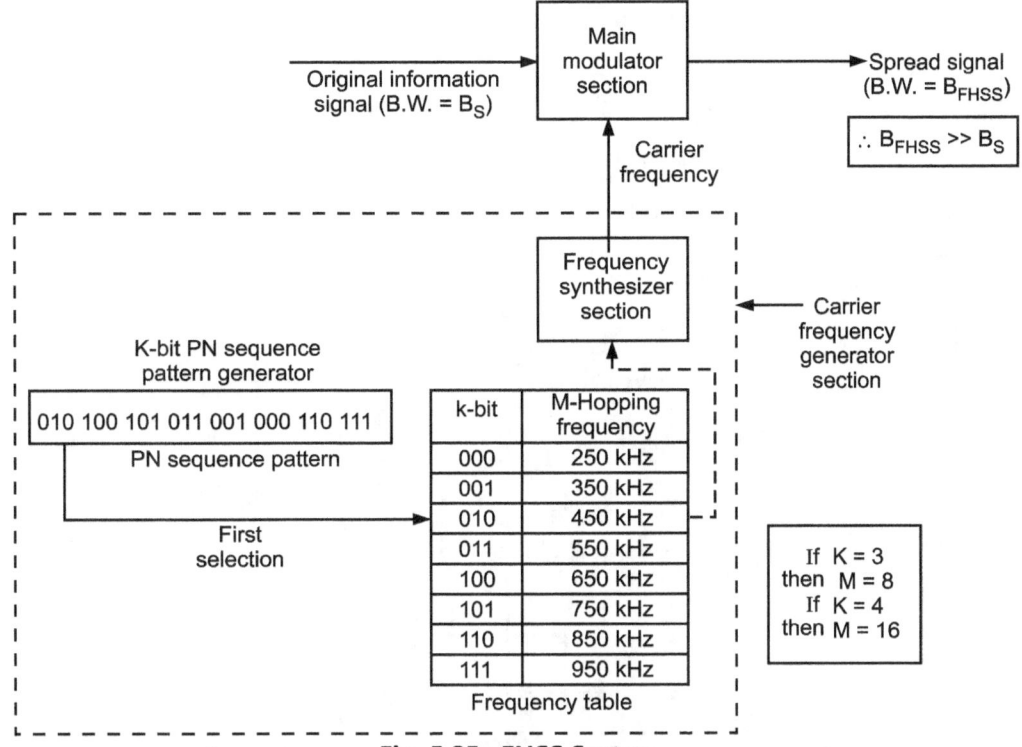

Fig. 5.25 : FHSS System

- Here at one moment original information signal modulates one carrier frequency, generated by PN sequence, frequency table and frequency synthesizer section. At the next moment the original information signal generates another carrier frequency as shown.
- Modulation is done by using only one carrier frequency at a time in the FHSS system.
- PN sequence generator generates k-bit pattern for every hopping period T_H.
- For every K-bit, M-hopping frequencies are generated.
- Also note that PN sequence pattern repeats after eight hoppings if K = 3 and   M = 8.
- PN sequence pattern will repeat after sixteen hoppings if K = 4 and M = 16.
- Consider K = 3 and M = 8 case, the frequency table is as shown in Table 5.3.

Table 5.3 : Frequency Table

K bit	M – Hopping frequencies
000	250 kHz
001	350 kHz
010	450 kHz
011	550 kHz
100	650 kHz
101	750 kHz
110	850 kHz
111	950 kHz

- Consider for cycle 1, the random PN sequence generated is

  010, 100, 101, 011, 001, 000, 110, 111.

- Consider for cycle 2, the random PN sequence generated is

  001, 111, 010, 110, 011, 101, 000, 100.

- Thus, for cycle 1 and cycle 2, the FHSS carrier frequencies selection for different hopping periods is as shown in Fig. 5.26.

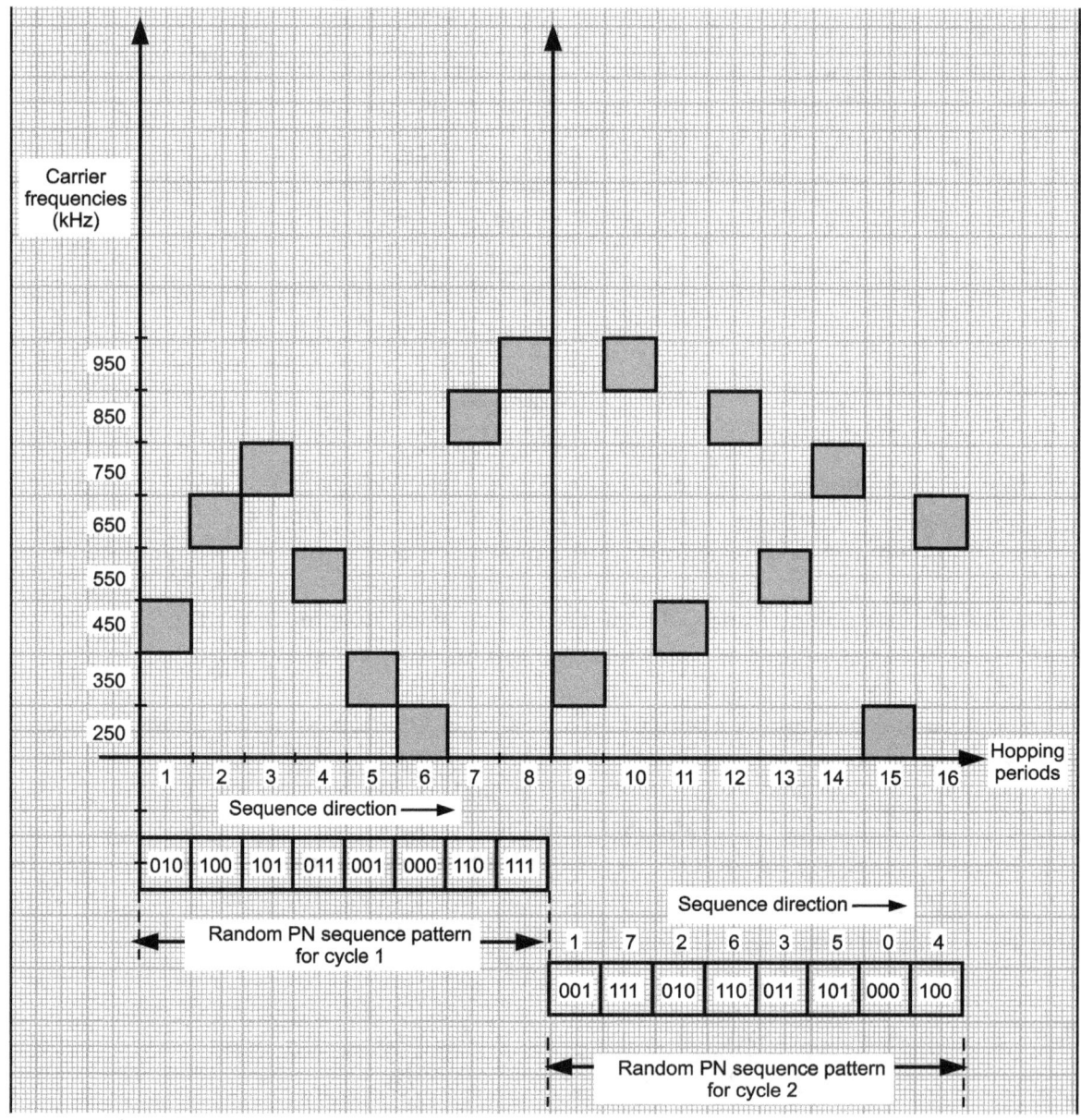

Fig. 5.26 : FHSS Frequency Selection for Different Cycles

- Thus, if hopping period is short, then transmitter and receiver can have privacy.

- If an intruder or hacker tries to intercept the transmitted signal, he can only access small amount of data because of unknown PN sequence at every next hop.

- Also anti-jamming provision is there in FHSS system, i.e. if intruder wants to jam the FHSS communication system, then he can jam the signal for only one hopping period randomly, but cannot jam for whole period.

- Also FDM and FHSS both act as bandwidth sharing application, but in different way.

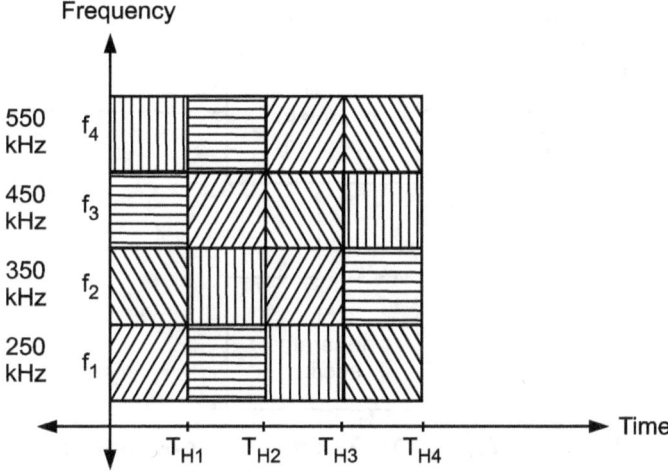

Fig. 5.27 : Typical FHSS System

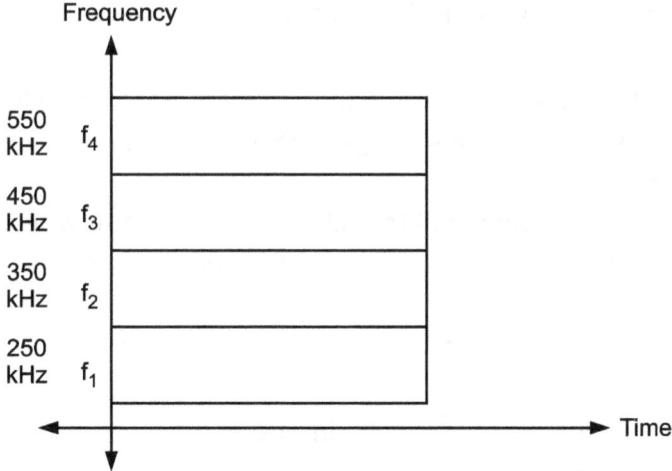

Fig. 5.28 : Typical 4-channel FDM System

5.8 DSSS (DIRECT SEQUENCE SPREAD SPECTRUM)

- In DSSS technique also, the signal is spread but the process is different.

- In DSSS each data bit is replaced with 'n' bits using a PN sequence code (or spreading code).

- Or we can say that each bit is assigned a code of n bits, called as chips.

- If   Chip rate $= C_R$

                                         Data rate $= D_R$

    then $C_R = nD_R$

- Typical DSSS communication system is as shown in Fig. 5.29.

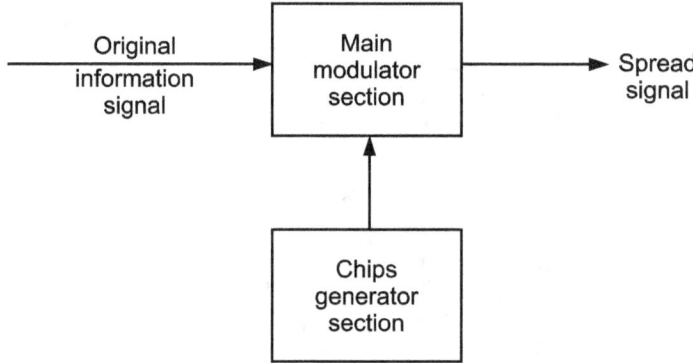

Fig. 5.29 : Typical DSSS Communication System

- In this technique, the PN sequence is applied directly to data entering the carrier modulator.

- The modulator therefore sees a much larger bit rate, which corresponds to the chip rate of the PN sequence.

- The result of modulating an RF carrier with such a code sequence is to produce a direct sequence modulated spread spectrum with $((sinx)/x)^2$ frequency spectrum, centered at the carrier frequency.

- The main lobe of this spectrum (null to null) has a bandwidth twice the clock rate of the modulating code, and the side lobes have null-to-null bandwidths equal to the code's clock rate.

- Illustrated below is the most common type of direct sequence modulated spread spectrum signal.

- Direct sequence spectra vary somewhat in spectral shape, depending on the actual carrier and data modulation used.

- Direct sequence systems are the best known and most widely used spread spectrum systems.

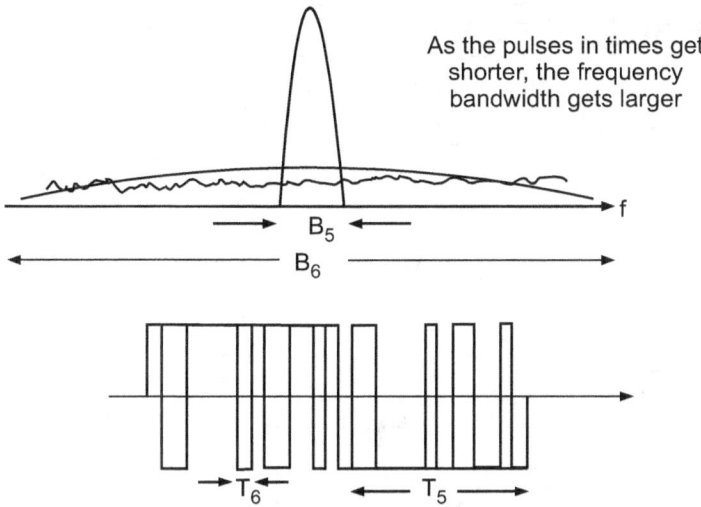

As the pulses in times get shorter, the frequency bandwidth gets larger

Fig. 5.30 : Spectrum Analyzer Photo of a Direct Sequence (DS) Spread Spectrum Signal
Note the original signal (non-spread) would only occupy half of the central lobe.

- This process is achieved by multiplying a radio frequency carrier with a pseudo noise.

- The pseudo noise (PN-code) is a binary signal which is produced at a much higher frequency than the data that is to be transmitted. Since this has a higher frequency, it has a large bandwidth, which spreads the signal in the frequency plane (i.e. it spreads its spectrum).

- The nature of this signal makes it appear as random.

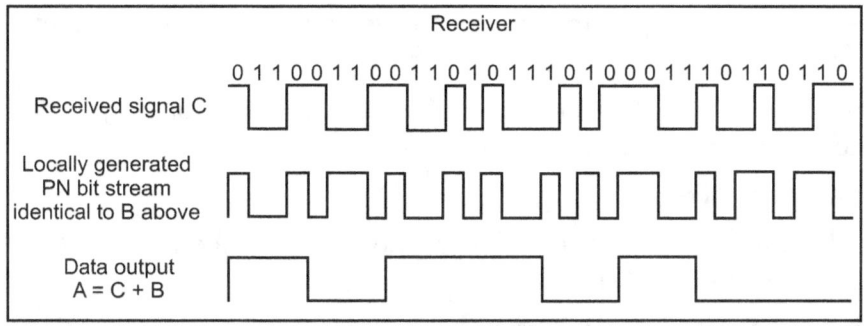

Fig. 5.31 : DSSS Coding

- Signals generated with this technique appear as noise in the frequency domain. The wide bandwidth provided by the pseudo noise code allows the signal power to drop below the noise threshold without losing any information.

- Special spreading codes like walsh code allow us to use DSSS in mobile communication and share bandwidth among several users.

5.9 MULTIPLE ACCESS COMMUNICATIONS

When number of users share the same medium for transmission as shown in Fig. 5.32, all the stations sharing the medium can hear transmission from any given station.

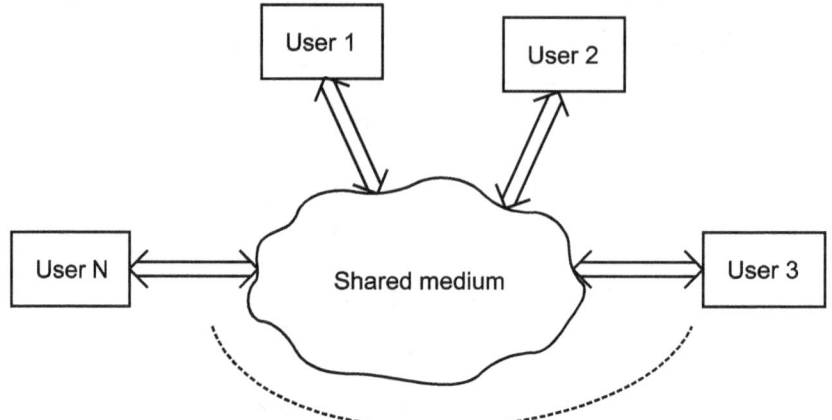

Fig. 5.32 (a) : Multiple Access Communication

If two or more stations try transmitting simultaneously their transmission will collide.

There are two schemes for allocating channels for transmission to a particular user.

(i) Static Channel Allocation :

It is static and collision free sharing of medium. If there are N users, the bandwidth of channel is divided into N subchannels and each user uses them separately. It is called Frequency Division Multiplexing (FDM).

FDM is efficient in case when all the channels have continuous traffic and inefficient when traffic is bursty.

Another static channel allocation method is Time Division Multiplexing (TDM) where each user is allocated a fixed time slot for transmission.

(ii) Dynamic Channel Allocation :

In situations where user traffic is bursty the channel is allocated on a per frame basis. This is called Medium Access Control Scheme.

There are two approaches of implementing this scheme :

- Scheduling
- Random Access

While allocating the channels dynamically, following assumptions are made :

- There are N independent stations which generate frames for transmission randomly. Once a frame is generated station is blocked i.e. it does nothing until frame is successfully transmitted.

- There is only one channel available.

- If two frames are transmitted simultaneously, it results into collision.

- Frame transmission can begin at any instant. Frames are transmitted in a fixed time slot.

- Stations can sense if channel is in use. If it is sensed busy no station will attempt to use it.

Stations cannot serve channel before use. Only after transmission they decide whether transmission was successful or not.

There are number of protocols devised to handle the multiple access over a shared channel. These protocols can be classified as :

- Random Access Protocols.

  e.g. Aloha, CSMA, CSMA/CD, CSMA/CA

- Controlled Access Protocols

  e.g. Reservation, Polling, Token Passing.

- Channelization Protocols

  e.g. FDMA, TDMA and CDMA.

5.10 ALOHA

- It is a random access scheme for transmitting information for terminals sharing the same channel.

- It is simple in operation.

- Information is transmitted over the shared channel as soon as it becomes available.

- If there is collision because of more stations transmitting simultaneously, they will wait for random amount of time before transmitting the information again. It is called back-off.

- Fig. 5.32 (b) shows frame transmission using ALOHA.

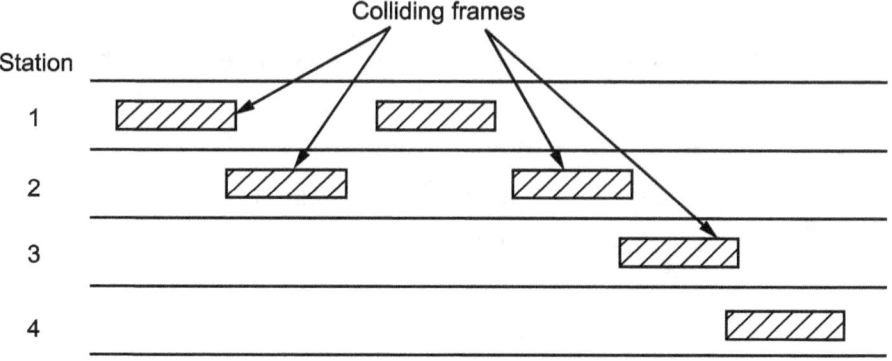

Fig. 5.32 (b) : ALOHA System

Efficiency of ALOHA :

Let L be the length of frame (bits) (constant).

R be rate of transmission.

$$\therefore \qquad \text{Frame time} \; = \; X = \frac{L}{R}$$

Let some frame arrive at time t_o and end at $t_o + X$.

This frame will collide if there is transmission from other stations between $t_o - X$ and $t_o + X$ as shown in Fig. 5.32 (c).

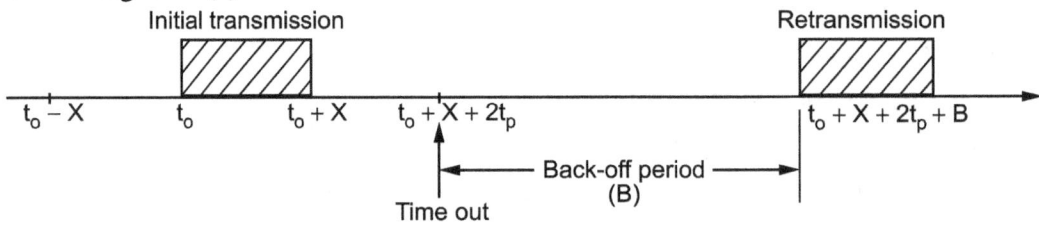

Fig. 5.32 (c) : ALOHA System

$$\therefore \qquad \text{Vulnerable time} \; = \; (t_o + X) - (t_o - X)$$

$$= \; 2X$$

Let G be the total arrival rate of the system in frames/X seconds. G is also throughput of the system. Let G be total arrival rate of the system in frames/X seconds. G is also called total load of the system.

With the assumption that the back-off spreads retransmissions such that new and repeated frame transmission are equally likely to occur, the number of frames transmitted in a time interval has Poisson distribution with average number of arrivals of 2G arrivals/2X seconds.

Hence, probability that k frames are generated during a given frame time are

$$P[k \text{ transmissions in 2X seconds}] = \frac{(2G)^k}{k!} \, e^{-2G}$$

Hence, throughput S is equal to total arrival rate G times probability of successful transmission.

$$\therefore \qquad S \; = \; P[\text{no collision}]$$

$$= \; P[0 \text{ transmissions in 2X seconds}]$$

$$= \; G \frac{(2G)^0}{0!} \, e^{-2G}$$

$$= \; Ge^{-2G}$$

The plot of S versus G is shown in Fig. 5.32 (d).

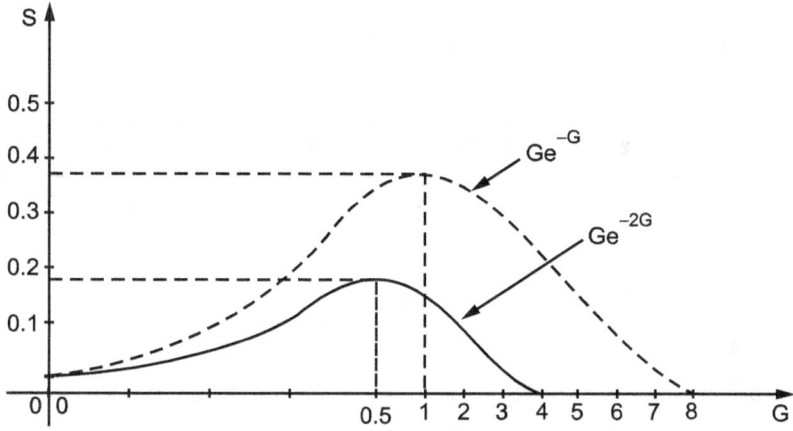

Fig. 5.32 (d) : Throughput Curve

It can be seen that the maximum value of S = $\dfrac{1}{2e}$ at G = 0.5. That is system can achieve throughput of 18.4% only.

Slotted ALOHA :

Performance of ALOHA can be improved by putting a restriction on time of transmission i.e. stations will transmit only at a fixed time (Synchronize fashion). Thus, reducing the probability of collisions.

All stations keep track of transmission time slots and are allowed to initiate transmission only at beginning of slot.

Vulnerable time i.e. time of collision reduces to $t_0 - X$ to X i.e. X second as shown in Fig. 5.33.

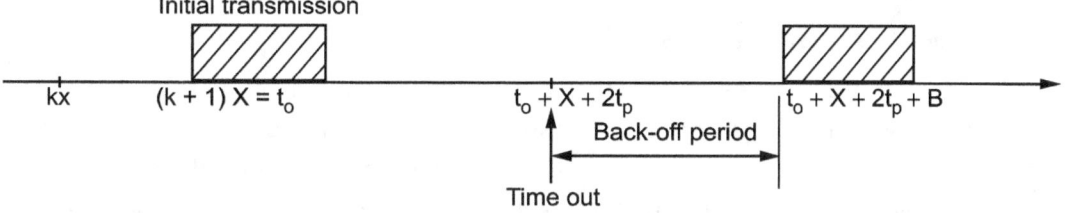

Fig. 5.33

There are G arrivals in X seconds, (G is total arrival rate)

$\therefore$
$$S = G \times P \text{ [no collision]}$$
$$= G \times P \text{ [0 transmission in X seconds]}$$
$$= G \times \frac{(G)^0}{0!} e^{-G}$$
$$= Ge^{-G}$$

Above equation is plotted in Fig. 5.33 (c). Slotted ALOHA has maximum   throughput of $\frac{1}{e} =$ 36.8% at G = 1.

5.11 CARRIER SENSE MULTIPLE ACCESS PROTOCOLS

Protocols in which stations listen for carriers and take suitable action are called Carrier Sense Protocols.

Following are some carrier sense protocols :

1. **1-Persistent CSMA :**
   - When a station has some data to send it listens to the channel.
   - If channel is busy it waits until it becomes free or idle continuously sensing the channel.
   - If channel is idle it transmits the frame.
   - It is called 1-persistent because whenever channel is idle the station transmits with probability 1.

2. **Non-Persistent CSMA :**
   - When station has some data to send, it listens to the channel and if channel is idle it sends data.
   - If channel is busy, it waits until it becomes free/idle.
   - But then it does not sense the channel continuously as in 1-persistent CSMA. It waits for random period and then again senses the channel.

3. **p-Persistent CSMA :**
   - It applies to slotted channels.
   - When a station is ready to transit data and channel is idle it transmits with probability p and decides not to transmit with probability q = 1 − p until next slot. If that slot is also idle it decides to transmit or defer with probability p and q. This process is repeated until either frame is transmitted or another station has started transmission.
   - If the channel is busy it waits until next slot and repeats above step.

5.12 CARRIER SENSE MULTIPLE ACCESS WITH COLLISION DETECTION (CSMA/CD)

A Shared Medium :

The Ethernet network may be used to provide shared access by a group of attached nodes to the physical medium which connects the nodes. These nodes are said to form a Collision

Domain. All frames sent on the medium are physically received by all receivers, however the Medium Access Control (MAC) header contains a MAC destination address which ensure only the specified destination actually forwards the received frame (the other computers all discard the frames which are not addressed to them).

Consider a LAN with four computers each with a Network Interface Card (NIC) connected by a common Ethernet cable.

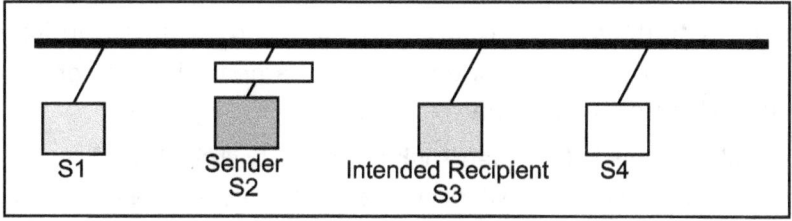

Fig. 5.34 (a)

One computer (S_2) uses a NIC to send a frame to the shared medium, which has a destination address corresponding to the source address of the NIC in the S_3 computer.

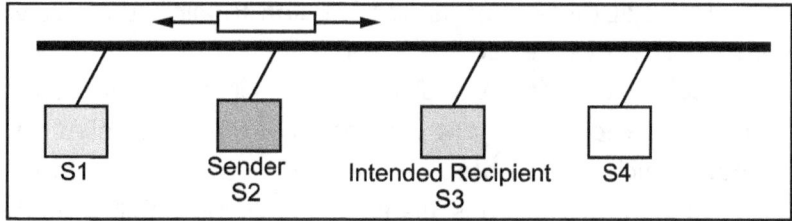

Fig. 5.34 (b)

The cable propagates the signal in both directions, so that the signal (eventually) reaches the NICs in all four of the computers. Termination resistors at the ends of the cable absorb the frame energy, preventing reflection of the signal back along the cable.

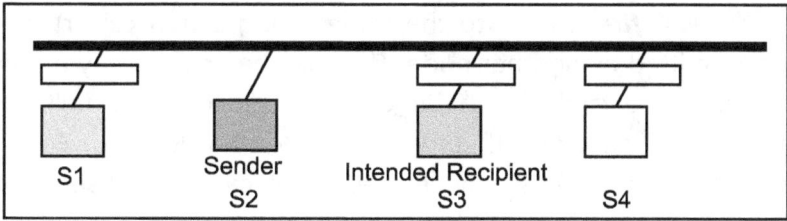

Fig. 5.34 (c)

All the NICs receive the frame and each examines it to check its length and checksum. The header destination MAC address is next examined, to see if the frame should be accepted, and forwarded to the network-layer software in the computer.

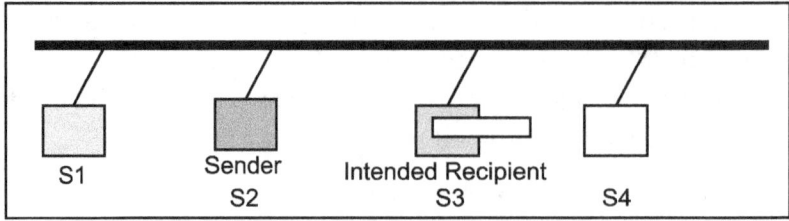

Fig. 5.34 (d)

Only the NIC in the computer S_3 recognises the frame destination address as valid, and therefore this NIC alone forwards the contents of the frame to the network layer. The NICs in the other computers discard the unwanted frame.

The shared cable allows any NIC to send whenever it wishes, but if two NICs happen to transmit at the same time, a collision will occur, resulting in the data being corrupted.

ALOHA and Collisions

To control which NICs are allowed to transmit at any given time, a protocol is required. As seen earlier, the simplest protocol is known as ALOHA (this is actually an Hawaiian word, meaning "hello"). ALOHA allows any NIC to transmit at any time, but states that each NIC must add a checksum/CRC at the end of its transmission to allow the receiver(s) to identify whether the frame was correctly received.

ALOHA is therefore a best effort service, and does not guarantee that the frame of data will actually reach the remote recipient without corruption. It therefore relies on ARQ protocols to retransmit any data which is corrupted. An ALOHA network only works well when the medium has a low utilization, since this leads to a low probability of the transmission colliding with that of another computer, and hence a reasonable chance that the data is not corrupted.

Carrier Sense Multiple Access (CSMA)

Ethernet uses a refinement of ALOHA, known as Carrier Sense Multiple Access (CSMA), which improves performance when there is a higher medium utilization. When a NIC has data to transmit, the NIC *first* listens to the cable (using a transceiver) to see if a carrier (signal) is being transmitted by another node. This may be achieved by monitoring whether a current is flowing in the cable (each bit corresponds to 18-20 milliAmps (mA)). The individual bits are sent by encoding them with a 10 (or 100 MHz for Fast Ethernet) clock using Manchester encoding. Data is only sent when no carrier is observed (i.e. no current present) and the physical medium is therefore idle. Any NIC which does not need to transmit, listens to see if other NICs have started to transmit information to it.

However, this alone is unable to prevent two NICs transmitting at the same time. If two NICs *simultaneously* try transmit, then both could see an idle physical medium (i.e. neither will see the other's carrier signal), and both will conclude that no other NIC is currently using the medium. In this case, both will then decide to transmit and a *collision* will occur. The collision will result in the corruption of the frame being sent, which will subsequently be discarded by the receiver since a corrupted Ethernet frame will (with a very high probability) not have a valid 32-bit MAC CRC at the end.

Collision Detection (CD)

A second element to the Ethernet access protocol is used to detect when a collision occurs. When there is data waiting to be sent, each transmitting NIC also monitors its own transmission. If it observes a collision (excess current above what it is generating, i.e. > 24 mA for coaxial Ethernet), it stops transmission immediately and instead transmits a 32-bit jam sequence. The purpose of this sequence is to ensure that any other node which may currently be receiving this frame will receive the jam signal in place of the correct 32-bit MAC CRC, this causes the other receivers to discard the frame due to a CRC error.

To ensure that all NICs start to receive a frame before the transmitting NIC has finished sending it, Ethernet defines a minimum frame size (i.e. no frame may have less than 46 bytes of payload). The minimum frame size is related to the distance which the network spans, the type of media being used and the number of repeaters which the signal may have to pass through to reach the furthest part of the LAN. Together these define a value known as the *Ethernet Slot Time*, corresponding to 512 bit times at 10 Mbps.

When two or more transmitting NICs each detect a corruption of their own data (i.e. a collision), each responds in the same way by transmitting the jam sequence. The following sequence depicts a collision :

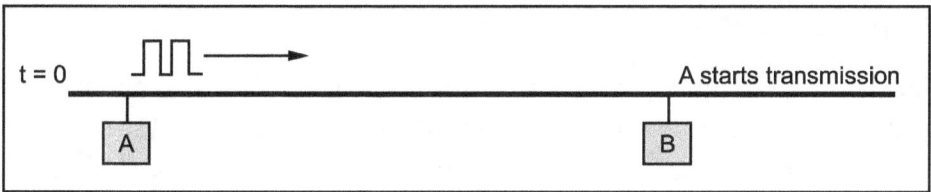

Fig. 5.35 (a)

At time t = 0, a frame is sent on the idle medium by NIC A.

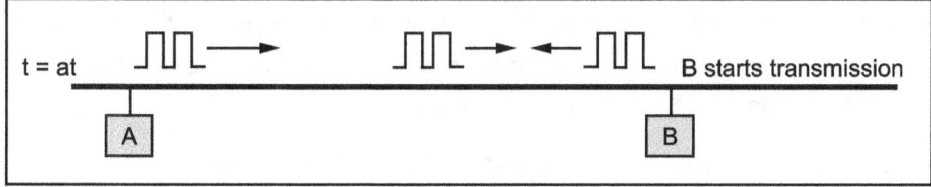

Fig. 5.35 (b)

A short time later, NIC B also transmits. (In this case, the medium, as observed by the NIC at B happens to be idle too.)

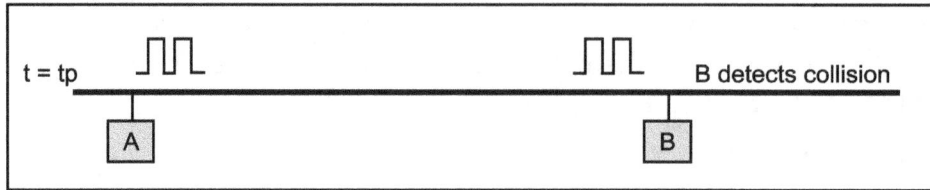

Fig. 5.35 (c)

After a period, equal to the propagation delay of the network, the NIC at B detects the other transmission from A, and is aware of a collision, but NIC A has not yet observed that NIC B was also transmitting. B continues to transmit, sending the Ethernet Jam sequence (32 bits).

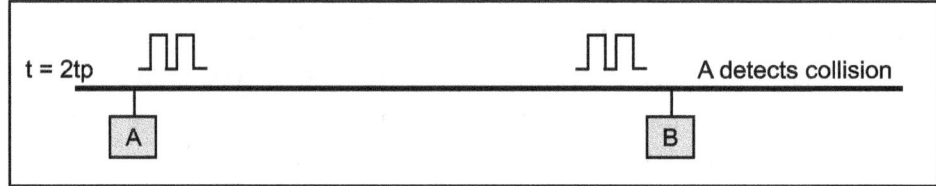

Fig. 5.35 (d)

After one complete round trip propagation time (twice the one way propagation delay), both NICs are aware of the collision. B will shortly cease transmission of the jam sequence, however A will continue to transmit a complete jam sequence. Finally the cable becomes idle.

Retransmission Back-Off

An overview of the transmit procedure is shown below. The transmitter initializes the number of transmissions of the current frame (n) to zero, and starts listening to the cable (using the carrier sense logic (CS) - e.g. by observing the R_x signal at transceiver to see if any bits are being sent). If the cable is not idle, it waits (defers) until the cable is idle. It then waits for a small Inter-Frame Gap (IFG) (e.g. 9.6 microseconds) to allow to time for all receiving nodes to return to prepare themselves for the next transmission.

Transmission then starts with the preamble, followed by the frame data and finally the CRC-32. After this time, the transceiver Tx logic is turned-off and the transceiver returns to passively monitoring the cable for other transmissions.

During this process, a transmitter must also continuously monitor the collision detection logic (CD) in the transceiver to detect if a collision occurs. If it does, the transmitter aborts the transmission (stops sending bits) within a few bit periods, and starts the collision procedure, by sending a jam signal to the transceiver Tx logic. It then calculates a retransmission time.

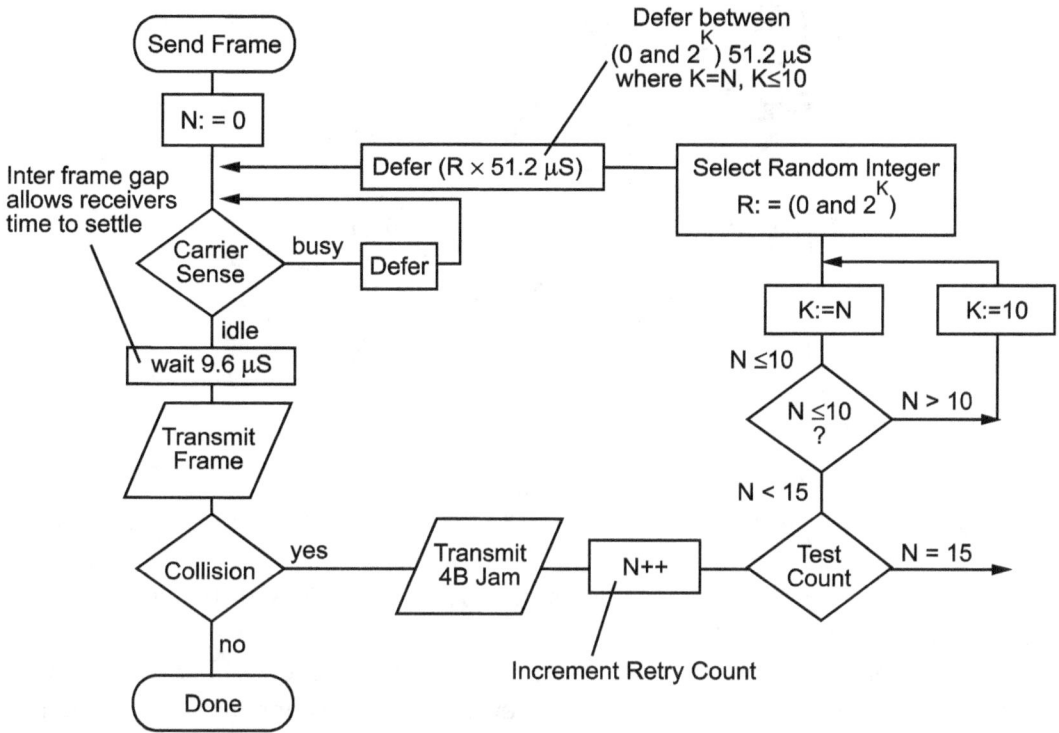

Fig. 5.36

If all NICs attempted to retransmit immediately following a collision, then this would certainly result in another collision. Therefore a procedure is required to ensure that there is only a low probability of simultaneous retransmission. The scheme adopted by Ethernet uses a random back-off period, where each node selects a random number, multiplies this by the slot time (minimum frame period, 51.2 µs) and waits for this random period before attempting retransmission. The small Inter-Frame Gap (IFG)   (e.g., 9.6 µs) is also added.

On a busy network, a retransmission may still collide with another retransmission (or possibly new frames being sent for the first time by another NIC). The protocol therefore counts the number of retransmission attempts (using a variable N in Fig. 5.36) and attempts to retransmit the same frame up to 15 times.

For each retransmission, the transmitter constructs a set of numbers :

   {0, 1, 2, 3, 4, 5, ... L} where L is ([2 to the power (K)]–1) and where K = N; K<= 10;

   A random value R is picked from this set, and the transmitter waits (defers) for a period.

   R × (slot time) i.e. R × 51.2 Micro Seconds

For example, after two collisions, N = 2, therefore K = 2, and the set is {0, 1, 2, 3} giving a one in four chance of collision. This corresponds to a wait selected from {0, 51.2, 102.4, 153.6} µs.

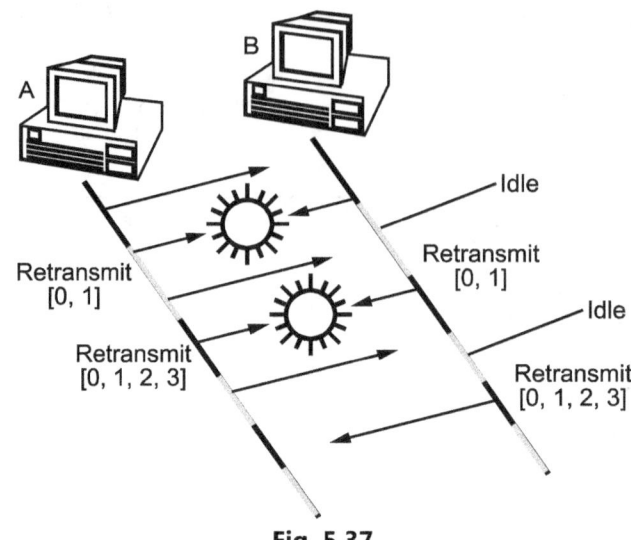

Fig. 5.37

After 3 collisions, N = 3, and the set is {0, 1, 2, 3, 4, 5, 6, 7}, that is a one in eight chance of collision.

But after 4 collisions, N = 4, the set becomes {0, 1, 2, 3, 4, 5, 6, 7, 8, 9, 10, 11, 12, 13, 14, 15}, that is a one in 16 chance of collision.

The scaling is performed by multiplication and is known as exponential back-off. This is what lets CSMA/CD scale to large numbers of NICs - even when collisions may occur. The first ten times, the back-off waiting time for the transmitter suffering collision is scaled to a larger value. The algorithm includes a threshold of 1024. The reasoning is that the more attempts that are required, the more greater the number of NICs which are trying to send at the same time, and therefore longer the period which needs to be deferred. Since a set of numbers {0, 1, ..., 1023} is a large set of numbers, there is very little advantage from further increasing the set size.

Each transmitter also limits the maximum number of retransmissions of a single frame to 16 attempts (N=15). After this number of attempts, the transmitter gives up transmission and discards the frame, logging an error. In practice, a network that is not overloaded should never discard frames in this way.

Late Collisions

In a proper functioning Ethernet network, a NIC may experience collision within the first slot time after it starts transmission. This is the reason why an Ethernet NIC monitors the CD signal during this time and use CSMA/CD. A faulty CD circuit, or misbehaving NIC or transceiver may lead to a late collision (i.e. after one slot time). Most Ethernet NICs therefore continue to monitor the CD signal during the entire transmission. If they observe a late collision, they will normally inform the sender of the error condition.

Performance of CSMA/CD

It is simple to calculate the performance of a CSMA/CD network where only one node attempts to transmit at any time. In this case, the NIC may saturate the medium and near about 100% utilization of the link may be achieved, providing almost 10 Mbps of throughput on a 10 Mbps LAN.

However, when two or more NICs attempt to transmit at the same time, the performance of Ethernet is less predictable. The fall in utilization and throughput occurs because some bandwidth is wasted by collisions and back-off delays. In practice, a busy shared 10 Mbps Ethernet network will typically supply 2-4 Mbps of throughput to the NICs connected to it.

As the level of utilization of the network increases, particularly if there are many NICs competing to share the bandwidth, an overload condition may occur. In this case, the throughput of Ethernet LANs reduces very considerably, and much of the capacity is wasted by the CSMA/CD algorithm, and very little is available for sending useful data. This is the reason why a shared Ethernet LAN should not connect more than   1024 computers. Many engineers use a threshold of 40% utilization to determine if a LAN is overloaded. A LAN with a higher utilization will observe a high collision rate, and likely a very variable transmission time (due to back off). Separating the LAN into two or more collision domains using bridges or switches would likely provide a significant benefit (assuming appropriate positioning of the bridges or switches).

Shared networks may also be constructed using Fast Ethernet, operating at 100 Mbps. Since Fast Ethernet always uses fibre or twisted pair, a hub or switch is always required.

Ethernet Capture

A drawback of sharing a medium using CSMA/CD, is that the sharing is not necessarily fair. When each computer connected to the LAN has little data to send, the network exhibits almost equal access time for each NIC. However, if one NIC starts sending an excessive number of frames, it may dominate the LAN. Such conditions may occur, for instance, when one NIC in a LAN acts as a source of high quality packetized video. The effect is known as "Ethernet Capture".

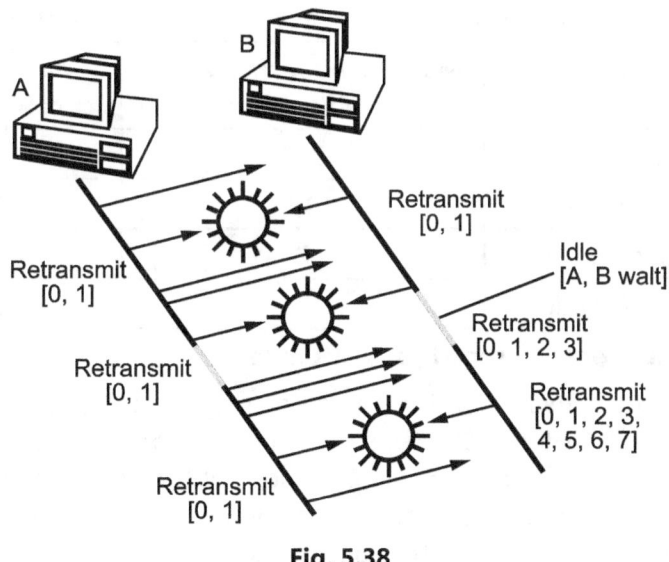

Fig. 5.38

Ethernet Capture by Node A.

Fig. 5.46 illustrates Ethernet Capture. Computer A dominates computer B. Originally both computers have data to transmit. A transmits first. A and B then both simultaneously try to transmit. B picks a larger retransmission interval than A and defers. A sends, then sends again. There is a short pause, and then both A and B attempt to resume transmission. A and B both back-off, however, since B was already in back-off (it failed to retransmit), it chooses from a larger range of back-off times (using the exponential back-off algorithm). A is therefore more likely to succeed, which it does in the example. A and B both attempt to send, however, since this fails in this case, B further increases its back-off and is now unable to fairly compete with A.

Ethernet Capture may also arise when many sources compete with one source which has much more data to send. Under these situations some nodes may be "locked out" of using the medium for a period of time. The use of higher speed transmission (e.g. 100 Mbps) significantly reduces the probability of Capture, and the use of full duplex cabling eliminates the effect.

Ethernet LANs may be implemented using a variety of media (not just the coaxial cable described above). The types of media segments supported by Ethernet are :

- 10 Base 5 Low loss coaxial cable (also known as "thick" Ethernet).

- 10 Base 2 Low cost coaxial cable (also known as "thin" Ethernet).

- 10 Base T Low cost twisted pair copper cable (also known as Unshielded Twisted Pair (UTP)).

- 10 Base F Fibre optic cable.

The network design rules for using these types of media are summarized below :

Segment type	Max Number of systems per cable segment	Max Distance of a cable segment
10 Base 5 (Thick Coax)	100	500 m
10 Base 2 (Thin Coax)	30	185 m
10 Base T (Twisted Pair)	2	100 m
10 Base F (Fibre Optic)	2	2000 m

Network Design Rules for Different Types of Cable

There is also a version of Ethernet which operates using twisted pair cabling or fibre optic links at 100 Mbps and at 1 Gbps. 100 Mbps networks may operate full duplex (using a Fast Ethernet Switch) or half duplex (using a Fast Ethernet Hub). 1 Gbps networks usually operate between a pair of Ethernet Switches. Many LANs combine the various speeds of operation using dual-speed switches which allow the same switch to connect some ports to one speed of network, and other ports at another speed. The higher speed ports are usually used to connect switches to one another.

5.13 CARRIER SENSE MULTIPLE ACCESS WITH COLLISION AVOIDANCE (CSMA/CA) :

In case of CSMA/CD, the transmitting station detects collision based on signal energy level. When there is no collision signal energy level will be minimum because only one station is transmitting. When there is collision energy level will be more.

In case of wireless transmission it is not possible to detect collision based on signal energy level. It is because there is more loss. Hence, the solution is avoid collision as it cannot be detected.

There are three strategies used to avoid collisions :

1. Interframe Space (IFS)
2. Contention Window
3. Acknowledgements.

1. Interframe Space (IFS) :

When a station wants to transmit and finds the channel is idle it waits for a period of time called interframe space (IFS). After the IFS time for a station is over and it finds that the channel is idle it can send, but not immediately it still waits for contention time. IFS can be variable for each station.

2. Contention Window :

A station that is ready to send waits for a time equal to random number of slots, the algorithm used to generate the random number of slots is binary back-off.

3. Acknowledgement :

If there is collision even with implementation of above, we can have the mechanism of acknowledgement where the transmitting station waits for acknowledgement from receiving station for a particular time. If time out occurs it can retransmit. Fig. 5.39 depicts the three strategies.

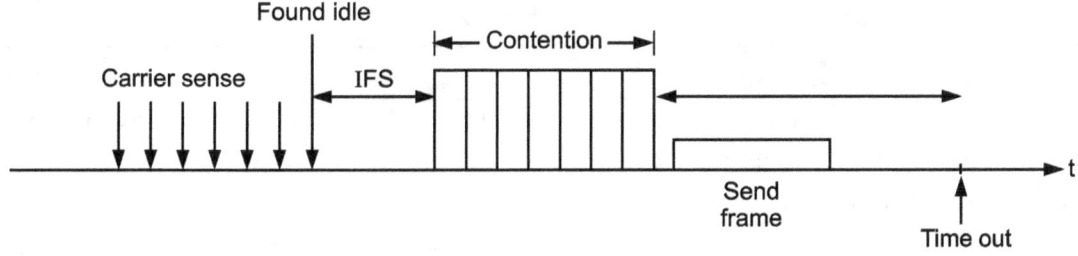

Fig. 5.39

The procedure is shown in flowchart below.

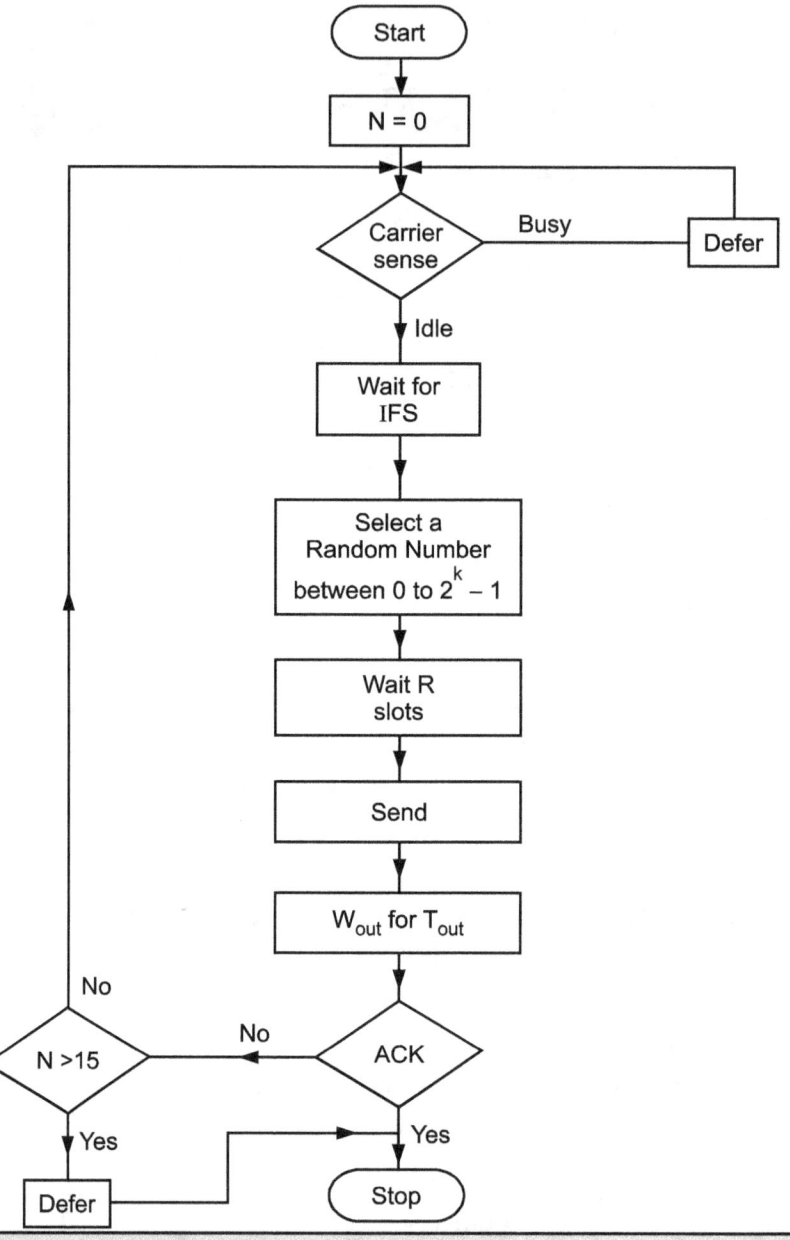

5.14 CONTROLLED ACCESS

In controlled access, the station consults one another to find which station has the right to send. We discuss three popular methods :

5.14.1 Reservation

In reservation method, a station needs to make reservation before sending data. Time is divided into intervals. In each interval, a reservation frame preceds the data frames sent in that interval.

If there are N stations in the system, there are exactly N reservation minislots in reservation frame. Each minislot belongs to a station. When a station needs to send data frame, it makes reservation in its own minislot. The stations that have made reservations can send their data frames after the reservation frame.

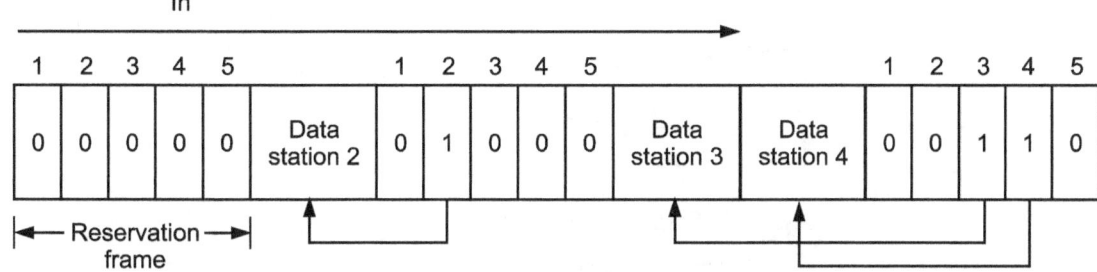

Fig. 5.40 : Reservation Access

In Fig. 5.40, it shows a situation with five stations and five minislot reservation frames. In the first interval, only stations 1, 3 and 4 have made reservations. In the second interval, only station 1 has made a reservation.

5.14.2 Polling

Polling works with topologies in which one device is designated as a primary station and the other devices are secondary stations. All data exchanges must be made through primary device even when the ultimate destination is a secondary device. The primary device controls the link. The secondary devices follow its instructions. The primary device is always the initiator of session.

If the primary wants to receive data, it asks the secondaries. If they have anything to send, this is called poll function.

If the primary wants to send data, it tells secondary to get ready to receive. This is called select function.

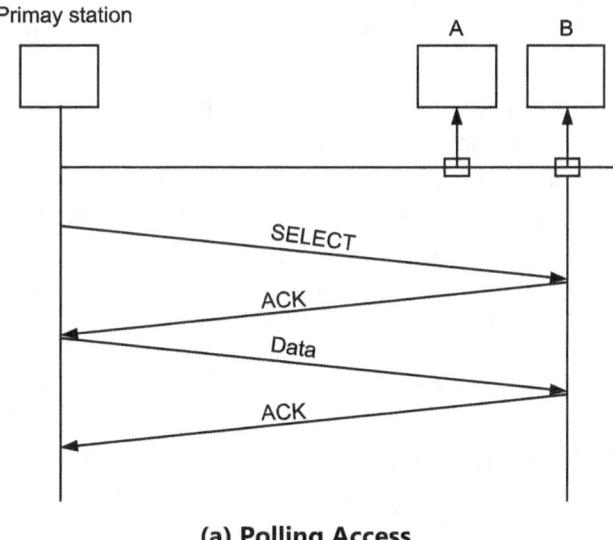

(a) Polling Access

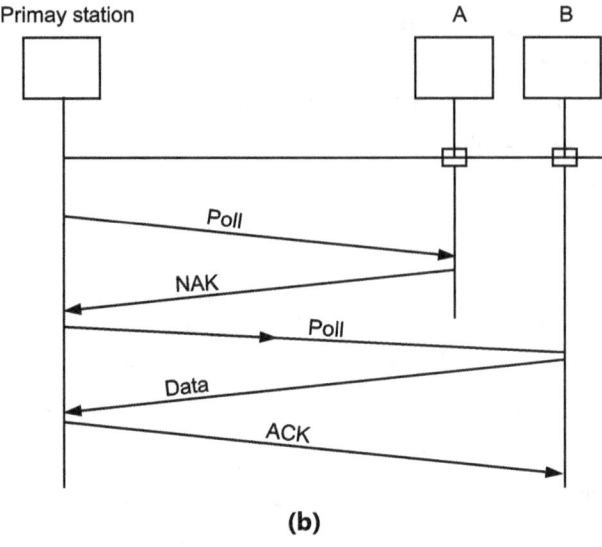

(b)

Fig. 5.41

5.14.3 Poll

The poll function is used for primary device to receive transmissions from the secondary devices. When the primary is ready for that, it must ask (poll) each device in turn if it has anything to send. When the first secondary is approached, it responds either with NAK frame if it has nothing to send or with data (in the form of data frame) if it does. If the response is negative (a NAK frame) then the primary polls the next secondary in the same manner until it finds one with data to send. When the response is positive (a data frame) the primary reads the frame and returns an acknowledgement (ACK frame) verifying its receipt.

5.14.4 Select

The select function is used whenever the primary device has something to send. The primary device controls the link. If the primary is neither sending nor receiving data, it knows the link is available.

If it has something to send, the primary device sends it. But however, it does not know, whether the target device is prepared to receive. So the primary must alert the secondary to the upcoming transmission and wait for an acknowledgement of the secondary ready status. Before sending data the primary creates and transmits a select (SEL) frame, one field of which includes the address of intended secondary.

5.14.5 Token Passing

In the token passing method, the stations in a network are organized in a logical ring. For each station, there is a predecessor and successor. The predecessor is the station which is logically before the station in the ring, the successor is the station which is after the station in the ring. The current station is one that is accessing to the channel now. The right to this access has been passed from the predecessor to the current station. The right will be passed to the successor when the current station has no more data to send.

A special packet called 'token' is used to pass the right to access from one station to another. The token keeps on circulating in the ring whichever station has the token it has right to access the channel. Whenever a station has data to send it waits for token. Whenever token is received it will send data. Whenever it has finished sending data, the token is passed to next station.

Token management is an important issue in this type of network. The network should ensure that the token is not lost because of some problem in the network. e.g. faulty station. Sometimes the data transfer may require priority assignments. The token can be used by stations as per their priority.

5.14.6 Logical Ring

- This standard evolved from the needs of companies like General Motors implementing terminals for factory automation.

- 802.3 was not suitable for them as a station in ethernet has to wait for a long time to send a frame in worst case. 802.3 frames do not have priorities which makes important frames waiting for unimportant frames.

- A token bus system is a medium access control technique for bus/tree stations form a logical ring around which a token is passed. A station receiving the token may transmit data and then must pass the token on to next station in the ring.

- Though it is similar to token ring it does not implement the ring physically as it has drawback of getting entire network down in case one terminal is down.

- If there are n stations in the token bus network and T_P seconds are required to send a frame, it will take not more than nT_P seconds to get a turn for a station.

- A token bus network is shown in Fig. 5.42.

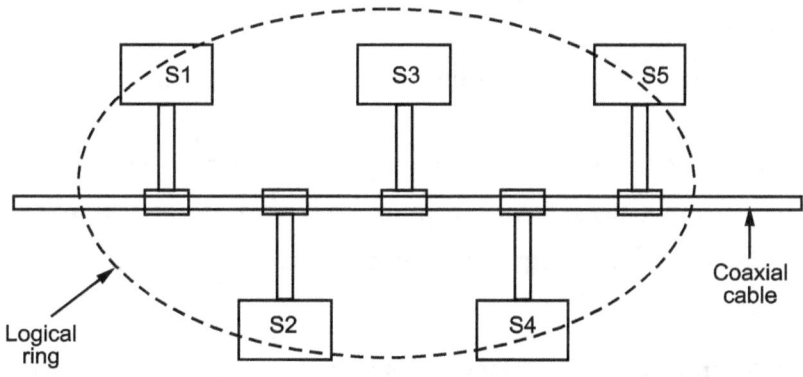

Fig. 5.42 : Token Bus

- The stations can be configured so that they can be part of the logical ring or may opt out of the ring.

- Initially highest number station gets the token. Then it passes the token to its neighbour (right or left).

- Token thus moves around the ring with token holder permitted to send the frame.
- If station has no data it must pass the token to next station.
- A 85 ohm broadband cable is used at physical layer.

5.15 MULTIPLE ACCESS TECHNIQUES

A transponder channel aboard may be fully loaded by single transmission from an earth station in Satellite communications. This is referred to as **single access** mode of operation. It is also possible for for a transponder to be loaded by a number of carriers. These may originate from a number of earth stations geographically separate and each earth station may transmit one or more of the carriers. This mode of operation is termed **multiple access.** The most commonly used methods of multiple access are FDMA, TDMA and CDMA.

5.15.1 FDMA :

- Frequency Division Multiple Access (FDMA) is the most common analog system.
- It is a technique whereby spectrum is divided up into frequencies and then assigned to users.
- With FDMA, only one subscriber at any given time is assigned to a channel.
- The channel therefore is closed to other conversations until the initial call is finished, or until it is handed-off to a different channel.
- A "full-duplex" FDMA transmission requires two channels, one for transmitting and the other for receiving. FDMA has been used for first generation analog systems.

5.15.2 TDMA

- Time Division Multiple Access (TDMA) improves spectrum capacity by splitting each frequency into time slots.
- TDMA allows each user to access the entire radio frequency channel for the short period of a call.
- Other users share this same frequency channel at different time slots.
- The base station continually switches from user to user on the channel.
- TDMA is the dominant technology for the second generation mobile cellular networks.

5.15.3 CDMA

- Code Division Multiple Access is based on "spread" spectrum technology.
- Since it is suitable for encrypted transmissions, it has long been used for military purposes.
- CDMA increases spectrum capacity by allowing all users to occupy all channels at the same time.

- Transmissions are spread over the whole radio band, and each voice or data call are assigned a unique code to differentiate from the other calls carried over the same spectrum.
- CDMA allows for a **soft hand-off**, which means that terminals can communicate with several base stations at the same time.

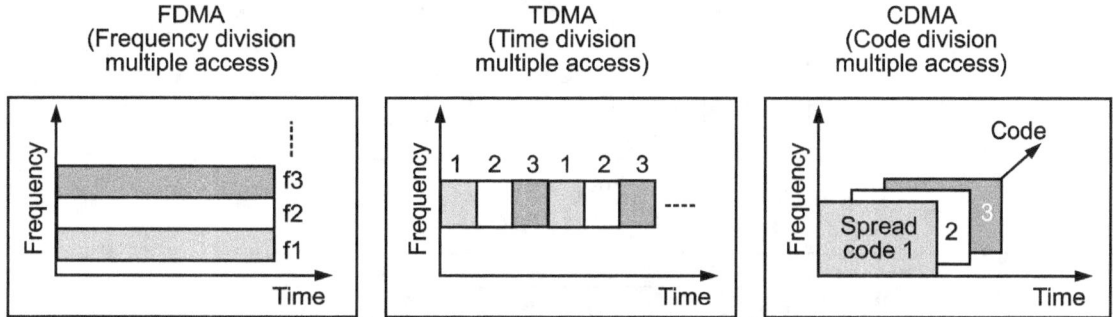

Fig. 5.43 : FDMA-TDMA-CDMA graphical representation

In addition to above multiple access techniques, we can have

- Fixed Assigned Multiple Access (FAMA) mode using either FDMA, TDMA, CDMA. In this mode, the format does not change even if traffic load changes.
- Demand Assigned Multiple Access (DAMA) mode using either FDMA, TDMA, CDMA. In this mode, the formats are changed depending on traffic demand. It is more efficient but costlier to implement and maintain.

Advantages of Digital Technology

All multiple access techniques depend on the adoption of digital technology. Digital technology is now the standard for the public telephone system where all analog calls are converted to digital form for transmission over the backbone. Digital transmission has a number of advantages over analog transmission :

- It economizes on bandwidth.
- It allows easy integration with personal communication systems (PCS) devices.
- It maintains superior quality of voice transmission over long distances.
- It is difficult to decode.
- It can use lower average transmitter power.
- It enables smaller and less expensive individual receivers and transmitters.
- It offers voice privacy.

5.15.4   How FDMA Works ?

- TDMA is basically analog's FDMA with a time-sharing component built into the system.
- FDMA allocates a single channel to one user at a time (see Fig. 9.13).
- If the transmission path deteriorates, the controller switches the system to another channel.
- Although technically simple to implement, FDMA is wasteful of bandwidth : the channel is assigned to a single conversation whether or not somebody is speaking. Moreover, it cannot handle alternate forms of data, only voice transmissions.

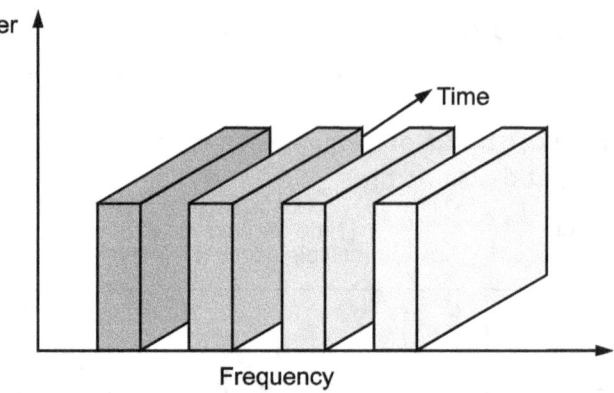

Fig. 5.44 : FDMA

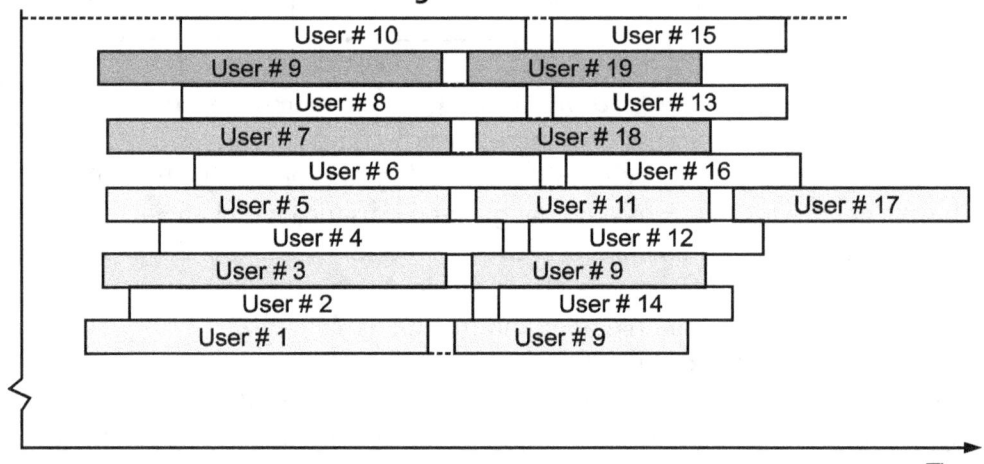

Fig. 5.45 : Schematic allocation of subscriber channels within an assigned frequency band (range)

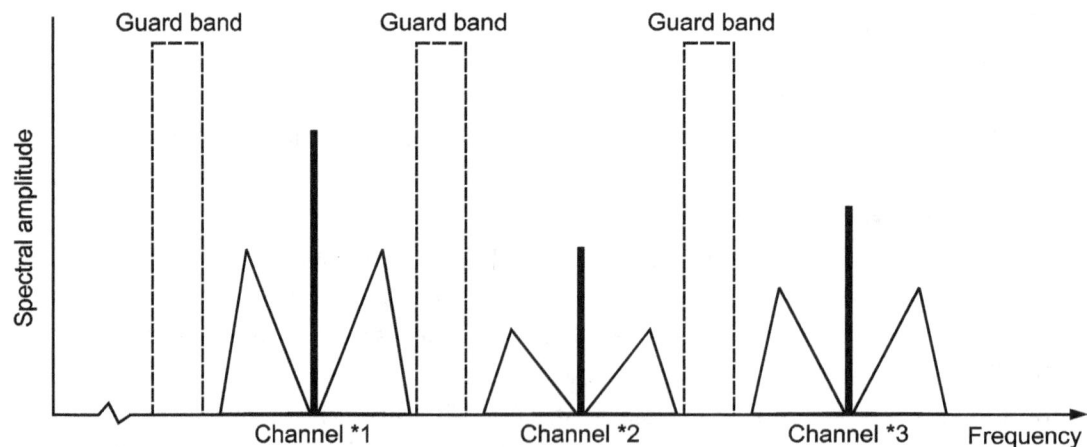

Fig. 5.46 : Schematic frequency spectrum of several subscriber channels

- Analog transmission is considered an "older" cellular phone technology.

- Analog technology was built in the early 1980's. Analog allows a cellular phone to transmit signals by sending voice, video, and data that are always changing, and so does the network systems.

- Analog is considered an older method of modulating voice or data information radio signals.

- Analog transmissions use FDMA technology. FDMA stands for "Frequency Division Multiple Access". FDMA is used exclusively for analog cellular systems, even though in theory FDMA can also be used with digital.

- Essentially, FDMA splits the allocated spectrum into many channels. In current analog cell systems, each channel is 30 kHz.

- When a FDMA cell phone establishes a call, it reserves the frequency channel for the entire duration of the call.

- The voice data is modulated into this channel's frequency band (using frequency modulation) and sent over the airwaves.

- At the receiver, the information is recovered using a band-pass filter. The phone then uses a common digital control channel to acquire channels.

- FDMA analog transmissions are the least efficient cellular networks since each analog channel can only be used one user at a time. Analog channels don't take full advantage of bandwidth.

- Not only are these FDMA channels larger than necessary given modern digital voice compression, but they are also wasted whenever there is silence during a cell phone conversation.

- . Analog signals are especially susceptible to noise and the extra noise cannot get filtered out. Given the nature of the signal, analog cell phones must use higher power (between 1 and 3 watts) to get acceptable call quality.

- Given these analog features, it is easy to see why FDMA is being replaced by newer digital networks such as TDMA and CDMA.

5.15.5 Advantages of FDMA

- If channel is not in use, it sits idle.

- Channel bandwidth is relatively narrow (30 kHz).

- Simple algorithmically, and from a hardware standpoint.

- Fairly efficient when the number of stations is small and the traffic is uniformly constant.

- Capacity increase can be obtained by reducing the information bit rate and using efficient digital code.

- No need for network timing.

- No restriction regarding the type of baseband or type of modulation.

5.15.6 Disadvantages of FDMA

- The presence of guard bands.

- Requires right RF filtering to minimize adjacent channel interference.

- Maximum bit rate per channel is fixed.

- Small inhibiting flexibility in bit rate capability.

- Does not differ significantly from analog system.

5.15.7   How TDMA Works ?

- TDMA relies upon the fact that the audio signal has been digitized; that is, divided into a number of milliseconds-long packets.

- It allocates a single frequency channel for a short time and then moves to another channel.

- The digital samples from a single transmitter occupy different time slots in several bands at the same time as shown in Fig. 5.56.

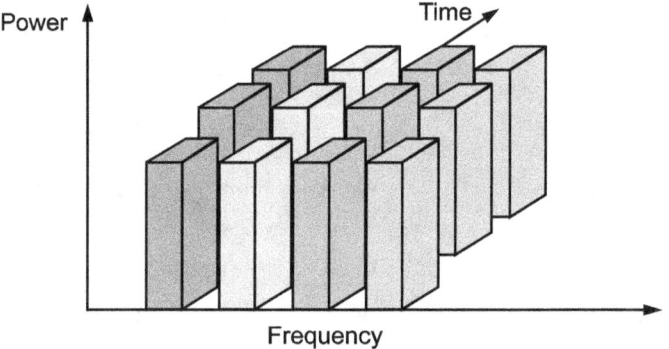

Fig. 5.47 : TDMA

- The access technique used in TDMA has three users sharing a 30 kHz carrier frequency.

- TDMA is also the access technique used in the European digital standard, GSM, and the Japanese digital standard, Personal Digital Cellular (PDC).

- The reason for choosing TDMA for all these standards was that it enables some vital features for system operation in an advanced cellular environment.

- Today, TDMA is an available, well-proven technique in commercial operation in many systems.

- To illustrate the process, consider the following situation. Fig. 5.48 shows four different, simultaneous conversations occurring.

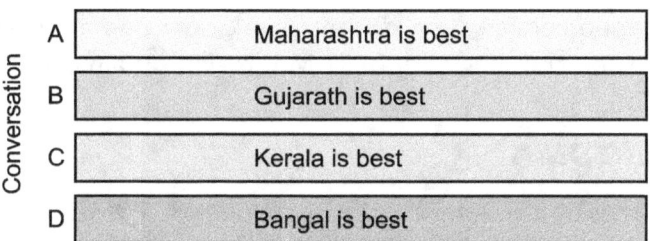

Fig. 5.48 : Four Conversations-Four Channels

- A single channel can carry all four conversations if each conversation is divided into relatively short fragments, is assigned a time slot, and is transmitted in synchronized timed bursts as shown in Fig. 5.49.

- After the conversation in time-slot four is transmitted, the process is repeated.

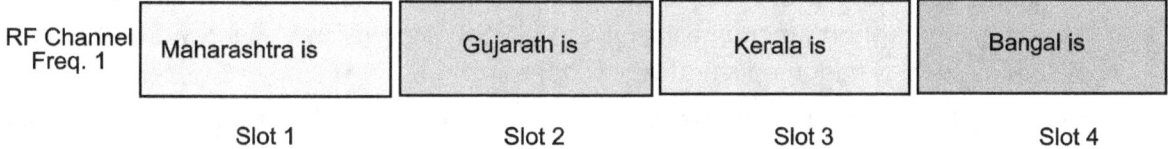

Fig. 5.49 : Four Conversations-One Channel

- Effectively, the implementations of TDMA immediately tripled the capacity of cellular frequencies by dividing a 30 kHz channel into three time slots, enabling three different users to occupy it at the same time.

- Currently, systems are in place that allow six times capacity. In the future, with the utilization of hierarchical cells, intelligent antennas, and adaptive channel allocation, the capacity should approach 40 times analog capacity.

5.15.8 Advanced TDMA

- TDMA substantially improved upon the efficiency of analog cellular.

- However, like FDMA, it had the weakness that it wasted bandwidth : the time slot was allocated to a specific conversation whether or not anyone was speaking at that moment.

- Enhanced version of TDMA Extended Time Division Multiple Access (ETDMA) attempts to correct this problem. Instead of waiting to determine whether a subscriber is transmitting, ETDMA assigns subscribers dynamically.

- ETDMA sends data through those pauses which normal speech contains.

- When subscribers have something to transmit, they put one bit in the buffer queue.

- The system scans the buffer, notices that the user has something to transmit, and allocates bandwidth accordingly.

- If a subscriber has nothing to transmit, the queue simply goes to the next subscriber. So, instead of being arbitrarily assigned, time is allocated according to need.

- If partners in a phone conversation do not speak over one another, this technique can almost double the spectral efficiency of TDMA, making it almost 10 times as efficient as analog transmission.

5.15.9 Benefits of TDMA

- In addition to increasing the efficiency of transmission, TDMA offers a number of other advantages over standard cellular technologies.

- First and foremost, it can be easily adapted to the transmission of data as well as voice communication.

- TDMA offers the ability to carry data rates of 64 kbps to 120 Mbps (expandable in multiples of 64 kbps).

- This enables operators to offer personal communication-like services including fax, voice band data, and short message services (SMSs) as well as bandwidth-intensive applications such as multimedia and videoconferencing.

- Unlike spread-spectrum techniques which can suffer from interference among the users all of whom are on the same frequency band and transmitting at the same time, TDMA's technology, which separates users in time, ensures that they will not experience interference from other simultaneous transmissions.

- TDMA also provides the user with extended battery life and talk time since the mobile is only transmitting a portion of the time (from 1/3 to 1/10) of the time during conversations.

- TDMA installations offer substantial savings in base-station equipment, space and maintenance, an important factor as cell sizes grow ever smaller.

- TDMA is the most cost-effective technology for upgrading a current analog system to digital.

- TDMA is the only technology that offers an efficient utilization of hierarchical cell structures (HCSs) offering pico, micro, and macrocells. HCSs allow coverage for the system to be tailored to support specific traffic and service needs.

- Because of its inherent compatibility with FDMA analog systems, TDMA allows service compatibility with the use of dual-mode handsets.

5.15.10 Advantages of TDMA

- Flexible bit rate.
- No frequency guard band required.
- No need for precise narrowband filters.
- Easy for mobile or base stations to initiate and execute hands off.
- Extended battery life.

- TDMA installations offer savings in base station equipment, space and maintenance.
- The most cost-effective technology for upgrading a current analog system to digital.

5.15.11 Drawbacks of TDMA

- One of the disadvantages of TDMA is that each user has a predefined time slot. However, users roaming from one cell to another are not allotted a time slot.
- Thus, if all the time slots in the next cell are already occupied, a call might well be disconnected. Likewise, if all the time slots in the cell in which a user happens to be in are already occupied, a user will not receive a dial tone.
- Another problem with TDMA is that it is subjected to multipath distortion. A signal coming from a tower to a handset might come from any one of several directions.
- It might have bounced off several different buildings before arriving (see *Fig. 5.50*) which can cause interference.

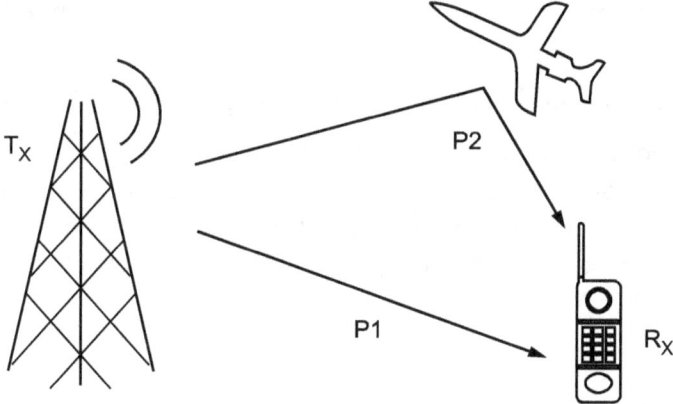

Fig. 5.50 : Multipath Interference

- One way of getting around this interference is to put a time limit on the system.
- The system will be designed to receive, treat, and process a signal within a certain time limit. After the time limit has expired, the system ignores signals.
- The sensitivity of the system depends on how far it processes the multipath frequencies. Even at thousandths of seconds, these multipath signals cause problems.

5.15.12 Disadvantages of TDMA in brief :

- Cross-link transmissions must occur one cross-link at a time.
- Time synchronization needed between all distributed users.
- Propagation delay corrections must be applied when cross-link signal path lengths vary in order to avoid signal collisions.
- The greater the number of spacecraft, the longer the duty interval for cross-link transmissions by a given spacecraft resulting in lowering the overall data throughput for the distribution.

- Changing the user distances of separation requires dynamic assessments of time slot allocations to compensate for variable signal delays.

5.15.13 How CDMA Works ?

- CDMA is a digital wireless technology.

- It is a general type of technology, implemented in many specific technologies.

- But the term "CDMA" is also commonly used to refer to one specific implementation : IS-95 - a mobile-phone technology that competes with technologies such as GSM. CDMA is a "spread spectrum" technology, which means that it spreads the information contained in a particular signal of interest over a much greater bandwidth than the original signal.

- *Code division multiple access,* CDMA, is a spread spectrum system in which two or more spread spectrum signals communicate simultaneously, each operating over the same frequency band.

- In a CDMA system, each user is given a unique sequence (pseudo-random code).

- This sequence identifies the user. For example, if user-A has sequence-a, and user-B has sequence-b, a receiver wanting to listen to user-A would use sequence-a to decode the wanted intelligence. It would then receive all the energy being transmitted by user-A and disregard the power transmitted by user-B. Fig. 5.51 shows CDMA in use in a cellular system.

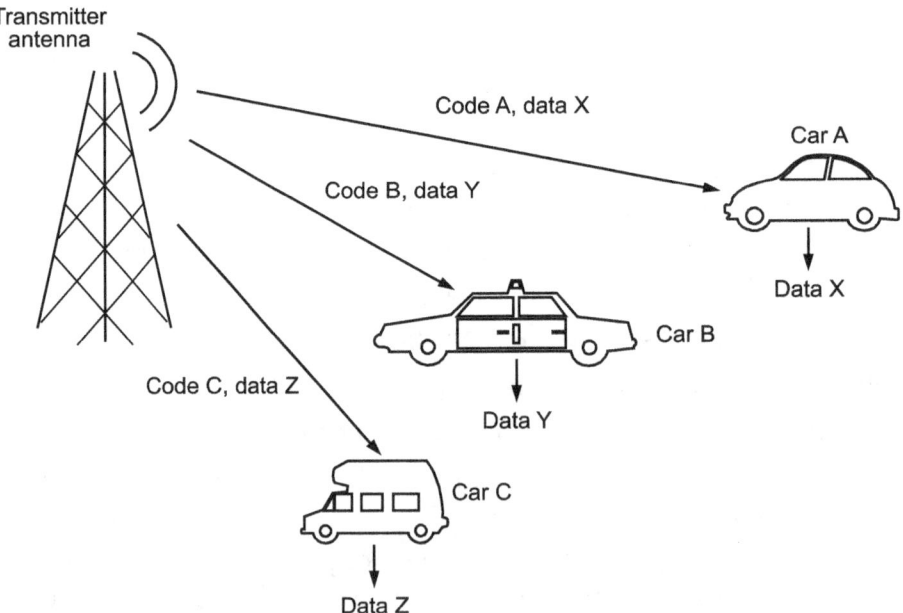

Fig. 5.60 : Spreading at Transmitter and De-spreading at Receivers

5.15.14 Some Benefits of CDMA

*   It has many advantages over TDMA.

*   CDMA is less prone to deep multipath fading caused by transmissions arriving at the receiver that have followed different paths. i.e. one signal direct, and another reflecting off a large object.

*   In fact, one approach in common use with CDMA systems, a rake receiver, takes advantage of multipath, normally a major source of interference and signal degradation in other systems. In a rake receiver, each receiver coherently combines the three strongest multipath signals to provide an enhanced signal with better voice quality.

*   Rake receiver : A rake receiver is a radio receiver designed to counter the effects of multipath fading. It does this by using several "sub-receivers" each delayed slightly in order to tune in to the individual multipath components. Each component is decoded independently, but at a later stage combined in order to make the most use of the different transmission characteristics of each transmission path. This could very well result in higher SNR in a multipath environment than in a "clean" environment.

*   CDMA can operate with much lower transmit powers leading to smaller handsets and smaller batteries and longer life. For example, some field trials in the different countries claimed to demonstrate that the average transmits power of CDMA phones averaged 6 mW, or roughly 10% of analogue phones for similar coverage.

*   CDMA can reduce interference between cells in cellular networks and improve 'hand-over' by summing and correlating transmissions from adjacent cells.

*   CDMA systems have the ability to co-exist with conventional narrow-band transmissions.

*   CDMA can simplify cell planning by removing the need to specify rigid frequency allocations to individual cells.

*   CDMA is claimed to provide higher spectrum efficiency compared to TDMA, although real verification of these claims is still lacking.

5.15.15 Advantages of CDMA in Brief

*   Multipath fading may be substantially reduced because of large signal bandwidth.

*   No absolute limit on the number of users.

*   Easy addition of more users.

*   Impossible for hackers to decipher the code sent.

*   Better signal quality.

*   No sense of handoff when changing cells.

5.15.16 Disadvantages of CDMA in Brief

• As the number of users increases, the overall quality of service decreases.

• Self-jamming.

• Near- Far- problem arises.

However, it seems clear that for the near future at least, TDMA will remain the dominant technology in the wireless market.

5.16 COMPARISON OF MULTIPLE ACCESS TECHNIQUES

TDMA	FDMA	CDMA
1. Users transmit inturn in their own unique time slots.	All users transmit at the same time but in unique frequency band.	Many users simultaneously transmit spread spectrum signals that occupy same frequency band.
2. Guard times are kept between two users.	Guard bands are kept between two users.	Both guard band and guard times are kept.
3. Power efficiency is high.	Power efficiency is low.	Power efficiency is highest.
4. Time synchronization is required.	Synchronization is not necessary.	Synchronization is not required.
5. Interference from adjacent users can degrade performance.	Interference from adjacent users can degrade performance.	Interference from adjacent users is negligible.
6. Implementation is complex.	Implementation is simple.	Implementation is complex.

SOLVED EXAMPLES

Example 5.1 : A group of N users share 56 kbps pure ALOHA channel. Each station outputs 1000 bit frame on an average of once every 100 sec., even if the previous has not yet been sent (buffered). What is maximum value of N ?

Solution :

For pure ALOHA,

Maximum throughput = 0.184

∴ Maximum usable channel bandwidth

$$R = 0.184 \times 56 \text{ kbps}$$

$$R = 10.3 \text{ kbps}$$

$$\text{Rate of transmission of stations} = \frac{1000}{100}$$

$$= 10 \text{ bps}$$

$\therefore$ Number of stations that can use the channel will be,

$$N = \frac{10.3 \times 10^3}{10}$$

$$= 1030$$

Example 5.2 : 10,000 Airline reservation stations are competing for the use of a single slotted ALOHA channel. The average station makes 18 requests/hr. A slot is 125 μsec. What is approximate total channel load ?

Solution : Total channel load is number of transmissions per slot.

Given : One station makes 18 requests/hr.

i.e. 18/3000 requests/sec.

    1/200 requests/sec.

$\therefore$ Number of requests made by 10000 stations in 1 sec

$$= 10000 \times \frac{1}{200}$$

$$= 50$$

i.e. 50 requests in 1 sec.

Hence, number of requests per time slot of 125 μsec = $125 \times 10^{-6} \times 50$

i.e.   Total load G = 0.006250

Example 5.3 : A large population of ALOHA users manages to generate 50 requests/sec. including both originals and retransmissions. Time is slotted in units of 40 msec.

    (a) What is the chance of success on first attempt ?

    (b) What is the probability of exactly k collisions and then a success ?

    (c) What is expected number of transmission attempts needed ?

Solution :

Given : Stations generate 50 requests/sec.

∴   Number of requests per time slot of 40 msec

$$= 40 \times 10^{-3} \times 50 = 2$$

∴   G = 2

(a) For slotted ALOHA,

Chance of success in first attempt will be

$$= e^{-G} \text{ (Poisson's Distribution)}$$

$$= e^{-2}$$

$$= 0.135$$

(b) The probability of exactly k collisions and a success

$$= (1 - e^{-G})^k \, e^{-G}$$

$$= 0.135 \times 0.865^{-k}$$

(c) The expected number of transmissions is,

$$e^G = 7.4$$

Example 5.4 : Calculate maximum throughput possible for ALOHA and pure ALOHA for a radio system with 9600 bps channel used for call setup request to base station. Let frame length be 200 bits.

Solution :

(i) The maximum throughput for pure ALOHA = 0.184.

Given :

Rate of transmission = 9600 bps

Frame length = 120 bits

∴   Number of frames per sec.

$$= \frac{9600 \text{ bits/sec.}}{120 \text{ bits/frame}}$$

$$= 80 \text{ frames/sec}$$

∴   Throughput = 80 × 0.184

$$= 15 \text{ frames/sec.}$$

(ii) For slotted ALOHA

Maximum throughput = 0.368

∴   Throughput   = 0.368 × 80

                                    = 30 frames/sec.

Example 5.5 : Measurement of slotted ALOHA channel with infinite number of users. Show that 10% of slots are idle.

(a) What is channel load G ?

(b) What is throughput ?

(c) Is the channel under loaded or overloaded ?

Solution :

(i) Given : $N = \infty$

                        Idle slots = 10%

∴ Probability of frame not generated = 0.1

Using Poisson's Law :

Probability that k transmissions are done in a slot is

$$= \frac{G^k \times e^{-G}}{k!}$$

∴ Probability that no frame generated

$$= \frac{G^0 e^{-G}}{k!}$$

$$= e^{-G}$$

∴ $0.1 = e^{-G}$

∴ $ln\, 0.1 = -G$

∴   Channel load, G = 2.3

(ii)   Throughput s = Ge^{-G}

                        = $2.3\, e^{-2.3}$

                        = 0.23

(iii) A channel is overloaded, if G > 1.

        Since G = 2.3. It is overloaded.

Example 5.6 : A CSMA/CD network running at 1 Gbps over 1 km cable with no repeaters. The signal speed in the cable is 200000 km/sec. What is minimum frame size ?

Solution :

Given :   d = 1 km

                                     v = 2×10^8 m/sec

$\therefore$ Propagation time (T_P) = $\dfrac{d}{v} = \dfrac{1000}{2 \times 10^8}$

                                        = 5×10^{-6} sec

For CSMA/CSD the frame must not be transmitted in time $2T_P$.

$\therefore$ $2T_P$ = 10×10^{-6} = 10 μsec.

                 Rate of transmission = 1 Gbps

$\therefore$ 1×10^9 bits are transmitted in 1 sec.

$\therefore$ Number of bits transmitted in 10 μsec.

                                        = $1 \times 10^9 \times 10 \times 10^{-6}$

                                        = 10×10^3

                                        = 10000 bits

$\therefore$ The frame size must be greater than 10000 bits which is minimum frame size.

Example 5.7 : At a transmission rate of 5 Mbps and propagation speed of 200 m/μsec to how many metres of cable is the 1 bit delay in token ring interface is equivalent ?

Solution :

                 Bit rate R = 5 Mbps = 5×10^6

                 Bit duration = $\dfrac{1}{R}$ = 2×10^{-7}

           Propagation speed = 200×10^6 m/s

                             = 2×10^8 m/s

Distance equivalent/bit

                          d = $v \times R$

                             = $2 \times 10^8 \times 2 \times 10^{-7}$

                             = 40 m

[i.e. if we add one more station it will introduce delay equivalent to 40 m cable].

EXERCISE

1. Explain the concept of multiplexing.

2. Explain the FDM with example in telephone system.

3. What is TDM ?

4. What is synchronous TDM ?

5. What is asynchronous TDM ?

6. Compare TDM Vs. FDM.

7. What is T-carrier system ?

8. Give the details of North American and CCITT digital multiplexing hierarchy.

9. What is T_1 carrier ? How PCM is used to get 1.544 Mbps speed ?

10. Draw and explain PCM-TDM transmitter system.

11. Draw and explain PCM-TDM receiver system.

12. What is the concept of CODEC used in voice communication ?

13. What is WDM ?

14. Explain advantages and applications of WDM.

15. Write short notes on :

    (a) Spread spectrum communication.

    (b) Difference between spread spectrum signal and normal signal.

16. How to classify spread spectrum communication system ?

17. Write short notes on :

    (a) FHSS system

    (b) DSSS system

    (c) Spread spectrum in wireless communication.

18. Explain the different advantages of SS system.

19. What are the different applications of SS system ?

20. State the protocols devised to handle multiple access communication.

21. Explain pure aloha.

22. Explain slotted aloha.

23. What are carrier sense multiple access protocols ?

24. Explain CSMA/CD technique.

25. How collision is detected in Ethernet ?

26. What is retransmission Back-off ?

27. Explain CSMA/CA technique.

28. What is controlled access ? How it is achieved ?

29. What is logical ring ? Explain.

30. State and explain various multiple access techniques.

31. Compare FDMA, TDMA and CDMA.

32. What are advantages and disadvantages of FDMA ?

33. What are advantages and disadvantages of TDMA ?

34. What are advantages and disadvantages of CDMA ?

PHYSICAL, MAC LAYER STANDARDS AND SWITCHING

6.1 CONNECTING DEVICES

- In LAN, MAN, WAN or Internet communication, different devices are required to connect different systems to each other.

- These devices works at different layers of ISO-OSI reference model as shown in Fig. 6.1.

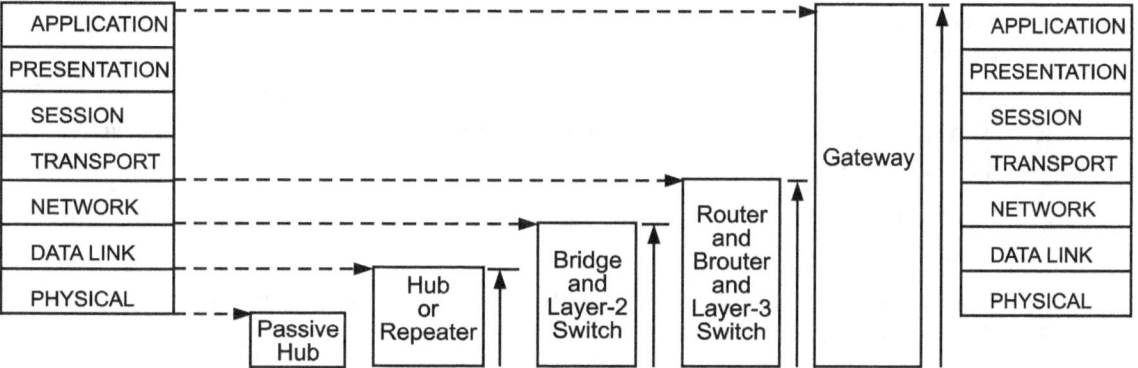

Fig. 6.1 : Connecting Devices as Part of Different Layers

- Passive hub (or connector) works below physical layer of ISO-OSI reference model.

- Hub or repeater works at physical layer of ISO-OSI reference model.

- Bridging device (Bridge) and other device like Layer-2 switch works upto datalink layer of ISO-OSI reference model.

- Router, Brouter (Bridge + Router) and Layer-3 switch devices work upto network layer of ISO-OSI reference model.

- Gateway works upto application layer of the ISO-OSI reference model.

6.2 LAYER-2 SWITCHING

- LAN switching is a form of packet switching used in local area networks. Switching technologies are crucial to network design, as they allow traffic to be sent only where it is needed in most cases, using fast, hardware-based methods.

- Layer-2 switching is hardware based, which means it uses the Media Access Control address (MAC address) from the host's Network Interface Cards (NICs) to decide where to forward frames.

- Switches use Application-Specific Integrated Circuits (ASICs) to build and maintain filter tables (also known as MAC address tables). One way to think of a layer-2 switch is as a multiport bridge.

- Layer-2 switches effectively provide the same functionality. They are similar to multiport bridges in that they learn and forward frames on each port. The major difference is the involvement of hardware that ensures that multiple switching paths inside the switch can be activated at the same time.

- Layer-2 switching provides the following :
  - Hardware-based bridging (MAC)
  - Wire speed
  - High speed
  - Low latency
  - Low cost

- Layer-2 switching is highly efficient because there is no modification to the data packet, only to the frame encapsulation of the packet, and only when the data packet is passing through dissimilar media (such as from Ethernet to FDDI).

- Layer-2 switching is used for workgroup connectivity and network segmentation (breaking up collision domains).

- This allows a flatter network design with more network segments than traditional 10BaseT shared networks.

- Layer-2 switching has helped develop new components in the network infrastructure :

- **Server Farms :** Servers are no longer distributed to physical locations because virtual LANs can be created to create broadcast domains in a switched internetwork. This means that all servers can be placed in a central location, yet a certain server can still be part of a workgroup in a remote branch, for example.

- **Intranets :** Allows organization-wide client/server communications based on a web technology.

- These new technologies allow more data to flow off from local subnets and onto a routed network, where a router's performance can become the bottleneck.

- There are three distinct functions of layer-2 switching :
  - Address learning
  - Forward/filter decisions
  - Loop avoidance

- **Address Learning :** Layer-2 switches and bridges remember the source hardware address of each frame received on an interface, and they enter this information into a MAC database called a forward/filter table.

- **Forward/Filter Decisions :** When a frame is received on an interface, the switch looks at the destination hardware address and finds the exit interface in the MAC database. The frame is only forwarded out to the specified destination port.

- **Loop Avoidance :** If multiple connections between switches are created for redundancy purposes, network loops can occur. Spanning Tree Protocol (STP) is used to stop network loops while still permitting redundancy.

- While layer-2 switch remains more of a marketing term than a technical term, the products that were introduced as "switches" tended to use microsegmentation and full duplex to prevent collisions among devices connected to Ethernets.

- **Microsegmentation** in computer networking is a term used to describe the segmentation of a collision domain into as many segments as there are circuits minus one.

    Segments = Circuits – 1

- This microsegmentation performed by the switch cuts the collision domain down so that only two nodes coexist within each collision domain. This way, collisions are decreased and only the two NICs which are directly connected via a point-to-point link are contending for the medium.

- By using an internal forwarding plane much faster than any interface, they give the impression of simultaneous paths among multiple devices.

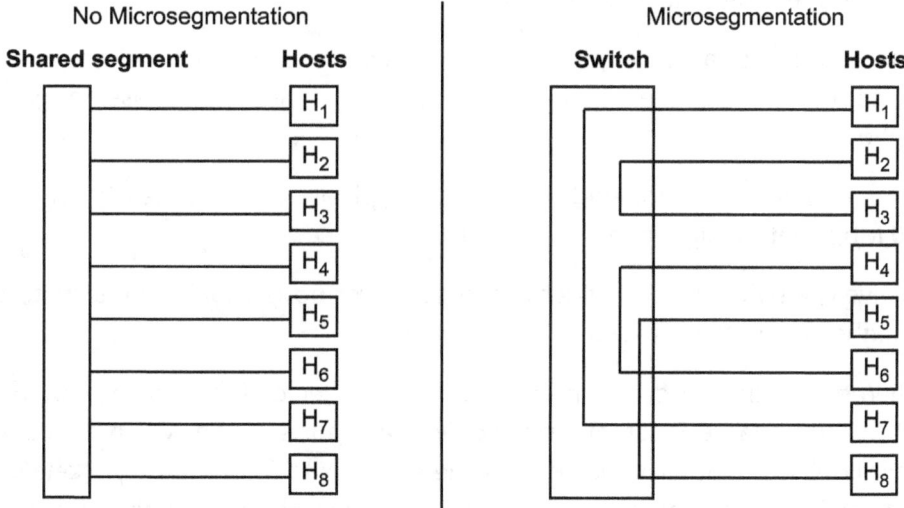

Fig. 6.2 : Microsegmentation and No Microsegmentation

- Once a bridge learns the topology through a spanning tree protocol, it forwards data link layer frames using a layer-2 forwarding method.

- There are four forwarding methods a bridge can use, of which the second to fourth methods are performance-increasing methods when used on "switch" products with the same input and output port speeds.

- **Store and Forward :** The switch buffers and typically performs a checksum on each frame before forwarding it on.

- **Cut Through :** The switch reads only up to the frame's hardware address before starting to forward it. There is no error checking with this method.

- **Fragment Free :** A method that attempts to retain the benefits of both "store and forward" and "cut through". Fragment free checks the first 64 bytes of the frame, where addressing information is stored. According to Ethernet specifications, collisions should be detected during the first   64 bytes of the frame, so frames that are in error because of a collision will not be forwarded. This way the frame will always reach its intended destination. Error checking of the actual data in the packet is left for the end device in Layer-3 or Layer-4 (OSI), typically a router.

- **Adaptive Switching :** A method of automatically switching between the other three modes.

- Cut-through switches have to fall back to store and forward if the outgoing port is busy at the time when the packet arrives.

- While there are specialized applications, such as storage area networks, where the input and output interfaces are at same speed, this is rarely the case in general LAN applications.

- In LANs, a switch used for end user access typically concentrates lower speed (e.g., 10/100 Mbps) into a higher speed (at least 1 Gbps).

- Alternatively, a switch that provides access to server ports usually connects to them at a much higher speed than is used by end user devices.

- An Ethernet switch is used to interconnect a number of Ethernet local area networks (LANs) to form a large Ethernet network. Different ports of the switch are connected to different LAN segments. The purpose of the switch is to forward the packets only to the desired destination segment of the network whenever possible, minimizing traffic on the network.

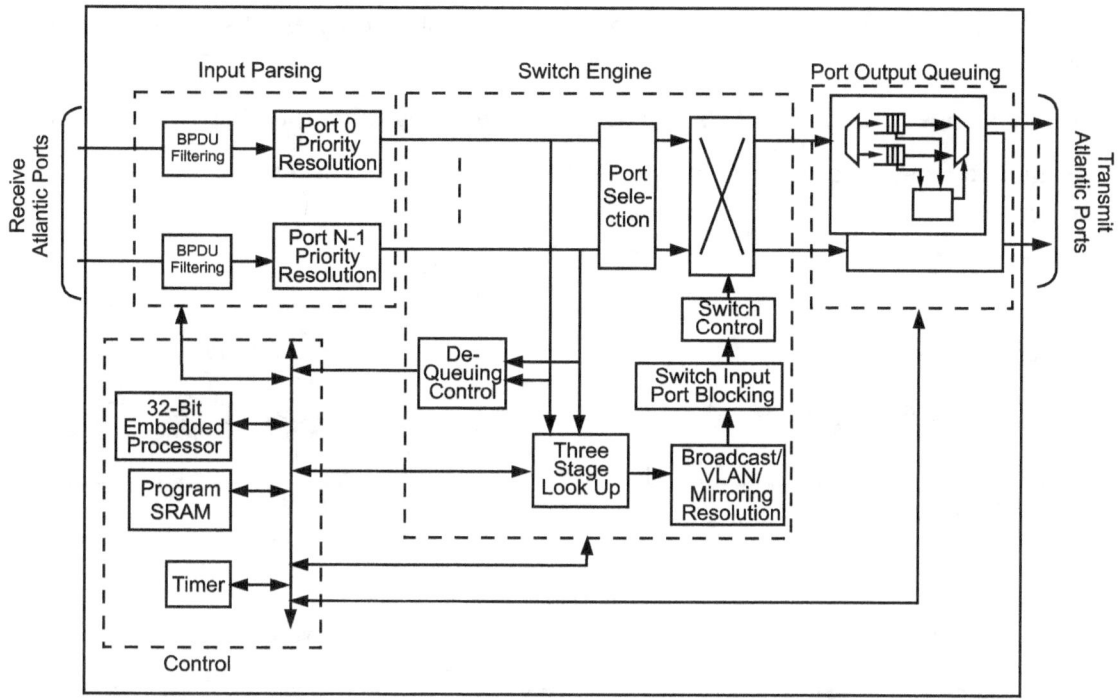

Fig. 6.3 : Ethernet Layer-2 Switch Block Diagram

Limitations of Layer-2 Switch

- Layer-2 switches have the same limitations as bridge networks. Remember that bridges are good if a network is designed by the 80/20 rule: users spend 80 percent of their time on their local segment.

- Bridged networks break up collision domains, but the network remains one large broadcast domain.

- Similarly, layer-2 switches (bridges) cannot break up broadcast domains, which can cause performance issues and limits the size of your network.

- Broadcast and multicasts, along with the slow convergence of spanning tree, can cause major problems as the network grows.

- Because of these problems, layer-2 switches cannot completely replace routers in the internetwork.

6.3 ROUTER

- Technically, a router is a networking device whose software and hardware are usually tailored to the tasks of routing and forwarding information.

- Router works upto layer-3 of ISO-OSI reference model means Physical + Data link + Network layer.

- Router routes the packets based on their logical addresses like host to host IP addressing.

- Router connects LANs to WANs and decision is taken by routing table maintained by it.

- Routers connect two or more logical subnets, which do not necessarily map one-to-one to the physical interfaces of the router.

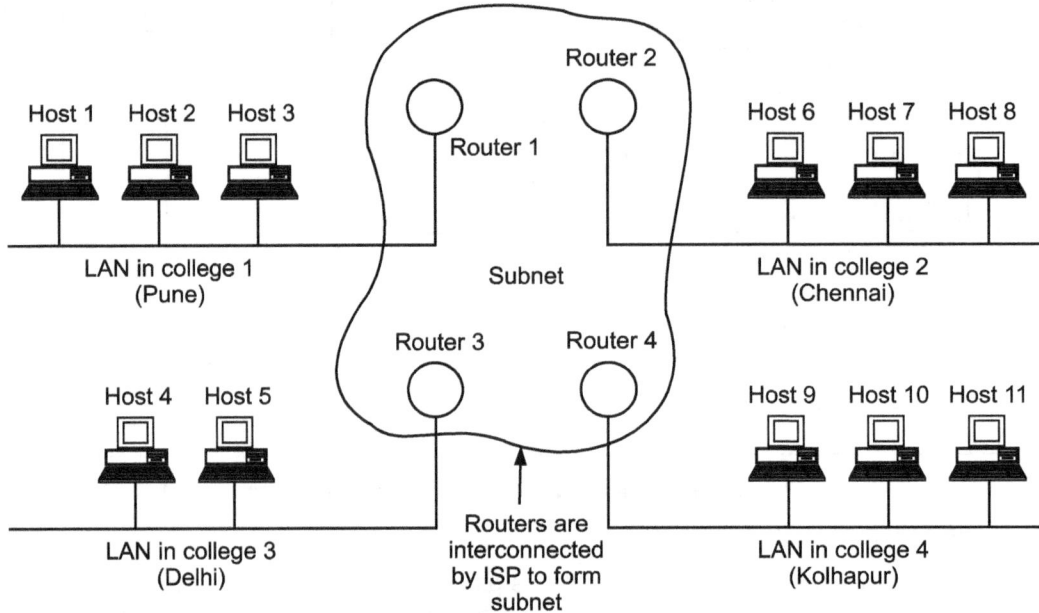

Fig. 6.4 : Typical Subnet (Host is not part of subnet)

- The term "layer-3 switching" is often used interchangeably with routing, but switch is a general term without a rigorous technical definition.

- In marketing usage, a switch is generally optimized for Ethernet LAN interfaces and may not have other physical interface types.

- In comparison, the network hub (predecessor of the "switch" or "switching hub") does not do any routing, instead every packet it receives on one network line gets forwarded to all the other network lines.

- Routers operate in two different planes :

  - **Control Plane**, in which the router learns the outgoing interface that is most appropriate for forwarding specific packets to specific destinations.

  - **Forwarding Plane**, which is responsible for the actual process of sending a packet received on a logical interface to an outbound logical interface.

6.4 TYPES OF ROUTERS

Routers may provide connectivity inside enterprises, between enterprises and the Internet, and inside Internet Service Providers (ISPs). The smallest routers provide connectivity for small offices and home offices.

1. Routers for Internet connectivity and internal use
2. Small Office Home Office (SOHO) connectivity
3. Enterprise routers
4. Access routers
5. Distribution routers
6. Core routers.

6.4.1 Routers for Internet Connectivity and Internal Use

Routers intended for ISP and major enterprise connectivity will almost invariably exchange routing information with the Border Gateway Protocol (BGP).

The several types of BGP-speaking routers are :

- **Edge Router :** Placed at the edge of an ISP network, it speaks external BGP (eBGP) to a BGP speaker in another provider or large enterprise Autonomous System(AS).
- **Subscriber Edge Router :** Located at the edge of the subscriber's network, it speaks eBGP to its provider's AS(s). It belongs to an end user (enterprise) organization.
- **Inter-provider Border Router :** Interconnecting ISPs, this is a BGP speaking router that maintains BGP sessions with other BGP speaking routers in other providers' ASes.
- **Core Router :** A router that resides within the middle or backbone of the LAN network rather than at its periphery.
- **Within an ISP :** It is internal element of Autonomous System (AS), such a router speaks internal BGP (iBGP) to that provider's edge routers, other intra-provider core routers, or the provider's inter-provider border routers.
- **Internet Backbone :** The Internet does not have a clearly identifiable backbone, as did its predecessors. Nevertheless, it is the major ISP router acting as a core element. These ISPs operate all four types of the BGP-speaking routers described here. In ISP usage, a "core" router is internal to an ISP, and used to interconnect its edge and border routers. Core routers may also have specialized functions in virtual private networks based on a combination of BGP and Multi-Protocol Label Switching (MPLS). Routers are also used for port forwarding for private servers.

6.4.2 Small Office Home Office (SOHO) Connectivity

- Residential gateways (often called routers) are frequently used in homes to connect to a broadband service, such as IP over cable or DSL.
- Such a router may also include an internal DSL modem.
- Residential gateways and SOHO routers typically provide network address translation and port address translation in addition to routing.

- Instead of directly presenting the IP addresses of local computers to the remote network, such a residential gateway makes multiple local computers appear to be a single computer.

- SOHO routers may also support Virtual Private Network tunnel functionality to provide connectivity to an enterprise network..

6.4.3 Enterprise Routers

- All sizes of routers may be found inside enterprises.

- The most powerful routers tend to be found in ISPs, academic and research facilities.

- Large businesses may also need powerful routers.

- A three-layer model is in common use, not all of which need be present in smaller networks.

6.4.4 Access Routers

- Access routers, including SOHO, are located at customer sites such as branch offices that do not need hierarchical routing of their own. Typically, they are optimized for low cost.

6.4.5 Distribution Routers

- Distribution routers aggregate traffic from multiple access routers, either at the same site, or to collect the data streams from multiple sites to a major enterprise location. Distribution routers often are responsible for enforcing quality of service across a WAN, so they may have considerable memory, multiple WAN interfaces, and substantial processing intelligence.

- They may also provide connectivity to groups of servers or to external networks. In the latter application, the router's functionality must be carefully considered as part of the overall security architecture. Separate from the router may be a Firewalled or VPN concentrator, or the router may include these and other security functions.

- When an enterprise is primarily on one campus, there may not be a distinct distribution tier, other than perhaps off-campus access. In such cases, the access routers, connected to LANs, interconnect via core routers.

6.4.6 Core Routers

- In enterprises, a core router may provide a "collapsed backbone" interconnecting the distribution tier routers from multiple buildings of a campus, or large enterprise locations. They tend to be optimized for high bandwidth.

- When an enterprise is widely distributed with no central location(s), the function of core routing may be subsumed by the WAN service to which the enterprise subscribes, and the distribution routers become the highest tier.

6.4.7 Routing Concept

- **Routing** is the process of selecting paths in a network along which to send network traffic. Routing is performed for many kinds of networks, including the telephone network, electronic data networks (such as the Internet), and transportation networks. This article is concerned primarily with routing in electronic data networks using packet switching technology.

- In packet switching networks, routing directs packet forwarding, the transit of logically addressed packets from their source towards their ultimate destination through intermediate nodes; typically hardware devices called routers, bridges, gateways, firewalls, or switches.

- General-purpose computers with multiple network cards can also forward packets and perform routing, though they are not specialized hardware and may suffer from limited performance.

- The routing process usually directs forwarding on the basis of routing tables which maintain a record of the routes to various network destinations.

- Thus, constructing routing tables, which are held in the router's memory, is very important for efficient routing. Most routing algorithms use only one network path at a time, but multipath routing techniques enable the use of multiple alternative paths.

- Routing schemes differ in their delivery semantics :

Unicast delivers a message to a single specified node;

Broadcast delivers a message to all nodes in the network;

Multicast delivers a message to a group of nodes that have expressed interest in receiving the message;

Anycast delivers a message to any one out of a group of nodes, typically the one nearest to the source.

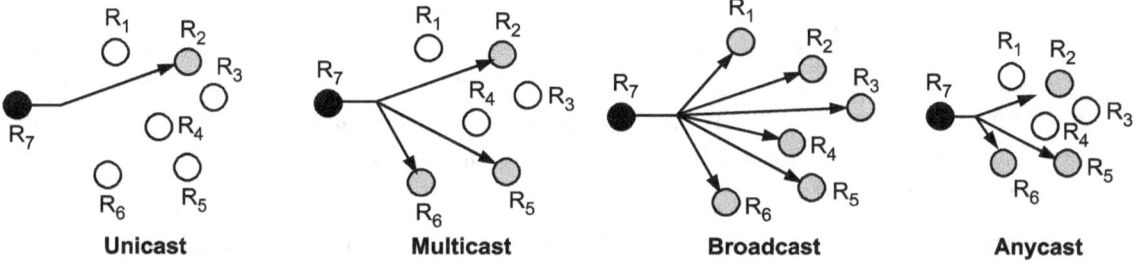

| Unicast | Multicast | Broadcast | Anycast |

Fig. 6.5 : Different Routing Schemes

6.5 GATEWAY

- Gateways work upto application layer of ISO-OSI reference model.
- Different network architecture systems like TCP/IP, Novell netware, Microsoft, Macintosh AppleTalk etc. can communicate with the use of Application Gateway.
- Application gateways, occasionally referred to as application proxies, are applications located between the end user and the Internet.

- Application gateways are used in unified communication. Also known as application proxy or application-level proxy, an application gateway is an application program that runs on a firewall system between two networks.

- When a client program establishes a connection to a destination service, it connects to an application gateway, or proxy.

- The client then negotiates with the proxy server in order to communicate with the destination service.

- In effect, the proxy establishes the connection with the destination behind the firewall and acts on behalf of the client, hiding and protecting individual computers on the network behind the firewall.

- This creates two connections : One between the client and the proxy server and one between the proxy server and the destination.

- Once connected, the proxy makes all packet-forwarding decisions. Since all communication is conducted through the proxy server, computers behind the firewall are protected.

6.5.1 Functioning Mechanism

- The end user directly contacts the application gateway.

- The application gateway performs the requested function on behalf of the user.

- The application gateway also acts as a firewall by intercepting any IP packets from the Internet.

- The application gateway can enforce the security policy since the end user never talks directly to a system on the Internet.

6.5.2 Pros and Cons

- **Security** - The application gateway runs on a secured host. Since the proxy stands between the user and the target system, they are not transparent to the users. Users will need to install custom applications to contact application gateways. No user accounts are saved on this host.

- **Simplicity** - The only function of the host running the application gateway is to proxy requests from end users.

6.5.3 Application Gateway Products

- Microsoft
- Cisco
- Nortel

6.6 PASSIVE HUBS (OR CONNECTOR) (BELOW PHYSICAL LAYER)

- Passive hub is nothing but simple connector unit as shown in Fig. 6.6.

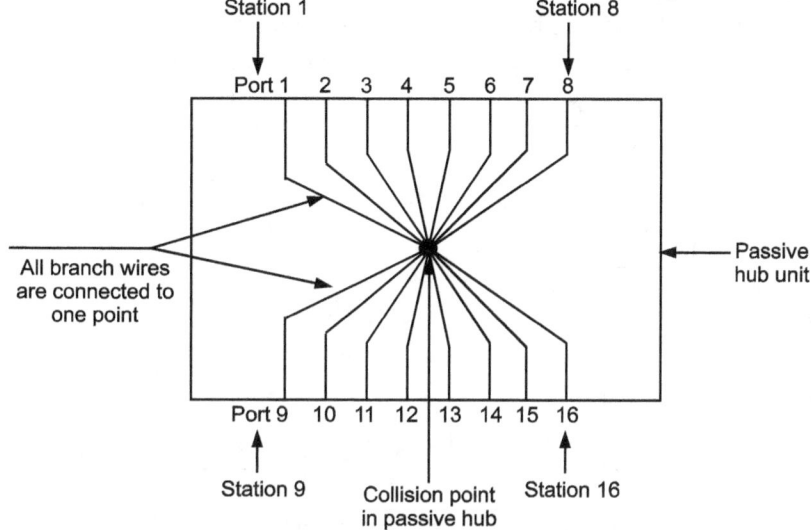

Fig. 6.6 : Typical Passive Hub Unit Internals

- This type of passive hub is basically a part of media.
- This passive hub is just like a wire connector and acts below physical layer of the ISO-OSI reference model.
- All the signals coming from station 1 to station 16, collides at collision point as shown in Fig. 6.6

6.7 REPEATERS AND ACTIVE HUB

- It works at physical layer of the ISO-OSI reference model.
- We have seen 10Base5 Ethernet length restriction upto 500 meters. To extend the length, we divide the cable into segments and install repeater section between two segments.
- Thus, repeater connects two segments of LAN, not two different LANs.

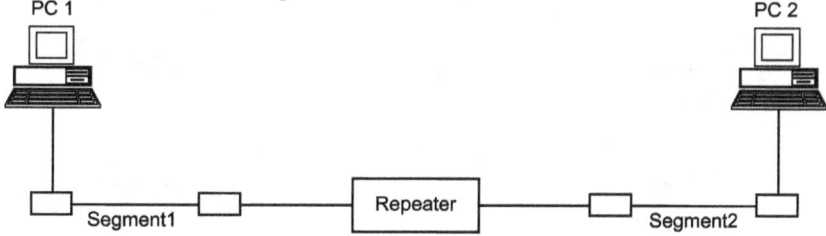

Fig. 6.7 : Repeater Connects Two Segments of LAN

- For long distance data communication, signal becomes weak or corrupted.
- This weakened or corrupted data is regenerated bit by bit using repeater. Hence, repeater is regenerator or it regenerates the copy of data i.e. weakened '0' $\rightarrow$ to right '0' and weakened '1' $\rightarrow$ to right '1'.

- Repeater is not an amplifier, because amplifier amplifies the signal as well as noise coming with signal and noise can replace the original signal.
- Thus, repeater is regenerator and regenerates the data '0' and '1' for weakened and corrupted '0' and '1' respectively.
- Thus, repeater is also known as hub device in networking.
- The repeater regenerates the corrupted signal as shown in Fig. 6.7.

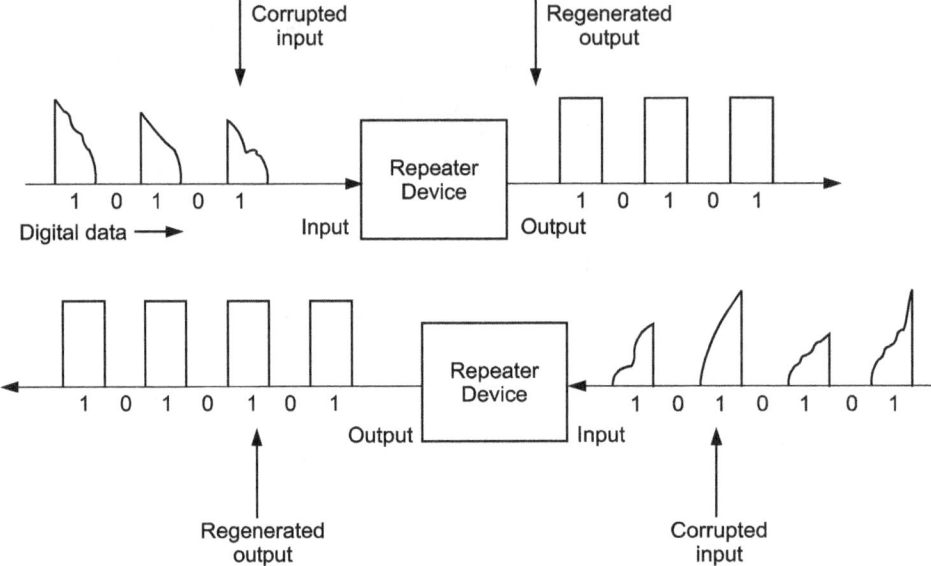

Fig. 6.8 : Function of Repeater Device

- Active hub is basically a multiport repeater as shown in Fig. 6.9.

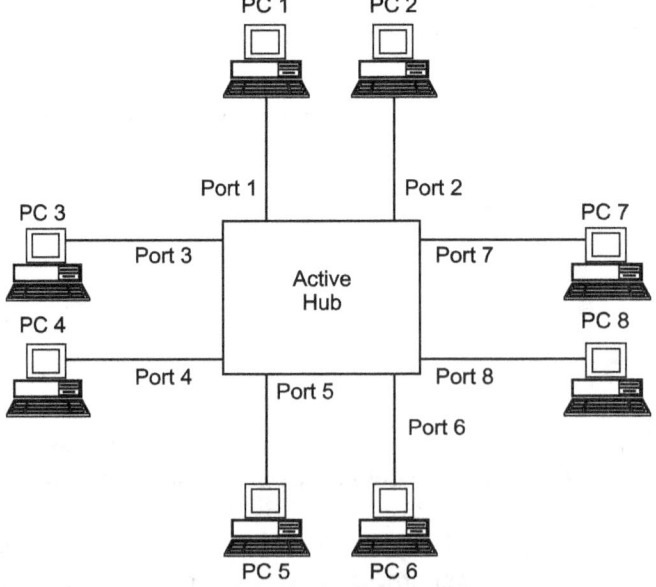

Fig. 6.9: Active Hub is basically a Multiport Repeater

6.8 BRIDGE DEVICE

- Bridge device works upto Layer-2 of the ISO-OSI reference model.

- Bridge device works upto Layer-2 means it works in both physical and data link layer of ISO-OSI reference model.

- A network bridge connects multiple network segments at the data link layer (Layer-2) of the OSI model, and the term Layer-2 switch is very often used interchangeably with bridge.

- Bridges are similar to repeaters or network hubs, devices that connect network segments at the physical layer; however, with bridging, traffic from one network is managed rather than simply rebroadcast to adjacent network segments.

- In Ethernet networks, the term "bridge" formally means a device that behaves according to the IEEE 802.1D standard—the popular term "switch" originated in marketing literature.

- Bridges tend to be more complex than hubs or repeaters. Bridges can analyze incoming data packets to determine if the bridge is able to send the given packet to another segment of the network.

- Since bridging takes place at the data link layer of the OSI model, a bridge processes the information from each frame of data it receives.

- In an Ethernet frame, this provides the MAC address of the frame's source and destination.

- Bridges use two methods to resolve the network segment that a MAC address belongs to Transparent bridging and Source Route Bridging.

Transparent Bridging :

- This method uses a forwarding database to send frames across network segments.

- The forwarding database is initially empty and entries in the database are built as the bridge receives frames.

- If an address entry is not found in the forwarding database, the frame is rebroadcast to all ports of the bridge, forwarding the frame to all segments except the source address.

- By means of these broadcast frames, the destination network will respond and a route will be created.

- Along with recording the network segment to which a particular frame is to be sent, bridges may also record a bandwidth metric to avoid looping when multiple paths are available.

- Devices that have this transparent bridging functionality are also known as *adaptive bridges*. **They are primarily found in Ethernet networks.**

- Transparent bridge must meet three criteria :

  1. Frames must be forwarded from one system to another.

  2. Forwarding table is automatically updated/made by learning frame movements in the LAN.

  3. Loops in the system must be prevented.

Source Route Bridging :

- With source route bridging, two frame types are used in order to find the route to the destination network segment.

- Single-Route (SR) frames make up most of the network traffic and have set destinations, while All-Route (AR) frames are used to find routes.

- Bridges send AR frames by broadcasting on all network branches; each step of the followed route is registered by the bridge performing it.

- Each frame has a maximum hop count, which is determined to be greater than the diameter of the network graph, and is decremented by each bridge.

- Frames are dropped when this hop count reaches zero, to avoid indefinite looping of AR frames.

- The first AR frame which reaches its destination is considered to have followed the best route, and the route can be used for subsequent SR frames; the other AR frames are discarded.

- This method of locating a destination network can allow for indirect load balancing among multiple bridges connecting two networks.

- The more a bridge is loaded, the less likely it is to take part in the route finding process for a new destination as it will be slow to forward packets.

- A new AR packet will find a different route over a less busy path if one exists.

- This method is very different from transparent bridge usage, where redundant bridges will be inactivated; however, more overhead is introduced to find routes, and space is wasted to store them in frames.

- A switch with a faster backplane can be just as good for performance, if not for fault tolerance. **They are primarily found in Token Ring networks.**

6.8.1 802.X to 802.Y Bridges and Variants

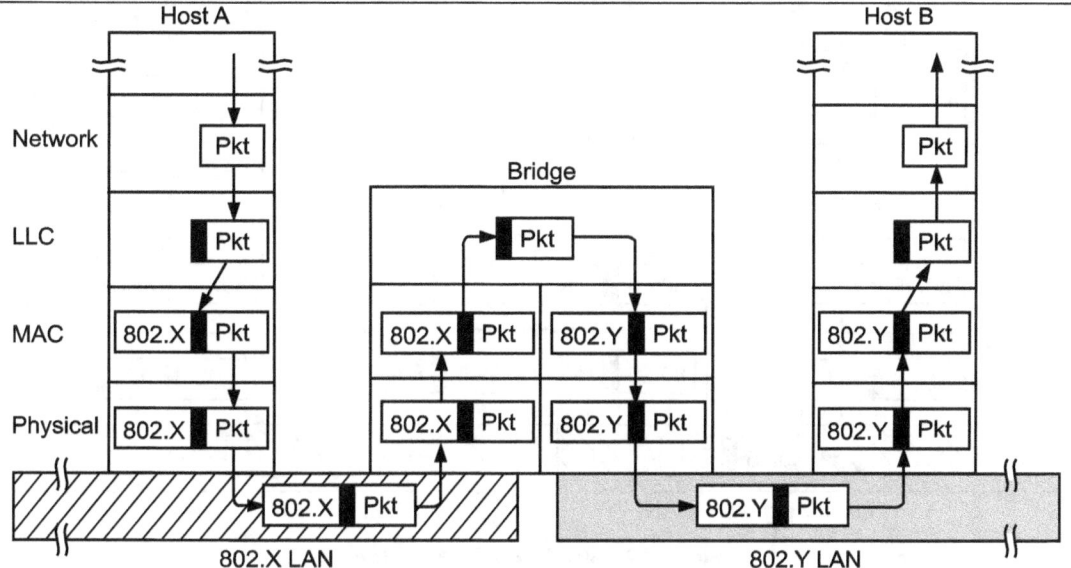

Fig. 6.10 : 802.X to 802.Y Bridge

- At Host 'A' network layer packet is indicated as packet. This comes to LLC layer and LLC header is added.
- At MAC Layer 802.X header is added to packet coming from LLC layer.
- At bridge end, 802.X header is removed and 802.Y header is added.
- Hence, at Host 'B', it understands only 802.Y header packet. Hence bridge converts 802.X to 802.Y header frame and communication of data is possible.

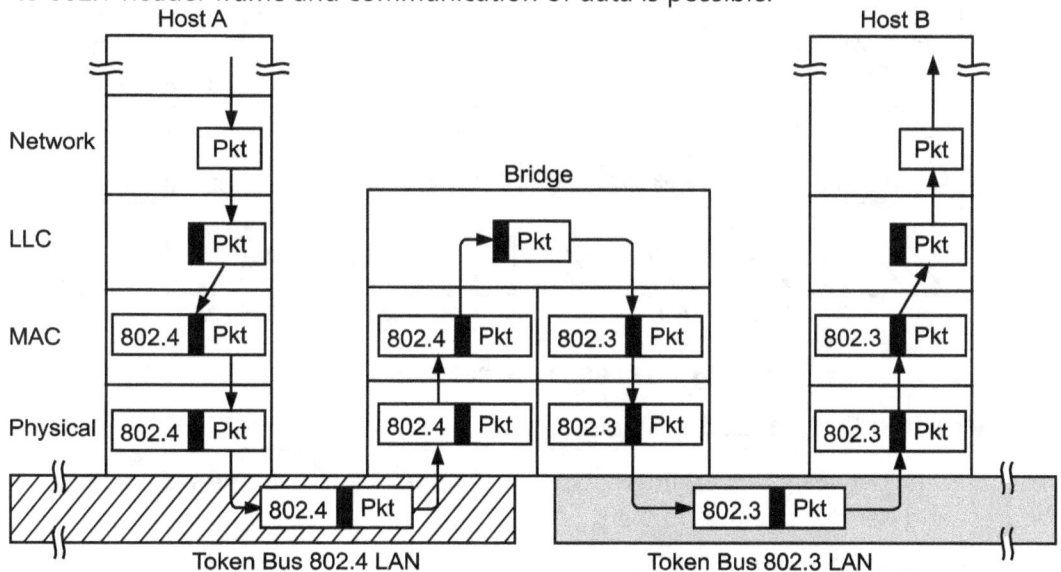

Fig. 6.11 : 802.4 to 802.3 Bridge

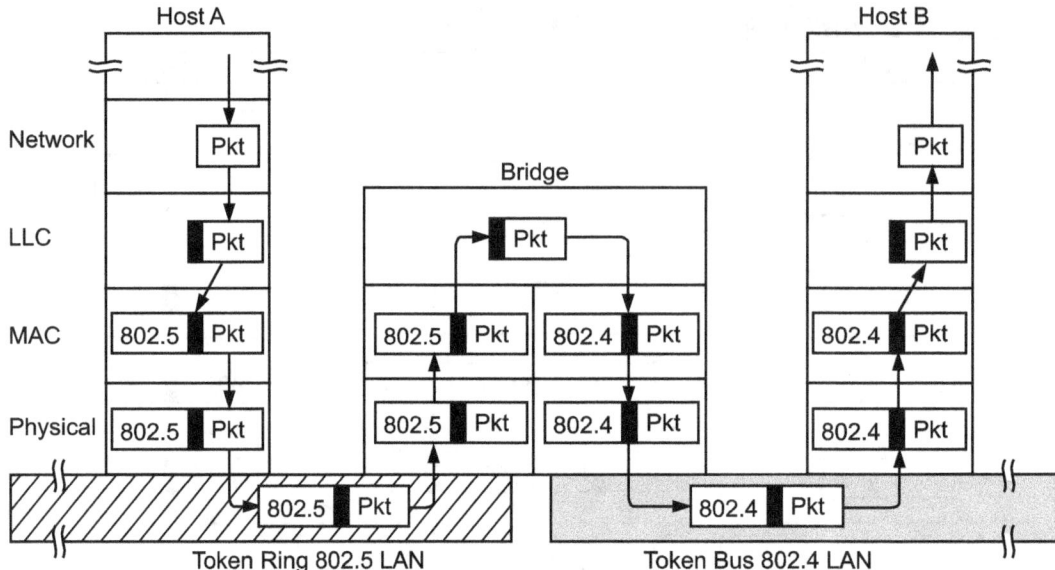

Fig. 6.12 : 802.5 to 802.4 Bridge

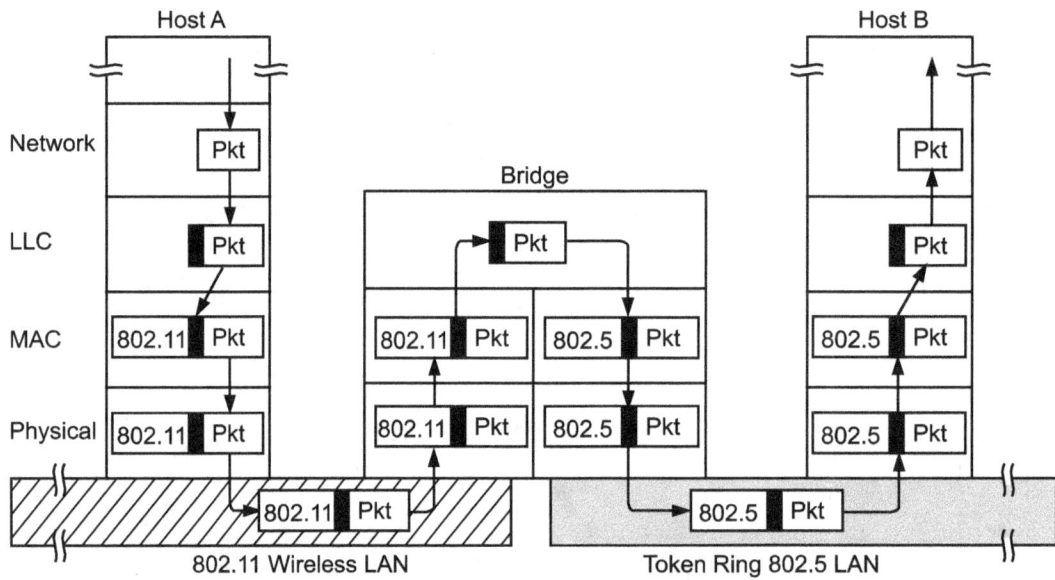

Fig. 6.13 : 802.11 to 802.5 Bridge

6.8.2 Filtering Database in Bridge

• To translate between two segment types, a bridge reads a frame's destination MAC address and decides to either forward or filter.

• If the bridge determines that the destination node is on another segment on the network, it forwards it (retransmits) the packet to that segment.

- If the destination address belongs to the same segment as the source address, the bridge filters (discards) the frame.

- As nodes transmit data through the bridge, the bridge establishes a filtering database (also known as a forwarding table) of known MAC addresses and their locations on the network.

- The bridge uses its filtering database to determine whether a packet should be forwarded or filtered. Bridge maintains the table which maps MAC addresses to the specific port.

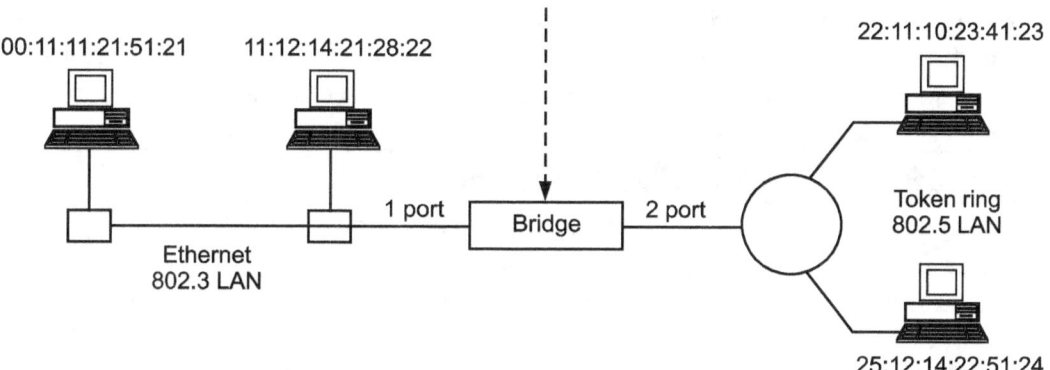

Fig. 6.14 : Bridge Table (MAC Address and Port Number)

6.8.3 Advantages of Network Bridges

- Self-configuring.
- Primitive bridges are often inexpensive.
- Isolate collision domain.
- Reduce the size of collision domain by microsegmentation in non-switched networks.
- Transparent to protocols above the MAC layer.
- Allows the introduction of management/performance information and access control.
- LANs interconnected are separate, and physical constraints such as number of stations, repeaters and segment length don't apply.
- Helps minimize bandwidth usage.
- Used to interconnect two LANs.

6.8.4 Disadvantages of Network Bridges

- Does not limit the scope of broadcasts.
- Does not scale to extremely large networks.
- Buffering introduces store and forward delays; on average, traffic destined for bridge will be related to the number of stations on the rest of the LAN.
- Bridging of different MAC protocols introduces errors.
- Because bridges do more than repeaters by viewing MAC addresses, the extra processing makes them slower than repeaters.
- Bridges are more expensive than repeaters.

Although infinite bridges (or Layer-2 switches) can be connected in theory, often a broadcast storm will result as more and more collisions occur. Collisions delay service advertisements, causes the hosts to back off and attempt to retransmit after a pseudo-random interval. Because bridges simply repeat any Layer-2 broadcast traffic, this can result in undesirable broadcast traffic consuming the network. An example would be a bridge in between adjacent office buildings. It is unlikely that the advantages of bridging would outweigh the loss of network bandwidth associated with all of the service advertisements.

Another major disadvantage is that any standards-compliant implementation of bridging cannot have any closed loops in a network. This limits both performance and reliability.

6.9 LAYER-1 HUBS VERSUS SWITCH

- A network hub, or repeater, is a fairly unsophisticated network device.
- Hubs do not manage any of the traffic that comes through them.
- Any packet entering a port is broadcast out or "repeated" on every other port, except for the port of entry.
- Since every packet is repeated on every other port, packet collisions result, which slows down the network.
- There are specialized applications where a hub can be useful, such as copying traffic to multiple network sensors.
- High end switches have a feature which does the same thing called port mirroring. There is no longer any significant price difference between a hub and a low-end switch.

	Hub	Switch
Definition :	An electronic device that connects many computers together to form a single computer network	A way of routing electricity and data flow patterns through circuits based on binary decisions.
Technical Specifications :	Hubs classify as Layer-1 devices in the OSI model	Network switches operate at layer-two (Data Link Layer) of the OSI model.
Cost :	Cheaper than switches	Costlier than hubs

Manufacturers :	Sun Systems, Oracle and Cisco	Sun Systems, Oracle, Belkin, Linksys, and Net Gear, Huawei.
Function :	To connect a network of personal computers together, they can be joined through a central hub	Network switches inspect data packets as they are received, determining the source and destination device of that packet, and forwarding it appropriately.

6.10 BRIDGING VERSUS ROUTING

- Bridging and routing are both ways of performing data control, but work through different methods.

- Bridging takes place at OSI Model Layer-2 (data-link layer) while routing takes place at the OSI Model Layer-3 (network layer).

- This difference means that a bridge directs frames according to hardware assigned MAC addresses while a router makes its decisions according to arbitrarily assigned IP addresses.

- As a result of this, bridges are not concerned with and are unable to distinguish networks while routers can.

- When designing a network, one can choose to put multiple segments into one bridged network or to divide it into different networks interconnected by routers.

- If a host is physically moved from one network area to another in a routed network, it has to get a new IP address; if this system is moved within a bridged network, it does not have to reconfigure anything.

- These days bridges are replaced with switches.

6.11 BRIDGE VERSUS LAYER-2 SWITCH

- Bridge frame handling is controlled in the bridge's software. Conversely,   layer-2 switch performs address recognition and frame forwarding with hardware. Similarly, a router and a layer-3 switch differ only by whether they forward in software, or hardware.

- A bridge can typically analyze/forward only one packet at a time, while a layer-2 switch has multiple parallel data paths and can handle multiple frames simultaneously.

- A bridge uses store-and-forward (it buffers the incoming frame, and then performs a CRC to ensure data integrity before forwarding the frame), while a layer-2 switch can be configured to either use store-and-forward, or to use cut-through (sending the frame as soon as the destination MAC address is realized, without checking the data for correctness).

- Because a layer-2 switch can incorporate the functions of a bridge, the bridge has suffered commercially. New installations typically include layer-2 switches with bridge functionality, rather than bridges. This has led to the general mixing of the two terms.

6.12 LAYER-2 VERSUS LAYER-3 SWITCH

- Essentially, a layer-2 switch is a multiport bridge.

- A layer-2 switch will learn about MAC addresses connected to each port and passes frames marked for those ports.

- It also knows that if a frame is sent out a port but is looking for the MAC address of the port it is connected and thereafter it drops that frame.

- Whereas a single CPU bridge runs in serial, todays hardware based switches run in parallel, translating to extremly fast switching.

- Layer-3 switching is a hybrid, as one can imagine a combination of a router and a switch.

- There are different types of layer-3 switching, route caching and topology-based switching.

- In route caching the switch requires both a Route Processor (RP) and a Switch Engine (SE).

- The RP must listen to the first packet to determine the destination.

- At that point the Switch Engine makes a shortcut entry in the caching table for the rest of the packets to follow.

- Due to advancement in processing power and drastic reductions in the cost of memory, today's higher end layer-3 switches implement a topology-based switching which builds a lookup table and populates it with the entire network's topology.

- The database is held in hardware and is referenced there to maintain high throughput. It utilizes the longest address match as the layer-3 destination.

6.13 ROUTER VERSUS SWITCH

- Routers and switches are both computer networking devices. They allow one or more computers to be connected to other computers, network devices, or to other networks.

- However, the functions of a hub, switch and router are quite different, even if at times they are integrated into a single device.

- Routers connect two or more logical subnets, which do not necessarily map one-to-one to the physical interfaces of the router.

- The term layer-3 switch is often used interchangeably with router, but switch is really a general term without a rigorous technical definition.

- In marketing usage, it is generally optimized for Ethernet LAN interfaces and may not have other physical interface types.

Definition	Router	Switch
Cost :	More expensive than hubs or switches.	Costlier than hubs.
Manufacturers :	Cisco, Juniper Networks, Belkin, Extreme Networks, Huawei, Netgear.	Sun Systems, Oracle, Belkin, Linksys, and Net Gear, Huawei.
Function :	Routers connect two or more logical subnets, which do not necessarily map 1-1 to the physical interfaces of the router.	Network switches inspect data packets as they are received, determining the source and destination device of that packet, and forwarding it appropriately.
Definition :	A router is a computer tailored to the tasks of routing and forwarding information. Routers generally contain a specialized operating system, RAM, NVRAM, flash memory, and one or more processors, as well as two or more network interfaces.	A way of routing electricity and data flow patterns through circuits based on binary decisions.
Technical Specifications :	Router works at layer-3 of ISO-OSI reference model.	Network switches operate at layer-two (Data Link Layer) of the OSI model.

6.14 ETHERNET

Local Area Network (LAN) is a data communications network connecting terminals, computers and printers within a building or other geographically limited areas. These devices could be connected through wired cables or wireless links. Ethernet, Token Ring and Wireless LAN using IEEE 802.11 are examples of standard LAN technologies.

Ethernet is by far the most commonly used LAN technology. Token Ring technology is still used by some companies. FDDI is sometimes used as a backbone LAN interconnecting Ethernet or Token Ring LANs. WLAN using IEEE 802.11 technologies is rapidly becoming the new leading LAN technology for its mobility and easy to use features.

Local Area Network could be interconnected using Wide Area Network (WAN) or Metropolitan Area Network (MAN) technologies. The common WAN technologies include TCP/IP, ATM, Frame Relay, etc. The common MAN technologies include SMDS and 10 Gigabit Ethernet.

LANs are traditionally used to connect a group of people who are in the same local area. However, the working group are becoming more geographically distributed in today's working environment. The virtual LAN (VLAN) technologies are defined for people in different places to share the same networking resource.

Local Area Network protocols are mostly used at data link layer (layer 2). IEEE is the leading organization defining most of the LAN protocols.

Protocol Structure - Local Area Network and LAN Protocols

The key LAN protocols are listed as follows :

LAN - Local Area Network Protocols	
Ethernet	Ethernet LAN protocols as defined in IEEE 802.3 suite
	Fast Ethernet : Ethernet LAN at data rate 100Mbps (IEEE 802.3u)
	Gigabit Ethernet : Ethernet at data rate 1000Mbps (IEEE 802.3z, 802.3ab)
	10Gigabit Ethernet : Ethernet at data rate 10 Gbps (IEEE 802.3ae)
WLAN	Wireless LAN in IEEE 802.11, 802,11a, 802.11b, 802.11g and 802.11n
	IEEE 802.11i : WLAN Security Standards
	IEEE 802.1X : WLAN Authentication & Key Management
	IEEE 802.15 : Bluetooth for Wireless Personal Area Network (WPAN)
VLAN	IEEE 802.1Q : Virtual LAN Bridging Switching Protocol
	GARP : Generic Attribute Registration Protocol (802.1P)
	GMRP : GARP Multicast Registration Protocol (802.1P)
	GVRP : GARP VLAN Registration Protocol (802.1P, 802.1Q)
Token Bus	IEEE 802.4 : LAN Protocol
Token Ring	IEEE 802.5 LAN protocol
FDDI	Fiber Distributed Data Interface
Others	LLC : Logic Link Control (IEEE 802.2)
	SNAP : SubNetwork Access Protocol
	STP : Spanning Tree Protocol (IEEE 802.1D)
	IEEE 802.1p : LAN Layer 2 QoS/CoS Protocol

6.14.1 Ethernet : IEEE 802.3 Local Area Network (LAN) Protocols

Ethernet protocols refer to the family of local-area network (LAN) covered by the IEEE 802.3. In the Ethernet standard, there are two modes of operation : half-duplex and full-duplex modes. In the half duplex mode, data are transmitted using the popular Carrier-Sense Multiple Access/Collision Detection (CSMA/CD) protocol on a shared medium. The main disadvantages of the half-duplex are the efficiency and distance limitation, in which the link distance is limited by the minimum MAC frame size. This restriction reduces the efficiency drastically for high-rate transmission. Therefore, the carrier extension technique is used to ensure the minimum frame size of 512 bytes in Gigabit Ethernet to achieve a reasonable link distance.

Four data rates are currently defined for operation over optical fiber and twisted-pair cables :

- 10 Mbps - 10Base-T Ethernet (IEEE 802.3)
- 100 Mbps - Fast Ethernet (IEEE 802.3u)
- 1000 Mbps - Gigabit Ethernet (IEEE 802.3z)
- 10-Gigabit - 10 Gbps Ethernet (IEEE 802.3ae).

The Ethernet system consists of three basic elements :

- The physical medium used to carry Ethernet signals between computers,
- A set of medium access control rules embedded in each Ethernet interface that allow multiple computers to fairly arbitrate access to the shared Ethernet channel, and
- An Ethernet frame that consists of a standardized set of bits used to carry data over the system.

As with all IEEE 802 protocols, the ISO data link layer is divided into two IEEE 802 sublayers, the Media Access Control (MAC) sublayer and the MAC-client sublayer. The IEEE 802.3 physical layer corresponds to the ISO physical layer.

The MAC sub-layer has two primary responsibilities :

- Data encapsulation, including frame assembly before transmission, and frame parsing/error detection during and after reception.
- Media access control, including initiation of frame transmission and recovery from transmission failure.

The MAC-client sub-layer may be one of the following :

- Logical Link Control (LLC), which provides the interface between the Ethernet MAC and the upper layers in the protocol stack of the end station. The LLC sublayer is defined by IEEE 802.2 standards.
- Bridge entity, which provides LAN-to-LAN interfaces between LANs that use the same protocol (for example, Ethernet to Ethernet) and also between different protocols (for example, Ethernet to Token Ring). Bridge entities are defined by IEEE 802.1 standards.

Each Ethernet-equipped computer operates independently of all other stations on the network : there is no central controller. All stations attached to an Ethernet are connected to a shared signaling system, also called the medium. To send data a station first listens to the channel, and when the channel is idle the station transmits its data in the form of an Ethernet frame, or packet.

After each frame transmission, all stations on the network must contend equally for the next frame transmission opportunity. Access to the shared channel is determined by the Medium Access Control (MAC) mechanism embedded in the Ethernet interface located in each station. The medium access control mechanism is based on a system called Carrier Sense Multiple Access with Collision Detection (CSMA/CD).

As each Ethernet frame is sent onto the shared signal channel, all Ethernet interfaces look at the destination address. If the destination address of the frame matches with the interface address, the frame will be read entirely and be delivered to the networking software running on that computer. All other network interfaces will stop reading the frame when they discover that the destination address does not match their own address.

When it comes to how signals flow over the set of media segments that make up an Ethernet system, it helps to understand the topology of the system. The signal topology of the Ethernet is also known as the logical topology, to distinguish it from the actual physical layout of the media cables. The logical topology of an Ethernet provides a single channel (or bus) that carries Ethernet signals to all stations.

Multiple Ethernet segments can be linked together to form a larger Ethernet LAN using a signal amplifying and retiming device called a repeater. Through the use of repeaters, a given Ethernet system of multiple segments can grow as a "non-rooted branching tree". "Non-rooted" means that the resulting system of linked segments may grow in any direction, and does not have a specific root segment. Most importantly, segments must never be connected in a loop. Every segment in the system must have two ends, since the Ethernet system will not operate correctly in the presence of loop paths.

Even though the media segments may be physically connected in a star pattern, with multiple segments attached to a repeater, the logical topology is still that of a single Ethernet channel that carries signals to all stations.

6.14.2 Standard Ethernet

MAC Layer : In standard Ethernet MAC layer performs two functions :

* Controls the access.

* Data received from network layer is used for preparation of frame to pass it to physical layer.

Ethernet MAC Data Frame for 10/100 Mbps Ethernet

Number of bytes	7	1	2/6	2/6	2	46-1500bytes	4
Name of field	Pre	SFD	DA	SA	Length/Type	Data unit + pad	FCS

* **Preamble (PRE)** - 7 bytes. The PRE is an alternating pattern of ones and zeros that tells receiving stations that a frame is coming, and that provides a means to synchronize the frame-reception portions of receiving physical layers with the incoming bit stream.
* **Start-of-Frame Delimiter (SFD)** - 1 byte. The SFD is an alternating pattern of ones and zeros, ending with two consecutive 1-bits indicating that the next bit is the leftmost bit in the leftmost byte of the destination address.

- **Destination Address (DA)** - 6 bytes. The DA field identifies which station(s) should receive the frame.
- **Source Addresses (SA)** - 6 bytes. The SA field identifies the sending station.
- **Length/Type** - 2 bytes. This field indicates either the number of MAC-client data bytes that are contained in the data field of the frame, or the frame type ID if the frame is assembled using an optional format.
- **Data** - Is a sequence of n bytes ($46 \le n \le 1500$) of any value. (The total frame minimum is 64 bytes).
- **Frame Check Sequence (FCS)** - 4 bytes. This sequence contains a 32-bit Cyclic Redundancy Check (CRC) value, which is created by the sending MAC and is recalculated by the receiving MAC to check for damaged frames.

Physical Layer :

There are several physical layer implementations. Some of them are :

1. 10Base5 : Bus, thick coaxial.
2. 10Base2 : Bus thin coaxial.
3. 10Base7 : Star UTP.
4. 10BaseF : Star, fibre.

6.14.3 10Base5 : Thick Ethernet

The first implementation is called 10Base5, thick Ethernet, or Thicknet. The nick name derives from the size of the cable, which is roughly the size of a garden hose and too stiff to bend with your hands. 10Base5 was the first Ethernet specification to use a bus topology with an external transceiver (transmitter/receiver) connected via to tap to a thick coaxial cable. Fig. 6.15 shows a schematic diagram of a 10Base5 implementation.

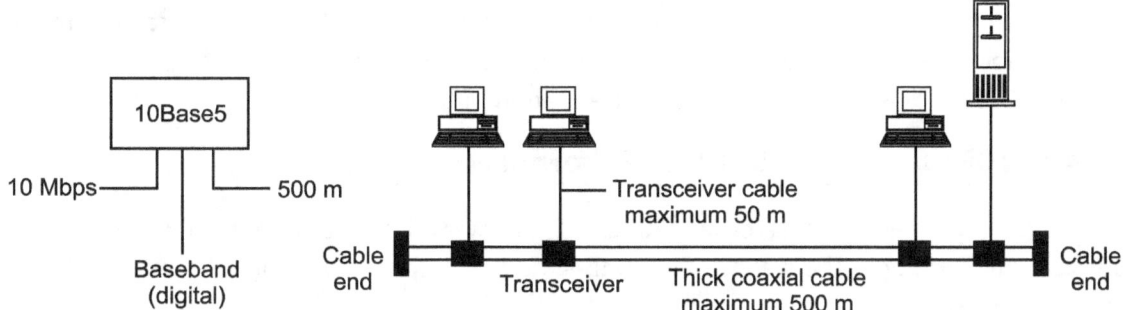

Fig. 6.15 : 10Base5 Implementation

The transceiver is responsible for transmitting, receiving and detecting collisions. The transceiver is connected to the station via a transceiver cable that provides separate path for sending and receiving. This means that collision can only happen in the coaxial cable.

The maximum length of the coaxial cable must not exceed 500 m, otherwise, there is excessive degradation of the signal. If a length of more than 500 m is needed, upto five segments, each a maximum of 500 meter, can be connected using repeaters.

6.14.4 10Base2 : Thin Ethernet

The second implementation is called 10Base2, thin Ethernet, or Cheapernet, 10Base2 also uses a bus topology, but the cable is much thinner and more flexible. The cable can be bent to pass very close to the stations. In this case, the transceiver is normally part of the Network Interface Card (NIC), which is installed inside the station. Fig. 6.16 shows the schematic diagram of a 10Base2 implementation.

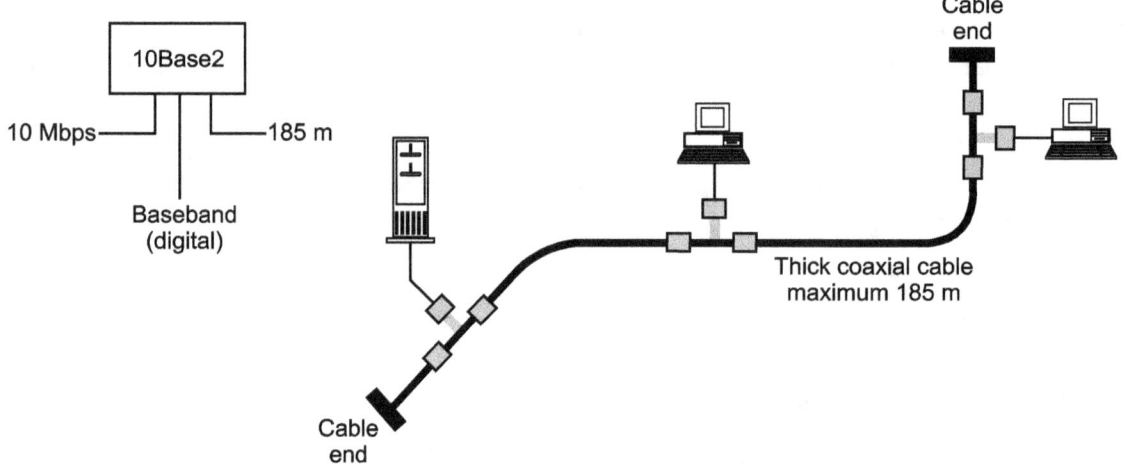

Fig. 6.16 : 10Base2 Implementation

Note that the collision here occurs in the thin coaxial cable. This implementation is more cost effective than 10Base5 because thin coaxial cable is less expensive than thick coaxial and the tee connections are much cheaper than taps. Installation is simpler because the thin coaxial cable is very flexible. However, the length of each segment cannot exceed 185 m (close to 200 m) due to the high level of attenuation in thin coaxial cable.

6.14.5 10Base-T : Twisted-Pair Ethernet

The third implementation is called 10Base-T or twisted-pair Ethernet. 10Base-T uses a physical star topology. The stations are connected to a hub via two pairs of twisted cable, as shown in Fig. 6.17.

Note that two pairs of twisted cable create two paths (one for sending and one for receiving) between the station and the hub. Any collision here happens in the hub. Compared to 10Base5 or 10Base2, we can see that the hub actually replaces the coaxial cable as far as collision is concerned. The maximum length of the twisted cable here is defined as 100 m, to minimize the effect of attenuation in the twisted cable.

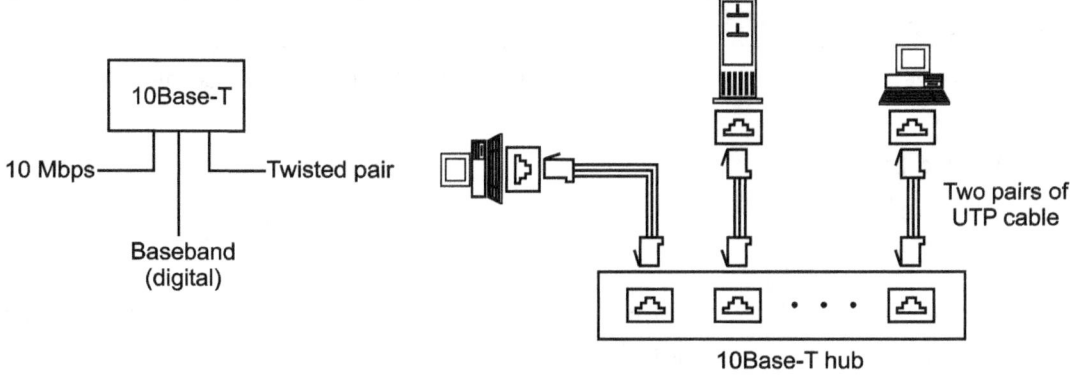

Fig. 6.17 : 10Base-T Implementation

6.14.6 10Base-F : Fiber Ethernet

Although there are several types of optical fiber 10 Mbps Ethernet, the most common is called 10Base-F. 10Base-F uses a star topology to connect stations to a hub. The stations are connected to the hub using two fiber-optic cables, as shown in Fig. 6.18.

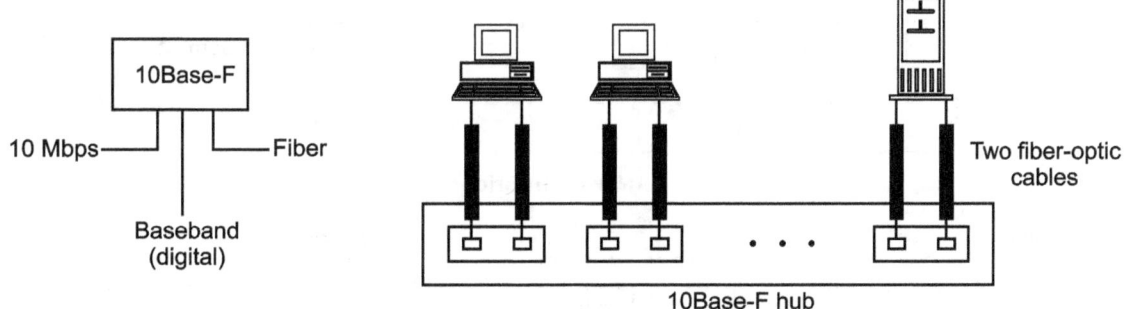

Fig. 6.18 : 10Base-F Implementation

Following table gives Comparison of Physical Layer Implementation of Ethernet.

Table 6.1 : Summary of Standard Ethernet Implementations

Characteristics	10Base5	10Base2	10Base-T	10Base-F
Media used	Thick coaxial cable	Thin coaxial cable	2 UTP	2 Fiber
length	< 500 m	< 185 m	< 100 m	< 2000 m
Line coding technique	Split phase Manchester	Split phase Manchester	Split phase Manchester	Split phase Manchester

6.15 BRIDGED ETHERNET

In order to have compatibility between 10 Mbps and 100 Mbps LANs, some changes were required. They are :

- Bridged Ethernet.

- Switched Ethernet.

- Full Duplex Ethernet.

The bridged ethernet divides LAN by bridges because of which there is improvement in bandwidth and separation of collision domains.

If we have 10 Mbps LAN and 10 nodes are there, the bandwidth will be divided among these nodes depending on need. e.g. if only one station wants to transmit entire bandwidth will be available to it. But if all of them want to transmit each one will have 1 Mbps bandwidth.

We can improve the bandwidth efficiency by using a bridge. If 10 nodes are divided into 2 groups of 5 each, each group will have an average bandwidth of 10/5 = 2 Mbps instead of 1 Mbps.

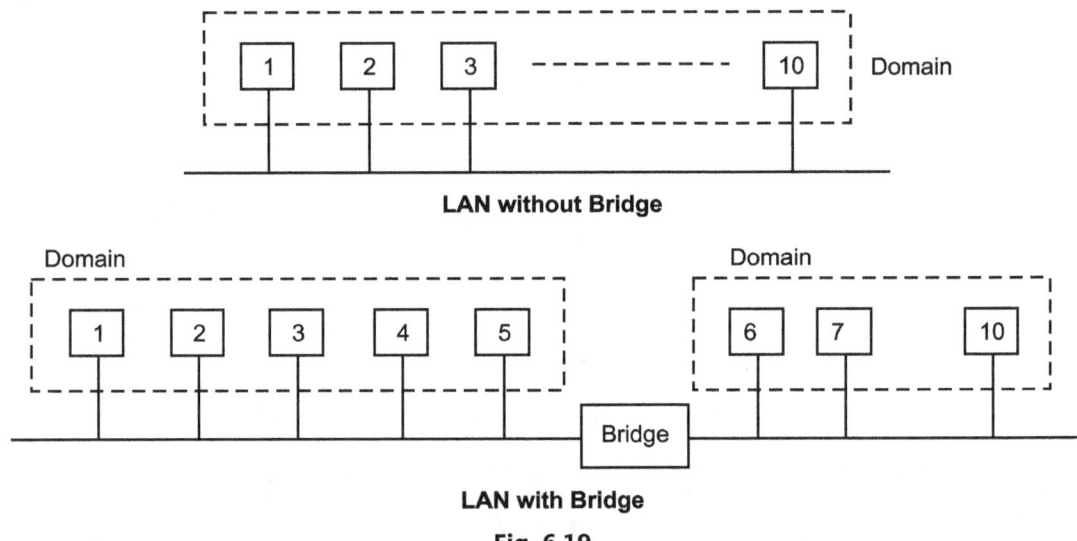

LAN without Bridge

LAN with Bridge

Fig. 6.19

Another advantage is number of nodes in collision domain are reduced and hence probability of collision reduces by 50%.

6.16 SWITCHED ETHERNET

If we divide the number of nodes in the LAN, there is improvement in bandwidth efficiency. We can have only single node in each network. If there are N nodes in LAN, there will be N networks. It is called switched LAN as shown below. The collision domain is also divided into N domains.

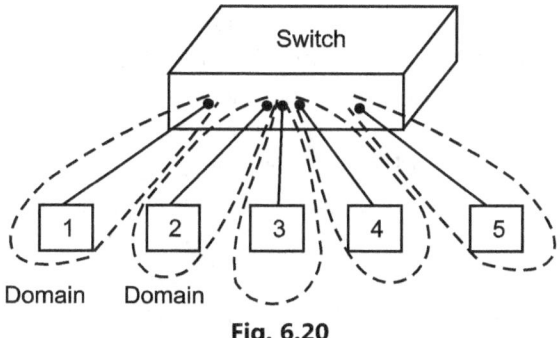

Fig. 6.20

The bandwidth will be shared between station and the switch (i.e. 5 Mbps each).

6.17 FULL DUPLEX ETHERNET

In half duplex a station can either send or receive. In full duplex mode Ethernet, send and receive operations can be done simultaneously. The capacity of each domain is doubled because of this. Two links will be used in such configuration.

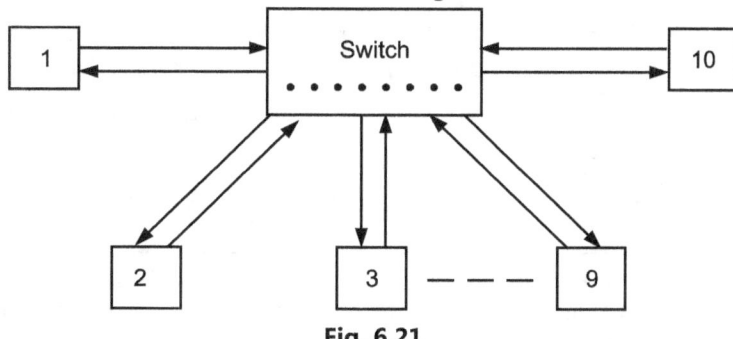

Fig. 6.21

In this mode, there is node of CSMA/CD, since each station is independent.

6.18 FAST ETHERNET : 100 MBPS ETHERNET

Fast Ethernet (100BASE-T) offers a speed increase ten times that of the 10BaseT Ethernet specification, while preserving such qualities as frame format, MAC mechanisms, and MTU. Such similarities allow the use of existing 10BaseT applications and network management tools on Fast Ethernet networks. Officially, the 100BASE-T standard is IEEE 802.3u.

Like Ethernet, 100BASE-T is based on the CSMA/CD LAN access method. There are several different cabling schemes that can be used with 100BASE-T, including :

- 100BASE-TX : Two pairs of high-quality twisted-pair wires.
- 100BASE-T4 : Four pairs of normal-quality twisted-pair wires.
- 100BASE-FX : Fiber optic cables.

The Fast Ethernet specifications include mechanisms for Auto-Negotiation of the media speed. This makes it possible for vendors to provide dual-speed Ethernet interfaces that can be installed and run at either 10-Mbps or 100-Mbps automatically.

The IEEE identifiers include three pieces of information. The first item, "100", stands for the media speed of 100-Mbps. The "BASE" stands for "baseband," which is a type of signaling. Baseband signaling simply means that Ethernet signals are the only signals carried over the media system.

The third part of the identifier provides an indication of the segment type. The "T4" segment type is a twisted-pair segment that uses four pairs of telephone-grade twisted-pair wire. The "TX" segment type is a twisted-pair segment that uses two pairs of wires and is based on the data grade twisted-pair physical medium standard developed by ANSI. The "FX" segment type is a fiber optic link segment based on the fiber optic physical medium standard developed by ANSI and that uses two strands of fiber cable. The TX and FX medium standards are collectively known as 100BASE-X.

The 100BASE-TX and 100BASE-FX media standards used in Fast Ethernet are both adopted from physical media standards first developed by ANSI, the American National Standards Institute. The ANSI physical media standards were originally developed for the Fiber Distributed Data Interface (FDDI) LAN standard (ANSI standard X3T9.5), and are widely used in FDDI LANs.

Protocol Structure - Fast Ethernet : 100 Mbps Ethernet (IEEE 802.3u)The basic IEEE 802.3 Ethernet MAC Data Frame for 10/100 Mbps Ethernet

Number of bytes	7	1	2/6	2/6	2	$612 <= n <= 1500$	4 bytes
Name of field	Pre	SFD	DA	SA	Length/Type	Data unit + pad	FCS

- **Preamble (PRE)** - 7 bytes. The PRE is an alternating pattern of ones and zeros that tells receiving stations that a frame is coming, and that provides a means to synchronize the frame-reception portions of receiving physical layers with the incoming bit stream.

- **Start-of-Frame Delimiter (SFD)** - 1 byte. The SFD is an alternating pattern of ones and zeros, ending with two consecutive 1-bits indicating that the next bit is the left-most bit in the left-most byte of the destination address.

- **Destination Address (DA)** - 6 bytes. The DA field identifies which station(s) should receive the frame.

- **Source Addresses (SA)** - 6 bytes. The SA field identifies the sending station.

- **Length/Type** - 2 bytes. This field indicates either the number of MAC-client data bytes that are contained in the data field of the frame, or the frame type ID if the frame is assembled using an optional format.

- **Data** - Is a sequence of n bytes ($612 \leq n \leq 1500$) of any value. Note that since transmission speed has increased from 10 Mbps to 100 Mbps, frame transmission time reduces by factor of 10. Hence, minimum frame size increases by a factor of 10 to 640.

• **Frame Check Sequence (FCS)** - 4 bytes. This sequence contains a 32-bit Cyclic Redundancy Check (CRC) value, which is created by the sending MAC and is recalculated by the receiving MAC to check for damaged frames.

6.19 GIGABIT (1000 MBPS) ETHERNET

Ethernet protocols refer to the family of Local-Area Network (LAN) covered by the IEEE 802.3 standard. The Gigabit Ethernet is based on the Ethernet protocol, but increased speed tenfold over the fast Ethernet, using shorter frames with carrier extension. It is published as the IEEE 802.3z and 802.3ab, supplement to the IEEE 802.3 base standards.

The Gigabit Ethernet standards are fully compatible with Ethernet and Fast Ethernet installations. It retains Carrier Sense Multiple Access/Collision Detection (CSMA/CD) as the access method. It supports full-duplex as well as half duplex modes of operation. Single-mode and multi mode fiber and short-haul coaxial cable, and twisted pair cables are supported. The Gigabit Ethernet architecture is displayed in Fig. 6.22.

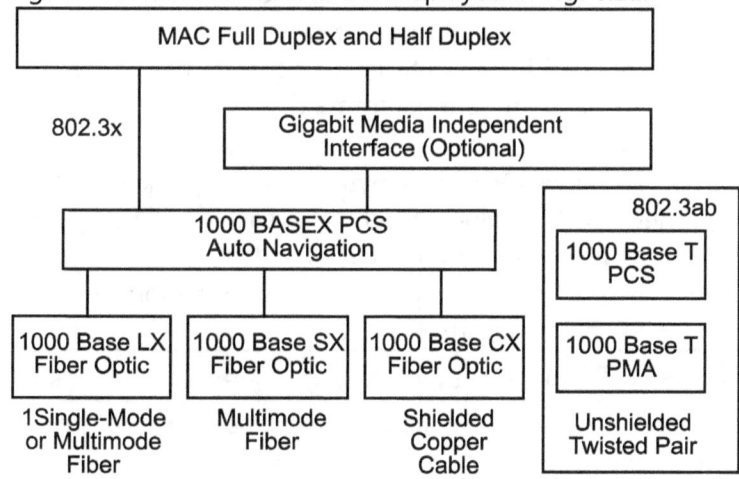

Fig. 6.22

The IEEE 802.3z defines the Gigabit Ethernet over fiber and cable, which has a physical media standard 1000Base-X (1000BaseSX - short wave covers up to 500 m, and 1000BaseLX - long wave covers up to 5 km). The IEEE 802.3ab defines the Gigabit Ethernet over the unshielded twisted pair wire (1000Base-T covers up to 75m).

The Gigabit interface converter (GBIC) allows network managers to configure each gigabit port on a port-by-port basis for short-wave (SX), long-wave (LX), long-haul (LH), and copper physical interfaces (CX). LH GBICs extended the single-mode fiber distance from the standard 5 km to 10 km.

6.19.1 Protocol Structure - Gigabit (1000 Mbps) Ethernet

1000Base-X has a minimum frame size of 416 bytes, and 1000Base-T has a minimum frame size of 520 bytes. An extension field is used to fill the frames that are shorter than the minimum length.

Number of bytes	7	1	6	6	2	494 <= n <=1500	4	Variable
Name of field	Pre	SFD	DA	SA	Length/Type	Data unit + pad	FCS	Ext

- **Preamble (PRE)** - 7 bytes. The PRE is an alternating pattern of ones and zeros that tells receiving stations that a frame is coming, and that provides a means to synchronize the frame-reception portions of receiving physical layers with the incoming bit stream.
- **Start-of-Frame Delimiter (SFD)** - 1 byte. The SFD is an alternating pattern of ones and zeros, ending with two consecutive 1-bits indicating that the next bit is the left-most bit in the left-most byte of the destination address.
- **Destination Address (DA)** - 6 bytes. The DA field identifies which station(s) should receive the frame.
- **Source Addresses (SA)** - 6 bytes. The SA field identifies the sending station.
- **Length/Type** - 2 bytes. This field indicates either the number of MAC-Client Data Bytes that are contained in the data field of the frame, or the frame type ID if the frame is assembled using an optional format.
- **Data** - Is a sequence of n bytes (494 <= n <=1500) of any value.
- **Frame Check Sequence (FCS)** - 4 bytes. This sequence contains a 32-bit cyclic redundancy check (CRC) value, which is created by the sending MAC and is recalculated by the receiving MAC to check for damaged frames.
- **Ext** - extension, which is an non-data variable extension field for frames that are shorter than the minimum length.

6.20 TEN-GIGABIT ETHERNET

It is the fastest Ethernet which use optical fibre cable. It is specified as IEEE 802.3ae standard. The goals of Ten-Gigabit Ethernet are :
- Upgradation of data rate to 10 Gbps.
- Make it compatible with other Ethernet standards.
- Use 48 bit address.
- Use same frame format.
- Make it compatible with other technologies such as ATM and frame relay.
- Keep same frame lengths (maximum and minimum).
- Allow existing LANs in WAN and MAN.

The specifications of MAC sublayer are full duplex mode of operation. Hence no contention. No need of CSMA/CD.

The physical layer specifications are :
- Fibre optic cables over long distance.
- Three different layers are :
  10GBase-S : Uses (300 m) short wave 850 nm multimode fibre.

10GBase-L : Uses (10 km) long wave 1310 nm singlemode fibre.

10GBase-E : Uses (40 km) extended 1550 nm single mode fibre.

6.21 SWITCHING INTRODUCTION

- When multiple devices want to communicate with each other, then simple solutions are :
  - Mesh network formation.
  - Bus network formation.

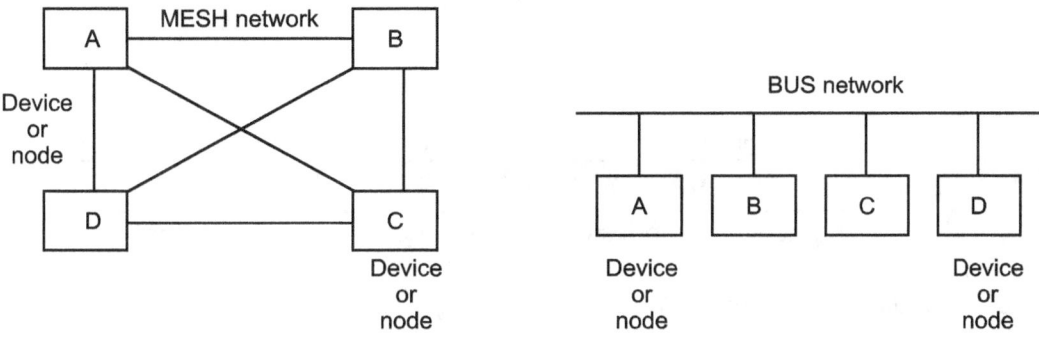

Fig. 6.23 : Interdevice Communication

- When above techniques are employed, it becomes impractical and wasteful when network size increases.
- Also network cost and maintenance becomes difficult for large network of devices.
- Then the solution to above problems is to use the switching system.
- Typical use of switch and switching system is as shown in Fig. 6.24.

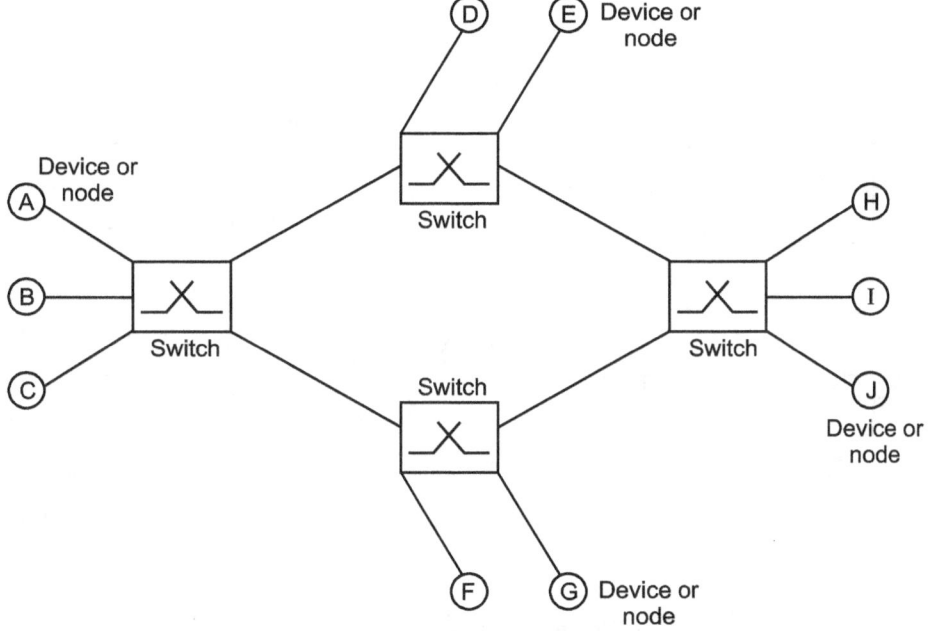

Fig. 6.24 : Typical Switch Based Network

- Thus, different devices/nodes can communicate with each other with the help of switches connected in the typical switch based network.
- The switches work on the principle of switching system.

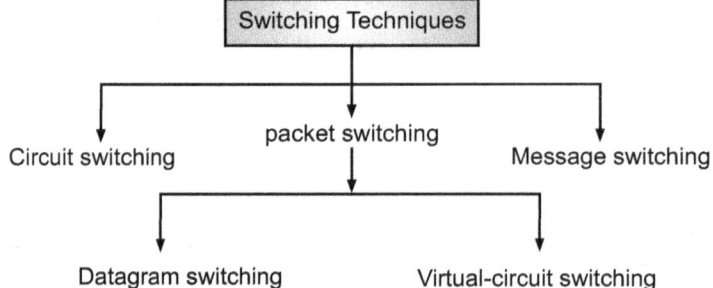

6.22 CIRCUIT SWITCHING NETWORKS

- In circuit switching networks, nodes or devices are connected to each other by physical links via switches.
- Typical circuit switched network is as shown in Fig. 6.25.

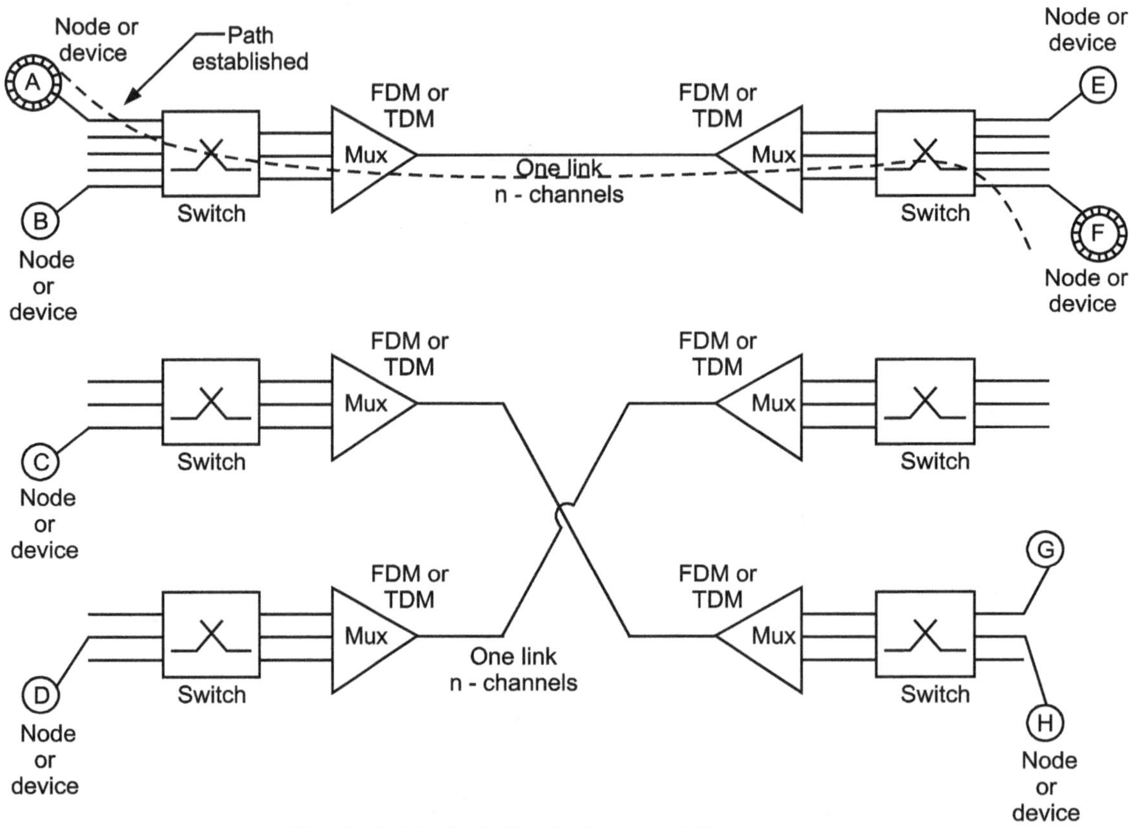

Fig. 6.25 : Typical Circuit Switched Network and Communication between Two End Systems A and F

- In this diagram, multiplexer (MUX) symbol is explicitly shown and it is implicitly included in switch fabric itself.
- The end system can be computer node or device like telephone set.
- In Fig. 6.25, the communication between two end systems A and F is highlighted.
- In circuit switched network, the communication between node 'A' and node 'F' is done through 3 phases as follows :
  - **Set-up phase (also known as connection establishment).**
  - **Data transfer phase.**
  - **Teardown phase (also known as connection release).**
- **In set-up phase a dedicated circuit** (i.e. combination of channels in links) needs to be established. For this node 'A' sends set-up request through switch fabric including multiplexer, to node 'F'. Then node 'F' receives this request and sends acknowledgement to node 'A' through same dedicated path. Thus, only after receiving this acknowledgement from node 'F', we can say that connection is established or set-up phase is completed. In this circuit switched network, end systems use addresses in TDM network whereas use telephone numbers in FDM network.

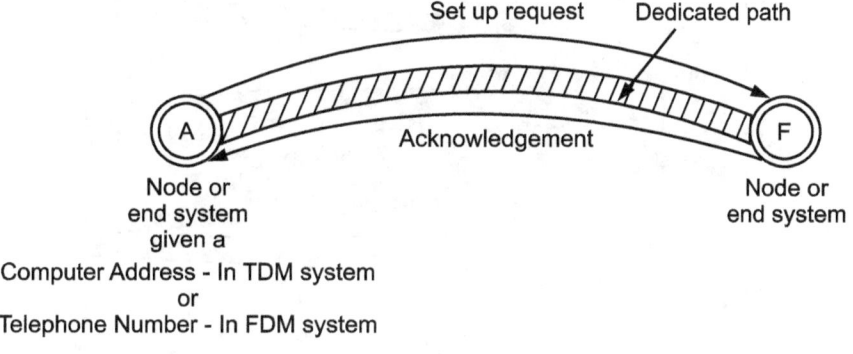

Fig. 6.26 : Typical Set-up Phase between End Systems A and F

- **In Data Transfer Phase**, end systems 'A' and 'F' can transfer data (or communication between two end systems is done).
- **In Teardown Phase (or connection release process)**, either 'A' system or 'F' system can stop the communication and release the common resources like dedicated link and switch etc.

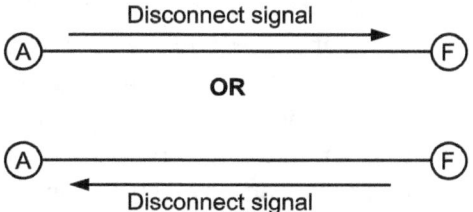

Fig. 6.27 : Teardown Phase (or Connection Release Process)

- **The circuit switched network is less efficient as compared to others** because network resources (switch and link) are allocated to 'A' and 'F' node and cannot be used by others or other connections are deprived.

- The total delay in communication between 'A' and 'F' end systems is given as :

Total delay	=	Connection establishment delay	+	Data transfer delay	+	Connection release delay

- Data transfer delay is also given as :

Data transfer delay = Propagation time delay + Data transfer time delay

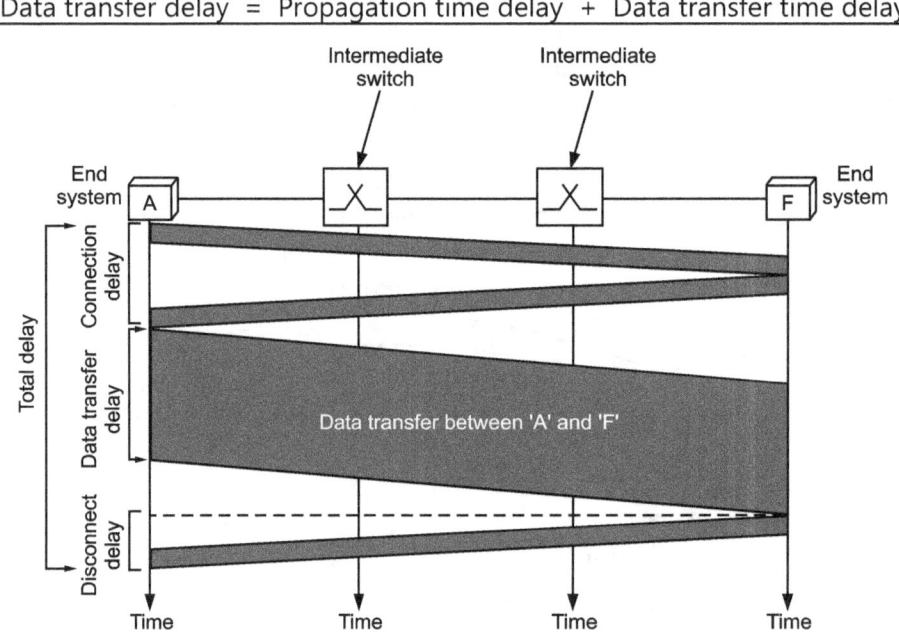

Fig. 6.28 : Typical Delays in Circuit Switched Network

(Here between two end systems like 'A' and 'F')

- Thus, typical example or application of circuit switched network in telephone communication is as shown in Fig. 6.28.

- There is a common misunderstanding that circuit switching is used only for connecting voice circuits (analog or digital). The concept of a dedicated path persisting between two communicating parties or nodes can be extended to signal content other than voice. Its advantage is that it provides for non-stop transfer without requiring packets and without most of the overhead traffic usually needed, making maximal and optimal use of available bandwidth for that communication. The disadvantage of inflexibility tends to reserve it for specialized applications, particularly with the overwhelming proliferation of Internet-related technology.

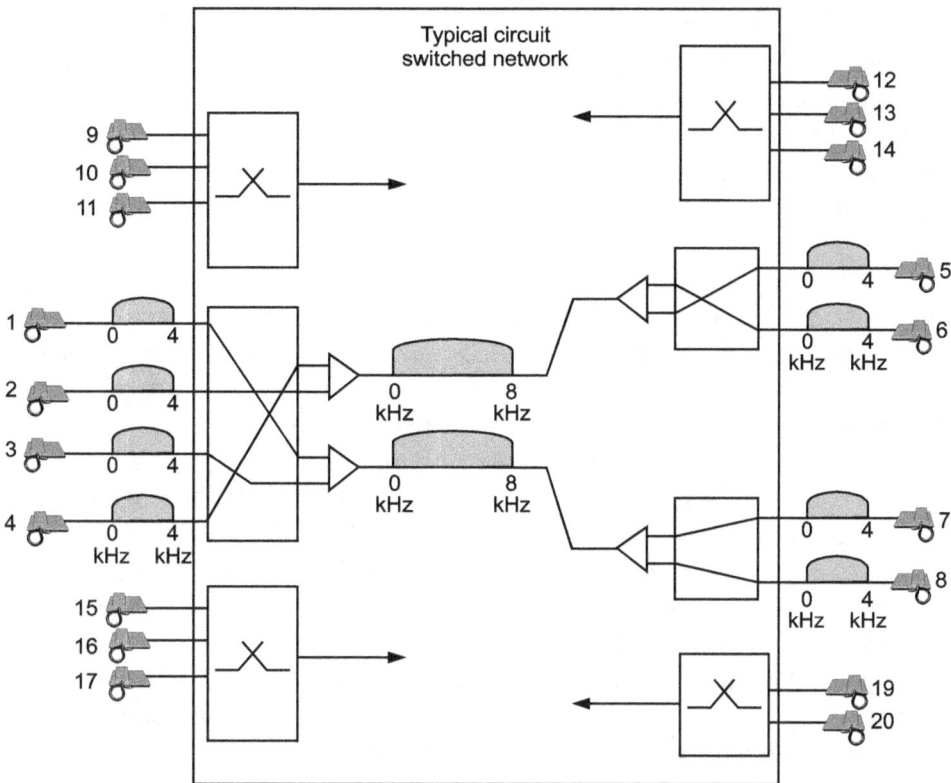

Fig. 6.29 : Typical Circuit Switched Network Example

- For call setup and control (and other administrative purposes), it is possible to use a separate dedicated signalling channel from the end node to the network. ISDN is one such service that uses a separate signalling channel while Plain Old Telephone Service (POTS) does not.

- The method of establishing the connection and monitoring its progress and termination through the network may also utilize a separate control channel as in the case of links between telephone exchanges which use SS7 packet-switched signalling protocol to communicate the call setup and control information and use TDM to transport the actual circuit data. Signalling System Number 7 (SS7) is a set of telephony signalling protocols which are used to set up most of the world's public switched telephone network telephone calls. The main purpose is to set up and tear down telephone calls

- Early telephone exchange is a suitable example of circuit switching. The subscriber would ask the operator to connect to another subscriber, whether on the same exchange or via an inter-exchange link and another operator. In any case, the end result was a physical electrical connection between the two subscribers's telephones for the duration of the call. The copper wire used for the connection could not be used to carry other calls at the same time, even if the subscribers were in fact not talking and the line was silent.

- Thus, generally, resources are frequency intervals in a Frequency Division Multiplexing (FDM) scheme or more recently time slots in a Time Division Multiplexing (TDM) scheme. The set of resources allocated for a connection is called a circuit. A path is a sequence of links located between nodes called switches. The path taken by data between its source and destination is determined by the circuit on which it is flowing, and does not change during the lifetime of the connection. The circuit is terminated when the connection is closed.

- In circuit switching, resources remain allocated during the full length of a communication, after a circuit is established and until the circuit is terminated and then the allocated resources are freed. Resources remain allocated even if no data is flowing on a circuit, hereby wasting link capacity when a circuit does not carry as much traffic as the allocation permits. This is a major issue since frequencies (in FDM) or time slots (in TDM) are available in finite quantity on each link, and establishing a circuit consumes one of these frequencies or slots on each link of the circuit. As a result, establishing circuits for communication that carry less traffic than allocation permits can lead to resource exhaustion and network saturation, preventing further connections from being established. If no circuit can be established between a sender and a receiver because of a lack of resources, the connection is blocked.

- A second characteristic of circuit switching is the time cost involved when establishing a connection. In a communication network, circuit-switched or not, nodes need to lookup in a forwarding table to determine on which link to send incoming data, and to actually send data from the input link to the output link. Performing a lookup in a forwarding table and sending the data on an incoming link is called forwarding. Building the forwarding tables is called routing. In circuit switching, routing must be performed for each communication, at circuit establishment time. During circuit establishment, the set of switches and links on the path between the sender and the receiver is determined and messages are exchanged on all the links between the two end hosts of the communication in order to make the resource allocation and build the routing tables. In circuit switching, forwarding tables are hardwired or implemented using fast hardware, making data forwarding at each switch almost instantaneous. Therefore, circuit switching is well suited for long-lasting connections where the initial circuit establishment time cost is balanced by the low forwarding time cost.

- The circuit identifier (a range of frequencies in FDM or a time slot position in a TDM frame) is changed by each switch at forwarding time so that switches do not need to have a complete knowledge of all circuits established in the network but rather only local knowledge of available identifiers at a link. Using local identifiers instead of global identifiers for circuits also enables networks to handle a larger number of circuits.

- Traffic Engineering (TE) consists in optimizing resource utilization in a network by choosing appropriate paths followed by flow of data, according to static or dynamic constraints. A main goal of traffic engineering is to balance the load in the network, i.e., to avoid congestion on links on a network while other links are under-utilized. To achieve such goals, traffic engineering methods can vary from offline capacity planning algorithms to automatic, dynamic changes. Since circuit switching allocates a fixed path for each flow, circuits can be established according to traffic engineering algorithms.

- On the other hand, circuit switching networks are not reactive when a network topology change occurs. For instance, on a link failure, all circuits on a failed link are cut and communication is interrupted. Special mechanisms that handle such topological changes have to be devised. Traffic engineering can alleviate the consequences of a link failure by pre-planning failure recovery.   A backup circuit can be established at the same time or after the primary circuit used for a communication is set up, and traffic can be rerouted from the failed circuit to the backup circuit if a link of the primary circuit fails. Circuit switching networks are intrinsically sensitive to link failures and rerouting must be performed by additional traffic engineering mechanisms.

Examples of Circuit Switched Networks

- Public Switched Telephone Network (PSTN).
- ISDN B-channel.
- Circuit Switched Data (CSD) and High-Speed Circuit-Switched Data (HSCSD) service in cellular systems such as GSM.
- Datakit [It supports file transfers, remote login, remote printing, and remote command execution. At the physical layer, it can operate over multiple media, from slow speed EIA-232 to 500 Mbit fiber optic links (called FIBERKIT)].
- X.21 (Used in the German DATEX-L and Scandinavian DATEX circuit switched data network).

6.23 DATAGRAM SWITCHING NETWORKS

- In packet switching networks, voice, video or data is converted into packet. Packet can be of fixed size or variable size, decided by network used and protocol used at both ends.
- In datagram switching, there is no resource allocation for a packet travelling from sender to receiver.
- This means there is no bandwidth reservation on links and no scheduled processing time for each packet.
- Thus, resources are allocated on demand and this allocation is done on a first come first serve basis.
- As a simple analogy consider two hotels (or restaurants). One which requires reservation and another that neither require reservation and nor accept them.
- For the hotel (or restaurant) which requires reservation, we have to go through the hassle of calling person of restaurant before we leave home and reach to restaurant.
- But when we arrive at restaurant we get table, can communicate with waiter and order for food.

- Thus, for the other restaurant which does not require reservation, we don't need to bother to reserve anything.

- In this restaurant when we arrive, we may have to wait for table, we may have to wait for communicating with waiter to order the food.

- Thus, restaurant with reservation and without reservation, this analogy is applicable for circuit switched network and datagram switched network respectively.

- The typical packet flow in datagram packet switched network is as shown in Fig. 6.30.

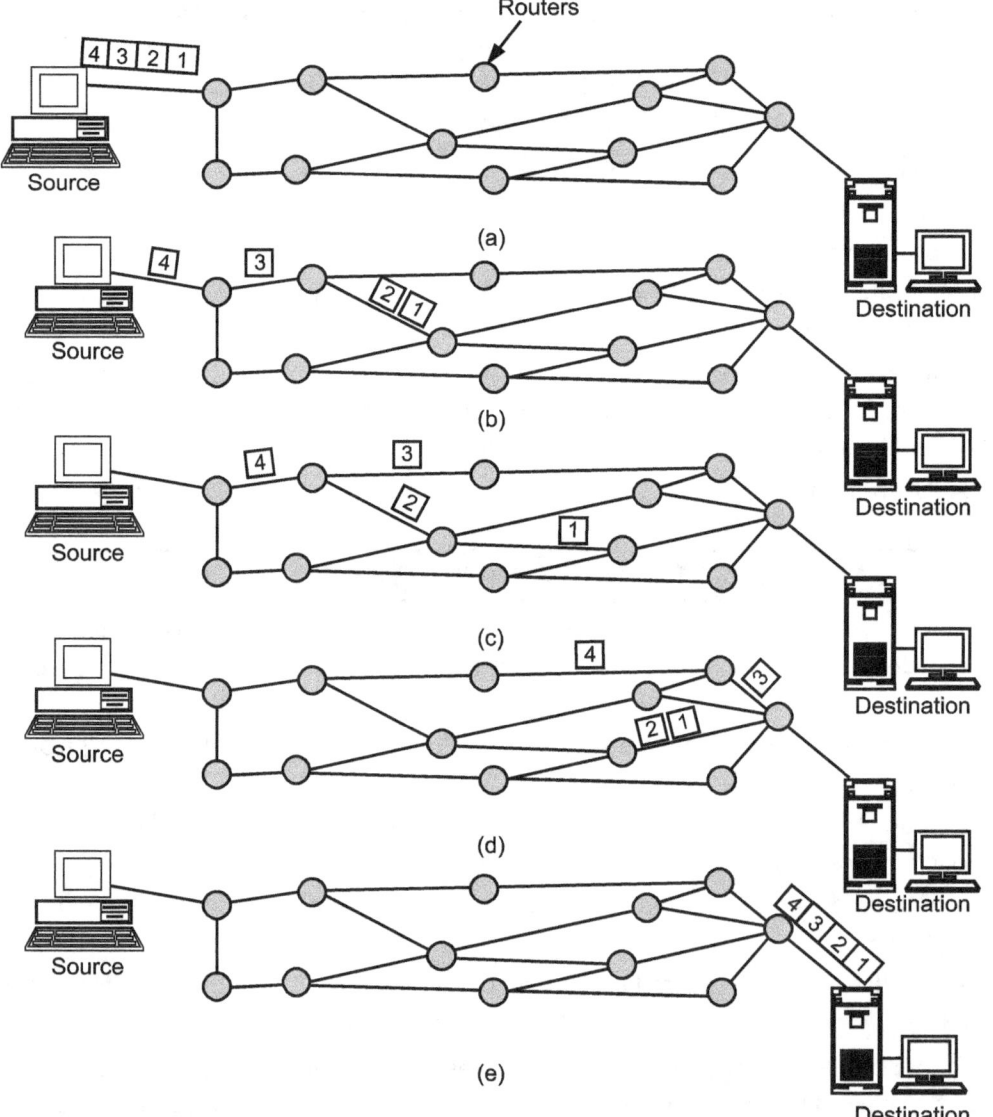

Fig. 6.30 : Datagram Network Packet Transfer from Source to Destination

Thus, in datagram packet networks, following characteristics are important :

- Each packet is treated independently.

- Packet can take any practical route.

- Packets may arrive out of order at destination router.

- Packets may go missing in the datagram network journey.

- Receiver at another end is responsible to reorder the packets and recover the missing packets.

- Transport layer at both (sender and receiver) ends is responsible to reorder the packet sequence and recover the missing packets.

- We have already discussed the connection oriented and connectionless services in first chapter. Datagram based networks are also known as connectionless networks.

- There is no set-up phase or teardown phase present in datagram switching network. When data is ready, it is transferred with full source and destination address from sender to receiver. For this each intermediate router maintains the routing table as shown in Fig. 6.31.

Routing Table maintained by Router Device

Destination address	Output port
12347	1
34569	2
22130	3
:	:
:	:
:	:
75759	4

Fig. 6.31 : Router Device uses Routing Table based on Destination Address

- The routing tables are dynamic in nature and are updated periodically. (Specific time is set by router administrator).

- The destination address is carried by the header among other information (or control information) of packet. This address remains same during the entire journey of the packet from source to destination or sender to receiver.

- Efficiency of datagram switch network is better than circuit switched network, because network resources are allocated only when there are packets to be transferred from source to destination.

- If source to destination packet transfer is finished or delayed then these resources can be used by other nodes or systems connected to this network.

- The delay between sender and receiver is given by,

$$\text{Total delay} \atop (T_D) = \text{Transmission delay} \atop (T_t) + \text{Propagation delay} \atop (T_p) + \text{Waiting delay} \atop (T_w)$$

- Typical datagram based packet switching network uses two routers in between sender and receiver as shown in Fig. 6.32.

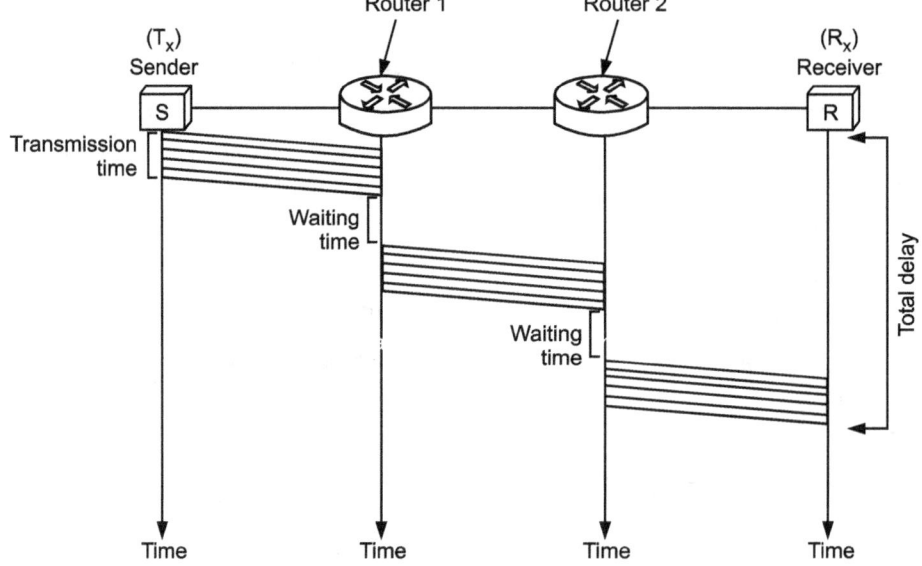

Fig. 6.32 : Delay present in Datagram Network

- Thus, total delay in above typical datagram network is given as,

$$T_D = 3T_t + 3T_p + T_{w_1} + T_{w_2}$$

where,

$3T_t$ = Three transmission times available (hence $3T_t$)

$3T_p$ = Three propagation delays available (hence $3T_p$)

$\left. \begin{array}{l} T_{w_1} \\ T_{w_2} \end{array} \right\}$ = Two waiting time delays available (hence T_{w_1} and T_{w_2})

- The best example of datagram network is Internet or TCP/IP protocol based LAN or Internet communication.

- Thus, a routing table contains a mapping between the possible final destination of packets and the outgoing link on their path to the destination. Routing tables can be very large because they are indexed by possible destinations, making lookups and routing decisions computationally expensive, and the full forwarding process relatively slow compared to circuit switching. In datagram packet switching networks, each packet must carry the address of the destination host and use the destination address to make a forwarding decision. Consequently, routers do not need to modify the destination addresses of packets when forwarding packets.

- Since each packet is processed individually by a router, all packets sent by a host to another host are not guaranteed to use the same physical links. If the routing algorithm decides to change the routing tables of the network between the instants two packets are sent, then these packets will take different paths and can even arrive out of order.

- Second, on a network topology change such as a link failure, the routing protocol will automatically recompute routing tables so as to take the new topology into account and avoid the failed link. As opposed to circuit switching, no additional traffic engineering algorithm is required to reroute traffic. Since routers make routing decisions locally for each packet, independent of the flow to which a packet belongs. Therefore, traffic engineering techniques, which heavily rely on controlling the route of traffic, are more difficult to implement with datagram packet switching than with circuit switching.

There are three primary types of datagram packet switches :

- **Store and Forward :** Buffers data until the entire packet is received and checked for errors. This prevents corrupted packets from propagating throughout the network but increases switching delay.

- **Fragment Free :** Filters out most error packets but doesn't necessarily prevent the propagation of errors throughout the network. It offers faster switching speeds and lower delay than store-and-forward mode.

- **Cut Through :** Does not filter errors; it switches packets at the highest throughput, offering the least forwarding delay.

- A datagram network is a best effort network. Delivery is not guaranteed. Reliable delivery must be provided by the end systems (i.e. user's computers) using additional protocols.

- The most common datagram network is the Internet, which uses the IP network protocol. Applications which do not require more than a best effort service can be supported by direct use of packets in a datagram network, using the User Datagram Protocol (UDP) transport protocol. Applications like voice and video communications and notifying messages to alert a user that she/he has received new email are using UDP. Applications like e-mail, web browsing and file upload and download need reliable communications, such as guaranteed delivery, error control and sequence control. This reliability ensures that all the data is received in the correct order without errors. It is provided by a protocol such as the Transmission Control Protocol (TCP) or the File Transfer Protocol (FTP).

6.24 VIRTUAL CIRCUIT NETWORKS (VC NETWORKS)

• Virtual circuit network is another type of packet switched network.

• Virtual circuit network is a cross between datagram switching network and circuit switching network. It has characteristics of both the networks.

Characteristics of Circuit Switched Network	Characteristics of Datagram Network
1. It has three phases like : • Set-up phase (connection establishment). • Data transfer. • Teardown phase (connection release). 2. Resources can be allocated during the set-up phase or connection establishment phase. 3. All packets follow the same path established during set-up phase or connection establishment phase.	1. Resource allocation can be on demand in VC networks. 2. In datagram packet header, destination IP addresses are mentioned, whereas in VC packet header next switch VCI (Virtual Circuit Identifier) number is mentioned.
In todays technology • Circuit switched network is implemented in physical layer. • Datagram switched network is implemented in network layer. • VC switched network is implemented in data link layer.	

• In VC switched networks, two types of addressing used are as follows :

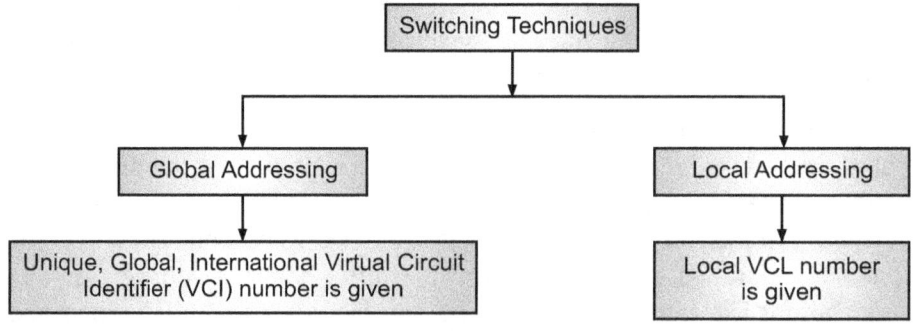

6.24.1 Virtual Circuit Packet Network

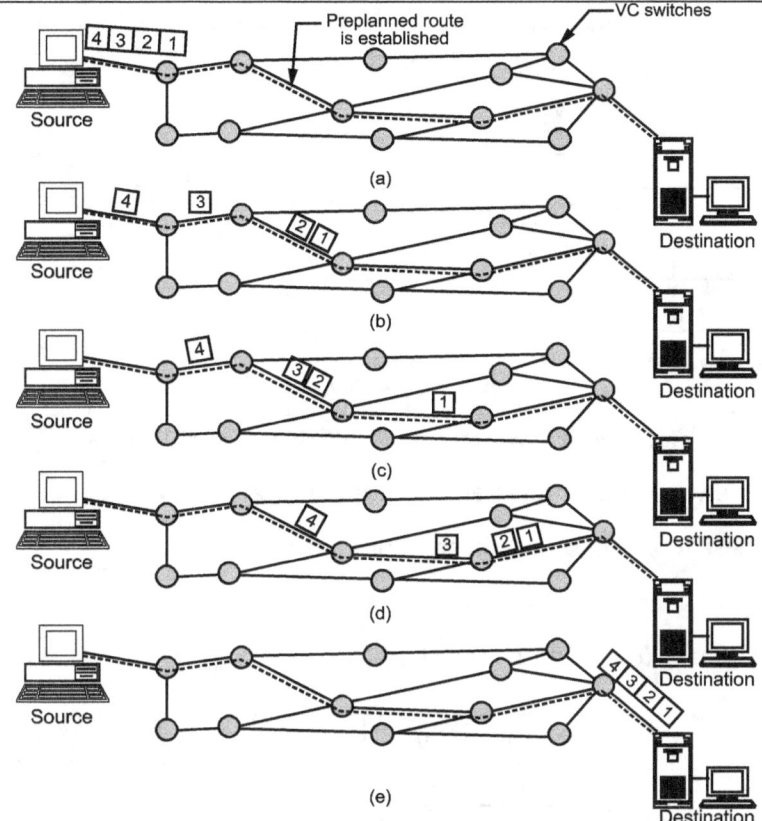

Fig. 6.33 (a) : Packet flow in Typical Virtual Circuit Packet Switched Network

- Typical VC switched network is as shown in Fig. 6.33 (b).

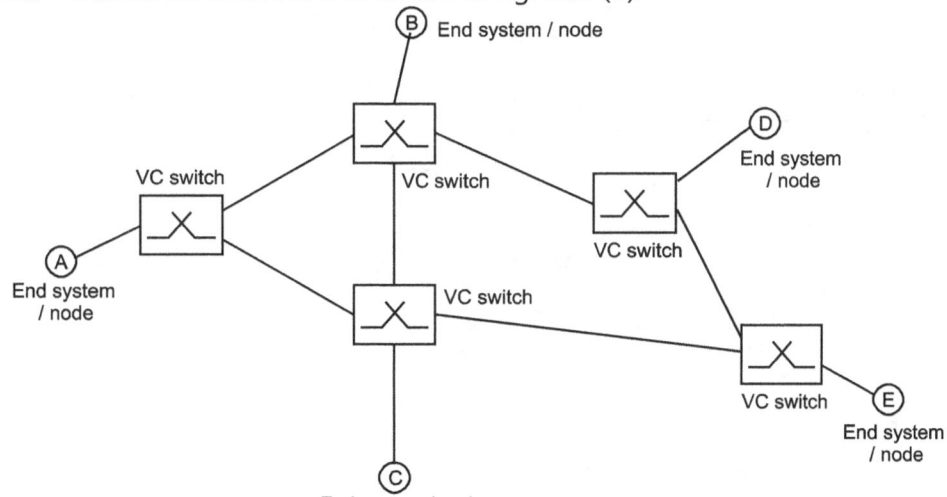

Fig. 6.33 (b) : Typical VC Switched Network

- **Virtual Circuit Identifier (VCI)** is used for data transfer from one end to another.

- VCI is used by frames between two VC switches. When frame arrives at one VC switch, it has a VCI, when it leaves it has a different VCI.

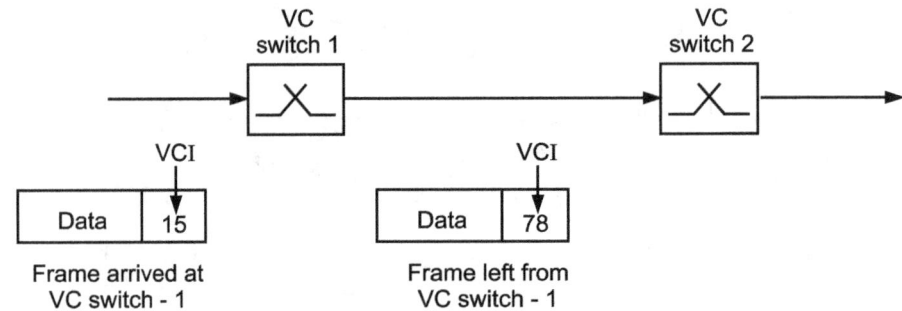

Fig. 6.34 : VC Switch decides VCI Number of Frames

The VC switched network uses three steps for communication :

- Set-up phase (connection establishment phase).

- Data transfer phase.

- Teardown phase (connection release phase).

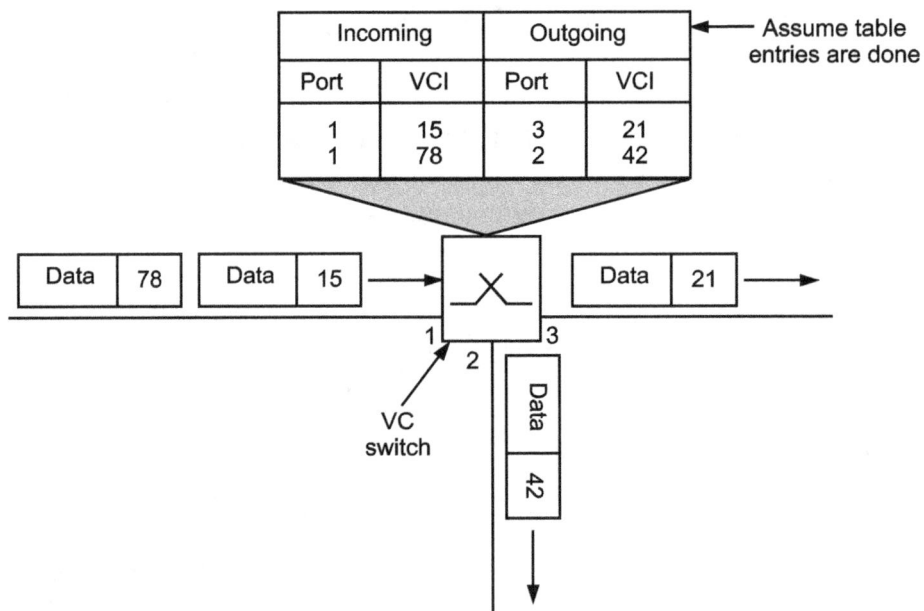

(a) Switching Table maintained by Typical VC Switch

(Assume that entries are done initially)

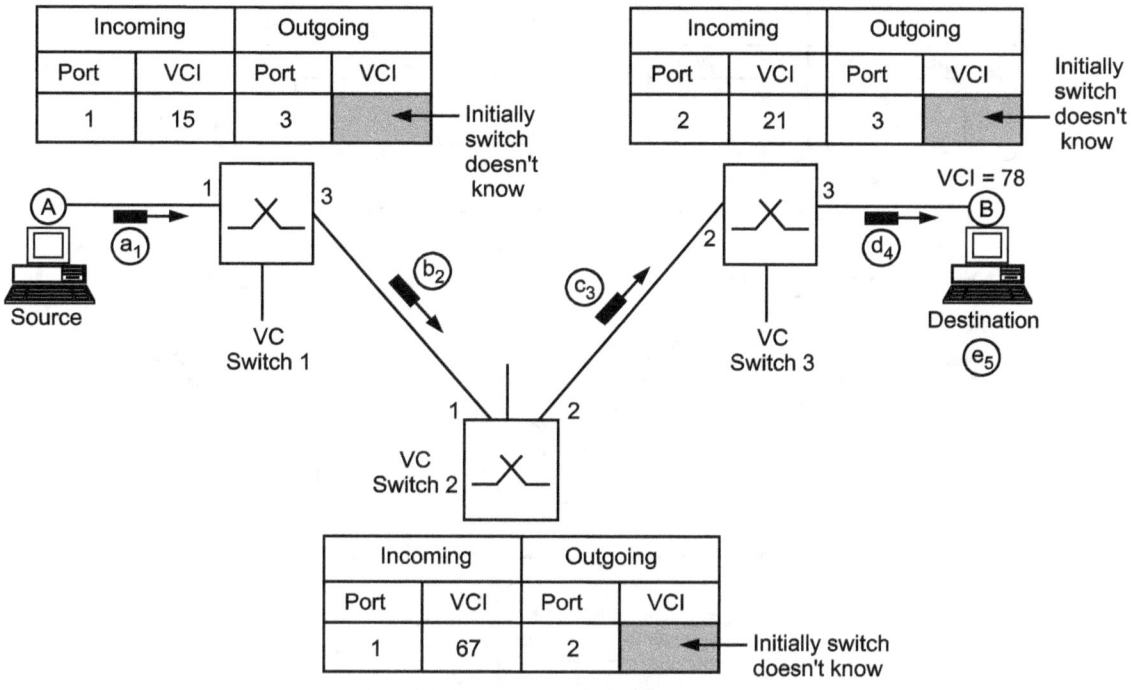

(b) Set-up Request Process from Source 'A' to Destination 'B'

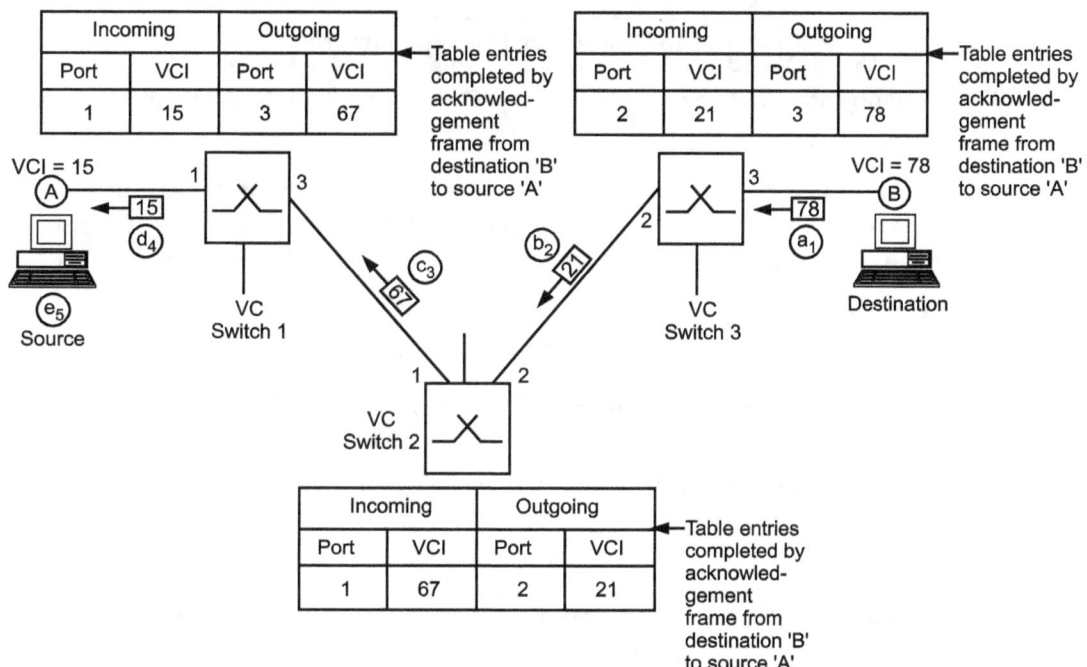

(c) Set-up Acknowledgement Process from Destination 'B' to Source 'A'

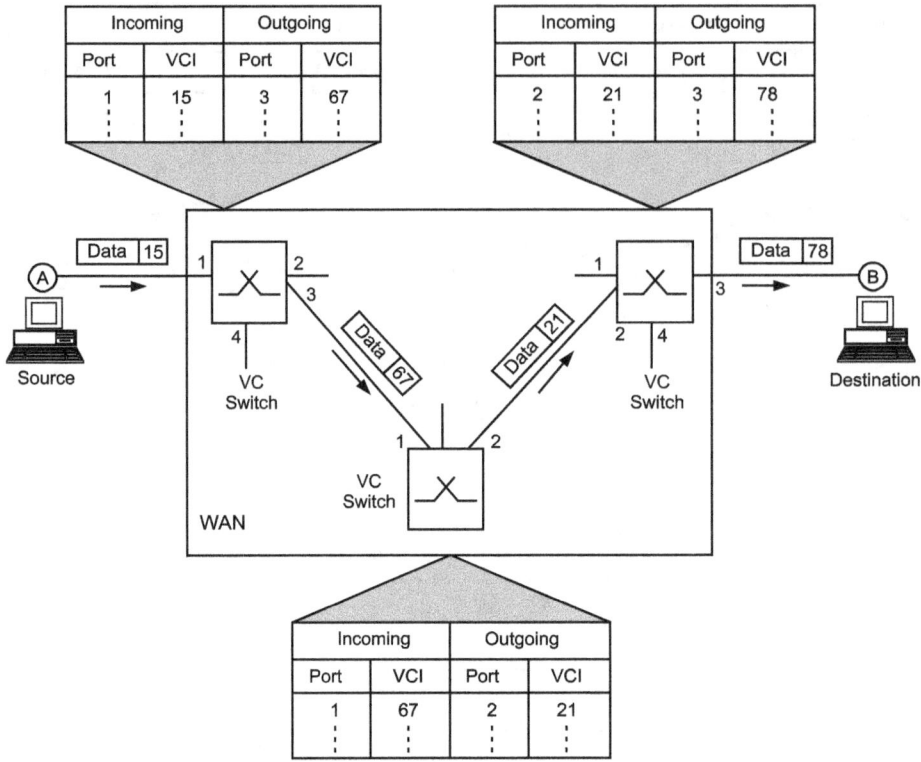

**(d) Source to Destination Data Transfer from
'A' to 'B' end system according to Updated Table Entries**

Fig. 6.35 : Communication between Source 'A' and Destination 'B' in VC Switched Network

- **Thus, Fig. 6.35 (a) says :**

  When incoming frame 1 with VCI = 15 and frame 2 with VCI = 78 arrives to VC switch, depending upon switching table entries mentioned, frame 1-VCI is changed from 15 → 21 and sent on port 3. Also frame 2-VCI is changed from 78 → 42 and sent on port 2.

- **Fig. 6.35 (b) says :**

  - Set-up request process from source 'A' to destination 'B'.

  - It clearly shows random incoming VCI number and undefined outgoing VCI numbers.

  - Set-up request starts from source 'A' → VC switch 1 → VC switch 2 →   VC switch 3 → destination 'B'.

- **Fig. 6.35(c) says :**

  - Special acknowledgement frame is sent from destination 'B' to source 'A'.

  - This special acknowledgement frame completes the table entries like

    VC switch 3 →   Outgoing VCI   =   78

	Incoming VCI	=	21
VC switch 2 →	Outgoing VCI	=	21
	Incoming VCI	=	67
VC switch 1 →	Outgoing VCI	=	67
	Incoming VCI	=	15

- Thus, source 'A' gets the VCI = 15 as source frame VCI number and hence source 'A' sends frame like ┃ data ┃ to immediate VC┃ 15 ┃ch 1 in data transfer phase.

- **Thus, Fig. 6.35 (d) says :**

    - Once table entries are confirmed the first frame generated from source 'A' is ┃ data ┃with VCI =┃ 15 ┃

    - Thus, data transfer takes place from source 'A' → VC switch 1 → VC switch 2 → VC switch 3 → destination 'B'.

- Hence, Fig. 6.35 shows communication between source 'A' and destination 'B' in VC switched network.

Where, set-up phase request process is given by Fig. 6.35 (b).

Set-up phase acknowledgement process is given by Fig. 6.35 (c).

Data transfer between 'A' and 'B' is given by Fig. 6.35 (d).

- Finally, when data transfer is completed between 'A' and 'B' systems then the remaining process is teardown process or connection release process. In this process or in this phase source 'A' sends a special frame called a teardown request to destination 'B'. Destination 'B' also responds with teardown confirmation frame and sends to source 'A'. Thus, all corresponding switching table entries are deleted from VC switches.

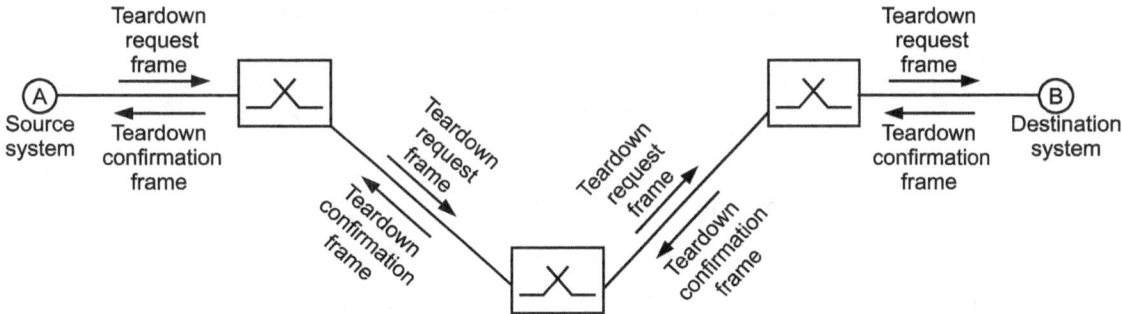

Fig. 6.36 : Typical Teardown Request and Confirmation set-up between Source 'A' and Destination 'B' after Data Transfer is Over

- Thus, the efficiency of the VC switched network is greater as compared to circuit switched network and datagram switched network.

- This happens because the main advantage of VC switched network is even if resource allocation is on demand, the source can check availability of the resources without actually reserving it.

- Thus, though path between source 'A' and destination 'B' is same, packets may arrive at the destination with different delays if resource allocation is done on demand as we discussed.

- The total delay in communication between source 'A' and destination 'B' is given by,

> Total delay = Transmission delay + Propagation delay + Set-up delay + Teardown delay

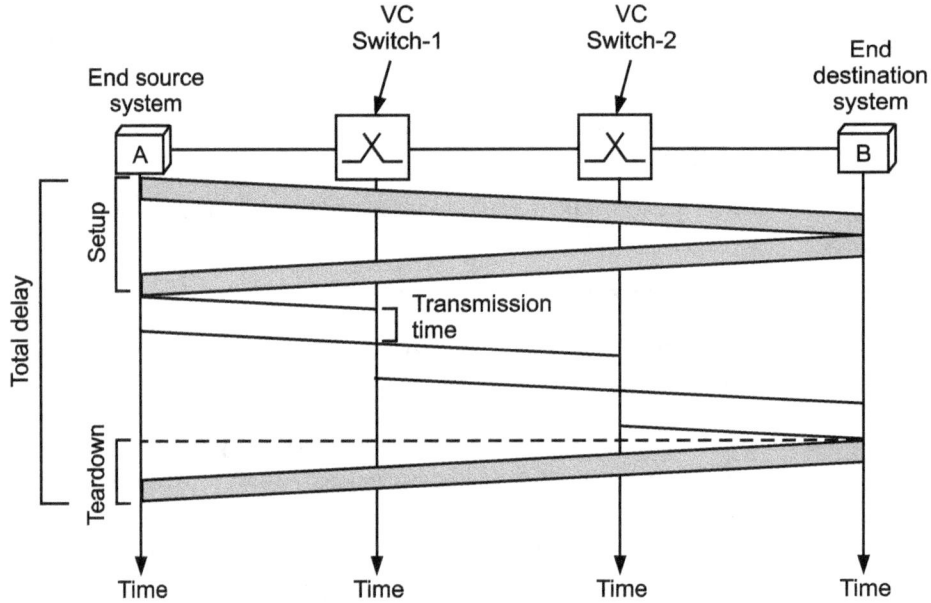

Fig. 6.37 : Delay Present in VC Switched Network

- Thus, total delay in above typical VC switched network is given as,

$$T_D = 3T_t + 3T_p + \text{Set-up delay} + \text{Teardown delay}$$

where,

$3T_t$ = Three transmission times available (hence $3T_t$)

$3T_p$ = Three propagation delays available (hence $3T_p$)

Set-up delay consists of request + Acknowledged process delay.

Teardown delay consists of request + Acknowledged process delay.

Following are the typical VC switched networks :

- X.25 VC switched networks.

- Frame relay VC switched networks.

- ATM (Asynchronous Transfer Mode) networks.

- MPLS (Multiprotocol Label Switching) networks.

6.24.2 Concept of Virtual Circuit

- A *virtual circuit* is a logical connection created to ensure reliable communication between two network devices.

- A virtual circuit denotes the existence of a logical, bidirectional path from sender device to another receiver device across an VC switched network.

- Physically, the connection can pass through any number of intermediate nodes, such as VC switches.

- Multiple virtual circuits (logical connections) can be multiplexed onto a single physical circuit (a physical connection).

- Virtual circuits are demultiplexed at the remote end, and data is sent to the appropriate destinations. Fig. 6.38 illustrates four separate virtual circuits being multiplexed onto a single physical circuit.

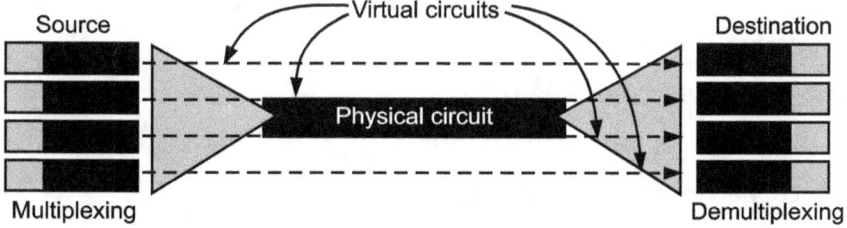

Fig. 6.38 : Virtual Circuits and Physical Circuit between Source and Destination

- Thus, we have seen the trade-off between connection establishment and forwarding time costs that exist in circuit switching and datagram packet switching.

- In VC switching, routing is performed at circuit establishment time to keep fast packet forwarding.

- Other advantages of VC switching include the traffic engineering capability of circuit switching, and the resources usage efficiency of datagram packet switching.

- Nevertheless, a main issue of VC switched networks is the behavior on a topology change.

- As opposed to datagram packet switched networks which automatically recompute routing tables on a topology change like a link failure, in VC switching all virtual circuits that pass through a failed link are interrupted.

- Hence, rerouting in VC switching relies on traffic engineering techniques.

6.24.3 Types of Virtual Circuits

• Switched Virtual Circuits (Physical connection is always present temporary logical connection is to be established every time for the data transfer) *Switched Virtual Circuits* (SVCs) are temporary connections used in situations requiring only sporadic data transfer between DTE devices across the Frame Relay network.

• Permanent Virtual Circuits (Physical connection is always present and permanent logical connection is already established so that any time data can be transferred) *Permanent Virtual Circuits* (PVCs) are permanently established connections that are used for frequent and consistent data transfers between DTE devices across the network. Communication across a PVC does not require the call setup and termination states that are used with SVCs. PVCs do not require that sessions be established and terminated. Therefore, DTEs can begin transferring data whenever necessary because the session is always active.

6.24.4 Typical Applications of VC Switched Networks

• File Transfer
  ➢ Character-interactive traffic (e.g. text editing)
  ➢ High Resolution graphics
• Access to Internet and Intranet
• Multimedia, Real Time Voice, Video, Fax
• LAN Peer-to-Peer, WAN Interconnection
• Multi-protocol networking applications
  ➢ ATM, SNA, TCP/IP
• Private backbone networks.

6.25 COMPARISON OF DIFFERENT SWITCHING TECHNIQUES

1. Now, we have seen the following switching techniques in detail.
   • Circuit switching.
   • Datagram switching.
   • Virtual circuit switching.

2. Let's compare the following :
   • Circuit switching Vs. Packet switching.
   • Datagram switching Vs. Virtual circuit switching.
   • Circuit switching Vs. Datagram switching Vs. VC switching Vs. Message switching.

6.25.1 Circuit Switching Vs. Packet Switching

Parameter	Circuit Switched	Packet Switched
Call setup requirement	Required	Not required
Dedicated physical path requirement	Yes, it is required	No, it is not required
Whether each packet follows the same path (route)	Yes, it follows the same path (route)	No, it does not follow the same path (route)
Bandwidth Available for Transmission	It is fixed	It is dynamic
Congestion can occur at	Setup time	On every packet
Bandwidth Wastage	Yes	No
Store and Forward transmission	Not available	Yes, it is available
Transparency in System	Yes, it is present	Not present
Charge applied	Per unit time	Per unit packet

6.25.2 Datagram (DG) Vs. Virtual Circuit (VC) Switching

Parameter	Datagram (DG) Network	Virtual Circuit (VC) Network
Requirement of Circuit Setup	Requirement of circuit setup is not needed	Requirement of circuit setup is needed.
Routing of Packet	Each packet is routed independently	Route is chosen when VC setup is over and all packet follows the same
Router failure	None	Less probability
If router fails	Packets are lost during the crash	All VCs that passed through the failed router are terminated
Achievement of Quality of service	It is difficult here	It is easy if enough resources can be allocated in advance for each VC
Congestion control	It is difficult over here	It is easy if enough resources can be allocated in advance for each VC
Examples of network	TCP/IP internet network	X.25, Frame Relay and ATM networks

EXERCISE

1. What are the different connecting devices used in computer data communication ?

2. Write short notes on following :

   (a) Passive hub

   (b) Hub or repeater

   (c) Bridge

   (d) Layer-2 switch

   (e) Router

   (f) Router

   (g) Layer-3 switch

3. Explain and correlate connecting devices with ISO-OSI reference model.

4. Explain 802.X to 802.Y bridge communication.

5. Explain the concept of filtering database in bridge.

6. What are different advantages of network bridges ?

7. What are different disadvantages of network bridges ?

8. What is Layer-2 switching ?

9. What is microsegmentation in switch ?

10. What are the limitations of Layer-2 switches ?

11. What is a router ? What are the different types of router ?

12. What is routing ? What are different routing schemes ?

13. What is "Gateway" connecting device ?

14. Compare Layer-1 hubs Vs. Switch device.

15. Compare Bridge Vs. Router.

16. Compare Bridge Vs. Layer-2 switch.

17. Compare Layer-2 switch Vs. Layer-3 switch.

18. Compare Router Vs. Switch.

19. State the protocols devised to handle multiple access communication.

20. Explain pure aloha.

21. Explain slotted aloha.

22. What are carrier sense multiple access protocols ?

23. Explain CSMA/CD technique.

24. How collision is detected in Ethernet ?

25. What is retransmission Back-off ?

26. Explain CSMA/CA technique.

27. What is controlled access ? How it is achieved ?

28. What is logical ring ? Explain.

29. State and explain various multiple access techniques.

30. Compare FDMA, TDMA and CDMA.

31. What are advantages and disadvantages of FDMA ?

32. What are advantages and disadvantages of TDMA ?

33. What are advantages and disadvantages of CDMA ?

34. What is Ethernet ?

35. State various forms of Ethernet based on data rate.

36. What is bridged ethernet ?

37. What is switched ethernet ?

38. Explain various physical layer implementations of 10 Mbps Ethernet.

39. What is Fast Ethernet ? Give its frame format.

40. What is Gigabit Ethernet ? Give its frame format.

41. Explain Ten Gigabit ethernet.

42. Classify the different switching techniques.

43. Write short notes on :

    (a) Circuit switching networks

    (b) Phases in circuit switching

    (c) Delay in circuit switching

44. Write short notes on :

    (a) Datagram switching networks

    (b) Delay in datagram networks

    (c) Types of datagram packet switches.

45. Write short notes on :

    (a) Similarities of VC switching with circuit switching and datagram networks

    (b) VC switching between source and destination

    (c) Virtual Circuit Identifier (VCI)

    (d) Phases in VC switching

    (e) Delays in VC switching networks.

46. What is Virtual Circuit ? What is SVC and PVC ?

47. Explain the different applications of VC switching.

48. Compare the following :

    (a) Circuit switching Vs. Packet switching

    (b) Datagram switching Vs. Virtual circuit switching

    (c) Circuit switching Vs. Datagram switching Vs. VC switching Vs. Message switching

SAMPLE QUESTION PAPER

End-Sem. Theory Examination

Time : 2 Hours   **Max. Marks : 50**

Instructions to the candidates :

    (i) Answer four questions.

    (ii) Neat diagrams must be drawn wherever necessary.

    (iii) Figures to the right indicate full marks.

    (iv) Assume suitable data if necessary.

---

1. (a) Draw the OSI reference model and explain the functions of different layers.   **[5]**

    (b) Explain the term frequency spectrum w.r.t. amplitude modulation and frequency modulation   **[5]**

OR

2. (a) Explain Shanon-Fano coding and Huffman source coding technique.   **[5]**

    (b) Explain in detail electromagnetic spectrum and applications of each spectrum.   **[5]**

3. (a) Explain following ARQ protocols with suitable   **[5]**

      (i)   stop_and_wait ARQ

      (ii)   Go_back_N ARQ

      (iii) selective_repeat ARQ

    (b) What is amplitude modulation? Discuss any two amplitude modulation techniques.**[5]**

OR

4. (a) Write a short note on   **[6]**

      (i)   Amplitude Shift Keying (ASK)

      (ii)   Frequency Shift Keying (FSK)

      (iii) Phase Shift Keying (PSK)

      (iv) Quadrature Amplitude Modulation (QAM)

    (b) What is hamming distance ? Explain with example.   **[4]**

5. (a) Consider building a CSMA/CD network running at 1 Gbps over a 1 km cable with no repeaters. The signal speed in the cable is 2,00,000km/sec, what is the minimum frame size ? **[5]**

(b) Differentiate between Synchronous Time-Division Multiplexing and Statistical Time-Division Multiplexing **[5]**

(c) Compare and explain the pure and slotted ALOHA system **[5]**

OR

6. (a) A large population of ALOHA users manages to generate 50 requests/sec, including both original and retransmission. Time is slotted in units of 40 msec. **[10]**

    (a) What is the chance of success on the first attempt ?

    (b) What is the probability of exactly k collision and the a success ?

    (c) What is the expected number of transmission attempts need.

(b) Explain various techniques of channelization **[5]**

7. (a) Differentiate between Repeater, Bridge, Router, Gateway along with suitable example. **[5]**

(b) Compare the data rates of traditional, fast and Gigabit Ethernets. **[5]**

(c) How does the Token Ring LAN operate? **[5]**

OR

8. (a) Write short note on 802.3 **[5]**

(b) Give the comparative analysis of fast, gigabit and 10-gigabit Ethernet **[5]**

(c) Compare Circuit switching network and datagram switch network. **[5]**